P9-BZN-075

NICOLE SHIFTED IN THE STUDY CHAIR, WONDERING WHERE THE MYSTERIOUS MARQUIS OF TYREHAM WAS . . .

. . . and wishing he'd hurry and make an appearance. The apprehension was almost more than she could bear.

Her disguise was flawless. She knew that. Her garb was that of a stable boy; every last hair swept up into a rigid knot beneath her cap, every sign of femininity concealed, as the binding around her breasts—which rivaled her corset in discomfort—could attest.

Clutching her father's note, she mentally rehearsed the speech she had prepared, reminding herself to further her cause by keeping her movements to a minimum during this, the sole one-on-one meeting she'd likely have to suffer with the man she meant to work for. After today, she'd be with the horses, training, and he'd be in his mansion doing whatever it was a marquis did.

But she wasn't leaving Tyreham without that job.

Behind her, a door swung open and she came slowly to her feet, unfolding from her chair like a man. It was time to convince him. She *had* to convince him. For her father's sake—and her own.

She turned to face her challenge.

"Mr. Stoddard? I'm the marquis of Tyreham. I understand you wish to see me."

My God, it was Dustin.

RAVES FROM BOOKSELLERS FOR ANDREA KANE'S SUPERB ROMANCE

EMERALD GARDEN

"A wonderful story. Characters you care about. A book I could not put down. Thank you for a joy of a read."
—Elinor, Best Sellers, Palos Heights, IL

"Ms. Kane has woven a warm and witty love story with just enough intrigue to keep you turning the pages. How wonderful to find a deep passion with your best friend."
—Denise Smith, Aunt Dee's Book Bag, Oxford, MI

"Each time I finish an Andrea Kane book I think 'she will never write one better than this.' Each time Andrea proves me wrong and I'm delighted."
—Adene Beal, House of Books, Tallahassee, FL

"Romance, intrigue, and humor have made *Emerald Garden* Ms. Kane's best book yet."
—Margaret Stilson, Paperback Exchange, Columbus, OH

"Andrea is brilliant! Brandi and Quentin tore at my heart and made me feel as if I were there. Andrea Kane books are definite keepers!"
—Linda Eisenberg, A Novel Idea, Bridgeton, NJ

"Brandi and Quentin's story is what romance is all about! Utterly touching, a sparkling gem of a book."
—Sharon Walters, Paperback Place, Mercer, PA

"Another jewel of a book to add to Ms. Kane's crown as a writer."
—Henrietta Davis, Waldenbooks, Pekin, IL

"Emerald Garden is, as all of Andrea Kane's books, stunning! She just gets better and better."
—Donita Lawrence, Bell Book & Candle, Del City, OK

"What an enchanting man and woman to accept each other unconditionally. . . . What a joyous garden of life and love!"
—Koren Schrand, K & S Paperback Exchange, Crescent Springs, KY

"This one has it all: romance, suspense, desire. It was breathtaking."
—Monika M. Schneider, The Paper Pad Bookstore, Port Charles, FL

"Just in time for Christmas sales! It will make my book recommendation easy. The perfect break from shopping stress. I couldn't put it down."
—Sharon Murphy, Paperback Trader, Houston, TX

"Another keeper in the unique style of Andrea Kane. Add a bit of *Gigi* and memorable secondary characters and a love that is destiny."
—Judy Spagnola, Waldenbooks, Cherry Hill, NJ

"Andrea Kane never disappoints. Our customers love her. Her stories are simply fabulous—please write faster!"
—Suan Wilson, Rainy Day Books, Olathe, KS

"Her best book yet. Riveting! I read it in one sitting—Quentin and Brandi were made for each other and Bentley deserves his own book. Bravo!"
—Marilyn Elrod, The Book Bag, Gadsden, AL

"Emerald Garden is like good chocolate. Delicious, delectable, a thing to savor. When Andrea Kane has a new book out, I get nothing done. A fine addition to any keeper shelf."
—Kevin Beard, Journey's End Bookstore, New Carlisle, OH

Books by Andrea Kane

My Heart's Desire
Dream Castle
Masque of Betrayal
Echoes in the Mist
Samantha
The Last Duke
Emerald Garden
Wishes in the Wind

Published by POCKET BOOKS

For orders other than by individual consumers, Pocket Books grants a discount on the purchase of **10 or more** copies of single titles for special markets or premium use. For further details, please write to the Vice-President of Special Markets, Pocket Books, 1633 Broadway, New York, NY 10019-6785, 8th Floor.

For information on how individual consumers can place orders, please write to Mail Order Department, Simon & Schuster Inc., 200 Old Tappan Road, Old Tappan, NJ 07675.

ANDREA KANE

Wishes in the Wind

POCKET STAR BOOKS

New York   London   Toronto   Sydney   Tokyo   Singapore

The sale of this book without its cover is unauthorized. If you purchased this book without a cover, you should be aware that it was reported to the publisher as "unsold and destroyed." Neither the author nor the publisher has received payment for the sale of this "stripped book."

This book is a work of fiction. Names, characters, places and incidents are products of the author's imagination or are used fictitiously. Any resemblance to actual events or locales or persons, living or dead, is entirely coincidental.

An *Original* Publication of POCKET BOOKS

A Pocket Star Book published by
POCKET BOOKS, a division of Simon & Schuster Inc.
1230 Avenue of the Americas, New York, NY 10020

Copyright © 1996 by Andrea Kane

All rights reserved, including the right to reproduce this book or portions thereof in any form whatsoever. For information address Pocket Books, 1230 Avenue of the Americas, New York, NY 10020

ISBN: 0-671-53483-1

First Pocket Books printing August 1996

10 9 8 7 6 5 4 3 2 1

POCKET STAR BOOKS and colophon are registered trademarks of Simon & Schuster Inc.

Cover art by Punz Wolff

Printed in the U.S.A.

Dedication

Three years ago I was submerged in the writing of *Echoes in the Mist,* agonizing over how to assuage Trenton's bitterness during those painful years before Ariana came into his life. My not yet ten-year-old daughter, Wendi, in an effort to ease my (and Trenton's) distress, offered some sage advice. "Mommy," she said, "what Trenton needs is a younger brother. Someone he can talk to who isn't so dark inside. Someone who has a good sense of humor, who looks like Trenton, and who loves horses. His name should be Dustin."

Thus, Dustin Kingsley was born, a hero who inspired a deluge of mail requesting his story, and whose powerful presence commanded that he receive just that.

So, Wendi, I gift *Wishes in the Wind* to you with all my love and thanks for your imagination, your affinity for horses, and your perception, wise beyond your years. Most of all, for being not only a fantastic kid and an extraordinary brainstorming partner but for being the very best friend a mom could ever "wish" for.

Acknowledgments

To those people who rode the tidal wave of deadline with me, each in their own incomparable way:

Pat, whose emotional support defies words.

Laura, whose encouraging countdown calls made my telephone answering machine a friend rather than a foe.

Helen, who researched obscure historical facts on a moment's notice and has yet to be unnerved by my urgency or to come up empty-handed.

Lisa, whose equestrian knowledge was surpassed only by her consummate faith and friendship.

Plunk, who reads each book as if it were her own and demands *almost* as much of me as I do of myself.

And most of all, to my family, who withstood the grueling weeks of absenteeism, exhaustion, and tension, and who ultimately cheered beside me when Nicole and Dustin's story turned out to be all I prayed it would be.

My thanks to you all.

Wishes in the Wind

One

Newmarket
Suffolkshire, England
April 28, 1875

Die, Aldridge.

The painted words pierced Nicole's soul like the fatal stab of a dagger.

Bloodred, they trickled down the stall's rear wall, sending shards of terror streaking up her spine. Unconsciously, she gripped Oberon's reins more tightly, unable to enter the thoroughbred's quarters, equally unable to back away.

All semblance of the past hour's reveling vanished in a heartbeat, the jubilant celebration spawned by her father's victory in the 2,000 Guineas forgotten in lieu of this grotesque spectacle.

Die, Aldridge.

Nicole's eyes squeezed shut—a futile gesture, for it could not erase the imprint of that pointed, sinister threat.

"Nickie?" From thirty feet away, Nicholas Aldridge sensed, rather than saw, his daughter's reaction. Extricating himself from his fellow jockeys, he made his way through Newmarket's stable to her side, patting Oberon affectionately as he passed. "What's wrong?"

His question died in his throat as he followed Nicole's gaze. "Damn," he swore softly.

"Papa," she managed, turning to face him. "What . . . ?"

"It's paint, Nickie. Only paint. Not blood."

"I realize that." She wet her lips with the tip of her tongue. "But its meaning is clear." Violet blue eyes studied her father astutely. "It's because of the race, isn't it? Because you wouldn't cooperate?"

Her father glanced furtively from side to side. "How did you know about that? Sullivan swore to me he wouldn't say a word."

"Sully told me nothing. He didn't need to. I'm not blind, Papa. Nor am I deaf. I've heard you tossing about at night, just as I heard your hushed conversations with Sully. Thus, I know what pressure you've been suffering these past weeks. But I had no idea the consequences of your refusal could be as serious as—" Nicole broke off, her tormented stare returning to the ominous crimson letters. "Who painted that?" she demanded. "Exactly who are these horrible men? Are they capable of making that threat a reality?"

"The scum who painted that message are merely pawns, Nickie. They deliver messages with their fists." Shoving back his cap, Nick dragged a forearm across his brow, then gulped at the bottle of ale he held. "As far as who issued their orders, I have no idea. But will he make sure they're carried out? I fear—" His mouth snapped shut.

Nicole needed no further reply. Her chin came up, determination overriding panic. "Then we must act. Now. Before they have time to do so first."

"Act?" Fatherly protectiveness surged to life in Nick's eyes. "Nicole, you don't understand what—who—we're up against. These men are experts at coercion. There's no way for me to escape. I knew that from the instant I was approached, just as I knew there'd be hell to pay if I didn't throw this race. My visitors made that very clear." His somber gaze returned to the painted message. "Consequences," he muttered. "Pursuit. Harassment. Hell, even a beating. I expected all that. I also figured they'd try to blacklist me. None of it would have worked. I'm too damned tough to whip into submission and too damned good at what I do to be banned from the course. But murder?" His expression grew haunted, as if by uttering the word aloud he'd made the prospect all the more tangible.

"Let's go, Papa." Nicole was already in motion, having

urged Oberon into his stall and untacked him with the skillful speed of a professional head lad. Snatching up a rag, she seized her father's bottle of ale, dousing the wall and vigorously scrubbing until the warning was no more than a muted blur. "There. Now no one will know the reason we fled."

"Fled?" Nick's head jerked around. "I just finished telling you—"

"Hey, Nick!" Gordon Sullivan's deep voice interrupted them. Seconds later he strode into Oberon's stall. "We're celebrating *your* victory. What's keeping you and the elf?"

Unsmiling, Nick turned to his longtime friend and colleague. "They were here, Sully. They left their calling card."

Sully's grin vanished. "Dammit. I was afraid this might happen." He broke off, his uncertain gaze flickering to Nicole.

"Say what you like," Nick supplied. "My clever elf has figured it all out."

An unsurprised nod. "What type of calling card?"

"A threat," Nicole supplied, inserting herself between the men. "Painted in red. Bloodred. Sully, they mean to kill Papa. I've got to convince him to get out of here. Before it's too late."

"Kill him?" Sully echoed. "They used those words?"

"Their precise message was, 'Die Aldridge.' That's terrifying enough for me."

Beads of perspiration broke out on Sully's brow. "Nick, something's not right here. You know as well as I do that these bastards don't kill. Pressure, thrash—yes. But kill? No." A flicker of apprehension. "Unless they're backed into a corner."

"You're talking about Redley," Nick supplied with a scowl of disbelief. "He was a bloody fool, Sully. Besides, we have no proof those lowlifes killed him."

"Don't we?" Sully's tone was ominously quiet. "You and I both ran the course at Doncaster last September. We both heard Redley boast to everyone within hearing distance that he'd thrown the St. Leger trial for himself, not for the scum who'd browbeaten him. He vowed to turn the tables, blackmail them out of thousands of pounds. Three days later, his quarters were ransacked and he was found dead."

"Oh, my God." Nicole went sheet white. "I thought he'd been robbed."

"It's possible he was." Nick wrapped a protective arm about Nicole's shoulders. "Stop it, Sully. You're scaring Nickie. Besides, the point is moot. I didn't give those hoodlums any cause for alarm. All I did was refuse to throw the race."

"Then why are they threatening to kill you?"

"The reasons don't matter," Nicole intervened. "Papa's safety does. I won't gamble with his life, Sully. I'm taking him away. Now."

Sully took in the all-too-familiar set of Nicole's jaw. "I agree, Nick must disappear, but not through your efforts, through mine."

"No." Nicole's veto was instant and fierce. "That would endanger your life as well. I won't have it."

"Nor will I," Nick concurred. "We'll find another way."

"Neither of you is thinking clearly," Sully accused with an exasperated shake of his head. "It's not my life that's at stake here. Nor is it solely yours, Nick." Scowling, he gave voice to the unpleasant truth. "These men aren't amateurs. They know everything about you—including the existence of your revered only child. If you're in danger, so is Nicole."

"Damn," Nick hissed, all the color draining from his face. "I never considered that."

"Even if that's the case, Sully, you won't ensure my safety by risking your own," Nicole interrupted, her mind racing for answers. "So please don't get involved. This problem is mine. Mine and Papa's."

"Really?" Sully arched a brow. "And how do you intend to handle it? By dashing off to parts unknown like a reckless filly, Nick in tow? By running away with no strategy or means of survival?" He assessed Nicole's mutinous expression in utter exasperation.

Raucous laughter reached their ears.

"We haven't time for this argument now," Sully pronounced, glancing swiftly over his shoulder to confirm that none of their fellow jockeys had drifted close enough to overhear him. Confident that, for the moment, they remained alone, he dug into his pocket and extracted a key.

"Take Nick to my quarters. They're less than a mile from yours and a whole lot safer. Undoubtedly, whoever left that message knows where you live. By tomorrow they might have figured out that you've taken off, and come looking for you. I'll slip into your rooms tonight, before that happens. I'll fetch your things and bring them to you. By morning we'll have devised a plan to get you out of Suffolk—both of you—to transport you somewhere secluded. And I do mean secluded, not London during the heart of the racing season. Once we get you settled, you'll stay put until those bastards find a new victim. They can't hurt you if they can't find you. Now go."

"No bloody way," Nick denounced with a hard shake of his head. "Sully, have you lost your mind? I'm a jockey. How do you suggest I ride if I'm stashed away like some hidden treasure?"

"I don't suggest you ride. I suggest you stay alive. For your sake—and Nicole's." Sully wasn't mincing words. "Now get the hell out of here before those ruffians come back to effect their threat." He groped in his jacket, pulling out several folded bills. "Take these. It's not much but it's all I've got, and, combined with your prize money, it'll be enough to buy you food and a place to stay."

"Keep your wages." Nick shoved his friend's hand away. "You're as noble—and as rash—as my daughter. Even if I were willing to give up racing and drop out of sight to protect Nickie, she and I need an income in order to survive. How long do you think we'd last on a few pounds?"

"We'll have an income, Papa," Nicole inserted, fists clenched at her sides. "I'll provide it."

Simultaneously, both men glared at her.

"What crazy idea are you thinking up this time, Elf?" Nick demanded, eyes narrowed in suspicion.

"It's not crazy. It's perfectly reasonable. Sully just claimed that I, as well as you, are in danger. Or rather, that Nick Aldridge and his daughter are. Well, I can eliminate both the danger and our lack of money."

"And how will you do that?"

"By ceasing to be your daughter."

Another silence, more ponderous than the first.

"Listen to me, Papa." Nicole gripped her father's forearms, excitement tingeing her cheeks as her plan took shape. "Those men will be hunting for Nick and Nicole Aldridge. Well, we won't be found. You'll be in hiding. And I'll no longer be Nicole Aldridge."

"And who, may I ask, will you be?"

An unconcerned shrug. "I haven't invented a name. At least not yet. But what I call myself doesn't matter. What matters is *what* I shall be, not *who*. And the answer to that is any one of a dozen things. A stable hand. A trainer. An apprentice to a trainer. I could go on and on. The point is, I'm qualified to perform any of those jobs. Better, in fact, than most any man in this stable. You, more than anyone, realize that's true. Not only did I grow up with horses, I learned from the best. Nick Aldridge. I can answer whatever equestrian ads the *Gazette* brandishes. Take any position at any stable, public or private." The tiniest of pauses. "I could even be a jockey."

Despite the refusal hovering on his tongue, Nick couldn't help but grin. "Ah, now we get to the truth. A jockey. Your greatest wish—to race. Is this your attempt to replace me in next month's Derby then?"

Nicole shook her head. "No one could replace you, Papa. You're the finest jockey in England. My wish is to race *beside* you, not in your stead."

"You underestimate yourself, Elf." Affectionately, Nick brushed a strand of ebony hair from her cheek. "Your horsemanship constantly amazes me. And that's a qualified assessment, not paternal pride talking. You have an incredible knack with horses."

"If so, it's because I'm your daughter."

"Not for long, according to the plan you've just spouted."

A tolerant sigh. "My pretense will only be for the world's prying eyes, Papa."

"I see. Tell me, then. This scheme of yours, hasn't it failed to take one very important detail into account?"

"The fact that I'm female."

"Um-hum."

"Well, I won't be. Not outside our home. When I go to seek employment, I'll be a man."

"A man," Nick repeated woodenly, ignoring the choked sputtering that emerged from Sully's throat.

"Yes." Nicole grinned impishly. "And a bloody good one at that."

Without looking away, Nick raised his palm, effectively severing Sully's oncoming verbal protest. "Elf," he continued, "that's absurd. Impossible."

"Why?"

"To begin with, there's nothing manly about you. Why, you're scarcely five feet tall and slender as a reed."

"And you're but a few inches taller and not many pounds heavier. As was my grandfather, and his father before that. The entire Aldridge line—all exceptional jockeys—were short and slight. An asset, I believe you said, in your line of work. I don't recall anyone questioning your masculinity."

"You're not only tiny, Elf, you're delicate and . . ." Flushing, Nick sought the right words, eventually abandoning his attempts and gesturing vaguely in the direction of Nicole's softly curving body. "You're twenty years old, Nickie. A grown woman. Although God knows I seem to forget that fact often enough."

"If I'm able to make *you* forget, the rest of the world will be easy to delude—especially once my disguise is complete. I'll pad my uniform, bind myself down. Believe me, Papa, no one will suspect I'm anything but an eager and adept young man."

"Hey, Sully! Where the hell are you?" came a shout from the far end of the stable. "Now we've lost you *and* Nick?"

With a start, Sully recovered both his voice and his awareness that precious minutes were ticking by. "Coming!" he called back, his worried stare fixed on Nick. "Go out through the rear," he hissed. "I'll tell the others Nicole took sick." Purposefully, he shoved the bills into Nick's hand, disregarding his friend's protest. "Don't be a bullheaded fool. You'd do the same for me. Now go. We'll talk later."

"Sully, I . . ."

"Go, dammit." Sully planted himself directly behind them, thereby obstructing any onlooker's view of their departure.

"Thank you, Sully," Nicole whispered.

In a heartbeat, they were gone.

Spraystone Cottage
The Isle of Wight

"Dustin, you're as restless as the waves of last night's storm," Ariana Kingsley declared, her turquoise eyes glimmering with humor, "and you have been ever since you arrived at Spraystone. It's been three days. And, while I never thought I'd say this, you're more insufferable than Trenton when you brood."

"That bad?" Dustin Kingsley returned with mock dismay. He rolled his brandy goblet between his palms, gifting Ariana with the melting smile that, according to countless affirmations, left a line of swooning women in its wake.

"Worse." Despite the levity of her tone, the duchess of Broddington studied her brother-in-law anxiously, wishing she could discern the cause of his unrest. Since the day they'd met, she and Dustin had been solid friends—and not only because of their mutual love for Trenton. Theirs was a caring, honest rapport, one that made Ariana feel as much Dustin's sister as if they were bound by blood.

Which made his uncustomary reticence all the more perplexing.

Blowing a wisp of auburn hair off her face, Ariana was on the verge of probing further when, from the corner of her eye, she spied a more immediate dilemma—one that propelled her from her armchair and sent her dashing across the sitting room in record time.

Deftly, she extracted her eight-month-old son, Alexander, from beneath the sideboard, scolding him as she gathered him in her arms. "And just what are you doing?"

Chuckling at his nephew's antics, Dustin leaned back against the cushioned settee, crossing one long leg over the other. "I believe he was on the verge of mastering the fascinating challenge that's been endlessly plaguing him. After days of eyeing the sideboard and all its bottles and fine crystal, he was hell-bent on inspecting them at close range. Had you delayed your interruption a scant moment longer, he would have pulled himself up and accomplished his feat."

"And my entire floor would be doused in madeira and garnished with slivers of glass," Ariana muttered. With an exasperated sigh, she glared at her innocent-looking son, striving to appear stern. "You," she informed him, marching back to her chair, "are an untamable tempest."

"I quite agree." Dustin flexed his shoulders, grimacing at the resulting stiffness. "Every muscle in my body aches from that tiny tyrant. I'm unused to such a whirlwind of activity."

"Now why don't I believe that?" Ariana responded dryly. "From the gossip I've heard thus far this season, it sounds as if you've attended every party and danced with every woman the *ton* has to offer. Soon you'll be forced to travel abroad in order to discover new prospects. Rather like you do with your thoroughbreds."

"An interesting concept." Surprisingly, Dustin sobered, staring pensively into his drink. "Unfortunately, however, I'm finding the allure of my thoroughbreds to be far more long-standing than that of my liaisons. I fear my brother snatched up the last real treasure in a vast array of shoddy imitations."

Ariana inclined her head. "Did something unpleasant happen at Newmarket?"

"Yes. My mare lost."

"Very amusing. That's not what I meant and you know it. You're not one to agonize over your losses—probably because they rarely occur. Now, are you going to answer my question?"

"Touché." Dustin raised his glass in tribute. "Very well. No, nothing happened at Newmarket—at least nothing tangible. But you're right. I am restless. Why? I haven't a clue. Perhaps it *is* time to travel abroad. I might not find intriguing women, but I'm sure I'll discover an Arabian or two."

Unfooled by his lighthearted quip, Ariana studied Dustin, wondering how her brother-in-law would react if she were to tell him what she believed to be not the immediate but the underlying cause of his malady. Was he ready to hear it? And was she the one to impart the fact that he was far too warm and loving a man to be eternally content with empty dalliances and profitable horse races?

Chewing her lip, Ariana resettled herself—and her son—in the cozy armchair.

Alexander was gone before she'd smoothed her skirts. He slid down the seat cushion, dropped to the rug, and crawled toward the sideboard—a miniature bandit intent on completing his crime.

He collided with his father's boots.

"Well, I see you've kept your poor mother occupied. All day, I suspect." Hoisting Alexander into his arms, Trenton Kingsley crossed over to his wife. "I'm home, misty angel." He bent, brushing her lips with his. "I missed you."

"I missed you, too." Ariana caressed her husband's jaw. "You've been gone forever. It was scarcely dawn when you left for Bembridge. Was the storm's destruction that severe?"

A tired nod. "Unfortunately, the village sustained quite a bit of damage. The good news, however, is that most of it is now in the process of being rectified."

"In other words, you spent all day securing the homes and providing for the families."

Trenton smiled tenderly at the blatant pride in her assertion. "It wasn't so remarkable a feat. After all, I have the money and the knowledge of the structures."

"You also have the heart," Ariana added fervently, love shining in her eyes. "You're incredible—and I don't mean as an architect or a duke. I mean as a man."

"And you're beautiful." Trenton frowned, stroking the shadows of fatigue beneath her lids. "But you look exhausted. In retrospect, I'm sorry we didn't bring Alexander's governess to Spraystone with us. At least you would have had some assistance."

"I couldn't do that to Mrs. Hopkins. She was more exhausted than I. Why, she nearly wept with joy when I told her to stay at Broddington for a much-needed rest. I suspect she'll sleep the entire week in anticipation of Alexander's return. Besides, I did have some help. Dustin was a savior."

Trenton's gaze flickered to his brother. "My thanks are twofold, then. One for helping Ariana with my rascal of a son, and one for remaining at Spraystone and keeping an eye on them both while I was away. I know you wanted to help out in the village, but when I left this morning, the skies were still ominous, the grounds were covered with splintered wood, and the base of the hill behind the cottage was badly flooded. I would never have left Ariana and Alexander alone, nor would I have trusted them into anyone's care but yours."

"My pleasure." Dustin waved away the thanks, one corner of his mouth lifting slightly. "Although, if you ask me, neither debris nor rushing waters are any match for your son. In truth, I believe that, had the storm chosen to resume, it would have survived a scant hour in Alexander's company before spinning out over the Solent as fast as its winds could whip."

Laughter rumbled in Trenton's chest. "You're probably right. What did my little villain do today?"

"You name it," Dustin replied, counting off on his fingers. "Painted the oriental rug in the library a vivid green, used the silver tea service as a thunderous new musical instrument, plucked stray feathers from your hens. He has a propensity for detail, your son. The uneven feathers seemed to offend him. So, once again, did the inexplicable existence of facial hair on human beings." Gingerly, Dustin touched the ends of his mustache and winced. "I take it I'm the only one he knows with one of these."

"Actually," Trenton replied thoughtfully, "I never before considered it, but yes. No wonder it baffles him so."

"Well, I've endured eight months of bafflement in the hopes that he'd come to accept it. But now he's graduated from bafflement to attempted obliteration. He spent the latter portion of the morning trying to detach my mustache from my upper lip. Thus, I've decided to concede and shave the bloody thing off the instant I return to Tyreham. At least that will leave one less part of me for Alexander to destroy." A wry grin. "In any case, by midafternoon Ariana had reached the point where she looked as if she were about to drop. So, I took over myself, confident that an eight-month-old's stamina was no match for a vigorous man of two and thirty. After three hours of frolicking in the barn and two hours of storytelling in the nursery, I'd altered my opinion. Your heir wasn't a bit fatigued, while I, on the other hand, fell asleep on the nursery floor, where I snored away the afternoon, awakening only when Ariana came to fetch me for dinner."

"I see." Trenton had to struggle to control his mirth. "And what, pray tell, did Alexander do during your well-earned respite?"

"Located a new diversion," Ariana sighed. "He squirmed down the stairs, feet first, only to discover the beloved haven you just completed for me. I spotted him as he crossed the conservatory threshold, eyes alight as he realized that it afforded him the same intriguing amusements as the conservatory at Broddington. By the time I'd dashed after him and crept through the pile of dirt he'd spilled, he'd already managed to upend three ferns and topple six geraniums."

Trenton's shoulders were shaking. "He's your son, Ariana. Inspired by flowers and animals."

"I beg to differ with you, Your Grace," Ariana retorted. "Alexander's propensity for getting into trouble is inherited from you. I was, and am, serene and content."

"Content, yes—after a fashion," Trenton concurred, having given the matter proper consideration. "But serene? Not until I've worn you out."

"Nevertheless," Ariana hastily interrupted, blushing as Dustin disguised his chuckle with a cough, "Alexander's devilish resolve is a Kingsley trait. Like all of you, he's intense, impatient, and perpetually in search of a challenge. I should know. I'm surrounded by Kingsley men."

Dustin stood to replenish his drink. "Why, Ariana, you cut me to the quick. Intense? Impatient? And here I thought I was remarkably easy to get along with; far more charming than Trent, and not nearly as moody or volatile."

"Normally, I'd agree." Trenton joined his brother at the sideboard. "But not this week. This week you've been testy as a bear and unsettled as hell."

Groaning, Dustin lowered the bottle with a thud. "First Ariana, now you. Well, you can both stop worrying. To my knowledge, nothing is wrong. Other than the fact that my trainer is retiring and my last three jockeys have been totally unable to win races." He shrugged. "Maybe I'm just becoming intolerant in my old age. Or maybe, as I told Ariana, it's time to go searching for new horses and horsemen to fill my stables."

"You have the finest thoroughbreds in Surrey—perhaps even in England," Ariana inserted quietly. "'Tis their owner who is out of sorts, not they."

Silently, Dustin traced the edge of the mahogany sideboard. "Perhaps you're right," he acknowledged.

That did it. Ariana's decision was made.

Rising, she transferred Alexander from Trenton's arms to her own, giving her husband a meaningful look. *Talk to him,* her eyes pleaded. *You're the only one who can.*

Wordlessly, Trenton nodded.

"Once again, I'm going to attempt to put Alexander to bed," Ariana stated. "And, given that it's after eight o'clock and his eyelids are drooping, perhaps I'll succeed. After which we can take a chance and sample our dinner. Since Clara was unable to get through Bembridge's flooded roads, I tackled the job of preparing today's meals. I'm encouraged by the fact that Dustin has consumed two of them and continues to live—a hopeful sign indeed. With a modicum of luck, we'll all survive the ordeal."

"You're a superb cook, misty angel."

"She'd be even better if you'd allow her more time in the kitchen," Dustin suggested, his mischievous grin revived. "Between satisfying Alexander's continual needs and your exhaustive ones . . ."

"That's it." Ariana scooted toward the door, her cheeks aflame. "I'm off to the nursery."

"Hurry back," Dustin called after her rapidly retreating back. "I look forward to continuing our discussion of your culinary skills."

Still chuckling, he turned to his brother. "She's quite a prize, Trent. Open and honest and so bloody in love with you that it's humbling. You're a lucky man."

"I know." Trenton sipped his madeira, his gaze fixed on Dustin's. "Care to talk about it?" he asked bluntly.

Dustin didn't pretend to misunderstand. "I would if I knew what it was." He sighed, humor eclipsed by uncertainty. "All I know is that lately everything seems so meaningless—the day-to-day rituals, the business arrangements, the competitions."

"The women?"

"Yes—them, too." Dustin abandoned his drink. "All in all, my life has become utterly tedious and predictable."

"Predictable?" Trenton's brows rose. "This from the man who changes partners more frequently than he changes clothes?"

"That's just sex, Trent, nothing more than a pleasurable distraction. Gratifying, yes, but distinctly unfulfilling."

"I could name a dozen women who's be thrilled to convert that distraction into a lifetime commitment."

"Marriage you mean?" Dustin shook his head. "I'm afraid you've spoiled me, Brother. After seeing what you and Ariana share, I won't settle for less. The women you're referring to regard me as a coveted prize. They like my money and the title Queen Victoria granted me. Well, perhaps that's enough for some, but not for me. At least sex is honest. Fleeting, but honest. It assuages the body but circumvents the heart. Surely you recall?"

"Yes, I recall," Trenton murmured with the quiet insight of a man who, thanks to his miraculous wife, knew the difference between lovemaking and sex.

"Then there's nothing else to say. I'm drifting, and I know it. But for the time being, I see no alternative."

Trenton nodded, shifting to another unsettled aspect of Dustin's life. "You mentioned several upsets in your staff. I know Banks's retirement comes as no surprise. Still, he's been training your thoroughbreds since you began breeding them to race. His resignation must pose a major setback."

"I'd be lying if I said otherwise. Banks is the best trainer in Surrey, perhaps in England. But I understand his decision. I'd probably make the same one, were I he. Trent, the man is nearing fifty. He's got a wife, children, even grandchildren. He's been training for twenty years, not to mention the ten years of riding he did prior to that. He's tired. Training is grueling as hell. I can't blame him for his choice."

"Nor can I," Trenton concurred. "Have you made arrangements for a new trainer?"

"I've interviewed five. Two of them are good. Damned good. I plan to meet with each once more. Then I'll make a decision."

"What about the ineffectual jockeys you mentioned?"

Dustin rolled his eyes. "Every one of the last three, while appearing to offer great promise when hired, has turned out to be a colossal disappointment."

"You'll rectify that."

"I already have. They've all been dismissed. Permanently. I'm finished tolerating indifference and mediocrity. My stables boast the finest thoroughbreds to date. I want an equally fine rider on their backs. In my mind, only one man fits that description—Nick Aldridge."

"I can't dispute that." Trenton nodded his approval. "Aldridge is one hell of a jockey."

"Indeed he is. With him in the saddle, my champions will take every race of the season."

"Then I presume Aldridge has agreed to your terms?"

"He will. Once I unearth him, that is."

"Unearth him? Didn't he just ride at Newmarket?"

"Yes, brilliantly. He won the Two Thousand Guineas by at least ten lengths. I fully intended to resolve things then and there by offering him a retainer—and a small fortune—to ride exclusively for me. However, as luck would have it, he was surrounded by a mob of well-wishers the instant he passed the winning post, after which no one seemed able to find him. I even sent a messenger to his home that night, but to no avail." Dustin shrugged. "He was probably out celebrating. I'm not concerned. I'll find him. I would have pursued the matter further, had I not been leaving for Spraystone. Upon my return, I plan to place an ad in the *Gazette*—one that clearly states Aldridge's name *and* the terms of my offer. I'm arrogant enough to believe he's heard of me, and that, between my reputation and the sum I'm willing to pay, *he'll* find *me.*" Dustin rubbed his palms together, a hint of the old Dustin surfacing in the challenging gleam that lit his midnight eyes.

"It sounds as if your tedium is about to come to an end."

"Yes, at least in business matters." The gleam vanished. "So, now that all my problems are resolved, we can ready ourselves for Ariana's excellent meal."

An enthusiastic squeal from the upstairs nursery negated that thought.

"You spoke too soon," Trenton muttered with a wry grin. "Evidently, my son has recouped his strength. I'd best go up and hasten this bedtime procedure, lest we starve."

Another squeal reached their ears, followed by Ariana's soft, loving admonishment.

Dustin swallowed, oddly shaken by the tender exchange between mother and son. "Trent, I'll be leaving Spraystone in the morning."

Silently, Trenton absorbed his brother's announcement. "That's a rather sudden decision, isn't it?"

"Sudden, but necessary."

"Why? You arrived only a few days ago."

"I know. And I've enjoyed every moment of my visit. But you need time alone with your wife and son. While I . . ." Roughly, Dustin cleared his throat. "I've a great deal on my mind and quite a bit to resolve. I'm restless as hell, which you and Ariana both noticed. I think it's best that I return to Tyreham and address that restlessness—at least the part that's within my ability to control. I've got to get on with my life, whatever the future may hold."

"I understand, perhaps better than you think. Although you know you're welcome here as long as you choose to stay." Trenton placed his hands on Dustin's shoulders, searching for just the right words. "Dustin, you, better than anyone, know how very little I believed in before I found Ariana. I was nothing more than a callous and embittered shell until that blessed day she stumbled into my life. And now? Now I'm whole. I believe in love, in trust, even in forever. If there's hope for an unyielding cynic like me, there's certainly hope for you."

"Thanks, Trent." Dustin didn't pretend to misunderstand. "However, waiting is fast becoming more than a mere inconvenience. To quote your wife, I'm intense, impatient, and perpetually in search of a challenge. A Kingsley trait, I believe she said."

A corner of Trenton's mouth lifted. "Ah, but the rewards are well worth the wait. Just look at how contented this Kingsley has become."

Warmth pervaded Dustin's gaze. "I have. And if ever I

doubted the existence of miracles, your transformation has long since erased those doubts. As for the love you and Ariana share, I could wish for no more." He arched a speculative brow. "Now if only I were sure that wishes are granted."

Miles away, gazing out the window, Nicole was pondering much the same thing—but for entirely different reasons.

Her eyes damp, she clutched a filigreed locket in her hand, seeing naught but dread in the starlit sky above. "I'm frightened, Mama," she whispered to the ubiquitous heavens. "So frightened. Papa's a wonderful man, and he's all I have. I don't know what I'd do if I lost him." Unsteadily, she wet her lips with the tip of her tongue. "Can you hear me, Mama? I'm wishing. Just as you taught me, I'm wishing—for Papa's sake, and for mine. If ever I needed the magic of my wishing locket, it's now. Please . . ." Nicole's voice faltered, her fist clenched tightly about the delicate piece of silver, "please let this wish come true."

Two

"Nickie, this is no life. Not for either of us."

Nick Aldridge swung away from the window, pacing his half of the room's modest floor. "I shouldn't have listened to you. Or to Sully, for that matter. Now I'm imprisoned in a bloody London inn, locked up like a caged rat for Lord knows how long. You and your crazy scheme."

"It isn't crazy, Papa," Nicole murmured, her voice muffled by the blanket they'd strung up to afford each a bit of privacy. She stepped around it, concentrating on the unfamiliar task of buttoning up a bodice. "The rumor we started makes perfect sense. As far as the world knows, you injured your leg during the last furlong of the Two Thousand Guineas and are now recuperating outside of Glasgow, at the home of relatives."

"We have no relatives in Glasgow."

A twinkle. "How would anyone know that? Besides, Mama had a Scottish cousin or two. That's why Sully and I chose Scotland. It's a perfectly plausible place for you to visit—and remote enough to keep any potential pursuers at bay. After all, you can do them no harm if you're away from England and the turf." Staring at herself in the looking glass, Nicole's twinkle vanished. "*This,* on the other hand, is totally implausible. Impossible, in fact."

18

"What is?" her father demanded, still prowling restlessly about.

"Me. This gown. I look—and feel—like a fool."

For the first time, Nick focused on his daughter. Abruptly, his pacing ceased, an odd light dawning in his eyes. "My God, Nickie. I'd forgotten . . . you look—" He broke off.

"That bad, is it?" Nicole sighed. "Well, 'tis a choice between this and the beige one. They're the only gowns I own, thank goodness. Were it not necessary that I blend in with the other women and be unrecognizable as Nicole Aldridge, I wouldn't even consider donning this absurd thing. Quite frankly, I don't understand why women submit to wearing them at all." She raised her pale yellow skirts, glaring down at the offensive layer of petticoats beneath. "It takes an hour to dress, after which you're too exhausted to move, too constricted to breathe, and too unwieldy to collapse in a chair." With a disgusted sound, she released the full skirts, letting them fall back into place. "I'll be grateful when I'm employed, back in the stables—and in breeches—where I belong."

Nick shook his head in disbelief. "You're blind, do you know that, Elf? You're beautiful. More than beautiful. Dressed like that, you're the image of your mother."

Now it was Nicole's turn to look incredulous. "Papa, I believe a week in seclusion has affected your vision. Mama was a lady—an elegant, fragile lady."

"Which you would be, too, if Alicia were alive to see to it." He swallowed. "She gave you so much I never could— her quick mind, her love of reading, and that fanciful imagination of hers. Thank God she lived long enough for that. But she died before you finished growing up. You were a girl. Now you're a woman. And I'm too rough around the edges to teach you anything about manners or social graces. I always assumed Alicia would do that."

Hearing her father's voice quaver with guilt and regret, Nicole went to him at once. "Stop it, Papa," she said quietly, taking his hands in hers. "You know as well as I do that Mama's death had nothing to do with the way I turned out. I've been in the stables, underfoot, since I could walk. The only time Mama managed to drag me away was for my studies. When she tried to interest me in more feminine pursuits, I fled the instant I could, scooting back to the stables in record time." A small smile. "Let's face it. I was hopeless."

"You were also a child."

"Not when Mama died, I wasn't. I was nearly thirteen when she contracted her influenza. And she'd long since accepted that I was, to quote her affectionate words, 'Nick Aldridge to be.' "

The sadness in Nick's eyes softened to a whisper of memory. "She was so bloody tolerant. Even though my job meant she could never have the traditional life she wanted."

"What she *wanted*, Papa, was you. She adored you just as you were." Nicole leaned up to kiss her father's cheek.

"She'd be proud of how lovely you've turned out. And she'd want me to see to your future."

"Fine." Nicole returned to the looking glass. "And you shall. But first we must see to yours."

Nick's lips twitched. "I think you should unbind your hair, for starters." He gestured to her thick sable mane, which was twisted into an expedient but less than ladylike braid. "Try to fix it somehow. However it is that women do."

Another sigh. "However indeed. It's nearly dusk. By the time I finish making myself presentable, twilight will have come and gone and all the newsstands will be closed. I wonder if it's really worth the effort just to fetch a newspaper that will doubtless offer as little in the way of employment as its three predecessors did."

"A job will come up, Elf," Nick soothed.

"One hopes before we run out of funds." Nicole chewed her lip. "If we had moved to the East End as I suggested, we could have saved half of what we're spending on this room. There's still time to . . ."

"No." Nick cut her off at once. "As it is, I worry every time you go out alone. But at least we're in a respectable section of town, not living in a filthy hovel, surrounded by drunks and highwaymen who would do Lord knows what to you the instant you stepped out the door." He shuddered. "No, Nicole. We stay put until you find a position."

Nicole recognized that tone of voice and conceded at

once, tugging her hair free and shaking it loose. "Then I'd best finish my chore and fetch today's *Gazette.*"

Two hours later, Nicole was no closer to finding a copy of the newspaper than she'd been at the onset of her excursion. Further, all the newsstands had shut down, as the fashionable world shifted from day to night.

She halted on the embankment road, her stomach lurching to remind her she'd eaten nothing since breakfast.

Breakfast.

A wave of panic accompanied the more dire realization that the lateness of the hour meant all the shops had closed for the evening. Besides the newspaper, she'd intended to purchase food. She and her father were down to a half loaf of bread and a bit of smoked meat—hardly enough to sustain them beyond tonight.

Beads of perspiration trickled down her back. What was she going to do?

Think. She had to think.

Unsteadily, Nicole made her way to the roadside and drew a deep calming breath—one that was instantly thwarted by the stubborn confines of her corset. Dizziness exploded in her head, and she clutched blindly at a nearby lamppost, determined to steady herself. All around her the sounds of night were unfolding at an alarming rate, a profusion of elegantly dressed people leaving their town houses for gala rounds of merrymaking. Originally, Nicole had counted on this very occurrence when she'd planned her jaunt, knowing that the throng of aristocrats would swallow up her presence as she made her way back to the inn. But her plan would backfire if she chose this moment to swoon, for amid this crowd someone was bound to notice a woman lying prone on the roadside.

The dizziness intensified as her corset stood its ground. In response, the collar of her gown seemed to tighten oppressively about her throat. *No,* she ordered herself silently, scrutinizing the passing carriages. *You will not faint. You can't risk calling attention to yourself.*

With staunch determination, Nicole pivoted, seeking a private spot, her gaze scanning the banks of the Thames.

Unthinking, she darted toward the river walk, which stretched between the embankment road and the river itself.

Thankfully, there was a secluded, empty bench behind a marble statue and a row of trees. She dropped onto it, forcing her breathing to become slow and shallow until the dizziness receded. *Damn this bloody corset*, she fumed. *Gown or no gown, I'll never again don one of these lethal stranglers.*

Twenty feet away, couples were milling about, but the lush line of trees acted as a shield between Nicole and the walkway's patrons. Safe and unseen in her tiny niche, she allowed herself to relax. She needed to plan her strategy, and she would—in a moment. But first her body needed to recoup its strength in order for her mind to function. And, in the absence of food, a brief respite would have to suffice.

Leaning her head back, she stared up at the sky, watching the twinkling of the stars as they appeared, one by one. This onset of night was magic—not just here, but everywhere. Even amid the chaos at the stables, everything seemed to slow at the spellbinding instant that twilight merged with darkness, as if to acknowledge the reverence of the occurrence.

A reminiscent smile played about Nicole's lips. This was also the hour of night when, as a little girl, her mother would tuck her in and tell her stories—wondrous, fairy-tale stories that made her heart sing and her imagination soar. She'd hang on to every word, awestruck, somehow believing it could all be. But then, her mother had the power to make one believe, and Nicole knew why. It was because Alicia Aldridge herself believed.

Do you know what stars really are, Nickie? She could almost hear her mother's voice. *They're bits of light offered to us by the magical sprites of happiness. They're reserved for special nights and equally special people, because only those who see—truly see them—can reap their magic.*

What is their magic, Mama? she'd ask. *And am I one of those special people?*

Her mother would smile that faraway smile. *Indeed you are. As for their magic, it's an offering. A precious offering to seize and to nurture. So remember, darling, every time you*

*see a star, you're being offered a miracle. Wish on it—wish
very, very hard, and that star, and all its enchantment, will be
yours.*

Forever, Mama?

Yes, my love, forever.

Two tears slid down Nicole's cheeks, and she wrapped her
arms about herself, capturing the memory as she studied the
sky. This was the kind of night her mother had alluded to:
clear, warm, and fragrant, alive with the blossoming buds of
spring.

And illuminated by a sea of dazzling stars.

Dreamily, Nicole focused on a star that seemed to call out
to her. It wasn't the largest nor even the brightest of the
heavens' offerings. But there was something extraordinary
about the way it glowed, as if trying to compensate for its
diminutive size, that drew her to it, held her captive.

I'm wishing, Mama, Nicole declared silently, *as I did on
my locket. Only this time I'm wishing for the magic offered
by that tiny star. Because, thanks to you, I still believe.*

Her throat constricted, and more tears trickled from the
corners of her eyes.

"May I offer my assistance?"

Nicole froze at the sound of the deep masculine voice,
dreams reverting abruptly to reality. She'd been discovered.
Someone knew she was here. She had to escape.

Inching to the edge of the bench, she mentally gauged her
distance to the road, preparing to bolt.

"Don't run off. And don't be frightened. I'm not going to
hurt you."

A hard hand closed over hers, and the bench shifted as
her unexpected companion sat down beside her.

"I'm not frightened," she heard herself say, keeping her
chin down. "I'm . . ." She broke off. *I'm what? Avoiding
detection?*

"I saw you clutching that lamppost. When you fled into
the trees, you were white as a sheet. I was concerned you
might faint."

"I'm fine." She stared at the tips of his polished evening
shoes, feeling the warmth of his palm over hers. "But I'd
best be on my way."

His grip tightened, and an instant later a handkerchief was pressed into her other hand. "Try this. I've been told it works wonders. Guaranteed to dry a lady's tears."

Nicole couldn't help it; she looked up, drawn to the husky teasing in his tone.

Her breath suspended—only this time her corset had little to do with it.

He was perhaps the most classically handsome man she'd ever seen, undoubtedly a nobleman, and not only because of his elegant evening attire. He had a bold straight jawline and patrician nose that screamed aristocrat, and thick black hair over a broad forehead and equally black brows, all set off by penetrating eyes the color of midnight—eyes that now assessed her with the practiced skill of a man who knew women . . . intimately.

His perusal was thorough, his approval obvious, even to a novice like herself. She could see it in his smile, his lips curving ever so slightly, and in his eyes, a glint of admiration in their deep blue depths, the dark brows lifting in surprised pleasure.

For the first time in her life, Nicole was grateful to be wearing a gown, outdated or not.

"You're far too beautiful to cry," he murmured, reclaiming the handkerchief and gently drying her cheeks. "Further, you're far too beautiful to be racing about London alone at night. Where were you headed?"

Nicole moistened her lips, her mind totally unable to formulate a suitable lie.

"What's your name?"

She blinked. "Pardon me?"

"Your name," he prompted. "You must have one."

"Oh. Yes. It's Nicole."

He smiled, and Nicole found herself wondering just how long someone could exist without breathing.

"Nicole," he repeated. "It suits you perfectly—beautiful and delicate. Have you a surname as well?"

That snapped her out of her reverie.

"I must be going." She made to rise. "I've already been away too long."

Those amazing midnight eyes narrowed. "Away? Away from whom?" His gaze fell to her left hand. "A husband?"

Nicole smiled at the expectant note in his voice. "No. I'm sorry to disappoint you, but I have no husband."

"Disappointed? *Au contraire,* my mysterious beauty, I'm elated." He caught her wrist, stroked it ever so lightly. "Sit. Just for a few minutes. Until the color returns to your cheeks."

She found herself complying. "Very well."

"Since we're exchanging only given names this evening, mine is Dustin."

"Hello, Dustin."

He grinned. "Hello, Nicole." His thumb traced the pulse in her wrist. "Why were you crying? Is it a man? If so, tell me his name and I'll beat him senseless."

She was uncomfortably aware of the heat his touch evoked, making her wrist tingle and burn. "No, it isn't a man. It's many things. Memories, mostly."

"Sad memories?"

"No, actually happy ones." She swallowed. "I was thinking about my mother."

"You lost her." It was a statement, not a question, and Nicole's eyes widened in surprise.

"Don't look so shocked," Dustin answered her unspoken thought. "I've worn that particular look myself."

"I see." Nicole inclined her head. "Why are you here?" she blurted.

A corner of his mouth lifted. "Is that a philosophical question or a specific one?"

"A specific one. Not 'here' meaning on this bench, but 'here' meaning on the river walk—alone."

"Is going for a solitary stroll so astonishing?"

"For a man like you? Yes."

"A man like me," he repeated. "What does that mean?"

"It means you're handsome, well bred, and devastatingly charming. Add to that the fact that it's the height of the London season and countless parties are in progress. So why aren't you there, surrounded by eager, adoring women rather than walking along the Thames by yourself?"

One dark brow arched. "I'm flattered. And dumbfounded. Are you always so honest?"

Nicole considered his question. "I think so, yes."

"Very well then, I'll be equally honest. I was invited to all those parties to which you refer, where I would mingle with all those women you just alluded to. And the very thought of spending another evening like that left me cold—cold and empty. So, instead I'm here, taking a solitary walk along the Thames. Now, have I shocked you?"

She studied his face, then shook her head. "As a matter of fact, no."

He leaned forward, tucking a stray curl behind her ear. "What nearly caused you to faint?"

"Exhaustion, I suppose. I haven't slept in several nights. I have a great deal on my mind."

"Obviously." His gaze intensified. "Would you like to talk about it? Perhaps I can ease your distress."

Nicole sighed. "Not unless you can undo events that have already occurred, or right life's wrongs and balance its inequities."

"Only that?"

He was teasing again, in that disarming way of his, and Nicole found herself responding by speaking the emotional truth that had gnawed at her all week. "Sometimes it all seems like too much. Sometimes I don't think I'm strong enough to overcome life's obstacles."

Dustin's smile vanished. "But you are. And it's not," he replied, somehow not needing to ask for clarification of her veiled declaration. "I have it on the finest authority that when a problem becomes unbearable, a solution appears. Therefore, the very fact that you're reaching your limit means your answer is near."

She started, taken aback by his profound assertion. "Is that a promise?"

"So I've been told." His forefinger traced the fine line of her jaw. "Let me help you."

"I can't." She eased away, knowing she must.

"At least let me see you home."

"No. It's . . . far."

"My carriage is parked just beyond these trees. My driver will take you anywhere you want to go."

"No."

"Very well, forget the carriage. I'll walk you home." He pressed a silencing forefinger to her lips. "I don't care if it's ten miles away."

"Dustin—please. I appreciate the offer, but I can't accept it."

His fingers captured her chin, those midnight eyes delving deep inside her. "I have one final request, then. A good-night kiss."

"What?"

His glance fell to her mouth, but he made no move to draw her near. "You don't have much experience with men, do you?"

"If you mean romantically, no. None."

"I thought not. You're too honest, too damned refreshing for it to be otherwise." His hand slid around to cup her nape. "If I promise to let you go immediately thereafter— no questions asked—may I kiss you, Nicole?"

She searched his face bewilderedly.

"I realize it's an outrageous request—outrageous and thoroughly improper—a request I have no right to make. But I'm making it nonetheless. And I want you to say yes."

"Yes," she heard herself whisper.

Tenderness flashed in his searing, midnight gaze. He framed her face between his palms, lowering his head until his lips brushed hers, once, twice, then settled on them for a slow, warm, exquisitely gentle exploration.

Nicole sighed, shifting a bit, unconsciously easing closer to the wondrous contact of his mouth.

He deepened the kiss slightly, molding his mouth to hers, nudging her lips apart to accept the initial penetration of his tongue. She made an inarticulate sound, swarmed by unfamiliar sensations, shivering with the awareness that she hovered on the brink of something new and dark and dangerous.

Slowly, Dustin raised his head. "Where do you live?"

The moment shattered, and Nicole leaped to her feet. "I must go. Now."

"Just tell me where you live."

"No more questions," she reminded him, backing away. "Your promise, if you recall."

Frustration drew his brows into a harsh, dark line. "How will I find you? I want to see you again, dammit."

"That's impossible." Gathering up handfuls of material, Nicole prayed her customary speed wouldn't be hindered by her gown. "Thank you for comforting me, Dustin. As you can see, the color has returned to my cheeks. Good night."

She bolted into the darkness.

"I hope this issue of the *Gazette* yields some results," Nicole murmured, dropping into a chair and unfolding the newspaper. "Especially given what I went through to find it."

Nick frowned, rubbing the back of his neck. "I was worried sick about you. Next time don't sprint off like an impulsive filly before you've checked to see if what you want is here—at the inn desk, of all places."

"An impulsive filly? You sound like Sully." Nicole flipped through to the ads. "But in this case you're right. What I did was stupid."

"Thank goodness, no harm came to you."

Nicole felt hot color suffuse her cheeks—color she carefully hid behind the printed pages. "It never occurred to me to check with the innkeeper to see if he had—" She shot up, nearly knocking Nick over. "Papa! Look at this!" Shoving the newspaper into her father's hands, she pointed to the first and largest paragraph on the personals page.

Nick Aldridge: As I've been unable to uncover your where-abouts so that we might talk face-to-face, I'm hoping to locate you through this personal. If you're reading it, come to Tyreham Manor, Surrey, at once to discuss an exclusive retainer. Name your price. The marquis of Tyreham

With a muttered oath, Nick gripped the page, rereading the lines several times before raising his head. "Lord Tyreham is the finest breeder in England."

"Breeder and racer," Nicole amended. "I know. I've heard his name spoken countless times at the stables." Her brows drew together. "Evidently, he placed this ad before word of your supposed injury reached him. I wonder what prompted him to place it now, of all times."

"That's no coincidence." Nick's scowl was grim. "Tyreham's gone through some disappointing jockeys lately. At least *he* believes they were merely disappointing. I know otherwise. The fact is that at least one of them—Alberts—was taking money from the bastards who attempted to blackmail me."

"He threw his races?"

"Exactly, a reality I'm sure the marquis is totally unaware of."

"That's all the more reason you'd be the ideal candidate for him," Nicole declared proudly. "You're not only the best jockey in England but the most ethical one as well."

"A lot of good that does me." Nick slapped the newspaper down. "Damn! Tyreham will have prime contenders in every race this summer—Epsom, Goodwood, the July Stakes at Newmarket. How can I miss this opportunity?" He raked a hand through his hair. "I swear I'd take my chances and resurface if I weren't so afraid those bastards would hurt you."

"Let me answer the personal."

Nick stared. "Nickie, are you insane? What would you tell the man? That you're Nick Aldridge?"

"No, of course not." Nicole interlaced her fingers, resting her chin atop her hands. "I'll tell him the truth."

"The truth?"

She grinned. "Well, a combination of the truth and the story Sully and I concocted—a story that has doubtless reached Lord Tyreham's ears by now and has, therefore, dashed his hopes of procuring your services any time in the near future." She paused. "Therefore, I shall ride to Surrey to interview with the marquis. I'll tell him I apprenticed under Nick Aldridge for fifteen years, since I was scarcely more than a tot. I'll tell him Nick and I have a very special rapport, that he taught me everything I know about horses. All of which is true."

"I see. And, given the close friendship you and Nick Aldridge supposedly share, I'm sure good old Nick must have told you exactly where he's staying. Have you thought about how you'll get out of sharing that information with the marquis?"

Her smile faltered, then reappeared. "Lord Tyreham won't expect me to divulge that information. He'll understand that you need rest—and privacy—to regain your strength. I'll divert his questions by offering him a temporary alternative to you. Me." Nicole glowed, warming to her story as she devised it. "I've just thought of the perfect plan! I'll arrive at Tyreham with a note addressed to the marquis and written in your hand. It will state that you sent me in your stead, to ride for him until you are able to travel to Surrey and take over. The note will then embellish on my versatility and my uncanny ability with horses."

A hearty chuckle vibrated in Nick's chest. "Now you not only look like your mother, you sound like her—the same quick mind and extraordinary imagination. Remember the stories she could invent out of thin air?"

Nicole smiled wistfully. "I remember. And she made every one of them sound plausible." Her gaze fell on the nightstand, and the precious wishing locket that lay upon it.

A symbol of dreams, like the star she'd wished upon earlier and the heart-stopping man who'd crossed her path.

Dustin.

Where was he now? Had he gone after her, or had he just dismissed their meeting as inconsequential and returned to the glittering world from which he'd come?

Hastily, she dismissed the questions together with the impossible memory that accompanied them.

"Nickie?" Her father's voice yanked her back to the subject at hand. *"Now* what are you thinking?"

She raised her chin. "I'm thinking that I might have inherited Mama's fanciful mind, but I also inherited your mule-headedness and spunk." She leaned forward, resuming her argument. "I can do this, Papa. I know I can. With your letter, the marquis won't dare turn me away. Oh, he might be reluctant at first, but he'll relent. After all, it's only temporary, and I am a close friend of yours." She held her breath. "Please, Papa."

Nick wrestled with his worry.

"Besides your spunk, I also inherited your strength," Nicole added softly. "I'm not frail like Mama was. I'm strong and I'm healthy. And, as you yourself claimed, I'm a damned good rider. An extraordinary rider, I believe you said." She squeezed her father's hand. "You've always taken care of me. Just this once, let me take care of you."

Releasing his breath on a sigh, Nick nodded. "Very well, Elf. Dress as a boy. Go to Tyreham. You can offer the marquis nearly the same level of skill as I can. But, Nicole . . ." His jaw set. "I won't allow this charade to go beyond the end of June. For both our sakes."

"You're thinking of the July meetings."

"Exactly. Oh, I have no doubt you'd place in every bloody race. But you're not traveling and sharing quarters with the other jockeys—men who, need I remind you, would believe you to be one of them?"

Nicole flushed. "I see your point. Very well then, the end of June. By that time, those greedy scoundrels will have found another victim."

"And by which time, you'll have driven the poor, unsuspecting marquis of Tyreham totally insane," Nick returned with an affectionate grin.

"Probably," she agreed. "Papa, what do you know of Lord Tyreham—other than his talent with thoroughbreds?"

Nick shrugged. "I've only spied him from a distance. He's a nice-looking fellow in his early thirties, I should say. He has quite a reputation with the ladies, from what I hear."

"Oh, splendid," Nicole muttered. "He's undoubtedly overbearing, arrogant, and thoroughly taken with himself."

A grin. "Then thank your lucky stars he'll think you're a man."

"My lucky stars," Nicole repeated, unable to squelch the memory those words evoked. "Yes, Papa, I will. And perhaps, if I'm truly lucky, those stars will reply."

Three

"Put down the bridle, Brackley. He's not ready yet."

Dustin leaned against the stable wall, frowning as he watched his head groom attempting to tack up Tyreham's newest stallion.

Brackley halted, exasperation etched on his face, while Dagger snorted and stomped about his stall. "It's been a fortnight since he arrived at Tyreham, and he still gets skittish every time I approach him."

"I'm aware of that. He's not much better with me."

"With all due respect, sir, I don't see how you can possibly enter him in the Derby even if the Jockey Club does grant you special permission to do so at this late date. No one can mount him, much less race him."

"The point's a moot one," Dustin stated flatly. "Because unless Nick Aldridge recovers from his leg injury, I'm withdrawing my request to add Dagger as a last-minute contender. I meant to win, not merely to enter. And that requires Aldridge. As for Dagger . . ." Dustin's eyes narrowed thoughtfully. "I purchased him for a reason. Every one of my instincts proclaimed him a champion. They still do."

"Your instincts are rarely wrong, my lord." Brackley

shook his head as he hung away the tack. "But this time . . . I don't know."

"Well, I do. It's up to us to determine the cause of Dagger's jitters and ease them. I don't give a damn how long it takes. We'll just have to be patient, even if it means deferring his racing victories until the fall meetings. Forcing ourselves on him won't work. We've got to earn his trust, win him over."

"All right, my lord," Brackley agreed dubiously. "If you say so."

"I do." Dustin turned on his heel. "I'll be back after lunch."

Striding through the stables, he silently berated himself for his brusqueness. It was totally unlike him, but he couldn't seem to snap out of this foul mood. Hell, he was as ornery as Dagger, the only difference being that, in his case, he knew the precise reason for his uncustomary black humor.

And that reason was an apparition named Nicole.

Dammit. He hadn't been able to concentrate on a bloody thing since he'd met her. He'd left London, gone home to Surrey in the hopes that he'd lose himself in his work: hire an exceptional jockey, select the right trainer, establish an affinity with Dagger.

Yet all he seemed to do was visualize a beautiful, anguished face, feel a soft, trembling mouth under his.

Nicole. Nicole what? Where was she from? How could he find her? They'd never crossed paths before—*that* was a certainty. But then, why would they? Her unadorned gown and total lack of artifice suggested she didn't travel in his circles, where the ladies were dazzling, wealthy, fashionable.

Contrived.

And so bloody shallow it sickened him.

She was different. And not just because she stood apart from the practiced members of the *ton*. It was she herself, a blend of innocence and wisdom whose beauty was as delicate and natural as the first buds of springtime. And yet, beneath that fragility, Dustin perceived a strength of character as rare as it was compelling.

How many years had it been since he'd met someone,

male or female, so totally lacking in pretense? When was the last time he'd talked, really talked, with a woman? Nicole's behavior diverged totally from what he'd come to expect: she seemed comfortable with him as a person, yet achingly self-conscious with him as a man.

What was she frightened of? Why had she run? Where the hell had she run to?

There had to be a way to find her. But how? Where should he search for a woman like Nicole? He couldn't knock on every door in London, though the idea grew more tempting by the minute.

He'd take out another personal.

That notion brought him up short. It was the only logical solution. He'd find the right words, make the ad so straightforward and earnest that it would convince her to meet him again—anywhere she chose.

Lost in formulating his message, Dustin exited the stables, his dark mood supplanted by anticipation.

"Tyreham. We've been waitin' for you."

The raspy voice brought him up short.

Blinking, Dustin shielded his eyes from the sunlight. A wary tingle shot up his spine as he regarded the two unkempt men blocking his path. "Who the hell are you?"

One muscular arm shot out, fingers grasping Dustin's shirtfront. "Friends. Here to warn you to stay out of trouble."

Shards of fury sparked in Dustin's eyes as he fought free of the punishing grip. "Get your hands off me. Now. Before I lose my temper."

He was shoved against the stable wall.

"You've been lookin' for Nick Aldridge. Don't."

Stepping purposefully away from the wall, Dustin advanced toward them, memorizing their faces and builds. The one who'd spoken was short, heavyset, with a ruddy complexion and glazed blue eyes. His companion was a few inches taller and a bit less muscular, with unruly black hair and a dark-slitted gaze.

"Your information is outdated," Dustin informed them, brushing off his collar. "Nick Aldridge is in Scotland recuperating from an injury, or haven't you heard?"

"Yeah, we heard." The shorter man began the deliberate

task of rolling up his shirtsleeves. "But if he should make a startlin' recovery and answer your ad, send him away."

"Why? Do you gentlemen have something against a man working for a living?"

"Some men, yeah. Aldridge is one of 'em."

"Who sent you here?"

"That's none of your business. Just do what we said and no one will get hurt."

A muscle flexed in Dustin's jaw. "I don't take kindly to threats. Nor do I take kindly to orders. Now get out of here and don't come back." He pushed past them and kept walking.

"That nephew of yours—what's his name, Alexander? He's a real tough little fellow. I'd hate to see that change."

Dustin froze in his tracks. Slowly, he pivoted to face his adversaries, fury washing over him. "If you come within ten miles of that child, I'll make you wish you were never born."

Surprise and a touch of fear registered on their unshaven faces. "Forget Nick Aldridge and we'll forget your brother's son," the second intruder advised.

"I said get out. I meant it." In two swift motions, Dustin shoved his own sleeves up and out of the way, his shoulders and forearms well-muscled from long years of horseman-ship. "And don't be fooled by my refined manners. If I need to show you the entrance gates by launching you through them, I shall."

"Just remember what we said. We won't be sayin' it again."

With that, they fled.

Blood continued to pound through Dustin's skull, his thoughts running rampant as he considered the ramifica-tions of what had just occurred. The bastards were common trash. Beating them senseless, satisfying as that might feel, would accomplish nothing. They were hired hands, paid for by someone they'd probably never seen, to do a job with no explanation other than how much money they'd make and who they should browbeat into submission.

Two things were certain: One, whoever hired those low-lifes was terrified of Nick Aldridge, and two, that bastard's determination to keep Aldridge off the turf was savage enough for him to threaten people's lives.

Which meant the stakes were high—most likely money or vengeance.

In either case, it raised new possibilities about Aldridge's sudden disappearance from England. Had it truly been spawned by an injury or was it incited by the more compelling need for self-protection?

Dustin rubbed his temples, qualms about Aldridge eclipsed by a more vital concern for Alexander. Not that he believed there was reason for worry, at least not while Aldridge remained in Scotland. Still, he didn't intend to take any chances. He'd wire Trent, alert him to keep a close eye on his son . . .

"Lord Tyreham?"

Dustin's head jerked around to see Poole, the distinguished Tyreham butler, standing a discreet distance away, hands clasped behind his back.

"Yes, Poole, what is it?"

The butler blinked—his only overt reaction to Dustin's curt tone. "Forgive me for intruding, sir. But you have a visitor."

"A visitor?" Entertaining was the farthest thing from Dustin's mind. "Send whoever it is away. I need to dispatch a telegram to Spraystone at once."

"Very good, sir. But I do think you'll want to meet with this lad."

"Lad?"

"Your visitor, my lord. It's a boy who's come in response to the personal you placed in the *Gazette.*"

Abruptly, Dustin became a captive audience. "The personal? Then it's—" He broke off. "Did you say a boy?"

"I did."

"Then it's not Nick Aldridge?"

"No, sir. But, according to the lad—whose name is Stoddard, by the way—Mr. Aldridge instructed him to come to Tyreham."

"Why?"

"To fill the proffered position."

Dustin's jaw dropped. "You're telling me Nick Aldridge sent a substitute jockey here in his place?"

"That's what I'm telling you, sir. Stoddard has a note

from Mr. Aldridge, which the boy insists will explain everything. However, he will show it only to you. In person."

"I'll see him immediately." Dustin took two strides toward the manor, then halted. "Poole." He pivoted to face his butler, lowering his voice to a terse, confidential murmur. "Send a telegram to Trent. Address it *only* to Trent. I don't want Ariana to read it. It will alarm her—probably without cause. Tell him that two men were here warning me not to hire Nick Aldridge. Tell him they mentioned Alexander in their threats. Urge Trent to keep an eye on his family but not to panic. I don't think my unwelcome visitors will dare approach my nephew—not given Aldridge's disappearance and not if they want to live."

All the color had drained from Poole's face. "Of course, sir," he replied, his voice unsteady. "Is there anything else I can do?"

"Tell me where I can find this Stoddard fellow. Because if he knows anything about what just happened here, I intend to find out."

"He's waiting in your study."

Nodding, Dustin clasped Poole's shoulder. "Not a word of this to anyone."

"No one, my lord."

"Thank you, Poole." His jaw set, Dustin stalked toward the manor.

Nicole shifted in the study chair, wondering where the mysterious marquis of Tyreham was and wishing he'd hurry and make an appearance. The apprehension was almost more than she could bear.

Her disguise was flawless. She knew that. Her garb was that of a stableboy; every last hair swept up into a rigid knot beneath her cap; every sign of feminity concealed, as the binding around her breasts—which rivaled her corset in discomfort—could attest.

Clutching her father's note, she mentally rehearsed the speech she'd prepared, reminding herself to further her cause by keeping her movements to a minimum during this, the sole one-on-one meeting she'd likely have to suffer with the man she meant to work for. After today she'd be with the horses, training, and he'd be in his mansion doing whatever it was a marquis did.

But she wasn't leaving Tyreham without that job.

Behind her the door swung open, and she came slowly to her feet, unfolding from her chair like a man. It was time to convince him. She *had* to convince him. For her father's sake . . . and her own.

She turned to face her challenge.

"Mr. Stoddard? I'm the marquis of Tyreham. I understand you wish to see me."

My God, it was Dustin.

For a split second, Nicole felt her legs give out, and she feared, yet again, she might swoon—a sensation she'd only experienced twice, both times in this man's presence.

Dustin—the marquis of Tyreham? How could this be happening?

"Stoddard?"

He was looking at her oddly, and she gave herself a mental kick. *Pull yourself together,* she commanded silently. *In Dustin's mind, nothing has changed since he walked through that door. He's a breeder seeking the best damned jockey in England, and I'm some obscure boy intruding on a job intended for another. And I want that bloody job— Dustin or not. So, I'd better say something. Now.*

"Yes—Alden Stoddard. Thank you for seeing me, my lord." Good, excellent. Her voice was calm and pitched lower than usual, more like a young man's than her own. She tugged at the brim of her jockey's cap, grateful that it covered not only her hair but most of her forehead as well. Firmly, she reminded herself that Dustin had met "Nicole" under cover of night and, therefore, had not gotten a thorough look at her; also that while he looked much the same then as he did now—other than a change from evening attire to riding clothes—she'd been someone else that night at the Thames, not only a different person but a different gender. Hence, not only wouldn't he see a resemblance, he wouldn't even be searching for one.

"You've certainly piqued my curiosity, Stoddard," Dustin was saying, simultaneously gesturing for her to be seated. He assessed her intently while she complied. Then he crossed over to his desk. "My butler tells me Nick Aldridge sent you."

"Yes, sir, he did." Nicole went taut as he walked past her, almost close enough to touch. Again she chided herself to forget that the man who was about to determine her future was the same man who'd invaded her dreams these past nights. If she didn't, she'd never survive this interview, much less acquire the position.

"Why?" Dustin perched on the edge of the desk, his midnight eyes fixed, once again, on her face. "Why did Nick Aldridge send you?"

"It's all here in this note, my lord." Composing herself, she extended her hand, staunchly stilling its trembling. "I assume you've heard about Nick's injury?"

"I've heard." He took the letter, making no move to unfold it.

Nicole cleared her throat. "Well, he was very disappointed that he couldn't accept your offer—at least not immediately. He sent me to fill in for him until he could ride."

One dark brow rose. "And who, may I ask, are you? The name Alden Stoddard means nothing to me."

Lord, he was formidable when doing business—a different man than the one who'd dried her tears. Well, perhaps that was better. It would make it easier for her to recall her purpose in coming. "I'm Nick's protégé," she said proudly. "I apprenticed under him for fifteen years."

"Fifteen years? You must have been riding before you could walk."

Angry color leaped to her cheeks. "I'm twenty, my lord. I was walking by the age of one and riding shortly thereafter."

"I see." A flash of amusement. "Go on."

"Nick is a brilliant and skillful horseman. I was lucky enough to reap the benefits of his teaching and talent. I'm fully qualified to act as your jockey until his return."

"That's quite an arrogant claim."

"It's not arrogance, sir. It's fact."

"I see." Dustin glanced down at the unopened letter in his hand. "I assume Aldridge has included your career summary in this recommendation."

"Career summary?"

"Yes. Where you've ridden, a list of specific races you've placed in . . . that sort of thing. And, of course, your license."

This was the part Nicole had dreaded most. Squaring her shoulders, she confronted it head-on. "No, he hasn't."

A look of feigned surprise. "Why not?"

"Somehow I think you've already guessed the answer to that, but, since you obviously wish to hear it from me, I'll comply. The truth is, I have no license. I've never raced professionally. My career, thus far, has been devoted to assisting Nick. But don't confuse opportunity with skill. When I *do* race—which I shall, be it for you or for another—I'll win. Not just once but every time I'm in the saddle."

"I applaud your confidence."

"Lord Tyreham—" Nicole took a deep, calming breath. "I'd appreciate if you wouldn't toy with me. If you've already made up your mind not to hire me, say so and I'll take my leave. However, if there's a possibility, no matter how slight, that you might reconsider—tell me. And I'll move heaven and earth to convince you to do so."

Dustin grinned. "Straightforward, honest, and very self-confident. I like that." He unfolded Nick's note, scanning it briefly. "Obviously, Aldridge has great faith in your abilities."

"If you require proof that the letter is written in Nick's hand . . ." Nicole reached into her pocket to extract the other samples of her father's handwriting she'd brought.

"I don't."

Her hand stilled. "What does that mean?"

"It means that moving heaven and earth won't be necessary. Save your strength for the turf. I'm convinced." Dustin rose. "When can you begin?"

"You're offering me the job?"

"Only until Aldridge returns from Scotland," he clarified.

"Of course." Nicole stood as well, cautioning herself not to shout out her elation. "I can start first thing tomorrow, sir." She gave him what she hoped was a self-assured smile.

"Good. Now, about living quarters—where are you from?"

"Pardon me?"

"Do you live far from Tyreham? If so, that will be a problem. In order for you to be ready for the remaining competitions this month, you'll need intensive training. The hours will be long, the work grueling. Perhaps you should move to Tyreham—that is, if your family doesn't mind."

Nicole's eyes widened. "You want me to race at the spring meetings—*this* year's spring meetings?"

"Of course. We're only in the first week of May. Most of the spring races have yet to take place. Newmarket's second set begins the eleventh—" Dustin frowned. "No, that's too soon. We'll need several weeks—you, to prepare, I, to meet with the Stewards of the Jockey Club about obtaining your license, getting special permission for last minute entries. Let's see, Bath and Somerset begin the eighteenth, as does Manchester. My instincts tell me to wait. You'll be ready for Epsom on the twenty-fifth."

"Epsom." Nicole breathed the word as if it were sacred. "Which race?"

A corner of Dustin's mouth lifted. "How good did you say you were?"

"Very good. Extraordinary, according to Nick."

"I see." Those incredible eyes were delving again. "Tell me, Stoddard, how are you at calming skittish horses?"

Nicole inclined her head, puzzled by the change in subject. "Horses are much like people, my lord. They're rarely skittish without cause. Why?"

"Because I've just purchased an amazing stallion who I believe can outrace every champion England boasts. I've seen him run, and he's incomparable, both in form and speed. However, during the fortnight he's been at Tyreham, he's balked whenever my head groom or I approach. Do you think you could bring him around?"

"And if I do?"

"Then you'll ride him in the Derby Stakes."

"I'll bring him around."

Dustin chuckled. "I take it the idea appeals to you?"

"My greatest dream has always been to ride in the Derby," Nicole answered honestly.

"Excellent. Then win Dagger over and your dream will become reality."

Nicole fought the urge to hug him. "Thank you for giving me this opportunity."

"You're welcome." His expression turned quizzical. "You never did answer my question about your living arrangements."

"I live in London. With my father."

"I see." A pensive silence. "Your father is welcome to move to Tyreham with you," he added, studying her reaction. "I can offer you a cottage on the far grounds where my tenants reside. It's small but furnished and private, and it will eliminate your need to travel to and from London each day."

Relief exploded in Nicole's chest. Not only a job that surpassed her wildest hopes but a home as well—and a safe place to hide her father. Perhaps her wishing locket had worked a miracle after all. "That would be ideal, my lord. Again, I thank you."

"And again you're welcome." He closed the distance between them, looming over her in a way that made her mouth go dry.

"I . . ." She swallowed, staring at his shirtfront. "I'd best be on my way. I have to pack. And tomorrow will be here before you know it."

"Indeed it will."

"You won't be sorry you made this decision, my lord."

"No, Nicole, I won't be." Dustin cupped her face, raising it to meet his gaze. "Because if you ride half as fast as you run, you'll put even Nick Aldridge to shame."

Four

Nicole's jaw dropped. "You knew?"

"The instant I saw you. Did you honestly think I wouldn't?"

She gave a small, bewildered shrug. "In truth, I didn't think at all. I hadn't time to. I had no idea who you really were until a quarter hour past." A mutinous spark. "Why did you put me through that grueling interview if you already knew who I was?"

"Because an incident occurred just before your arrival, and I had to decide if your visit was in any way related."

"What incident?"

Dustin answered with a question of his own. "Your father—the man who will accompany you to Tyreham—it's Nick Aldridge, isn't it?"

Fear flashed in her violet eyes—eyes more exquisite than he'd been able to fathom in the darkness of night—as frantically, she sought an explanation. "He's . . . I'm . . ."

"So, he's not in Scotland at all," Dustin mused aloud.

"My lord, please." She'd gone sheet white.

"It's all right, Nicole." Dustin captured her fingers, warming them in his. "Your secret is safe. Your father will be, too. I'll make certain of it. I promise."

Satisfaction inundated him as he saw her visibly relax.

43

"Is my disguise so transparent then?" she asked in a small voice.

"Only to me, and only because I've done nothing but visualize your face since we met. If it's any consolation, my butler, Poole, who is known for his discerning eye, never doubted for a minute that you were a boy. So I commend you on a job well done."

He was rewarded with a hint of a smile. "You've comforted me yet again, my lord, and this time without need of a handkerchief."

"I'm honored," Dustin replied. Soberly, he assessed her delicate features, thinking to himself that even disguised as a boy, she was breathtaking—all that he'd remembered and more.

On impulse, he reached out, tugging at the brim of her cap, frowning when it wouldn't budge. "Did you cut your hair?" he demanded.

She shook her head. "No. I wanted to. It would have been prudent, given the circumstances. However, Papa became irate at the prospect. So I compensated by pinning the cap on so securely it cannot fall free."

"Take it off."

"Lord Tyreham . . ." She glanced uneasily at the door.

His eyes darkened. "Two days ago it was Dustin."

"That was before I knew who you were."

"I'm the same man you met on the river walk. Only now you have a title to put alongside the name." Swiftly, he crossed the room, turning the key to lock the door and protect Nicole's secret. "I also have a surname. It's Kingsley. As yours is Aldridge. Now, does that conclude all aspects of our introduction?"

"You've made your point, my lord—Dustin," she amended, detecting the clenching of his jaw. "Now what is it you want from me?"

"From whom? Nicole Aldridge or Alden Stoddard?"

"Both."

"Very well." He walked slowly toward her. "From Alden Stoddard, I want answers."

"That's what I was afraid of, once you mentioned this mysterious incident you have yet to disclose." Sighing,

Nicole resettled her cap more firmly on her head. "So you *were* toying with me when you offered me the job."

"You didn't let me finish. I also want first place in the Derby. And I believe Stoddard is the man to hand it to me."

"You were serious then?" Her chin shot up. "The job is mine?"

"Um-hum." He stifled a grin—as well as a nearly unbearable urge to haul her against him and kiss her senseless. "If your father says you're that good, you must be." He continued toward her, halting only when mere inches separated them. "Is everything you said about being Aldridge's protégé true?"

"Yes. I practically grew up in the stables."

Dustin searched her face. "Why?"

"Because I adore horses. Because I come alive when I ride."

"That wasn't the question I wanted answered."

"I suspected as much." Nicole's fists knotted at her sides, steeling her to deliver the necessary reply. "Which why did you require an answer to? Why am I dressed this way? Because the marquis of Tyreham couldn't be expected to take me seriously as a female jockey. Why is my father taking this risk? Because he believes, as I do, that I'm a damned good rider. And why now? Because Papa's life depends on it. Does that cover all your whys?"

Despite the menacing significance of her final words, Dustin chuckled. "You and Dagger should be a good match. You're as fiery as he."

Nicole blinked. "Nothing I just said surprised you, did it?"

"No." He raised her clenched fist to his lips, unable to resist teasing her. "But I do think you owe me an apology for assuming I'd dismiss your riding abilities simply because you're a woman."

Now she looked totally stunned. "Have you given any thought to the consequences of allowing me to ride in the Derby?" Guilt tinged her cheeks as she realized how true her words were. "If not, you must. You're renowned and respected on the turf. You could be disqualified, penalized, if someone should see through—"

"They won't." His breath grazed her knuckles. "But I thank you for your integrity and your concern." Kissing a path to her wrist, he smiled at the way her pulse accelerated at his touch. "I know what I'm doing, my fervent Derby contender. Fret not. Beneath my"—he raised his head, giving her a wicked grin—"handsome, well-bred, and devastatingly charming exterior lies a shrewd businessman, one who is hell-bent on winning. And winning means taking risks. I'm taking one with Dagger. I'm taking another with you. Both will pay off."

"And you called me arrogant?" Nicole murmured, shivering a bit as he nuzzled the sensitive underside of her forearm. Lashes lowered, her expression was an open contradiction of dazed awareness and stubborn denial as she struggled to retain her train of thought. "Dustin, what I said about Papa—you knew, didn't you? That he's in trouble, I mean. Whatever occurrence preceded my arrival, it alerted you to that fact."

"Yes. I knew." He hesitated. "Two men called on me this morning just prior to your visit. It seems they spotted my personal in the *Gazette* and would prefer I not hire your father. They told me so in no uncertain terms."

"They threatened you?"

"More or less." A wave of tenderness swept through him at the sight of her worried expression. "Fear not, love. I can take care of myself." His glance turned meaningful. "And my houseguests, as well."

"If Papa and I stay here, we'll be endangering you."

"No you won't." Dustin pressed his forefinger to her lips, silencing her protest. "Guaranteed. Now, tell me what your father's done to anger the wrong people enough to pursue him and to necessitate your taking the drastic step of masquerading as a boy."

That distracted her, and she stiffened, sparks of anger igniting her eyes. "I'm not masquerading. Other than the difference in gender, Alden Stoddard is Nicole Aldridge. This"—she indicated her attire—"is who I am. The person you met the other night was a facade. She doesn't really exist."

"Doesn't she?" Dustin drew her closer. "You've haunted me for two nights you know. Which leads me to another

46

why. Why did you run away? Did you think I meant you or your father harm?"

"It wasn't you. I would have run from anyone who approached me." She hesitated.

"Nicole, if you'll forgive my bluntness, I already know far more than you originally intended. You might as well tell me the rest. And, sweetheart, you can trust me."

Slowly, she nodded. "I do trust you. I have from the start. I'm not certain why, but I do." She inhaled sharply. "There are horrible men after Papa—and all because he's honest and won't succumb to their demands to forfeit races."

"Money. Why am I not surprised?" Dustin's jaw tightened fractionally. "Have you seen these men?"

"No, but I've witnessed their threats firsthand." In a rush, she detailed what had happened after the 2,000 Guineas when she discovered the ominous message in Oberon's stall. "Papa and I fled Newmarket then and there. The thought of losing Papa—I was terrified. I still am. Then I met you, and your kindness meant more than I can say. But when you pressed for my full name, I panicked. Given Papa's fame, I knew you'd recognize the surname Aldridge the instant I said it. And, being that Sully had just circulated the rumor that Papa was recuperating in Scotland, I couldn't risk your guessing that if Nick Aldridge's daughter were still in London, Nick would be, too. So I bolted."

"'Sully'?" Dustin pounced on her reference.

"Gordon Sullivan. The only other person who knows Papa's whereabouts."

"Ah, yes, Sullivan." A nod. "I've seen him race. He's a fine jockey."

"He's also our closest friend. He helped us locate safe quarters, then spread the news of Nick Aldridge's supposed injury. The rest was up to me."

"Up to you?"

"Yes. I convinced Papa to entrust me with the responsibility of earning our wages, at least for a time. After fifteen years, I was more than able to fulfill the requirements of any job in the thoroughbred world."

"As a boy."

"As a boy," Nicole confirmed. "But first, I had to find an available position. In order to do that, I had to pore over the ads of every newspaper I could get my hands on, which meant I had to venture onto the streets of London to buy those newspapers." She grimaced. "So I dressed the only way I could to ensure concealment—in the reprehensible apparel I had on the night we met."

"You looked lovely." Dustin couldn't help but grin at her shudder of revulsion—the complete antithesis of any reaction he'd ever received from a lady. "The only way you could ensure concealment . . ." he repeated. "Am I to conclude you don't often don conventional attire?"

"Never, if I can help it. I only own two gowns, and those I bought just to appease Papa. Only for him would I have suffered the misery of wearing that ridiculous day dress. Not to mention that torturous corset, which nearly succeeded in suffocating me to death."

Laughter rumbled from Dustin's chest. "So that was the cause of your near swoon."

"Corsets should be declared illegal," she informed him with a lift of her chin.

"I couldn't agree more." He caressed her nape, keenly attuned to her tiny quivers of pleasure. "I'll remember never to suggest that you wear one." His voice grew husky. "We have yet to probe the question, what do I want of Nicole?"

"I'm afraid to ask."

"Don't be." He tipped her head up to his. "One kiss," he urged, nipping at her lower lip. "The same one we began but never finished."

"Dustin—" The bewildered expression was back on her face. "Given the circumstances, I don't think that's wise."

"Probably not," he agreed. "But, as I told you, I believe in taking risks, especially when my instincts scream out that I should." He drew her close.

"My instincts are shouting just the opposite," she whispered, wide-eyed.

"In that case, let's listen to mine."

With that, his mouth closed over hers, silencing her protests and completing the awakening that had begun two nights before, on a private bench along a moonlit walk.

A kiss—Dustin knew it only as a prelude to passion, the

preliminary step in an age-old dance that culminated in bed.

Not so with Nicole.

The sweetness of her mouth, the hesitant parting of her lips as she silently granted him entry, was a breathtaking entity unto itself, as foreign as it was humbling. Trembling with emotion, Dustin enfolded her in his arms, deepening the kiss in deliberate, gradual shimmers of sensation. His tongue glided inside, softly stroking every velvety surface, learning every delicate texture. Then it sought hers, melding in an exquisite, shattering caress more poignant than anything he'd ever experienced.

Nicole felt the impact, too, for she stiffened, clinging and retreating all at once.

"Don't." Dustin breathed the protest into her open mouth, tightening his embrace even as he ordered himself to slow, to remember her innocence, her inexperience with men.

He felt as inexperienced as she.

"Stay." His lips circled hers. "Just a moment longer—stay."

She paused, and he could actually feel her indecision.

Cautiously, he repeated the caress, his tongue penetrating, sliding sensuously against hers.

She melted, moaning softly and entwining her arms about his neck.

"Yes," he managed, shuddering at the unbearable beauty of the contact. "Nicole . . . kiss me." He molded her against him, feeling the pounding of her heart, the fragility of her form, the awakening of her response.

On and on the kiss went, tenderness melding with fire, the intensity escalating until it was nearly unbearable.

Abruptly, Nicole pulled away. "No."

"Yes." He reached for her, scowling as she backed off.

"I can't," she gasped, wildly shaking her head as if searching for a rational reason for her actions. "W-we come from different worlds." She continued to retreat; Dustin continued to advance. "I work for you," she tried, feeling the door behind her, tugging at the handle only to recall he'd locked it. "I'm supposed to be a man," she burst out.

That had the desired effect.

Halting, Dustin stared at her, the ironic significance of her words sinking in. "Damn." He raked a hand through his hair, his gaze roving restlessly from her jockey's attire back to her kiss-swollen lips, the contrast slapping him like a douse of cold water.

Sharply, he inhaled. "We have a problem, Derby."

The affectionate term brought frustrated tears to her eyes. "Don't retract your offer," she entreated. "Let me ride for you—and not just because of my dreams to race. Because of Papa. Please, Dustin. I'll stay away from you. We'll never kiss again—I promise."

Whatever he'd been about to say vanished in the wake of her ludicrous vow. "What did you say?"

"I said we'll never kiss again. You have my word."

His chuckle erupted with a will all its own. "And you have my word we *will* kiss again. As for your unfounded apology, let me remind you that you didn't initiate the kiss. I did."

She contemplated that truth. "Very well, then, I promise to unman you if you ever initiate another."

Dustin's shoulders shook. "How comforting. I appreciate the warning, Derby. I'll be sure to protect myself against oncoming injury the next time I take you in my arms." Noting her drawn expression, he sobered, a wave of tenderness constricting his chest. "Alden Stoddard—what made you choose that name? The Alden, I assume, you derived from Aldridge."

A flicker of hope invaded Nicole's eyes. "Yes, I did. I wanted a bit of Papa with me when I raced. As for Stoddard—" She smiled. "It means 'keeper of horses.'"

"Most fitting." Dustin extracted his handkerchief, gently drying her eyes. "It appears my handkerchief is being put to use after all."

"It appears so."

Their gazes locked.

"Well, Stoddard," Dustin emphasized the name, glancing over to consult the clock, "I suggest you take your leave. You'll need time to collect your belongings and your father, then return to Tyreham for a good night's sleep. I'll have the cottage stocked with food. Training begins tomorrow at six A.M."

Nicole's smile was radiant. "Thank you, Dustin," she whispered. Self-consciously, she cleared her throat, lowering her voice to a slightly deeper pitch. "Six A.M., my lord," Alden Stoddard replied with a nod. "I'll be at the stables—ready to train for our victory at Epsom."

"Coop? We're here."

In the process of grooming his chestnut mare, Farley Cooper gave no sign that he'd heard the muffled proclamation. To the contrary, he kept his gaze fixed on the horse rather than raising it to the two men who'd, moments ago, entered his darkened stables.

Approaching boots plodded through the muck, then fell silent, alerting Coop to his visitors' proximity.

"Did you hear me?" the heavyset man pressed. "We're back from Tyreham. We had our chat with the marquis."

"I heard you, Parrish." Coop smoothed his horse's velvet coat. "But before I listen to another word, did you make sure no one saw you come in here?"

"It's nearly midnight, Coop. Who the hell would be at your stables except us and the horses?"

"I said, did you make sure?" Coop snapped.

"Yeah, we made sure," the second visitor piped up. "The place is deserted. So are the grounds."

"Good." The brush stroked downward and paused. "So, what did you learn from Lord Tyreham?"

"That he doesn't like to be threatened." Parrish scowled, remembering the marquis's surprisingly muscular build, his lethal reaction to the very mention of his nephew. "He's sure as hell not soft like most blue bloods. In fact, he's damned menacing when he's mad."

"I didn't ask for an assessment of his character," Coop spat. "I asked what you learned from him. Did Aldridge answer Tyreham's ad or not?"

"Not accordin' to the marquis." Parrish shook his head. "And even if I thought he was lyin', which I don't, Archer and I have been snoopin' around that estate for two days now. Especially the stables. And neither one of us saw any sign of Aldridge."

"I don't see why Tyreham would hire a jockey he means to stash away, Coop," Archer commented, scratching his head. "Maybe Aldridge really is in Scotland."

"Maybe." Coop abandoned his task, dragging a scarred forearm across his brow, and veering slowly to face them. "But we know damned well he's not hurt. Scared probably, but not hurt."

"Who cares?" Parrish shrugged. "Wherever he is, he's not racin'. So who needs him? I say we let him rot."

"*You* say?" A warning flashed in Coop's eyes. "You're not paid to think, Parrish, you're paid to act. And *I* say we try a different approach to unearth Aldridge."

Parrish scowled, failing to hear or heed the implicit threat in Coop's reprisal. "There's no point," he persisted. "Aldridge is useless to us if he's not in the saddle. So why are we wastin' our time . . ."

He never completed his statement.

In one motion, Coop whipped a blade from his boot and shoved Parrish against the wall, the knife at his throat. "Shut up, you stupid fool," he hissed. "Or I'll carve you into little pieces. I said I want Aldridge. More specifically, our employer wants Aldridge—no matter where he is or what he's doing. The reasons don't matter, the outcome does. So, if you both want to stay healthy"—his glance darted to Archer, watching him flinch as the blade nicked Parrish's skin, drawing a drop of blood—"you'd better find him. Fast. Have I made my point?"

"Yeah, Coop. You made it," Parrish squeaked.

An instant later he was freed, and he leaned against the wall, snatching up a nearby cloth and pressing it to his neck. "You want us to go to Glasgow and search?"

"Search where, you dimwit? Glasgow is a city, not a village. What would you do, comb the streets asking each passerby if he'd seen a wayward jockey?"

"What about startin' with Aldridge's relatives—you know, the cousins of his dead wife? Wouldn't he be stayin' with them like the rumors say?"

"First of all, rumors are rarely fact—especially if they're started by a man who chooses not to be found. Second, our employer has used all his resources to uncover these supposed cousins. They've vanished from the face of the earth, if they ever existed at all. So, we're back where we started. Even if Aldridge is in Glasgow, we don't know where he's hiding. He might very well have assumed a disguise and a new identity to keep from being found. Besides"—Coop's lips curved into an ugly smile—"my guess is there's a much easier way to get our hands on him. Rather than scour the whole British Isles, we'll simply get him to come to us."

"And how do we do that?" Archer asked cautiously.

"Through Sullivan."

"Sullivan?" Parrish blinked. "He's Aldridge's best friend. He's sure as hell not goin' to help us find him."

"Not willingly. But with a bit of persuasion."

"You want us to rough him up a little?"

"No, I want you to rough him up a lot. And not only with your fists. Use whatever tools you need. Make it messy, but not fatal. We need Sullivan alive. I want news to reach Aldridge that, just to discover his whereabouts, you thrashed his buddy within an inch of his life. As for Sullivan, I want him coherent and so terrified that, if he does know where Aldridge is, he'll happily furnish us with the address. Or at the very least, he'll wire Aldridge on his own and plead with him to reemerge."

"What if Sullivan doesn't know Aldridge's hidin' place?"

"Then we wait. It shouldn't take long for Aldridge to get wind of Sullivan's brutal beating. I expect he'll be on the next rail home."

"You think so?"

"I do indeed. Remember, Aldridge has just two weaknesses, his daughter and his old pal Sully. And since the little chit Nicole is tagging along with her father, Sullivan is our only remaining bait. Further, devotion aside, you know how *honorable*"—the word was a bitter sneer—"Aldridge is. If he won't throw a race, he sure as hell won't sacrifice his friend's life to save his own neck."

"You're probably right."

"I *know* I'm right." Pensively, Coop regarded the tip of his blade. "Grab Sullivan at home, not the stables. That would be too risky, especially given how thorough a job you need to do and how much time it'll take to do it right. You know where he lives." His gaze shifted back to his henchmen. "Now get on it."

Glancing at Archer, Parrish shifted uncomfortably, still holding the cloth to his neck. "Uh, Coop—I know you're busy"—he wet his lips—"but you did say we'd get our money after we finished with Tyreham."

"No," Coop corrected, a paralyzing gleam reigniting his eyes. "I said you'd get a *portion* of your money after you finished with Tyreham. How much of it depended on how much information you unearthed—which, in this case, is nil. What's more, I have a strong aversion to greed, especially when the bastards who display it haven't done a thing to earn their keep." His grip on the knife tightened until his knuckles were white. "And I have an even stronger aversion to being pressured."

"C-Coop . . ." Sweat broke out on Parrish's brow. "—we didn't mean . . ."

"Don't do it again." Coop shoved his free hand into his pocket, extracting several five-pound notes. "Here." He tossed the money at Parrish's feet, waiting until the frightened thug had snatched it up. "Split that with Archer," he commanded. "It's all you're going to see until you've finished this job. Now get the hell out. And don't come back until Sullivan's been taken care of and Aldridge is on his way home."

"Okay, Coop." Archer had already begun backing off.

Parrish glanced at Archer, then at the meager amount he held. Hastily, he straightened, abandoning all thought of arguing the insufficient sum. "Thanks, Coop," he muttered, inching away a hairbreadth behind Archer. "We'll take care of everything."

"You'd better. I react even more violently to being failed than I do to being pressured." With callous deliberation, Coop stared down at his scarred forearm, kneading the disfigured skin. "Needless to say, so does our employer."

Five

"Papa, I've taken care of everything." Nicole glanced out the cottage window, noting that the sun was beginning to peek its head up over the horizon. "Why are you behaving like an ornery tiger?"

"Because I feel like one, that's why."

With an exaggerated sigh, Nicole tucked the final pin into her upswept hair, tugging at her cap to make certain it wouldn't budge.

"Why not clamp your hair down with steel bands?" Nick muttered, glaring at her over the rim of his coffee cup. "You've already done that to your chest."

Nicole bristled, unused to her father's disapproval—or his explicit references to her figure. "I'm doing what I must." She eyed herself critically, making certain the binding beneath her shirt was doing its job. Satisfied that her curves were totally concealed, she crossed the cottage's small but cozy kitchen and poured herself some coffee. "What's more, you knew what I intended when I responded to the marquis's ad. Disguising myself as a boy was a crucial part of my plan. I wore this binding when I left for my interview yesterday, and you did no more than grumble. So why have you been ranting since I returned with the news that I'd gotten the position?"

55

"Because a few unexpected changes accompanied you back from Tyreham," Nick retorted, slamming his cup to the table. "None of which I had time to consider during our flight from the inn. Hell, I scarcely had enough time to wire our new address to Sully. But I've had plenty of time to think since then. And I'm furious at myself for allowing you to push me into this insanity."

"Papa, I thought you'd be pleased with this cottage. It's more than adequate for our needs, and Lord Tyreham has generously offered it free of charge."

"I'm not talking about the cottage and you know it. I'm talking about the reasons why we had to move here in such a blasted hurry. If you remember, your plan in trying to get this job was to buy us time—and wages—until I could resurface from this bloody seclusion I'm confined to. We agreed you would train in my stead to *pretend* to compete in the summer meetings. *Pretend,* Nickie. I made it plain that I refuse to allow you to actually enter those races. So what happened? Lord Tyreham was so impressed by my letter and your skills that he decided to speed up our schedule. To have you run the Derby. *This* year's Derby, the one that's taking place in three weeks. Needless to say, you were thrilled and agreed straightaway, without even consulting me. Like a tempest, you whirled us up, swept us off to Tyreham, and now intend to begin full-time training in"— he glanced at the clock—"a quarter hour. Well, dammit Nicole, I'm still your father. And I can still forbid it."

"But you won't," Nicole replied softly. "Because you, better than anyone, know how much running the Derby means to me. Oh, Papa, it's been my dream ever since you sat me on my very first horse. I can feel it, taste it, savor the sensations of crossing that line. It's one race, Papa. How dangerous can it be?" She gave him an impish grin. "Besides, if I'm half as extraordinary as you claim, maybe I'll win."

"You *are* extraordinary. But you're also a woman, whether or not you care for the idea. You're also my daughter"— his voice faltered—"all I have left in the world. And I know you, perhaps better than you know yourself. You think running the Derby will satisfy your passion, but it'll only feed it, make you want more. It'll whet your appetite, sink into your blood like a heady dose of brandy. And, speaking of brandy, let's not forget that you'll be gallivanting about with a bunch of raucous jockeys who believe you're one of them. You'll also be prancing onto the racing scene at the precise time when those crooked bastards who threatened my life are avidly seeking a new target and in hot pursuit of their old one—me. According to what you told me last night, they've gone so far as to threaten Lord Tyreham—at his own home, no less—should he ever consider hiring me."

"Papa," Nicole squeezed his hand, "even if those animals happen to be at Epsom when I run, it won't matter. They'll never realize you and I are related, much less that I'm your daughter. They'll never even suspect I'm a woman. As for their illegal offerings, should they approach me, I'll make it clear from the start that I cannot be bought. And, as the Derby will be my one and only riding event"—she gave her father an I-promise-you look—"they won't receive a second chance to twist my arm."

Nick sighed, his heart weighted by a foresight his daughter had yet to acquire. "Let's put aside the issue of your racing but once," he said lightly. "Apart from all the possible danger, you have one hell of a task ahead of you—readying this thoroughbred for the Derby. I needn't tell you that if he's really as skittish as the marquis says, he'll require calming in order to be tacked and mounted, much less raced."

"I know, Papa. And I'll use all the skills you've taught me. I'll make you proud, you'll see."

"I'm already proud, Elf. But I'm also worried. Not about the horse—if anyone can bring him around, it's you—but about the situation." Tension drew grim lines about Nick's mouth, cast shadows of doubt across his face. "You mean the world to me, Nickie."

"As you do to me. I'll prevail, Papa. I promise."

"You'll be alone. Neither Sully nor I will be there to watch over you."

That did it. Feeling her father's pain, his need to simultaneously offer his blessing and withhold it, Nicole knew what she had to do. No, she silently amended, what she *chose* to do.

All night long she'd tossed and turned in her new bed, grappling with whether or not to tell him the truth: that Dustin knew precisely who—and what—she was. Her instincts had screamed yes. Her father deserved to know. She'd never before kept anything from him, and she so badly wanted to divulge the details of Dustin's kindness, his vow to protect them. It would put her father's mind at ease and, at the same time, somehow validate the unfathomable emotions Dustin evoked inside her.

Yet, her intentions could backfire. Given Dustin's reputation, her father might balk when he learned that the womanizing marquis of Tyreham had realized from the start that his new jockey was female. Worse than balking, he might order her away—from Tyreham, from the Derby . . . and from Dustin.

The very thought spawned an unwelcome constriction in Nicole's chest, one that had nothing to do with her binding and everything to do with her emotional and physical attraction to Dustin Kingsley. With great difficulty, and for the umpteenth time, she tried to squelch her flustered uncertainty. Flustered because—after but two kisses—she was already in over her head. Uncertain because, not only was she treading in uncharted waters, she was doing so with a man so devastating, so proficient in his charm, she could scarcely stay afloat.

"Nickie?" Her father was gazing expectantly at her, a myriad of questions in his eyes.

Abruptly, Nicole returned to the here and now, accosted by a cold dose of reality. *This* was what mattered, her conscience cried out, guilt rearing its ugly head. Her father's safety, their future, her commitment to the weeks ahead. She had no room in her life for a casual dalliance. Especially now. And especially with the man who'd just hired her and now held her fate in his hands.

Once again, reality intruded, refusing to allow such self-deception. Who was she kidding? Nicole thought with a resigned sigh. A casual affair? She? Under any circumstances? Even with a man as sinfully tempting as Dustin? Never. The prospect was as inconceivable to her as lying or stealing, as unnatural as the corset she'd been forced to wear. Essentially, she was just too honest, too principled.

Too provincial.

And Dustin, warm and intuitive though he might be, was anything but provincial. *That* she'd deduced instantly, despite her sexual innocence. One didn't need firsthand experience to recognize charisma like Dustin's. It was a tangible entity—innate, unmistakable, bone-melting. As was the self-assuredness of his technique. The resulting message was clear: Dustin Kingsley *knew* women—intimately and often. In contrast, Nicole was a green schoolgirl, one who understood only the kind of fidelity and commitment her parents had shared, and who wasn't equipped to handle the aftermath of Dustin Kingsley.

So, yes, the timing was irreconcilable.

But so were she and Dustin.

Nicole drew a slow, inward breath. There was no choice. She'd have to forget those heart-stopping moments in his arms. They'd been a dream, an illusive taste of forbidden fruit.

She couldn't risk another bite.

"Elf?" By this time Nick sounded alarmed. "What is it? There's something you're not telling me. Is it about those thugs who threatened Tyreham?"

"No, Papa, nothing like that." Nicole raised her chin, determined to give her father the truth, or at least the part that might appease him.

On the other hand, it might explode in her face.

Reflexively, her fingers skimmed her pocket, grazing the comforting outline of her wishing locket.

"I won't be alone," she plunged in. "Even without you or Sully to look after me, I'll be in good hands." *Here goes.* "Lord Tyreham will see to my safety. He understands what you and I are up against. He's vowed to protect us."

"You've lost me."

"He knows, Papa."

Silence. Then, "Exactly what is it he knows?"

"Everything. That Nick Aldridge is my father. That you're right here at Tyreham, rather than in Scotland." A pause. "And that Alden Stoddard is Nicole Aldridge—and a woman."

Her father's jaw dropped. "You told him?"

"Of course not. But then, given the circumstances, I didn't need to."

"I think you'd better explain."

"All right." Nicole paused only to take a fortifying gulp of coffee. "Do you recall what I told you about the last night in London when I went searching for a copy of the *Gazette?*"

"You said you became dizzy from dashing up and down the streets. I remember."

A semblance of a smile. "Actually, I think it was more the fault of my strangling undergarments. In any case, I found a private bench along the river walk, where I sat waiting for my light-headedness to subside. During that time, a gentleman wandered by and offered his assistance." Nicole met her father's gaze. "The man was the marquis of Tyreham."

"Bloody hell." Nick blinked. "You never mentioned this. Why?"

"At the time, it didn't seem important."

"Not important? Nickie, it's not like you to be so shortsighted. If you'd already met Tyreham—if *Nicole* had already met Tyreham—how on earth did you hope to fool him during your interview?"

"Simple. I had no idea that the gentleman who offered me aid—and who introduced himself only as Dustin—and the renowned marquis of Tyreham were one and the same person."

"I need something stronger than coffee." Nick shoved aside his cup but made no move to fetch the spirits he'd alluded to. Instead, he froze, waylaid by a sudden, unpleasant possibility. "When, during this interview of yours, did the marquis recognize Stoddard as Nicole Aldridge?"

The very question she'd most dreaded. Bracing herself, Nicole replied, "At the onset."

"Dammit." The very reaction she'd expected. Fiercely, Nick's fist struck the table. "You're telling me Lord Tyreham hired you knowing you were a girl?"

"Yes. He didn't proclaim me an imposter until after he'd engaged Stoddard's services. He wanted to make certain there was no connection between my arrival at Tyreham and the unexpected appearance of those hoodlums, but, yes, Lord Tyreham knew who I was the instant he saw me."

A muscle worked in Nick's jaw. "You knew how I'd react,

didn't you? That's why you conveniently neglected to tell me all this."

"I rather suspected, yes. I hated keeping it from you, Papa, but . . ."

"Well." Nick was lost in his own reasoning. "This certainly clears up the mystery of why the marquis hired you on the spot, no questions asked. I'd be willing to bet, given the marquis's notorious reputation with women, that he'd have offered you the job without benefit of my glowing letter of recommendation."

Nicole flinched. "That's not fair, Papa. Be angry with me for not telling you everything. Be concerned about how I'll keep up my pretense now that Lord Tyreham knows the truth. But don't cheapen me or my abilities by suggesting that the marquis offered me this job simply so he could seduce me. I'm far from stupid, and he is far from desperate."

The quaver in her voice offset Nick's anger. "Elf, this is no reflection on you, not your character or your skill. Your horsemanship is outstanding, your character impeccable." He broke off, grappling to find the right words. "But, as for Tyreham's intentions—well, frankly, Nickie, I'm not sure you'd recognize seduction if it clubbed you over the head."

"I grew up in the stables, Papa. I have eyes and I have ears. I know the minds of men better than I do those of women."

"Growing up amid an army of jockeys who regard you as their surrogate child does nothing to prepare you for . . ." Again, he paused. "What I'm saying is, despite your experience with men, you have *no* experience with men. Least of all with those as accomplished as the marquis of Tyreham."

Nicole felt a stab of unreasonable jealousy. "For all we know, Lord Tyreham's conquests are no more than rumor. You told me yourself your description was based on hearsay."

"No, what I told you was that I'd heard Tyreham has quite a reputation with the ladies. By 'I heard,' I didn't mean through idle chatter. You know me better than that. My sources are men who've worked with the marquis—jockeys, grooms, even some of his own colleagues. Like the earl of Lanston. Surely you recall his name?"

"I recall," Nicole replied flatly. "You rode his mare in last summer's meeting at Goodwood."

"Exactly. Well, the earl and his friends nearly brought *me* to blushing with their constant jabber about Tyreham and his women. They spent more time and money wagering on who Tyreham's next paramour would be than they did on the upcoming races. I'd repeat some of their banter, were it appropriate for your ears. Suffice it to say that Tyreham's status—and his popularity—among women is common knowledge. Need I elaborate further?"

"No." Nicole was suddenly and inexplicably furious. "I don't want to hear anymore. Moreover, I don't know, or care, how Lord Tyreham behaves with his paramours. But in my case, he's been positively heroic. He came to my rescue on the river walk, then again in his study when he offered me the job. Papa, you can't deny that he's putting himself, and his reputation, at risk in order to protect us. His reputation with thoroughbreds, not women," she clarified quickly. "He could be disqualified by allowing me to race, or harmed if those criminals uncover the fact that he's helping you. Yet, he listened to the details of our dilemma, then insisted upon hiring me *and* upon my moving to Tyreham—with you." Her brows rose. "Perhaps I'm being naive, but if all the marquis wanted were to seduce me, wouldn't he be undermining his own plan by boarding me amid scores of tenants, accompanied by my father, no less?" She gestured about the tiny cottage. "In quarters as small as these, I think he'd find it difficult to avoid discovery while conducting a private tyrst."

"All right, Nickie, you've made your point." Nick rubbed his forehead. "I'm not proud of my thoughts. But I'm also not ashamed of wanting to shield you. From everything."

Nicole's fingers caught her father's, wrapped around his calloused palm. "And I'm not proud of having kept this from you. It was cowardly, and for that I apologize. But Papa—" Her gaze grew fervent, silently begging him to understand. "I was so afraid you'd forbid me to race. This opportunity means more to me than anything, save you. It's the only chance I'll ever have to run the Derby. So, please, don't say no. I'm aware you have every right to, and if you do, I'll march out to the stables this instant and tell Lord

Tyreham I must resign. But I'm asking you to give me this chance. Please, Papa, I've wished for it forever."

A tender smile. "Is this one of the dreams kept tight in your wishing locket?"

"One of my first."

With a hard squeeze, Nick released her fingers, intuition whispering that he was yielding far more than his authority. He was, in some unfathomable way, relinquishing his little girl to become all he had raised her to be.

Roughly, he cleared his throat. "I want to meet with Tyreham." Holding up his hand, he checked Nicole's mortified protest. "Don't worry, Elf. I won't blurt out my qualms about his reasons for hiring you. If he's the kind of man you say he is, I won't need to—he'll assuage them on his own. Moreover, my concern for you is only part of what I want to discuss with the marquis. Given the fact that he's now been thrust into this whole shady blackmail scheme, I want to mull over our best course of action."

"Very well," Nicole agreed cautiously, experiencing a flicker of hope at her father's ever-so-subtle relenting. "I'll tell Lord Tyreham you've asked to see him."

"Good. As soon as possible. Today."

Hope was eclipsed by fear. "Papa, you can't leave the cottage. If someone should see you—"

"They won't and I won't. I'll stay safe inside these walls while I wait for the marquis's visit. Tell him I'll expect him around noon." Nick gave the brim of Nicole's cap a gentle tug. "That, Elf, should give you more than enough time to have his testy stallion eating out of your hand."

"Papa, are you saying . . . ?"

"I'm saying that the Derby is little more than a fortnight away. So if you want to win it, you'd better go start your training."

With a whoop of joy, Nicole flung her arms about her father's neck.

Dustin prowled the stable floor, lost in thought. Arising before dawn had posed no problem today, for he'd never gone to bed. What's more, he wasn't the least bit tired.

What he was, was frustrated.

Frustrated and stymied.

Nicole Aldridge. The most breathtaking, unexpected distraction ever to walk into his life.

Refreshing, beautiful, unconventional—if he'd been preoccupied with her before, he was obsessed with her now. Like a lovesick schoolboy, he'd spent half the night reliving the moments she'd spent in his arms, recalled the feel of her: soft and delicate, eager and innocent. As fervent in her masquerade as she was in her awakening. Except that the masquerade was intentional, the awakening unconscious. Unconscious, unintentional, and, as of yet, unfinished.

God, how he wanted to finish what they'd scarcely begun.

He could actually visualize her in his bed, her eyes alight with lavender fire, her skin like silk beneath his hands.

She'd shiver and breathe his name as he went into her . . .

Dammit.

With a grimace, Dustin halted, shifting to relieve the sudden constriction of his breeches. This was madness. In all his life, he'd never behaved like this, not even as an adolescent with his first woman. Yet now, after but two meetings, he could think of nothing but Nicole, his senses in turmoil, his body rigid to bursting.

He had to stop this insanity. If not for his sake, for Nicole's. The last thing she needed during the next few critical weeks was to be perpetually reminded that he wanted her and that she wanted him, too. He'd vowed to protect her, to keep her and her father safe. Accordingly, he'd hired Alden Stoddard and, by doing so, shouldered the task of helping Nicole convince the world she was a boy.

Something he could hardly do if the very sight of her—clad in jockey garb or not—made him randy enough to howl at the moon.

What in hell's name had he gotten himself into?

For starters, an unpalatable mystery that, he was beginning to suspect, delved far deeper than he'd originally assumed. Whoever wanted Aldridge off the turf wanted it badly enough to threaten his life . . . and the lives of all who aided him. Why?

And at the heart of this thickening mystery was a beautiful woman who made Dustin feel too many conflicting emotions to recount, much less understand.

Hell, even that which he understood was unrivaled in its intensity. Desire, commonly the most uncomplicated motivator, elemental as the physical craving of one body for another, took on a new dimension when it came to Nicole. He wanted her with a gnawing hunger that would tolerate no substitute, a hunger that defied control or alleviation.

And that was but the fringe of his bafflement. Because, beyond her body, he wanted to hold her, to help her, to envelop her in a cocoon of safety. At the same time, he wanted to fling open the world's portals to her, offer her every iota of reckless freedom she'd be offered as a man and denied as a woman.

He wanted to understand the dreams in her eyes and find a way to make them reality.

How in God's name could he feel so much, so soon? They'd spoken but twice, their conversations brief, shrouded in secrets, their kisses broken fragments of temptation that were a lifetime from fruition.

The truth was, he didn't even know her.

And yet he did.

Rubbing his eyes, Dustin tried to assess the situation rationally. He was a grown man, one who'd lived two and thirty years and was seasoned enough to know that experience shaped character. It also molded outlook and modified expectations.

Yes, he was searching.

He'd told as much to Trent. But wishes and certainties were worlds apart. That he retained a flicker of hope was inevitable, particularly after witnessing Trent's transformation beneath Ariana's healing love. But a more extensive idealism? A true conviction that a similar fate awaited him as well?

That flicker had long since begun to extinguish.

He was jaded. Or perhaps self-protective was a better word. In either case, it was easier merely to exist than to withstand the constant ache of loneliness. So, unconsciously, he'd blanketed his heart in a tangible, if not unbreachable, layer—a layer he was ambivalent to allow anyone to pare away.

All the more reason to balk at these powerful feelings.

Then why wasn't he balking?

Because the same wisdom that recoiled from vulnerability recognized the rarity of a miracle like Nicole. And that wisdom shouted that whatever obstacles blocked his path, he couldn't let her go.

Nor could he hurt her.

Which led to his ultimate dilemma. How could he have her without hurting her?

"Good morning, Lord Tyreham."

The object of his thoughts hovered uncertainly in the stable doorway. "I'm not late, am I?"

"No, of course not." Dustin strode over, absorbing her from head to toe, recalling the perfect curves of her now-disguised body as they'd been the first night they'd met. "In fact, your timing is perfect. My head groom, Brackley, is exercising Dagger—or trying to. As soon as they return, I'll introduce you to your defiant mount."

Nicole glanced about, more speculative than concerned. "And the rest of your employees—stableboys, grooms . . . ?"

"Derby, if you're asking if we're alone, you can relax. The answer is no. My stables are huge, as is my staff. They're scattered about, attending to their jobs."

"Actually, I was wondering if we *could be* alone. Only for a minute," she was quick to add.

His curiosity was thoroughly piqued. "Of course. Come with me." He led her into a small, private room at the head of the stables. "This is my equivalent of an office," he explained, closing the door behind them and turning to lean back against it. "I keep schedules, papers, and various records here. It's convenient. It also serves as a bedchamber when one of my horses has a long and difficult night."

"Do you sleep here when they're ill?"

"Ill or foaling. Does that surprise you?"

"Surprise me, no." She shook her head. "But I am impressed. Such dedication is rare, especially with a man who can well afford to hire others to keep vigil for him."

"Wealth does not preclude commitment, Derby. It's true I was raised with money. But I was also raised with principles. My father believed the former was a matter of chance, the latter, of character."

Visibly, Nicole relaxed. "I'm glad to hear that. It should make the chat we're about to have that much easier."

Dustin cocked a brow. "Is that what we're about to have—a chat?"

"Yes." Again, her gaze darted about.

"We're alone," he confirmed. "Now what's troubling you?"

"The weeks ahead." For the first time since entering the stables, Nicole abandoned Stoddard's lower-pitched voice in favor of her own. "I think we should clarify the situation so there are no misunderstandings."

Damn, her eyes were beautiful. Luxurious amethysts, breathtaking as a rare indigo sunset. Dustin's gaze swept lower, deliberately focusing on her boyish attire to remind himself that it was Stoddard he faced, not Nicole. Based on her appearance, that should have been easy. Men's breeches, boots, shirt, cap: her disguise was good—damned good. No one would be able to see through it.

No one but he.

"Lord Tyreham, I insist we state our positions."

"Which positions in particular?" he managed in a husky voice. "We can explore as many as you like."

She blinked, innocence rendering her oblivious to his double entendre. "I'd like to discuss a few details of my employment."

"Details?" He inclined his head. "As I understood it, you're going to win the Derby for me. What more is there to clarify? Wages? How many hours a day you'll train?"

"Neither. I'm grateful for the opportunity you've given me. I'll train for as long as it takes and accept whatever wages you deem fair."

"Then what details are you referring to?"

"I'm referring to the fact that I can't do my job effectively if I'm anxious, not to mention that Dagger will sense and take on my unease."

"Spoken like a true horseman." Dustin couldn't help but grin. "And I quite agree. The questions that arise are, what's causing your anxiety and how can I relieve it?"

"The cause and the solution are the same." Nicole raised her chin. "You."

"I?"

67

"Yes. Without your cooperation, this entire plan is doomed to failure. I need to know you were sincere when you vowed to safeguard Papa and me."

"I was and I am."

"Then it's crucial that you support my efforts. You must perceive me and treat me as Alden Stoddard."

"Derby—" Dustin lowered his voice, an added precaution to ensure they were not overheard. "Stop worrying. I don't make promises I don't mean to keep. I'll protect your secret, as well as your father's. Trust me not to betray you."

"I do trust you—I have from the onset. But there are several points I must emphasize. First, recognize that I shall always address you formally—as 'my lord' or 'Lord Tyreham.' It would be totally inappropriate for Stoddard to use your given name."

"Agreed."

"Next, cease eyeing me as if I'm some delightful confection you plan to gobble up."

Dustin's lips twitched. "I wasn't aware I was doing that. But, rest assured, the way I eye you when we're alone will differ greatly from the way I eye you among others."

Confusion clouded her face. "That's not what I meant."

"Nevertheless, it's the truth. My demeanor with Alden Stoddard will be completely businesslike. In fact, I'll go one step further." Dustin considered the drastic vow he was about to make, then pushed onward, praying he'd have the strength to see it through. "Even when we're alone, I'll let you dictate the terms of our relationship. Until and unless you proclaim otherwise, you are Alden Stoddard and I am your employer. Fair enough?"

"Yes." Nicole looked surprised, dazed, and—best of all—disappointed.

"That should eliminate your anxiety, Derby. You now know that I won't leap upon you like some sacrificial lamb to be devoured against your will. Incidentally," he added with a wry grin, "even under the best of circumstances, I don't devour innocent women. Or boys of any kind, innocent or otherwise."

A flicker of humor. "I'm relieved, my lord. I *was* told that innocent women are the only sort who remain safe from your allure. However, I'd heard nothing about boys. I'm delighted to hear that they, too, are excluded from your list of potential prey."

Laughter rumbled from Dustin's chest. "I'm going to have to accustom myself to that rapier wit and forthright tongue."

"If Papa's complaints about me are valid, you have quite a challenge ahead of you."

"I knew that from the start. But, Derby—" His gaze delved deep inside her. "Remember that challenges are my forte. Especially those as well worth embracing—and savoring—as you."

Her lashes swept her cheeks, now flushed in response to his blatant message.

"Continue with your details," Dustin murmured, easing her back to safe ground. "What else can I do to assuage your anxiety?"

"Only one thing more." The toe of Nicole's boot traced lines in the dirt. "My father wants to see you," she announced uncomfortably. "Today. I told him what happened between us in your study . . . no!" Her head came up, her expression mortified as she realized what she'd just implied. "I don't mean I told him what we . . . that we . . ." Agitated, she sought the right words. "What I meant was that I explained the outcome of my interview, that you'd deduced who I was and why."

"I understood what you meant." Rather than amusement, Dustin felt a surge of acute tenderness at her plight. When was the last time he'd seen a woman try so hard to circumvent any mention of what amounted to no more than a chaste, albeit soul-shattering, kiss? "And I concur wholeheartedly with your decision. The more intimate moments of our exchange should be kept private, not only because hearing about them would upset your father but because there aren't words to describe the magic that occurs when you're in my arms."

He could actually see the tiny shiver that ran through her. "It's never going to happen again," she whispered, her tone as unconvincing as her pledge.

"Oh, yes it is." Dustin's need to hold her was a palpable ache in his chest—one he refused to succumb to. "Not just again, but again after that. It's as inevitable as dawn, as compelling as darkness. However, it will be up to you to determine when and where."

She was struggling to stay afloat. Guilt apprised him that he wasn't helping.

"Let's get back to the subject at hand," he suggested, heeding his inner voice. "Why does your father want to see me?"

"Partially, to discuss the men who are after him. Partially to . . . to . . ." Her flush deepened.

"To make certain I won't take advantage of his daughter," Dustin finished for her.

She looked startled, her eyes widening in reaction.

"As I told you, Derby, I was raised by a highly principled man. I well understand honor." He met and held her gaze. "You said that you trust me."

"I do."

"Then trust me not to take advantage of you or hurt you in any way. Even if it means sacrificing my own needs. And yours."

A current of sensual awareness ran between them, softening Nicole's eyes to a smoky violet. "All right."

God, how he wanted her. "What time would your father like to meet?"

"At noon. Papa says that's all the time I'll need to win Dagger over."

Dustin chuckled. "I suspect he's right."

Nicole didn't return the smile. "Dustin," she murmured, unaware she'd even used his given name, "At the risk of overstepping my bounds, would *you* go to *him?* I know that's an unusual request. You must be accustomed to summoning others, rather than vice versa. But I'm terrified that if Papa leaves the cottage . . ."

"He should never venture outside that house," Dustin inserted at once. "Not until we've resolved this threat to his life, and how far-reaching it really is. Of course I'll go to him."

"Thank you." She nearly sagged with relief. "I seem to be perpetually thanking you."

"Then stop. If you want to thank me, win the Derby. I'll consider that to be a splendid token of your appreciation."

"You really mean that, don't you?"

"I wouldn't say it if I didn't. Not to you." Dustin hesitated, determined to explain that final statement and, by doing so, to explore his unprecedented pull toward her. "Candor is an unusual trait for me, at least where women are concerned."

"Why is that?"

"Because, in my experience, women prefer to hear anything other than the truth."

"Perhaps you're associating with the wrong women."

"Perhaps. Which brings me to my request—a request that involves those hours when you're off duty. I'd like to call on you, to enjoy the pleasure of your company. On those occasions, I don't care if you dress in breeches or gowns, nor do I care if our topics are as complex as the philosophy of life or as fundamental as the breeding of horses. You decide. Moreover, I'll visit on your terms—at the cottage, with your father present if you wish. That should ease your mind, not only about my intentions, but about the risk of discovery, which will be nil. Anyone who sees me come and go will think I'm simply visiting my jockey to plan our strategy. May I have your permission?" He hesitated. "Nicole's permission?"

Silence.

At last, she replied, "You promised to let me set the rules. Yet earlier, you insisted that our . . . embrace will happen again. I don't understand how such conflicting assurances are feasible."

"Don't you?"

He saw her breath catch.

"Derby—" Staunchly, Dustin struggled to retain his final shred of control, the one that kept him from damning his vows and dragging her into his arms. "You *will* set the rules." Who was he convincing, her or himself? "That was my vow, and I intend to keep it." God help him. "As for our kisses, their future is in your hands. Yours, and fate's."

Nicole's expression was an exquisite kaleidoscope of emotions. "And if I refuse your visits? Will Alden Stoddard be scratched from the Derby?"

"I'll repeat what I said yesterday. Whatever Nicole decides will have no bearing on Stoddard's position. My alliance with each of them is entirely separate, neither being contingent upon the other."

"Why?" she whispered. "Given the strict constraints that would define our visits, why do you want to see me?"

"Many reasons. Some of which I supplied on the river walk, when I explained why I was out walking alone rather than immersing myself in the season's balls. One of which I supplied a moment ago when I admitted how seldom I've employed honesty in my dealings with women. And others of which I can't supply at all, for they're beyond my comprehension." He frowned. "Do you know I can't recall the last time I shared a meaningful conversation? Offered something more profound than a practiced compliment or a senseless nicety? Not just with women but with *anyone,* save Trent and Ariana. Yet with you—" He shook his head in amazement. "You remind me there's more. Even after three fleeting chats. I can't explain it any better than that, for I'm not sure I fully understand it myself."

"Who is Ariana?"

Dustin started. He'd become so absorbed in his explanation, he'd nearly lost track of what he'd said. "What?"

"Ariana," Nicole repeated cautiously. "Is she a . . . friend?"

There was no mistaking it. Nicole was bothered by the possibility.

Abruptly, Dustin wanted to whoop with joy. "Yes, Derby, she's a friend. But not in the way you mean. She's my sister-in-law, married to my brother Trenton."

"Oh." Relief, vivid as the dismay that had preceded it, flashed across her face.

"She's a very special young woman. We became friends the instant we met—the very day she married Trent. If there's such a thing as a marriage made in heaven, they have it."

"I see." Nicole looked puzzled. "Is she dishonest?"

He blinked. "No. She's remarkably sincere."

"Then why do you assume she's unique?"

"Because I've known quite a few women. And, believe me, I know of what I speak."

Nicole chewed her lip thoughtfully. "I'm sorry, then. For

so sophisticated a man, you've had very limited experiences with women. I've been fortunate. In my case, just the opposite is true. Despite my narrow circle of acquaintances, I've always found men to be engaging companions, unpretentious in both discussion and recreation."

Rage. Dustin nearly jolted at its unfamiliar intensity. More staggering still was its cause: jealousy. Fierce, undiluted jealousy. He wanted to choke the life out of every nameless, faceless bastard who'd come near her. "What men?"

"Pardon me?"

"What men? And what recreation?"

Stunned comprehension dawned. "The kind one partakes in outside the bedchamber," Nicole retorted, her chin set in that mutinous way Dustin was coming to recognize. "With men who have assets more meaningful than a betting book of wagers on who their next paramour will be." She folded her arms across her chest. "Bear in mind, my lord, that unlike you, I haven't spent the better part of my life between the bedsheets. I grew up in the stables, amid fine men like Papa, Sully, and all the other jockeys and trainers I've been fortunate enough to know. And, before your eyes once again darken to that fierce shade of blue-black, I mean 'know' in the fellowship sense, not the biblical one."

Dustin's lips twitched. "I'm glad," he said without a shred of remorse. "Because, despite the fact that I'm not a violent man, I felt suddenly compelled to kill each and every male who's ever so much as touched you."

"Once again, I appreciate your concern for my welfare. Although this time that concern was most unnecessary. To be blunt, the only male who's ever touched me, as you put it, is you."

Abruptly, the world looked brighter.

"Good. I intend to keep it that way." He glanced up at the sound of approaching footsteps. "Dagger is back, having either received his exercise or provided Brackley with his. Before I take you out there and perform the introductions, may I have Nicole's answer?"

She was frowning, evidently still pondering the undue severity of his reaction. Hell, he didn't blame her. He'd been equally astonished himself.

"Dust . . . Lord Tyreham." She searched his face. "You and I are worlds apart."

"That, Derby, is not an answer."

Another pause. "You did agree that I would race Dagger, no matter what my answer might be?"

"Only if Dagger agrees."

"He will."

A chuckle. "Then, yes. You'll race Dagger. Regardless of your decision. You have my word."

"All right." Nicole sighed, looking eager and reluctant all at once. "Four o'clock. At the cottage. Come for tea." An impish twinkle. "By the way, I'd suggest you eat beforehand. I have it on the best authority that my scones are more lethal than bullets. As for attire, you'll have to endure my wearing breeches. And not only to avoid discovery. As I explained—"

"I remember." Triumph, more intoxicating than brandy, surged through Dustin's veins. "You don't wear gowns."

"Or corsets," she reminded him.

"Or corsets."

Their eyes met.

"Nicole . . ." Her name was as intimate as a caress, deliberately used to underscore what hovered between them. "Thank you."

"You're welcome," she managed.

Clearing his throat, Dustin reached behind him, turning the door handle to lead Stoddard to his future. "Have we covered everything, Derby?"

"I believe so, yes."

"Excellent. Then, let's go. You're about to meet your match."

"It's too late, my lord." Passing through the doorway, Nicole brushed by him—and shivered. "I fear I already have."

Six

"How was he today, Brackley?" Dustin asked, striding into Dagger's stall. "Did our glimmer of hope hold out?"

The groom shook his head. "Unfortunately, no, my lord. When I saw you manage to tack him up, I thought finally we were making some progress. I even succeeded in walking him—calmly—for a quarter hour or so. But then I attempted to mount him and, well, he wanted no part of that. He started his usual rearing and fussing like a scared cat." Brackley frowned. "If you'll forgive my saying so, sir, I don't see much chance of competing in the Derby. Perhaps if Banks hadn't retired just now, things would be different. Banks had a unique way of soothing mounts like Dagger. I'm afraid I haven't that same ability. And with the Derby just weeks away, I don't know if the dramatic transformation you seek is possible, my lord."

"Well, we're about to find out." Dustin gestured for Nicole to join them in Dagger's stall. "This is the lad I told you about." Not even a heartbeat of hesitation accompanied the introduction. "Brackley—Stoddard, our new jockey. If Nick Aldridge's recommendation holds true, Stoddard will easily match Banks's rapport with horses and, thus, make remarkable headway with Dagger. After which,

I'm convinced they'll ride to a well-deserved victory in the Derby."

"Stoddard." Brackley inclined his head at Nicole, his expression friendly but dubious. In fact, he looked about as certain of Dustin's prediction as a magistrate being assured a pickpocket had successfully mended his ways. "I sure hope you know what you're doing."

"Nice to meet you, Brackley—and I do." Relief rushed through Nicole. Brackley might doubt her skill, but he didn't doubt her gender.

The latter was all that mattered.

The former she'd combat . . . and rectify.

So saying, she turned her attention to the sleek challenge now stomping about before her. "Hello, Dagger," she murmured, walking, slow and easy, toward the magnificent deep brown thoroughbred.

Dagger's head jerked around, and he eyed her cautiously, ears erect as he listened to the sound of her voice.

"Stoddard, I don't know how much Lord Tyreham's told you," Brackley inserted. "But you've got quite a job ahead of you."

"The marquis has prepared me for Dagger's skittishness." Nicole paused, glancing from one man to the other. "May I spend a few minutes alone with him?" she requested. "He'll trust me sooner if he can concentrate solely on me. Distractions will slow down that process. And, as we all know, we haven't the luxury of time."

For a long, thoughtful minute, Dustin assessed her from beneath hooded lids. Then he nodded. "All right. Brackley and I will wait in my office."

The groom's jaw dropped. "My lord? Are you sure that's wise? Dagger's a handful, even for me to control alone, and I'm twice Stoddard's size."

"Our new jockey is right," Dustin replied, gazing intently at Nicole in silent conveyance of his faith. "Drastic circumstances call for drastic action. Therefore, if Stoddard feels he can handle Dagger on his own, let's give him a chance. He'll call us if he needs assistance."

"I certainly will. Thank you, my lord," Nicole responded, gratitude shining in her eyes.

Brackley scowled but said nothing further, following Dustin from the stall.

Nicole waited until their footsteps had faded into the distance. Then, she turned her attention to Dagger.

The thoroughbred stared at her, ears forward, tail swishing nervously as if he were preparing to balk at the slightest provocation.

"You're frightened," Nicole noted softly, wondering what scoundrel had abused this beautiful stallion to make him so apprehensive. "I'm sure you have good reason. But no one here is going to hurt you." Inching closer, she placed a sugar cube on her palm and extended it for his inspection.

Dagger sniffed at her hand, then leaned forward warily before snatching up the treat and gobbling it down.

With calculated deliberation, Nicole remained as she was, making no sudden moves either to shift her palm to stroke him or to snatch her hand away. "The marquis is right about you," she concluded, surveying the thoroughbred's powerful body and long, lean limbs at close range. "You are extraordinary. Now we need only reaccustom you to trusting your rider, and victory will be ours. My instincts are never wrong, Dagger. We're going to be incomparable together, you and I."

The horse never blinked. But Nicole could actually sense his fear abate.

Why? she mused. She'd scarcely spent five minutes alone with him, not nearly enough time—skillful though she might be—to accomplish the arduous task of winning him over.

"You're not afraid of me, are you, Dagger?" she confirmed aloud, taking the risk and lifting her fingers to caress his muzzle, purposely keeping her hand where he could scrutinize her every motion.

In response, Dagger whinnied softly, announcing his approval.

Nicole smiled, continuing to stroke the jagged white streak that spanned his muzzle from top to bottom; a stark contrast against his chocolate brown coat. "You were aptly named," she told him, tracing the bold marking with her forefinger. "This does indeed resemble a dagger. But you're not dangerous. You're proud and devoted—*if* you're treated with the respect you deserve. If only you could tell me who mishandled you. It certainly wasn't Lord Tyreham, nor was it Brackley. The marquis is a wonderful man who believes in you, and who is as devout a horseman as I. And, as for Brackley, I know his manner is curt, but his concern for you is genuine. Yet you don't trust either one of them, not completely. Is it their size? Was the man who hurt you tall?"

In response, the thoroughbred nuzzled the side of Nicole's neck.

Man.

Her own word reverberated in her mind, and comprehension erupted.

"What a fool I'm being," she exclaimed. Glancing about, she leaned close to Dagger's ear, lowering her voice to a breath of sound. "You know who I am—or rather, what I am, don't you? Of course you do. I can fool people, but they haven't your keen instincts. You know I'm a woman. That's why you're unafraid. Of course whoever unnerved you was a man—who else would be tending to you? Well, you need no longer fear such abuse. Lord Tyreham would only hire men as kind and compassionate as he. And he is kind. Believe me, I know." Nicole's nod was emphatic. "He'll look out for you just as he's looking out for me. As will I. Your future is secure, my friend. But, Dagger," she whispered, "in return, you must keep my secret. We'll let them think it's my size that soothes you—and my skill, of course," she added with an impish grin. "But the fact that I'm female must remain between us. Us and Lord Tyreham. Agreed?"

Nudging her pocket, Dagger hunted for another cube of sugar.

"Blackmail, h-m-m?" Nicole's brows rose, and she offered her coconspirator what he sought. "Very well. Our bargain is sealed. Now, shall we walk the course together? I'd like to have you trotting by day's end and cantering by tomorrow. That way, we'll be galloping by midweek and exploring the training grounds at Epsom by week's end. How does that sound?"

Another whinny.

"Excellent. Let's go."

Forty-five minutes later, Nicole and Dagger were taking Tyreham's course at a brisk trot, the fluidity of Dagger's gait astounding even to Nicole.

"Splendid," she praised, patting the stallion's neck and slowing him to a walk. "You could win this Derby even with a less experienced rider on your back. Your trot is so graceful, I can hardly wait to see your canter. However"— Nicole's jaw set, long years of training supplanting enthusiasm—"wait I shall. Until tomorrow. We've done enough for today, given how long it's been since you were ridden. It's time to cool down and head back to the stables."

For the first time since she'd mounted, Nicole relaxed her concentration enough to take in her surroundings. With a start of surprise, she realized she had an audience.

Dustin and Brackley stood at the end of the course, beaming from ear to ear. Brackley was shaking his head in welcome astonishment, wiping his brow and muttering under his breath.

But it was the look on Dustin's face that made Nicole's heart leap.

Pride, pure and abundant, transmitted itself to her, coupled with a victorious gleam of pleasure.

"Incredible," he called, saluting as she and Dagger approached. "You've humbled us, Stoddard."

"You sure as hell have." Brackley was still shaking his head. "I'd never have believed it if I hadn't seen it with my own eyes."

"I got lucky," Nicole answered. "Whoever intimidated Dagger was obviously big. I'm short and slight and too young for my voice to be threateningly deep." She tossed them a saucy grin. "True, I'm also a superb rider. And Dagger is a superb mount. The combination is unbeatable. Now, if you'll excuse us, Dagger and I will meet you at the stables."

"You were right, my lord," Brackley stated as their new jockey urged Dagger off. "Stoddard is everything Aldridge claimed he'd be."

"He certainly is." Dustin nodded, his penetrating gaze fixed on Nicole. "Everything Aldridge claimed and more."

Abruptly, he turned away, taking out his timepiece and glancing at it. "Brackley, show Stoddard around the stables, and introduce him to the rest of the staff. I've an interview with a prospective trainer in an hour and a meeting at noon."

"Of course, my lord."

Disregarding Brackley's puzzled expression, Dustin headed off, never pausing until he'd reached the manor, crossed the hall in long, uncompromising strides, and locked himself in his private study.

He was in trouble. Deep trouble.

Pouring himself a drink, Dustin stared out the bay window, oblivious to Tyreham's magnificent wooded acres. Instead all he saw was Nicole, sitting straight-backed in the saddle, as natural astride Dagger as if she'd been born there. She'd handled herself and Dagger with all the finesse of a seasoned jockey, not a novice. Novice? Hell, his last three jockeys, each boasting a decade of experience, would have benefitted greatly from her instruction, she was that good. His practiced eye had seen Nick Aldridge's influence in every facet of her performance: stature, technique, fluidity, coordination. Even her judgment when it came to assessing a horse's limitations. She was indeed her father's daughter, reflecting every iota of Aldridge's intuitive skill in the tactics she'd taken with Dagger. In less than an hour, she'd transformed him from an unapproachable tempest to the champion he was meant to be.

She was superb.

But, contrary to Nicole's misgivings, that wasn't the cause of Dustin's inner turmoil.

His lips curved into a mirthless smile. Nicole had accused him of undervaluing her abilities because she was a woman.

She couldn't be more wrong.

Not only did he recognize her exceptional talent, he had no trouble accepting and heralding her as the best damned rider he'd ever seen. In truth, he'd be willing to bet more than his reputation; he'd bet his entire fortune and his whole line of thoroughbreds that she'd win the bloody Derby.

Further, he wouldn't deprive her of that victory for anything on earth.

Thus, her concerns were unfounded. Between her skill and his resolve, he'd easily convince the entire racing world that Nicole was Alden Stoddard.

But deluding the public was one thing. Deluding himself was quite another.

This brought Dustin to his true quandary, the reality of which had struck him, full force, as he watched Nicole complete Tyreham's course, her face flushed with the thrill of victory.

He could herald her as a jockey, but he could never—not even for the shortest of durations—view her as a man.

Biding his time had suddenly become an untenable option.

Tossing off his drink, Dustin stared broodingly into the empty goblet.

He'd expected Nicole's masquerade to present difficulties; but never had he anticipated his feelings for her to be so powerful that he'd be unable to squelch them, even for a day. Yet, that's precisely what was happening. Just now, seeing those amethyst eyes alight with triumph, her half-hidden face so spontaneously beautiful—jockey cap or not—his conscience and determination had waged major battle with his instincts. Ultimately, he'd needed every ounce of self-control not to haul her off Dagger's back and into his arms, to feel her joy and hail her accomplishment as the wondrous feat it was.

To seal their elation in a dance as old as time.

All of which characterized the very avenue he'd promised Nicole he wouldn't pursue.

So where the hell did that leave him? He couldn't elude his feelings, nor could he act upon them. At least not until Nicole made the next move—an unlikely possibility, to say the least. Even under the best of circumstances, a sexual overture would be as foreign to Nicole as the donning of a corset. And now? Given that she spent every waking moment disguised as a man, coupled with the fact that the rare visits she'd agreed to allow him would occur in her cottage under her father's watchful eye?

The prospects were less than grim.

And Dustin's time was short.

Because once the culprits who'd threatened Nick Aldridge had been unearthed, the cause for Nicole's disguise would be eliminated. At which point, there was every likelihood that she would vanish from Dustin's life as swiftly as she'd materialized, and not only for propriety's sake, for her own sake as well. Dustin could feel her confusion as palpably as he could her awakening. She was overwhelmed by the intensity of what hovered between them. Hell, so was he. But Nicole was young, inexperienced. Headstrong. Her misgivings would win out over her new-found emotion and drive her away.

It was up to him to get through to her first.

But how?

With a muttered oath, Dustin refilled his glass, silently berating himself for erecting his own insurmountable barriers. In attempting to put Nicole at ease, he'd succeeded in digging his own proverbial grave. *Think,* he commanded himself, lowering the bottle of madeira. There had to be a way. A way to keep his promises to Nicole without letting the miracle of what was between them slip through his fingers. A way to maximize their time together; to get her alone without jeopardizing her disguise.

There was.

Dustin's head came up, determination pulsing through his veins. The plan he'd just conjured up involved taking a hell of a risk, one that could backfire and wrench Nicole from his grasp forever. On the other hand, it could be just the answer he sought—his only answer.

It was a risk he had to take.

Abandoning his drink, Dustin once again consulted his timepiece, his mind racing ahead. He'd conclude his morning interview posthaste, especially since his final decision was virtually made. Both trainers vying for the position at Tyreham's stables had flawless records and came with glowing recommendations. But Raggert, the candidate who was returning to Tyreham today, had been referred to Dustin by the earl of Lanston, a colleague whose instincts were second only to his own. Lanston had sung Raggert's praises to the skies—a fact that weighed heavily on the fellow's behalf. So, if Raggert were amenable, Banks's job would finally be filled, and Dustin's attention could return where it belonged.

To the Derby.

And Nicole.

Crossing over to his desk, Dustin collected the necessary papers. He would expedite the business ahead. After which, he intended to make his way over to the tenants' section of the estate to hold a discussion whose potential impact eclipsed all else from his mind.

A discussion that could very well determine his future.

No one answered Dustin's knock.

Given the situation, that came as no surprise.

Waiting until he'd given the cottage resident ample time to reach the door and be silently poised to listen, Dustin knocked again, this time quietly announcing, "It's I, Tyreham."

The lock slipped free of its bolt, and the door eased open a bit, then halted, as the still-unseen occupant assessed his visitor from within. A heartbeat later, the door swung wide. "Come in."

Dustin entered the cottage and faced the slight, dark-eyed man he recognized immediately as Nick Aldridge. "Throw the bolt," he advised. "No sense taking chances." He waited until Nick had complied, then extended his hand. "Aldridge. 'Tis a pleasure."

"An honor to meet you, my lord," Nick replied, gripping Dustin's fingers. "There aren't words enough to thank you for your help."

Waving away the thanks, Dustin glanced about.

"We can talk in the sitting room," Nick supplied. He led the way to a small but cozy chamber. "What can I offer you?" A scowl. "Neither Nickie nor I are very adept in the kitchen. I can't vouch for the refreshments—other than our liquor, of course."

Recalling Nicole's description of her culinary skills, Dustin stifled a grin. "No refreshment is necessary. I ate a large breakfast not too long ago. Besides, I'd rather not waste time. You and I have a lot to discuss."

"Indeed we do." Nick gestured for Dustin to be seated, after which he lowered himself into an armchair.

"First, let me apologize for arriving early," Dustin began, perching at the edge of the settee. "I realize you weren't expecting me until noon. But my morning interview was as brief as it was successful, and, given that I was most eager to meet with you, I took the liberty of coming directly to your cottage. I hope I haven't inconvenienced you."

"Of course not." Nick shook his head, leaning forward with avid expectation. "You had time for a morning meeting? Does that mean the elf—" Awkwardly, he cleared his throat. "Nicole—brought your stallion around?"

The term of endearment was as touching as the paternal pride that accompanied it. "In record time," Dustin reported with a grin. "Within an hour she and Dagger were trotting, moving together as if they'd been a team for months rather than minutes. Your daughter's abilities are staggering."

Pride glowed on Nick's face. "She is extraordinary, isn't she? A born rider from the time she was a tot."

"So you said in your letter of recommendation."

Nick's smile faded. "I'm sorry for the deception. Had there been another way—"

"There was no deception," Dustin interrupted. "You might have fabricated the name Alden Stoddard, but the many claims you made about him were true."

"Let's not play games, my lord, well-intentioned or not. Your assumption was that Stoddard was male. There are no female jockeys."

"There are now."

"No one knows that, except Nicole and me. And now you." With that, Nick shifted in his chair. "Pardon my bluntness, sir, but before we delve into Alden Stoddard or the circumstances that necessitated inventing him, we need to discuss Nicole and your expectations of her."

"I agree. We do." Dustin's tone was equally candid. "You're her father. Air your concerns and I'll address them."

"Fair enough." A flicker of surprise—and perhaps admiration—flashed in Nick's eyes. "To begin with, I'm worried about the idea of Nickie racing."

"You don't think her capable?"

"Capable? Hell, she's better than nearly every jockey I've

84

ever been up against. What I'm worried about is her well-being."

"Her well-being?" Dustin frowned. "How will competing in the Derby jeopardize that? Are you concerned it's too much too soon? That the pressure on her will be too great?"

An ironic snort. "Quite the opposite. Not only does Nickie ride like she was born for it, she thrives on pressure. I expect she'll stay calm long after the others are sweating profusely."

Well-being. A sudden, unnerving thought struck Dustin. "Do you have reason to suspect the bastards who threatened you will recognize Nicole?"

"Definitely not," Nick answered with the kind of conviction that suggested long hours of contemplation. "To my knowledge, those men have never laid eyes on Nickie. And even if they have, they'll believe what everyone else does—that she's in Scotland. With me. Tending to my injury. Besides, they'd never see through her disguise. It's too bloody good. Nickie made sure of that—given she'd have to get by the other jockeys, most of whom are my friends and have known the elf since she was a tot. She took extra precautions to fool them, lowering her voice, altering her mannerisms, and . . . er, binding herself down." Nick flushed. "Anyway, combine all that with the cap she wears that hides half her face, and my colleagues would have to be looking damned close to see a glimpse of the real Nickie, which they won't be. Not at Epsom. All their attention will be focused on their own mounts." A troubled pause. "At least, I pray that's the case." Nick rubbed his palms against his breeches. "My nagging fear is for the time immediately preceding the race. Nickie will need to weigh out a quarter hour before the Derby's onset, draw a lot for her starting position, line up at the gate. That's when she'll be most vulnerable. Stoddard is new to the turf. The *Racing Calendar* will have printed his name as your stallion's jockey of record, so speculation will be rampant. It's only natural for the other jockeys to want to size up an unknown competitor. If they should stare long enough . . ."

"They won't have the opportunity."

"What?"

"I'm not without influence, Aldridge. I intend to make

special provisions to eliminate the possibility you just described. Nicole won't arrive at Epsom until the Derby is about to commence. She'll be weighed out *alone.* Then she and Dagger will be ushered to their position at the gate just before the starter's flag is lowered. The other riders won't have time to scrutinize them."

"Thank God." Nick sagged with relief. "I can't tell you how that's preyed on my mind."

"Well, you can put it to rest. Now tell me precisely what else is causing you to worry about Nicole's well-being."

Again, Nick stiffened. "I'll be blunt, my lord. I never meant for Nickie's scheme to go this far. We needed an income. I needed to 'disappear.' She was only to get a job and support us until the buzzards stopped circling me. I expected she'd stay at Tyreham, train for the summer races, and never put that training to use. July is a full two months off, more than enough time for those bastards to lose interest in me and cast their eye on a more cooperative source. Once that happened, I planned to resume my life and have my daughter resume hers." His mouth set in harsh, stubborn lines. "I won't have Nickie living the life of a jockey—a man among other men. Traveling, living, sleeping in the same quarters."

"Nor will I." Dustin's expression was as steely as his tone. "I never even considered such a prospect. You have my word, Aldridge. Nicole will be shielded, separate, not only at the starting gate but in every aspect of her job."

"And, with all due respect, how do you intend to arrange such thorough overseeing?" Boldly, Nick met Dustin's gaze. "Or should I ask, who's going to provide it—you?"

"I take it you find that notion disagreeable?"

"Disagreeable? No. Unthinkable." Nick inhaled sharply, struggling to temper his reaction. "I realize I've got a lot of nerve speaking to you this way, given all you've done for us. As I said earlier, I'm grateful as hell for your assistance and your protection. Further, I have no grounds for questioning your motives. Not according to Nickie, who swears you've been not only kind but a perfect gentleman. I'm also aware I'm blatantly overstepping my bounds, given who you are and who I am. My only excuse is that Nickie is the most important part of my life."

"You're Nicole's father. Which, in this case, far outweighs any meaningless title or rank. Now speak your mind."

"Very well. Nickie's grown up in the stables among men who treat her with all the teasing affection of fathers to their child. Consequently, she's had no cause to view herself through the eyes of a suitor. The fact is, she doesn't even realize that over the past few years she's grown to be an extraordinarily beautiful young woman—the image of her mother. I myself didn't perceive the transformation until several days ago when she actually donned a gown. 'Twas the night she located your ad in the personals. You recall the evening you and she met."

"I recall."

"I'm certain you do," Nick returned dryly. "Which is precisely why I'm a bit uneasy."

"Because I met Nicole as herself prior to meeting her as Stoddard?"

"No, because of your quick and avid interest in her. Because Nicole is bloody beautiful and innocent, and your reputation is as black as Satan himself."

Dustin found himself chuckling. "I begin to see where Nicole inherited her forthrightness."

"And are you equally forthright?"

"Apparently, I'm destined to be—at least when it comes to the Aldridges. So, yes. I intend to be uncharacteristically frank, but not only for your sake, for mine as well." Dustin paused. "And for Nicole's." With staunch determination, he leaned forward, muscles taut. "I don't customarily discuss my private life. This is an exception. Partly because you're indirectly involved and partly because I need your help."

"My help?"

A nod. "First, let me assure you—as I seem to be perpetually assuring your daughter—the issue we're about to broach is separate and apart from both Nicole's entry in the Derby and from my proffered assistance in your dilemma. I'm committed to your safety *and* Nicole's victory, regardless of the outcome yielded by this morning's talk."

"You've discussed this matter with Nickie then?"

"Several times."

"I see. Very well, I'll accept your statement as sincere."

"Good. Now on to the subject at hand—Nicole. To be blunt, I've never known anyone quite like your daughter. From the moment we met, my feelings have been ... intense is the only word I can muster. And, believe me, that in itself is telling. Because, while I cannot muster emotions at will, I can always muster words. It's an art I've perfected over more years than I care to recall."

"With women, I presume you're implying."

"With nearly everyone. But, yes, with women."

"Don't bother elaborating. I've heard how accomplished you are at your various liaisons."

"Accomplished?" Dustin repeated with a bemused shake of his head. "That's an ironic choice of words. Because with Nicole, I feel anything but accomplished. To the contrary, I find myself unsure in ways I never imagined. I wonder how to proceed so as not to hurt her; how to avoid frightening her away; how to convince her that what I'm feeling is entirely real and entirely new—rooted in something far deeper than attraction.

"I'm aware of my reputation. Unfortunately, I can't prevent the spreading of gossip. But I can attest to the fact that my past has nothing to do with Nicole nor with my sentiments where she's concerned. Which leads me to my request. If I give you my word that I won't compromise Nicole's values or ask anything of her that would threaten her happiness, will you give me permission to call on her? Here. With you as a chaperone, if need be."

"Why would you ask my permission?" Nick countered, having watched Dustin intently as he spoke. "In fact, knowing that I'm privy to your notorious reputation, why not avoid dealing with me altogether? Surely you'll have ample opportunity to see Nicole during her next few weeks of training."

"No, I'll have ample opportunity to see Alden Stoddard," Dustin corrected. "And, given that I've promised Nicole to treat Stoddard as the young man he allegedly is, I'll have no chance to get to know Nicole Aldridge. Unless I find a way to visit her in a place other than the stables, somewhere entirely separate from her life as Stoddard and where she needn't fear discovery."

"I see." Nick's eyes narrowed. "You said you've spoken to

Nickie. Well, she's not mentioned a word of it to me. Given that fact, I'm curious. What are her feelings on this matter?"

"The ones she's aware of or the ones she isn't?"

Nick didn't pretend to misunderstand. "Both. Although I have my doubts about adopting the latter as truth, being that it's coming from you. Frankly, you haven't known Nickie long enough, or well enough, to perceive her feelings before she does."

"I disagree. Nevertheless, here's your answer. Nicole is confused. She trusts me, and she's drawn to me, and she's intimidated as hell by both. In my opinion, this pull between us is more than she's ready to handle yet. In fact, unless I convince her otherwise, I fully expect her to bolt the instant your circumstances alter." A corner of Dustin's mouth lifted. "Unless, of course, that change in circumstances should occur before she's won the Derby. In which case she'll delay her departure until after she's passed the winning post."

Tenderness flashed in Nick's eyes, followed by a faraway look and a weighted sigh. "I can't pretend to fathom the way you titled people live, Tyreham. I met my wife when I was in my teens, fell deeply in love, and married her as soon as I'd saved enough money for us to get by. She meant—everything to me. Oh, I thrive on racing, I always have. It's in my soul, the spark that drives me. No one understood that better than Alicia." Nick's voice quavered. "But although riding was my spirit, Alicia was my heart. When she died, a part of me died with her. Nicole is all I have left, the miracle Alicia blessed me with." A faint smile. "I see so much of Alicia in Nickie—the dreamer, the romantic, the eternal light of joy. I know Nickie thinks she's just like me, but she's not. Not outside the stables. Her heart is like her mother's—fragile. And I won't allow you, or anyone else, to shatter it."

"I don't intend to shatter it. I intend to win it."

Silence.

"Give me time to consider all you've said," Nick stated at last.

"All right. But, in the interim, Nicole's invited me to tea. Today. At four o'clock." Despite the intensity of the moment, Dustin found himself grinning. "Accompanied by inedible scones. I accepted her invitation. Is that permissible?"

"I suppose if Nickie's already asked you to come . . ."

"She has. With stipulations, of course." Dustin counted off on his fingers. "First, I had to reiterate my vow that she would race Dagger whether or not she agreed to my visits, which I did. Second, I had to promise to eat beforehand, so I shan't perish from the ponderous weight of her scones. And last, I had to accept her decision to greet me in her customary attire of breeches and shirt, rather than gown and slippers."

This time Nick chuckled. "That sounds like Nickie. Evidently, she enjoys your company. Very well, Tyreham, four o'clock it is. After which, perhaps I'll be in a better position to address your request."

"Fair enough." Having accomplished his goal—or, at least, a portion thereof—Dustin shifted to the next crucial topic. "Now let's get to your quandary."

"Agreed. I take it you have questions. What can I tell you that Nickie hasn't already relayed?"

"The men who blackmailed you, what did they look like?"

Nick frowned, recalling every detail he could. "I only saw them twice—both times at the stables, both times for no more than two minutes. They were foul-looking and stinking of ale. The shorter one was more muscular. He was heavyset and flushed, with pale eyes. The other one was taller, not by a lot, and less brawny. His hair and eyes were black."

"The same two men who paid a little visit to Tyreham." Dustin stood and began prowling the room. "They were exceedingly anxious to find out if you were working for me. In fact, my gut tells me they didn't just want you off the turf. They wanted you. Badly enough to risk exposure by coming to see me. Badly enough to take the time to unearth my one weakness in order to scare me into producing you if the rumors were false and you were employed at my stables." Seeing Nick's questioning look, Dustin added, "My nephew Alexander, my brother's infant son. They threatened to harm him if I hired you."

"Dear God." Nick dragged a forearm across his brow. "I had no idea . . ."

"They're serious, Aldridge. They intend to find you. The question is, why?"

"I've racked my brains for that answer, but to no avail. However, I agree with your assessment. They mean to do much more than blacklist me. They mean to kill me. That's why I got away as fast as I could."

"Then why do you assume they'll eventually give up?"

"Because the only time they've ever killed was when one of the jockeys involved vowed to retaliate. Openly. Stupidly. As a result, he was silenced."

"Who was that?"

Nick hesitated.

"Whatever you tell me will stay in this room," Dustin assured him.

A terse nod. "Redley. After the St. Leger Trial last fall. Although nothing was ever proven."

"Damn." Dustin's hands balled into fists. "I remember. Redley was killed at home, allegedly during a robbery. He worked for those animals?"

"Initially, yes. But I was there along with a dozen other men when he announced his intentions to beat the blackmailers at their own game. Three days later he was dead."

"And, knowing this, you still think they'll lose interest in you and disappear?"

Nick averted his gaze. "My situation is entirely different from Redley's. I'm not a fool. I have no intention of seeking vengeance. What's more, I don't possess a shred of information that might intimidate them or make them fear exposure."

"What makes you think Redley did?"

"The way he spoke. Why else would he have been so cocky, boasting that he'd thrown the race for his own purposes and that he now had the ammunition to get even?"

"You said it yourself—he was stupid. That doesn't mean he had anything other than greed to back it up."

"Nevertheless, he conspired with those criminals. I didn't. Sooner or later, they'll realize I'm no threat. At which point they'll forget me."

Dustin absorbed Nick's words, his rigid profile. "You don't believe that any more than I do."

A hard swallow. "I have to believe that. For Nickie's sake." Rising, Nick faced Dustin, a bleak look in his eyes. "Since I fled Newmarket a week ago I've felt nothing but rage. Anger clouded my reason, and it was only today during the quiet hours when Nickie's been at the stables that I've begun pondering the situation rationally. The truth is that if I ignore those bastards' threats, go charging back to the turf like a self-righteous fool, I'll be jeopardizing Nickie's life. She's my heart, Tyreham. If they hurt her—" Nick's voice broke. "I couldn't endure it. And if they killed me, who would Nickie have left? Therefore, I've come to the conclusion that to be heroic is to be reckless. I've got to wait this thing out until they give up and divert their energies elsewhere. Time is my only hope."

"You're deluding yourself," Dustin countered. "What's more, you know it. And, by doing so, you're not protecting Nicole, you're exposing her to even greater danger." Adamantly, he shook his head. "As for tactics, I'd never suggest you pursue these men. That would be downright suicidal. But they're not going to give up, Aldridge. Not until they find you. So denial is not the solution. Discovery is."

"Discovery?" Nick repeated. "How do you suggest I unearth facts while in hiding?"

"I don't. But then, *you're* in hiding. *I'm* not."

Nick studied Dustin for a long, thoughtful minute. "Who are you doing this for, your nephew or Nickie?"

"Both. And for the whole bloody lot of us who refuse to allow scum to corrupt the turf." Dustin frowned in thought. "Clearly, this is no amateur scheme. It's too vast and too ruthless. Which means there are pieces missing. Such as, who do those two lowlifes you described work for? They're certainly not acting on their own. So who's issuing their instructions, aiming to make a fortune on fixed races evidently as far back as last September?"

"Not just aiming. Succeeding." Nick gave a resigned sigh. "You really believe this is the prudent course of action, don't you, Tyreham?" He waited only for Dustin's nod. "I hope to God you know what you're doing. But since you're determined to try to stop these men, you'll need all the help

I can give you, prisoner though I am. I'm privy to more details than you are. For example, I know several jockeys who cooperated by throwing races. One, in fact, rode for you."

"Who?"

"Alberts."

Dustin inhaled sharply. "So, it wasn't incompetence. My assessment of his riding abilities was right."

"Indeed, he's one hell of a jockey. He's also a greedy scoundrel who collected a thousand pounds for forfeiting the fall races. And he's far from alone. I can give you names, racing events . . . the incidents are widespread, involving a handful of riders and Lord knows who else."

"Has no one tried to stop them?"

"Last September a group of us jockeys speculated over ways to put an end to the situation. But then Redley was murdered, and our desire for justice was eclipsed by our desire to stay alive."

"A group of you . . . I gather your friend Sullivan was part of that group."

Nick's brows rose. "Nickie discussed Sully with you?"

"Only to say that he's your closest friend and that he helped spirit you from the turf."

"He did. He also gave us every pound he had in order to keep us hidden."

"I'll replenish every cent—in person."

"You intend to see him?"

"With your permission, yes. He's the only one, other than Nicole and me, who knows your true whereabouts. Also, he's not only your trusted friend but a fellow jockey, someone who's far closer to the riders in question than I. Perhaps he can help, maybe add to the list you provide me."

Nick considered the request. "What if those bastards are watching you? They'll see you meet with Sully. I don't want them connecting him with my disappearance."

"Aldridge," Dustin replied soberly, "given your long-standing friendship with Sullivan, do you honestly believe they haven't already connected him with your disappearance?"

"You're right. I'm sure they have." Nick massaged his temples, wearily crossing over to a small desk from which he extracted paper and pen. "Sully's quarters are in Suffolk," he informed Dustin, scribbling down the address. "Here. At least you'll be able to tell him that Nickie and I are well. I don't dare communicate with him myself."

"No, you don't." Dustin slipped the paper into his pocket. "I'll assure him you're both quite safe. In fact, I'll ride to Suffolk first thing tomorrow." A thoughtful pause. "On the return trip, I think I'll drop in on the Viscount Preighbrook, ask him a few questions about Redley."

Nick blinked. "I'd nearly forgotten. Redley rode Lord Preighbrook's filly Nightingale at the St. Leger Trial."

"Which was his last race," Dustin reflected aloud. "I remember how upset Preighbrook was by Nightingale's performance. In truth, we were all somewhat stunned, given that she was the overwhelming favorite. But then, no one expected Redley to fall behind on that last lap." Dustin nodded decisively. "Yes, I'll definitely pay a visit to Preighbrook on my way home. His estate is right here in Surrey."

"Is that wise? Inevitably, word will get out that you're dredging up the circumstances surrounding Redley's death."

"I hope so." A steely glint lit Dustin's eyes. "In fact, I'm counting on it. The sooner those two lowlifes realize I'm delving, the sooner they'll reappear on my doorstep. At which time I intend to unsettle them enough so they'll race off to whoever pays their wages—with me at their heels, alert and undetected. If I'm successful, we'll be one step closer to resolving the crimes and resuming our lives." Dustin's gaze drifted to the window, over the path that led to the stables. "Our lives and our futures."

Seven

"Papa?"

Nicole shut the cottage door behind her, tugging pins from beneath her cap as she walked through the hallway.

"Ah, if it isn't my brilliant prodigy, Alden Stoddard." Eyes twinkling, Nick strolled out to greet her. "Your day must have been successful. You're beaming from ear to ear."

"Are you alone?" Nicole demanded, her hand pausing in its task.

"I am. Lord Tyreham left a half hour ago."

"So Dustin—Lord Tyreham did remember your meeting." Searching her father's face, Nicole resumed, yanking impatiently at the next layer of pins.

"He certainly did. He arrived early, in fact." Her father's raised brows were the only indication he'd noted her unintentional use of Dustin's given name. "Lord Tyreham was very impressed with your skill. Evidently, you won his stallion over posthaste."

"Oh, Papa, I wish you could have been there!" At last, Nicole's cap came free, releasing her disheveled tresses in a wild cascade down her back and shoulders. "Dagger is magnificent. He's the most incredible thoroughbred I've ever seen. And he's not hard to handle, he's just apprehensive—with good cause. Obviously, he's been abused." She paused to catch her breath and blow wisps of hair from her face. "The ironic part is that I didn't need to do a thing to win him over, other than be myself, not because of my affinity for horses but because of my gender. Dagger's keen senses told him at once that I was a girl, which put his mind at ease, since whoever harmed him was undoubtedly a man. Thus, after two minutes of conversation and an equal number of sugar cubes, we became fast friends. And when we rode, oh, Papa, we were extraordinary together. It was magic. Part of me was itching to break into a gallop, but I could hear your voice in my head reminding me that it was Dagger's first training session in Lord knows how long and that I should bring him along slowly. So I curbed my enthusiasm. But tomorrow we'll canter, and by week's end we'll be galloping and ready to run at Epsom. Papa, you would have been so pleased!" Nicole dropped her cap to the floor and hugged her father.

"I'm more than pleased," Nick declared, chuckling as he embraced her. "I'm bursting with pride. What's more, I don't think you realize how significant your accomplishment was, any more than you recognize the true extent of your rapport with horses. You're one of a kind, Elf. And, while I'm sure everything you surmised about Dagger's past is true, rest assured that he wouldn't have taken so quickly and totally to every woman. Like any responsive, intelligent thoroughbred, he senses someone special." Gently, her father held Nicole away from him, studying her flushed cheeks and sparkling eyes. "Worried though I am, I'm equally as thrilled for you, Elf. Thrilled that you're getting the opportunity to feel the elation you're experiencing now and the rush of victory you'll experience when you and Dagger pass the winning post." His grip tightened. "This one time," he added in an uncompromising tone.

"This one time," Nicole repeated without hesitation. "But what a glorious one time. The Derby." Determination surged through her. "I'm going to win it, Papa."

"I haven't a doubt." He paused. "Evidently, neither has Lord Tyreham."

Nicole tensed. "Did he say that?"

"He said many things, that being one of them. He was amazed by your ability, and effusive with his praise."

Relief swept through her. "He left the course rather abruptly. I thought perhaps he was angry that I'd taken it upon myself to mount and ride Dagger without summoning anyone."

"He was far from angry. As for his leaving abruptly, when he arrived at our cottage, he mentioned something about a morning appointment. I presume that appointment was what rushed him from the course. In any case, it certainly wasn't disapproval of your actions."

"I'm glad." Nicole brightened. "In Lord Tyreham's absence, his head groom, Brackley, showed me around the stables. They're enormous, Papa, and the marquis's horses are the finest I've ever seen. Even his staff is exceptional—every attendant right down to the stableboys. I spent hours committing the entire stable to memory, getting acquainted with the horses, and trying to grasp all the details of day-to-day procedure. The staff was generous with their knowledge and patient with my dozens of questions." Nicole tossed her father an impish grin. "All the while not one of them suspected Alden Stoddard was anything but male."

"Excellent." Nick cleared his throat. "You haven't asked what Lord Tyreham and I discussed."

Her grin faded. "I assume you discussed the men who blackmailed you."

"We did—among other things."

"Other things?" Nicole stared at the toe of her boot.

"Um-hum. For example, the marquis asked my permission to come to tea today. Evidently, you invited him."

Nicole's gaze snapped back to his. "Do you mind?"

"I don't know. Should I?"

A heartbeat of silence ensued.

"Nickie," her father said quietly, "we need to have a talk." He glanced at the grandfather clock standing just outside the sitting room.

"I'm filthy, Papa." Nicole blurted out the first excuse that came to mind. Her feelings about Dustin were too raw, too baffling to discuss, especially with her protective—and opinionated—father. "I need a bath. Also, I'm famished.

Why, I believe I could even manage to swallow one or two of my scones."

"Given the amount of food Lord Tyreham stocked the cottage with, we can find something more substantial and far better tasting for you to eat than your scones." Her father's tone told her he was unfooled by her attempts at evasion. "We'll talk while you eat. You'll have more than enough time to bathe before your guest arrives."

Like a condemned prisoner, Nicole nodded, following her father into the kitchen.

What in God's name was she going to tell him when she herself didn't understand these careening emotions, much less how to squelch them?

Frowning, Nicole filled a plate with cold chicken and apple pudding. More unsettling still, what had Dustin said to pique her father's curiosity?

Apparently, she was about to find out.

Her appetite gone, Nicole leaned against the counter, nibbling at her meal and trying to swallow past the lump in her throat. "This is delicious," she announced, pushing the food about on her plate.

"Yes it is. Although I'm surprised you noticed, given you've scarcely downed two mouthfuls." Her father folded his arms across his chest and faced Nicole squarely—a decisive gesture she'd seen him use countless times with others, rarely with her. "Tell me about Lord Tyreham and your feelings toward him."

Nicole stopped chewing. "What did Dustin tell you?"

"That's the second time you've referred to your employer by his given name. When did you become so well acquainted?"

She could actually feel her cheeks flame. "I explained to you that when Lord Tyreham and I met, he introduced himself only as Dustin—not out of disrespect or because he was making advances," she added hastily, "but because I'd only supplied him with my given name. Which, as you can guess, was to conceal my identity. He merely responded in kind. So that explains why I occasionally slip and refer to him as Dustin."

"I see. Does that also explain why you refuse to meet my eyes and are blushing profusely?"

Nicole's flush deepened. "If you're worried about my jeopardizing my disguise, don't be. I'm very mindful that Alden Stoddard addresses Lord Tyreham by title."

"How reassuring," her father returned dryly. "But it isn't Stoddard's welfare that's troubling me. It's my daughter's. A daughter, I might add, who has never been less than straightforward with me."

Sighing, Nicole gave up all semblance of eating . . . and hedging. "Papa, it might seem otherwise, but I'm not intentionally keeping anything from you. I'm just not certain how to respond."

"Respond with the truth. Do you have feelings for this man?"

"I don't know." Nicole shook her head in frustration. "I shouldn't. I can't."

"But you do," Nick concluded.

"Yes," Nicole whispered. "I do." She stared out the window. "Papa, right now I'm fighting to keep you safe. Until this ordeal is over, I haven't the strength to contend with emotional upheaval. And that's precisely what giving in to my attraction for Dustin Kingsley would be. I can't do it—not now. Maybe never. He and I are worlds apart not only in social position but in values, in ways of life. The complications are vast, possibly insurmountable."

"True. Yet, knowing all this, you invited him for tea."

Her lashes lowered. "I can't explain it."

"I believe you just did." Nick crossed over, lifting Nicole's chin with his forefinger. "There's a voice inside me commanding me to forbid you from associating with a man whose reputation is as black as Tyreham's. A man who's not only a womanizer but an aristocrat whose life is far removed from the one you know, and who has the wealth and power to break your heart without ever breaking stride. But judging from what you just said, you're already aware of who he is and what's at stake."

"I do—in here." Nicole tapped her head. "Unfortunately, I can't seem to convince my heart to be equally as pragmatic."

"So I gathered." Nick appeared to weigh his options, and his words. "I know I can't keep you a child forever. However, nor can I stand by and watch you get hurt.

Therefore, I'll honor Lord Tyreham's visit. As for his request, that remains to be seen. Now go have that bath. Should your guest arrive early, which I strongly suspect he might, I'll entertain him."

His request?

Nicole blinked, comprehending that whatever permission Dustin had sought clearly involved more than an invitation to tea. "Exactly what is it Lord Tyreham requested?" she asked cautiously.

"The opportunity to become better acquainted with you, or rather, with Nicole Aldridge, not Alden Stoddard. The right to call on you with some degree of frequency. In this sitting room, under my watchful eye."

Her heart skipped a beat. "And how did you respond?"

"I intended to refuse. But the marquis was very convincing."

"Convincing." Nicole moistened her lips. "In what way?"

"Let's just say that either the man is the most accomplished of liars, or he genuinely cares for you—whatever, in his realm of thinking, 'caring' means. Based on what I've seen of bluebloods, I remain wary. Only time will tell if my misgivings are unfounded where Tyreham is concerned. The important thing is I believe he's sincere about not *meaning* to hurt you. He was also entirely honorable in his approach. After hearing him out, I relented—a bit—agreeing *only* to his first visit. From there on, I reserve judgment."

"Thank you, Papa." Nicole kissed his cheek.

"Don't thank me yet," Nick said gruffly. "I'm far from reassured, because, no matter how sincere Tyreham is, his good intentions can't eliminate the obstacles that, as you yourself pointed out, are vast. Nor can they alter the glaring contrast between your way of life and his." Nick scowled. "In any case, once I've had the chance to think and to personally assess Tyreham's behavior toward you, I might very well revert to my original impulse, to toss him out and barricade the doors. The marquis might be a very persuasive man, which he is about many things, but so am I."

Her father's last statement brought Nicole up short. "About many things," she repeated. "Are you referring to the blackmail situation?"

A reluctant nod.

"Papa, don't shield me. I'm as involved as you are. What did you and Dustin discuss?"

"Lord Tyreham is determined to uncover the entire scheme, complete with whoever's at its helm."

Fear gripped Nicole's stomach. "Won't that endanger you?"

"Not the way the marquis intends to handle it." Her father's gaze met hers, and he gave a resigned sigh. "Very well, Nickie. I'll tell you the rest. The last thing I want is for you to worry. Lord Tyreham's plan consists of his doing the probing while I stay in hiding and supply him with details, at least those I'm aware of, such as the names of crooked jockeys and occasions when they threw their races. I've compiled a list. I'll give it to him this afternoon. He intends to ride to Suffolk first thing tomorrow to see Sully and, if possible, to add to my list. After which, he means to call on the necessary parties."

Nicole's fear intensified. "Those steps can hardly be kept secret, especially in light of Dustin's reputation on the turf. The entire racing circuit will be buzzing with news of his investigation. He'll be a walking target."

"That's what he's counting on. He wants to lure the lowlifes who threatened him back so he can follow them to their employer, then expose him. By the way, Tyreham and I compared descriptions. The men who warned him away from me are the same ones who tried blackmailing me and, doubtless, the same ones who left me that friendly greeting on Oberon's stall."

"I assumed as much." Nicole clutched her father's forearms. "Papa, this whole thing scares me to death. Maybe we should just leave matters alone, stay in hiding until more time has passed. Then you and Lord Tyreham will both be safe."

"Stay in hiding?" Nick teased gently, patting her cheek. "And have you replace me on the turf? Never." Seeing her ashen expression, he sobered. "Nickie, this situation won't go away by itself. We have to put a stop to it. Now."

"I know." With a small nod, Nicole relented, realizing there was no choice, terrified by the prospect.

"Go have that bath of yours. The marquis will be arriving in less than an hour."

"All right." Uneasily, Nicole made her way from the kitchen, up the stairs to her room. Leaning against the door, she battled the apprehension that knotted her gut, reassured herself that fate would intercede and set things right.

But fate alone was too mercurial, its path too uncertain. It needed wishes to fortify its magic.

Instinctively, Nicole's hand slid into her pocket, extracting her wishing locket and placing it in her palm. With infinite love, she traced the pattern etched into the burnished silver, recalling that special night fifteen years ago when she'd held the necklace for the first time.

Do you like it, Nickie?

Oh, Mama, it's beautiful. Is there a photograph inside?

No, darling, there's a far greater treasure kept tight within this locket's walls.

What is it? Oh, Mama, let me see.

Nicole smiled softly, remembering how she'd fumbled with the catch, mastering it at last and tugging it free.

Acute disappointment had surged through her five-year-old heart when she'd found the locket to be empty.

There's nothing here, Mama, she'd murmured, her eyes brimming with tears.

You're wrong, love.

I'm not wrong. It's empty.

Only because you're looking with your eyes, not your heart. If your heart were to peer inside, it would see that this is no ordinary locket. It's a wishing locket. Inside is a bottomless cache made especially for wishes, with enough room for every dream you've ever dreamed, still more for all those wishes yet to be wished.

Really? Nicole had looked more closely. *How does it work?*

First, you must think of what it is you're wishing for—and focus on it very, very hard. Then close your eyes and squeeze the locket tight between your hands. And, lo and behold, your wish will be captured by the locket's magic and stored inside.

Until when?

Until the locket deems it time to set that wish free, and make it come true.

When will that be?

Ah, Nickie, only the locket knows the answer to that. When it decides to grant a particular wish, it will cast it from its depths, transforming that wish to reality. But you must trust in the locket's wisdom and never stop believing in its magic.

But what if it takes years and years and years for a wish to come true?

Then that wish's time has yet to be.

What if, in the meantime, the locket gets too crowded and runs out of room for new wishes? How will I know?

That's part of the locket's wonder. It never runs out of room. It can hold as many cherished dreams as can your heart.

You're sure?

I'm sure, my darling.

Savoring the memory, Nicole gazed down at her legacy, two tears trickling down her cheeks and dropping onto the locket's shimmering surface.

"I hope you're right, Mama," she whispered aloud, wiping the silver dry. "I hope my locket truly does hold infinite wishes because I have another to entrust to its magical depths." Her fingers closed around the necklace, clasping it tightly, her eyes squeezed shut. "I've already prayed for Papa's safety. Now I must pray for Dustin's, as well. Because if anything were to happen to him . . ." She choked back more tears. "I couldn't bear it. So please, wishing locket, take care of him. Take care of them both."

At half after three, Dustin's last thread of patience snapped.

Abandoning his drink, his study, and his pacing, he strode out of the manor and headed in the direction of the Aldridges' cottage. Waiting was pointless. He'd done nothing but think of Nicole since morning, anticipating this mere visit with more fervor than he had all his former and most ardent liaisons combined.

Single-minded though he might be, however, he was still acutely aware that this tea signified far more than a social chat—not only to him but, for altogether different reasons, to Nick Aldridge. Nicole's father had made it clear that this was to be a trial visit, one that would determine whether or not he would sanction Dustin's courtship of Nicole. Further, Dustin realized that while he and Aldridge had gotten on famously this morning, Nicole's father still viewed him as one of "them": a nobleman and a libertine. Accordingly, while Dustin had made enough headway for Aldridge to permit today's call, nothing more permanent than that had been secured.

In short, grudging allowance was a long way from open-armed welcome.

It was up to Dustin to convert the former to the latter.

Tread lightly, he cautioned himself, as he reached the front door. *You want Aldridge's sanction, not his censure. Go slowly, very slowly. For your sake—and Nicole's.*

Taking a determined breath, he knocked. "It's Tyreham," he announced after a moment's pause.

"So I gathered." With a terse nod, Nick admitted him, his demeanor friendly, yes, but aloof, assessing—a wary father protecting his child. "Come in."

"I'm early—again. Is that inconvenient?"

"No. This time I expected it, so I was prepared. Have a seat." Nick gestured toward the sitting room. "Nickie should be down in a minute. She was a bit disheveled from her hectic morning."

Dustin paused in the sitting room doorway. "Did something happen after I left the course?" he asked, concern knitting his brows. "When I last saw Nicole, she was cooling Dagger down, looking utterly exhilarated."

"She was. She still is." Nick relaxed a bit, affection lacing his tone. "But riding Dagger was only the beginning. She then went on to tour your stables end to end, meet every one of your thoroughbreds, and bombard your staff with questions. She didn't return to the cottage until well after two."

"Ah, then she enjoyed herself."

"She most assuredly did," Nicole replied, descending the stairs to join them. "Thank you for the opportunity you've afforded me, my lord. Dagger is all you claimed and more."

So are you, Dustin wanted to say, drinking her in like a fine wine.

Dressed in the promised breeches and shirt, her face was devoid of cosmetics, her throat adorned only by a delicate silver locket. And her hair, loose and unencumbered by a jockey's cap, was just as he'd remembered it—a cloud of rich black silk.

He clenched his fists to keep from reaching out and running his fingers through it.

"You rode superbly," he said instead. "I haven't spoken to Brackley since I left the course, but my guess is he won't stop muttering and shaking his head for weeks. That's how astonished you've rendered my impervious groom."

"Fear not," Nicole returned. "Brackley recovered. He was quite composed when he showed me around the stables. Nevertheless, I appreciate the praise. I also apologize."

"For what?"

"For taking Dagger out without summoning both you and Brackley. It was wrong of me. My only excuse is that Dagger and I had begun to relate so well, and I didn't want to take a chance . . . that is, I thought perhaps . . ."

"You can be frank," Dustin finished for her. "You thought perhaps Brackley and I would appear and destroy the rapport you'd established with Dagger. And you would have been right. That's precisely what we would have done. Hence, your apology is unnecessary but accepted. I would, however, be interested in hearing what method you used to bring my reticent stallion around. I tried everything experience has taught me and barely managed to break the surface. The fear he brought with him to Tyreham was deeply ingrained."

"I wish I could boast some miraculous secret, but I can't. The truth is, I'm a woman. You know that. I know that. And now Dagger knows that. Since whoever abused him was undoubtedly male, his fear does not extend to me. I had only to wait for him to perceive my gender, then coax him into trusting that I had the best of intentions. The rest came naturally." She shot Dustin a shrewd look. "Further, I'm certain you realized all this long before I offered my explanation. You're a renowned horseman. And, since what I've just told you is both obvious and elementary, I have to wonder why you asked me to clarify my methods. Is this a test of my knowledge or my candor?"

Dustin heard Nick's sharp, astonished gasp. "Nickie . . ." he began.

"It's all right, Aldridge." Dustin waved away the interception. "Nicole's question is entirely justified." He met her defensive gaze. "The answer is neither. It's my careless attempt to appear gallant by praising you. As I've mentioned, I'm unaccustomed to people who prefer truth to flattery."

The fire in her eyes banked, softening their color to a warm, smoky violet. "'Tis a pity, my lord. Frankness suits you far better than artifice. You should try it more often."

"I'll do that," Dustin promised. "In fact, I'll begin right now. Might I trouble you for some refreshment—more specifically, your scones? After hearing your colorful description, I'm impatient to sample them."

"You picked an unfortunate subject on which to test your newfound candor." Nicole's grin was impish. "Once you've tasted my scones . . ." She shuddered. "Suffice it to say that your eagerness will be transformed to nausea."

"I'll take my chances. After all, what is life without risk?"

Their gazes met.

"Very well, my lord." Nicole looked away first, heading for the kitchen. "You and Papa go to the sitting room and await your undoing."

"Not I," Nick called after her. "I'll have some of that delicious gingerbread Tyreham's cook sent over. If the marquis chooses to die, that's his business."

Nicole's shoulders began to shake. "A wise decision, Papa," she commended over her shoulder. "I'll bring enough gingerbread for two—plus a bit extra, should Lord Tyreham live long enough to change his mind."

Thoughtfully, Nick watched his daughter disappear from view, then led Dustin into the sitting room. "Tyreham," he said the instant they were within, "I appreciate your taking Nickie's insolence in stride. I don't know what came over her. I've never heard her speak that way. Oh, she's forthright as hell, but never rude, certainly not to my employers. Or, in this case, to *her* employer."

"I don't think the remark was aimed at her employer," Dustin answered quietly, settling himself on the settee. "It was aimed at me. Or rather, the inbred highborn in me." A faint smile. "In case you haven't noticed, Nicole is no fonder of the nobility—or its affectations—than you are."

"Oh, I've noticed. Actually, a good part of that intolerance is my doing. And I'm not apologizing for it. The truth is, I have little regard for frivolous living and no respect for those who are uncommitted to their family and their work. Nickie's grown up listening to my convictions and forming her own. I'm proud to say that she, too, has little use for lazy, unprincipled people."

"Not all noblemen are lazy and unprincipled."

"No, they're not. Or rather, not when it comes to business. When it comes to women, however, I've seen just the opposite." Nick shrugged. "At least that's been my observation."

"I won't argue. For the most part, you're right. However, there are exceptions. There are also those of us who would like to become exceptions—transgressors awaiting the right opportunity or the right incentive to reform."

"I suppose." Obviously uncomfortable with the turn the conversation was taking, Nick cleared his throat. "I wonder what's keeping Nickie."

"You forget how heavy my scones are, Papa," Nicole replied, making her way into the room. "I could scarcely hold up under their weight." So saying, she deposited a tray of tea, gingerbread, and what looked to be lumpy balls of browned dough, on the side table. "Refreshment," she announced, transferring one dough ball to a plate and handing it to Dustin. "How do you take your tea, my lord?"

"Hmm?" Dustin was rotating the dish, staring at the scone in utter amazement.

"I asked how you took your tea."

Hearing the laughter in her voice, Dustin raised his head and regarded her dazedly. "Today? Strong. Very strong."

"I anticipated that," she returned with a bright smile, filling his cup to the brim. "Here. Hold this saucer while you take your first bite of scone. Then you'll be able to drown out the flavor instantly."

Dustin nodded, biting into the scone and chewing what tasted like a clump of sand. He swallowed, gasped in a breath, then downed the entire cup of tea.

"Shall I serve you another scone, my lord?"

"No," Dustin managed, shaking his head. He handed her his empty cup, gesturing for her to refill it.

She complied, then passed it back.

He gulped it dry.

"Is something wrong, my lord?"

Dustin caught his breath. "You don't, by chance, employ a cook?" he croaked. "Ordinarily, I mean?"

"Of course not. Since Mama died, Papa and I have fended for ourselves."

"How long has that been?"

"Seven years."

Dustin shook his head in disbelief. "In that time, how is it that one of you hasn't perished?"

"That's an easy one," Nick cut in. "I do most of the cooking." He turned to Nicole. "I'll have a slice of that gingerbread, Elf. And some tea."

"Certainly, Papa." Nicole served her father what appeared to Dustin to be the most magnificent piece of gingerbread he'd ever seen.

"Would you care for a slice, my lord?" she inquired, inclining her head in his direction. "Or are the scones to your liking?"

"Oh, the scones are delicio—" Dustin caught Nicole's eye, and the two of them dissolved into laughter. "Actually," he amended, "I'd kill for that gingerbread. This"—he gestured toward the scone—"was perhaps the most dreadful substitute for food I've ever tasted." He cocked a brow. "Honest enough?"

"Bravo." Nicole served him an enormous slice of gingerbread. "As a reward, I'm giving you the largest piece. Soon the scone will be no more than a horrid memory."

"Nickie's mutton isn't bad," Nick commented, "and she does fairly well with eggs. However, her beef is as tough as a horse's tack, and her pastries . . ."

"Enough honesty, Papa," Nicole interceded. "I think we've made it clear that my culinary skills are lacking."

"But your riding skills make up for it," Dustin informed her. He placed his teacup on the table, leaning forward. "In keeping with my newly tried candor, let me say that while you were right about my guessing why Dagger didn't fear you, you were wrong if you assumed my praise to be insincere. I never imagined you'd make such startling headway in one morning. Oh, I'd hoped that your being a woman would ease Dagger's apprehension. But calming a horse is one thing, winning his trust and reestablishing his confidence quite another. Not to mention matching your cadence to his, moving as if you're a born team when in fact you're virtual strangers. The last is an accomplishment with any mount, skittish or even-tempered. It normally takes months to achieve. You did it in under an hour and with a very difficult mount. No, Nicole, your way with horses is astounding. Astounding and innate." Dustin's nod was decisive. "You and Dagger are going to win that Derby. I can feel it in my bones."

Excitement tinged Nicole's cheeks. "As can I. Your instincts about Dagger were right, my lord. He's an exceptional mount—a true winner."

"As is the rider who will inspire him to victory."

"Thank you." A spark of humor danced in Nicole's eyes. "This time for praise that is not only genuine but, in my opinion, accurate." Sobering, she chewed her lip, clearly uncertain about how to phrase her next words. "I realize it's none of my business," she said at last, "but who was Dagger's former owner?"

"That's not where Dagger's fears originated." Dustin shook his head, instantly grasping Nicole's train of thought. "You're wondering who abused him. I've asked myself that same question. But the mistreatment took place before Dagger's previous owner bought him. The reason I know that is because Lanston—the previous owner in question—happens to be a long-standing colleague of mine. He told me about Dagger's reckless nature and deep-seated apprehension. And, by the way, this situation is very much your business. Everything concerning Dagger is."

"Lanston?" Nick put in. "The earl of Lanston?" Seeing Dustin's nod, he added, "I ran for the earl at last summer's meeting at Goodwood. He's a sharp fellow. Pleasant, too."

"He's also a fine breeder," Dustin supplied. "He bought Dagger at Tattersall's two years ago. I missed that particular auction or I would have given my colleague some healthy competition. Like any breeder worth a damn, he perceived Dagger's potential instantly, despite the fact that he'd obviously been mistreated."

"He was scarred?"

"Not outwardly, no. But, according to Lanston, he was wild, unapproachable. For two years the earl tried to rectify the damage that had been done. He badly wanted to race

Dagger. On one or two occasions, he actually did. But those were minor events. Lanston just couldn't risk it. Dagger was too bloody unpredictable. One moment he was galloping like a champion, the next he was rearing, stomping, and tossing his rider. Finally, Lanston lost patience and sold Dagger to me. I was delighted to try my hand at bringing him around. Having seen him run, I knew how good he was. I was determined, come hell or high water, to transform him into the winner he was born to be. Fortunately, Lanston had made greater strides than he realized. Not once since arriving at Tyreham has Dagger been so unruly that Brackley or I couldn't handle him. Nervous and reticent, yes. But wild? Uncontrollable? No."

Nicole frowned. "I can't picture Dagger being either wild or uncontrollable. He's frightened and confused, both of which I intend to remedy. Trust me, my lord. Whatever horrible treatment Dagger received is behind him now. He'll know nothing but respect and affection, not only from his owner but from his jockey."

"A most fortunate horse." Dustin found himself envying his recalcitrant stallion.

"The earl of Lanston," Nicole repeated thoughtfully. "That name is somehow familiar."

"You heard me say it a dozen times last summer," Nick broke in swiftly. "Remember? Like I just told the marquis, I rode for Lanston at the Goodwood Stakes."

"No, that's not it." Nicole shook her head. "I heard his name recently. Quite recently. I just can't remember when and in what context."

"Perhaps you heard me mention the earl to Brackley today," Dustin suggested. "Lanston referred a superb trainer to me. Raggert's his name. I hired him this morning. He'll begin at Tyreham in a day or two. I think you'll enjoy working with him—or rather, Alden Stoddard will."

"I've met Raggert," Nick said, looking strangely relieved by the turn the conversation had taken. "Seen him work, too. He's good."

"No, it wasn't this morning, and it wasn't in connection with a trainer," Nicole maintained. "Although I'm pleased you've hired one who inspires your confidence. But I recall hearing the name Lanston . . ." Comprehension struck, followed by a deep, heated blush.

"Go on," Dustin pressed, feeling an equal measure of puzzlement and uneasiness. Had Nicole met Lanston during a recent racing event? He was a nice enough looking fellow—and certainly available. Had he approached her with his famous charm? "Where did Lanston's name come up?"

"I—I'm not certain. I think it was at the stables. Yes, that's it. A few of the jockeys were discussing him." Nicole turned to her father. "You're out of tea, Papa. May I pour you more?"

"Yes. Please do." Nick thrust his cup at Nicole.

"Did the jockeys' comments embarrass you?" Dustin persisted.

Averting her gaze, Nicole said nothing.

"Was Lanston present at the time?" Dustin's ire was increasing by the minute.

Nicole's color intensified.

"Tell me." Puzzlement was gone, supplanted by icy fury. Dustin gripped his knees, awaiting her reply. Had that womanizing friend of his made advances toward Nicole? If so, Dustin would throttle him. "Have you met Edmund?" he demanded.

"Edmund?"

"The earl of Lanston. Have you met him?"

"No, my lord, I have not."

"Are you certain? He spends a fair amount of time with his contenders prior to each race."

"So I understand," Nicole blurted, obviously reaching her limit. "Most of that time, I've heard, is spent placing wagers on the identity of your next paramour."

Nick groaned and slid down in his chair.

Dustin sucked in his breath. "What?"

"You heard me, my lord." Nicole poured herself some tea, her hand shaking so badly that hot liquid sloshed into the saucer. "Your reputation precedes you."

"Nicole . . ." Dustin felt a slash of pain, coupled with a potent combination of guilt and regret: guilt for the fact that he was causing Nicole anguish; and regret that her exposure to the aristocracy had been sordid enough to dishearten her and to reinforce her belief that all noblemen were lechers.

Most specifically, he.

At that moment, Dustin wanted nothing more than to be able to deny Lanston's implications, to negate the existence of the women in his past, even though their memories had crumpled to dust the night he'd met Nicole.

But the truth was, he couldn't.

"Aldridge, let me speak to Nicole alone." Dustin vaulted to his feet, the demand issued of its own accord. "Please," he added, gentling his tone in response to the faint narrowing of Nick's eyes. "Five minutes. That's all I ask. You can pace the length of the hallway and watch the bloody clock the whole time, for all I care. But I need to talk to Nicole." He gave Aldridge an exasperated look. "Rest assured, even *I* have yet to ravish a woman in five minutes, much less with her father standing outside the door."

Nick's glance flickered to Nicole. "Elf?"

Head bent, Nicole nodded. "It's all right, Papa. I have a few things I need to tell the marquis, as well."

Slowly, Nick stood. "Five minutes." He stalked across the room, pausing in the doorway. "I'll be right outside—in case my daughter needs me," he added with a meaningful glare. As if to further illustrate his point, he crossed the threshold and pulled the door partway shut behind him, leaving enough space to overhear any commotion that might arise.

Dustin wasted not an instant.

"Nicole, about Lanston's comments . . ."

"I have no right to judge you," Nicole murmured, staring at her lap. "I apologize for my outburst."

"And I apologize for my past." Dustin took her hand, pulling her to her feet. "How can I convince you those women don't matter?"

"You shouldn't have to. The way you conduct your life is none of my concern." She kept her gaze level with his shirtfront, plainly unwilling to meet his. "I don't know what possessed me to speak to you like that. I'm not normally ill-mannered."

"And I'm not normally an awkward schoolboy. Yet with

you, I am. And it is your concern." He gripped her elbows, drawing her closer. *"I'm* your concern. As you, Derby, are mine." He glanced from the slightly open door to the clock on the mantel. "We haven't much time. Your father is like a bloody sentry. So ask me."

"Ask you?" She peeped questioningly up at him from beneath her lashes.

"Yes. Ask me. To kiss you."

"To kiss . . ." She looked utterly dazed—and utterly exquisite. "Dustin, we're alone here to discuss our differences—why I react so badly to your way of life, your artificial facade."

He shook his head, tipping up her chin. "No, Derby, we're alone here to reaffirm what happens when you're in my arms, which is the very thing that makes you want to run away, to declare us unsuited for each other. Well, we're not. We're more perfectly suited than you realize. And I don't want you to be afraid."

"I am," she whispered.

"Nicole." He threaded his fingers through her hair, savoring the texture he'd ached to explore. "I won't hurt you. I swear it. Nor am I trying to seduce you. I want more than that from you. But for now, I'll settle for a kiss, a kiss that I vowed not to initiate until—unless—it was what you wanted. Do you want me to kiss you, Nicole?"

A flush stained her cheeks as she grappled with her decision. "Yes," she breathed in a tiny voice.

Dustin's hands were shaking as he gathered her against him, enfolding her in his arms and covering her mouth with his.

He hadn't realized how badly he'd needed her, how desperately he'd wanted to taste her again. Sensations, unknown before Nicole, erupted instantly, submerging him in the same unchartered waters he'd been drowning in since the night they'd met.

Her lips trembled under his, soft and hesitant and so sweet Dustin nearly groaned aloud. He didn't rush her, taking only as much as she offered, contenting himself with damp, chaste kisses that demanded nothing, yet sought more than he could ever explain.

Slowly, like a tentative flower, Nicole's lips parted, opening to Dustin's penetration, silently seeking a deeper joining.

He gave it to her—gave it to them both.

"Nicole." He murmured her name, his tongue sweeping inside to capture hers, to claim every tingling surface before entwining with hers once more. He lifted her closer, melding her against him, possessing her with an urgency that transcended the mere physical, delved down to his very soul. Her taste was heaven, the feel of her—small, delicate, shivering with her own response—more bloody right than even his memories could preserve. He enveloped her in his embrace, thinking that just holding her, kissing her like this, was enough to bring him to his knees. It was magic, as unique as her candor, as intoxicating as her beauty.

"Dustin . . ." Nicole's hands slid up his shirtfront, then paused, knotting against him as if deciding whether to continue their path to his shoulders or to propel her to freedom—now, before it was too late.

Unwilling to consider the latter, Dustin snatched the choice away, capturing her arms and bringing them around his neck. "Hold me," he commanded, his voice rough with emotion. "Feel what I'm feeling. Dammit, Nicole, don't run away from me."

Her eyes opened—those drowning smoky amethysts—and she stared up at him, her gaze searching, struggling . . . losing. In a rush, she relented, whispering his name and leaning into him, her muscles taut with inner turmoil even as she twined her arms about him, kissed him back with all the fervor he longed to awaken.

For one perfect moment they remained as such—locked together, breathing each other's needs, sharing each other's wants.

Then, abruptly, Nicole wrenched herself away.

"This can't happen." She backed off, scarcely able to speak.

"Why?" Dustin own voice sounded shattered, his heart hammering so hard against his ribs that it hurt. "Because your father's in the hall? We'll find another time, another place—"

"No!" Nicole cut him off, shaking her head wildly. "It's

not because of my father." Turning away, she wrapped her arms around herself, trying to still her body's shaking. "It's because of this." She indicated her fierce reaction. "You want to know why I'm afraid? This is why, Dustin. I'm out of my league, a novice."

"A novice who's made a mockery of every kiss I've ever experienced," he answered quietly. "One who makes me feel things I never imagined feeling."

"Don't say that." She bowed her head, her hair veiling her expression like a black satin curtain. "This can't happen. We can't allow it to happen."

"We can't stop it from happening." He came up behind her, moving her disheveled tresses aside to kiss her nape. "Nor do I want to."

"Dustin, please. Think of who you are. Who I am."

"Who am I, Nicole?" He nuzzled the side of her neck.

She broke away, pivoting about to face him. "A nobleman. My employer." Her lips trembled. "A man who's taken more women than he has races."

"Damn Lanston!" Dustin erupted, teeth clenched against the impotent rage escalating inside him. He didn't dare shout. The last thing he needed was for Nick Aldridge to come running to Nicole's rescue. "Damn Lanston," he growled again. "And damn his insipid gossip."

"Is it untrue? Exaggerated?"

"Does it matter?" Dustin caught her shoulders. "Nicole, feel me. I'm shaking as much as you are. What difference does it make who I am, how I've lived?"

"Because it does," she answered, wearing that same wistful expression she'd worn the night they'd met, gazing into the starlit skies, tears of emotion glistening on her lashes. "Because I'm an idealistic child who believes in love and fidelity and commitment. Because you live a life that defies every one of those values. Because I refuse to become your next publicly acclaimed paramour or even your discreetly kept one. And, based on all the reasons I've just spouted, because unless we stop this attraction before it's too late, I'll be forced to leave my job and Tyreham—which, as you know, could be disastrous for Papa."

Dustin's thumbs caressed her collarbone, soothing her with gentle, sweeping motions. "I understand your fears.

This is all happening very fast. But sweetheart, you've got to trust me. Not only here . . ." He brushed his knuckles across her forehead. "But here." His fingertips grazed that part of her shirt that covered her heart. "Give me a chance. Give *us* a chance."

"There can be no 'us,'" she said in a small, shaken voice. "There can only be Lord Tyreham and Alden Stoddard."

"Is that really what you want?"

Silence.

"Honesty, Nicole. You're the one teaching it to me."

Tears wet her lashes. "No, it's not what I want, God help me. But, under the circumstances, it's what I must do not only for Papa's sake but for mine. I haven't a choice."

"Yes, you have." Purposefully, Dustin reached into his pocket, withdrew his handkerchief, and tenderly wiped away her tears. "Derby, you *do* have a choice. Give me the trust I'm requesting. Let me prove to you that I'm not the incurable hedonist you've proclaimed me to be." He framed her face between his palms. "Can you honestly tell me you don't come alive when we're together? Not only when we touch but when we talk? When we laugh? Even when we argue?"

She shook her head. "You know I can't tell you that. I'd be lying." Pride interceded, and her small jaw set. "However, in your case, I'm sure you've enjoyed such sensations countless times in the past."

"Never." His lips feathered across her cheekbones. "Not in two and thirty years. Not with anyone but you."

Her eyes searched his. "I'm terrified," she whispered.

"I'm not. I'm certain. As certain as I am that the sun will set tonight and rise tomorrow. Trust me, Nicole. If I'm wrong, then once I've resolved this mystery and your father is safe, I promise to let you walk away. Intact," he added pointedly. "But if I'm right . . ." He smiled, sifting strands of her hair through his fingertips. "Ah, Derby, if I'm right, then perhaps we can right life's wrongs and balance its inequities together."

A soft light illuminated her face. "You remembered."

"Our first conversation? Every word. Every dream in your eyes. Every hope in your smile." He held her gaze. "Give me a chance."

A long pause . . . followed by a tiny nod. "I'll try."

Lord, had he ever known such bone-melting relief? "Good. Start by telling me you'll see me again."

Another nod, this one more decisive than the last. "Unless Papa . . ."

"He won't refuse you. He loves you too much."

"He would if he believed you'd hurt me."

"And do you think he believes that?"

Again, Nicole shook her head. "No."

"Then it's settled." Dustin bent, brushed her lips with his. "Speaking of your father, he's probably about to burst in and toss me out. Besides, I'd best get back to the manor. I need to pack. I'll be away for a day or two."

A shadow crossed Nicole's face. "You're going to see Sully." Her fingers bit into Dustin's sleeves. "Papa told me your plans to bait those horrible men who threatened you. I needn't tell you how dangerous that might be." Frustration laced her tone. "I dragged you into this situation. I came to you looking for a job, and now you're immersed in a dilemma that, by all rights, should be mine to contend with. It's *my* father they want. *I'm* the one who should be incurring the risks."

"And aren't you?" Dustin reminded her quietly. "Didn't you take the ultimate risk the day you walked into Tyreham as Alden Stoddard, determined to protect your father at all costs? There are all types of risks, Derby. Yours is greater than most. It requires restraint, selflessness, and a lot more courage than it would take to go charging recklessly out, seeking some unknown enemy who could, in turn, destroy the very man you've vowed to protect." Dustin captured Nicole's hand in his. "Never doubt the importance of what you're doing. It's ultimately you, not I, who is shielding your father."

"I realize that. It's only . . ." She swallowed. "Dustin, please . . . be careful."

Dustin pressed her palm to his lips. "I will. You just concentrate on readying Dagger for the Derby. I'll concentrate on freeing your father of this noose that's hanging around his neck—and the turf of ruthless criminals who profit off frightened, greedy men. Together, you and I will set things right. Agreed?"

A faint smile. "Agreed."

"Good." Dustin's gaze fell to her mouth. "Now, since we won't be alone together for heaven knows how long, ask me."

"Ask you what?"

"You know damned well what. Ask me to kiss you."

Nicole's smile deepened. "I already did."

"Do so again."

The tip of her tongue wet her lips. "Must it always be my initiative?"

"Today, yes. After today, no bloody way. I've fulfilled the terms of that insane promise I gave you."

Shyly, she leaned into him. "Very well. Please, Dustin, kiss me."

"My pleasure, Miss Aldridge."

He fused their mouths for a brief, shattering instant, easing away only when she'd gone weak in his arms. "As of now," he muttered huskily, "the rules have officially altered. I suggest you alert your hopes and dreams to that fact. Tell them I intend to make each and every one of them a reality."

Eight

"You've been whistling since you walked in the door," Nick noted, lowering his newspaper. "Who's the cause of your fine mood, Dagger or his owner?"

Nicole flushed, securing the pins beneath her cap as she prepared to return to the stables. "I haven't seen Dustin since he left the cottage yesterday, Papa. By now, he's probably in Suffolk, meeting with Sully."

"I know where he is. But that still doesn't answer my question, now does it?" Nick tossed the paper aside, abandoning all pretense of reading. "You've avoided me since Tyreham took his leave. First, you were exhausted and needed rest—at six o'clock, mind you. You didn't even emerge for dinner, and if you ate breakfast, I never heard you. You were gone by the time I awoke—at sunrise, by the way. You returned a half hour ago, gulped down some food, and are now preparing to bolt again."

"Dagger and I are training for the Derby."

"You needn't remind me. Now, do you intend to answer me? Or are we never going to discuss the marquis?"

Uneasily, Nicole perched on the arm of her father's chair. As always, when it came to Dustin, her thoughts were in a breathless, convoluted jumble. Oh, she'd yearned to share with her father the exhilaration resulting from those five precious minutes in the sitting room. But she'd needed time alone. Time to think, to absorb the significance of the monumental step she'd taken—a step that had transported her from meager resistance to wary acceptance—to relive the transitional moments in Dustin's arms when she'd given up the struggle and yielded the battle.

God help her if she lost the war.

Long into the night she'd remained awake, sitting up in her bed, arms wrapped about her knees, wishing locket clutched in her hand. Innocent though she was, she understood—perhaps better than Dustin—the extent of what her concession could cost her. By lowering her emotional guard, granting him entry to her life, she was affording him the opportunity to do what Dustin Kingsley did best: charm his way into—and out of—her heart. Just as he had dozens of women in the past.

With one difference. Those women had been raised like Dustin: wealthy, sophisticated, marrying for money, straying—albeit discreetly—for pleasure. There seemed to be a tacit understanding among noblewomen that they remained chaste until their wedding day and then, once married and having presented their husbands with a requisite heir, they could seek amusement elsewhere, so long as their indiscretions remained undiscovered. And, in Dustin's case, they were evidently willing to reverse that order, whether to lure him down the aisle or simply because the pleasure was worth more than the sacrifice, Nicole wasn't certain. In either case, the whole prospect was unthinkable to her. The gifting of her body was integrally tied to the gifting of her heart. And her heart could be offered but once, accompanied only by the fervent prayer that it not be shattered.

How, from any perspective, could Dustin avoid shattering it? To begin with, Nicole failed to see any way for him to bridge the gap between them—a gap that, to her, appeared insurmountable, no matter how fervently he professed otherwise. Further, even if he succeeded, what precisely did he want of her? What was Dustin Kingsley's idea of a commitment? For a provincial commoner like herself, there was but one answer: marriage. Was he prepared to offer that? Or did his notion of permanence extend no further than a long-term mistress or lover?

That incited another worry. Dustin had declared he wanted more from her than seduction. Did that mean he planned to await her invitation for lovemaking, just as he had her request for a kiss? Or did it mean he intended to keep himself to chaste kisses and caresses, rather than ask for more? The latter was doubtful. But even if such were the case, did he honestly believe that by sparing her virtue, he'd leave her unscathed when they parted? If so, he was wrong. For even if her body remained intact, her soul would not.

"Nicole." It was her father's no-nonsense tone, one that jerked her back to the present and reminded her of the conversation at hand. "I take it by your silence that you're not ready to discuss Lord Tyreham. Well, I'm sorry to hear that, but I am. In case you've forgotten, the man left here yesterday with my permission to continue calling on you. And, given that I'm your father—and that every one of my paternal instincts is berating me for my decision—I want your assurance that it was the right one."

"I'm sorry, Papa." Nicole sighed, covering her father's hand with hers. "I never intended to exclude you from my thoughts. I just needed a few hours to sort them out. This is all very new to me." She squeezed his fingers. "First, thank you for granting Dustin permission to continue his visits. I prayed you'd give your approval."

"So I noticed," Nick said gruffly. "Why do you think I relented? And I do mean relented. I'd hardly term it approval." He massaged his temples. "Lord knows, I'm having second—and third—thoughts. I don't know what possessed me to give in so easily. Just because you looked at me with those pleading eyes of yours shouldn't have been enough to make me welcome Tyreham with open arms."

"No, it shouldn't have." Nicole's lips curved. "Nor was it. Admit it, Papa. You like him."

"You're damned right, I like him. He wouldn't have set foot in here the first time if I didn't—job or no job. Not only do I like him but, for whatever it's worth, I believe he's sincere." A speculative pause. "Apparently, so do you."

She could actually feel her heartbeat accelerate. "Yes, Papa, I do—like him *and* believe he's sincere. I can't explain why, but I've trusted Dustin from the instant we met. What's more, I can't seem to stop thinking about him nor longing to be in his company." Her lashes lowered. "I, better than anyone, realize that for any one of a hundred reasons, it would be better for all of us if I severed this before it began. The fact is, I can't seem to do it."

"Maybe that's because it's already begun."

Nicole's startled gaze met her father's.

"Nickie." Nick's expression was sober, his voice rough as gravel. "There's another reason I'm sticking to my decision about Tyreham's visits, other than your obvious feelings and my respect for the man. A reason that didn't come to me till dawn. All night I lay awake, alternately reminding myself how decent and honest he's been, then remembering his bloody reputation and deciding to change my mind and turn him away. By sunrise, I found myself at a loss, staring off into space and wishing your mother were alive. That's when it came to me." Nick drew a slow, unsteady breath. "If Alicia were here, I know exactly what she'd say. She'd say I had no business coming between you and what could be the future fate has in store for you. Fate, she'd remind me, was wiser than logic and passion combined, more profound than logic, more objective than passion."

"I remember," Nicole replied softly. "Wishes and fate. Mama trusted in both."

A spark of memory lit Nick's eyes. "Wishes and fate. That's what she said the day I proposed to her. I knew bloody well I hadn't the right to make her mine; her being a well-bred young lady and my being a jockey with scarcely a shilling to my name. But Alicia never hesitated. She said we were meant to be, that she'd wished us to be. She left a respectable family to marry a man with nothing to offer but his love and his dreams."

"You realized those dreams, Papa," Nicole defended at once. "You became the most renowned jockey in England. And in the interim, it was that love that sustained us."

"I know, Elf." Nick patted her hand tenderly. "All the more reason that if Tyreham really is the right man for you, I'd be a bloody hypocrite to deny you the same chance at happiness your mother and I had. Two different people from different worlds who loved each other enough to get by. Oh, don't get me wrong—it was hard as hell sometimes. I was used to taking care of myself, coming and going as I pleased with no one home worrying about me. Alicia was used to staying put, going to church on Sundays, and eating a family dinner at seven o'clock each night. We each gave a little, took a little, and somehow it all worked out. In your case, the adjustment would be even harder. Tyreham's a marquis, for God's sake. A marquis with a lot of money and a lot of women." Shaking his head, Nick muttered, "Half of me wants to call him out now and shoot him before it's too late. But for your sake, for your mother and the magic she brought to my life, I'll wait, let you follow your heart, and pray—should it lead to Tyreham—that he doesn't break it. Because if he does, so help me, if he hurts you in any way, he'll answer to me, title or no title."

"Thank you, Papa." Moved beyond words, Nicole hugged her father fiercely. "You're a wonderful man. Mama made a superb choice—the only choice."

Nick swallowed. "We were blessed, your mother and I. But as I said, it wasn't easy. It took strength and patience and grit—all of which you have and which I prayed you'd never need." He gripped Nicole's arms, held her away from him. "Are you scared, Elf?"

"Terrified."

"Good. You should be." He tugged lightly at the rim of her cap. "Be careful, Nickie. You've got my spunk, but your mother's heart. Guard it well—it's the only one you've got." With an awkward cough, he came to his feet. "Now go exercise that stallion of yours. Have you got him cantering yet?"

"As of this morning, yes." Taking her father's cue, Nicole jumped up, perceiving his tacit need to change the subject. "Dagger moves with such grace, it's more like sailing than riding. I plan to take a few low fences this afternoon, just to reinforce our timing and technique. If all goes well, I'll accelerate the pace tomorrow and gallop the length of the course. Brackley can time us." A triumphant grin. "Dustin will return from Suffolk, *and* his new trainer will arrive to find Dagger and me ready for Epsom—a full week earlier than expected."

Rather than sharing her excitement, Nick scowled, his

eyes darting restlessly about the room. "I hope Tyreham will have learned enough to end this farce and get me back on the turf where I belong."

Nicole's elation faded. "Papa, I know you're fidgety . . ." she began.

"Fidgety? I'm losing my bloody mind. That list I gave your marquis, together with whoever else Sully adds to it, had better yield some results."

"It will," Nicole assured him. "If there are answers, Dustin will find them."

Dustin was hoping much the same thing.

Leaning forward, he glanced out the carriage window, taking in the rolling countryside of Suffolkshire.

He'd arrived at his destination.

For the umpteenth time, he unfolded the list Aldridge had given him, wondering where this investigation would lead. With any luck, to the truth. Then Aldridge would be free and Nicole would be his.

He grinned at his own arrogance. Oh, it wouldn't be easy. Nicole was as stubborn as she was beautiful. But eventually, if he had to move heaven and earth, he would make it happen.

Tenderly, Dustin recalled yesterday's kiss, the dazed wonder in Nicole's eyes and the all-too-transparent emotion on her face as she'd granted him the permission he sought. God, how he wanted to make that look last forever.

He had his work cut out for him. Winning Nicole over, convincing her that his motives were as decent as hers, was going to be a mammoth task, especially given her denigrating view of his reputation. Still, he'd achieved his initial victory: persuading her to accept his visits. *Two* victories, he amended silently. Not only had Nicole invited him back, so had her father.

Recalling the uncertainty on Aldridge's face, the warring emotions in his eyes, Dustin felt a wave of compassion. The man obviously adored his daughter. 'Twas no wonder he felt reluctant to place her in the hands of a notoriously wanton aristocrat.

Well, those misgivings would vanish soon enough.

"Here we are, sir," Dustin's driver called out, bringing the carriage to a halt.

Snapping out of his reverie, Dustin shoved the list back in his pocket and, without waiting for assistance, opened the carriage door and climbed down.

At first glance, the half-timbered cottage looked to be deserted. Dustin scowled. Aldridge had said nothing about Sullivan traveling elsewhere after Newmarket. Assumably, he was home. That being the case, Dustin had dispatched a rather cryptic message late last night, advising Sullivan of the pressing need for them to meet early this morning. It should have been enough. After all, though the man wasn't aware of Dustin's role in all this, he did know Aldridge was living at Tyreham. Therefore, he had to have guessed that the subject of the meeting pertained to his friend.

So where the hell was he?

Dustin raised his fist and knocked.

The door, of its own accord, swung open.

A warning bell sounded in Dustin's head, and he stepped inside. "Sullivan?"

No answer.

Puzzled, he glanced about the narrow hallway, plagued by the nagging feeling that something was amiss. Other than the partially opened door, there was no evidence to support his suspicion. The furnishings, so far as he could see, were intact, showing no evidence of an intruder. Still . . .

"Sullivan!" he called again.

Was it his imagination, or had he heard a rustle from farther within?

He hesitated, knowing he was trespassing, weighing his options.

A low moan reached his ears.

Tossing caution to the wind, Dustin stalked the sound, which led him into what appeared to be the cottage's sole bedchamber.

"Sulliv—" He broke off, seeing the crumpled form lying in the center of the room. "Dammit." He reached the man's side in an instant. Kneeling, he eased him gently to his back to assess the extent of the jockey's injuries.

They were bad.

Blood covered much of his face and head, his clothing torn, his eyes swollen shut. The only sign of a struggle was the lamp overturned alongside the bed and the pile of bedcovers Sullivan had apparently been clutching when he went down. Evidently, he'd been either surprised or overpowered. The latter, at the very least, Dustin guessed. If the assailants were the same burly hoodlums who'd visited Tyreham, Sullivan's slight jockey's build would be no match for their strength.

"Sullivan, can you hear me? It's Tyreham."

With the greatest of efforts, one eye slitted open. "Tyre . . . ham."

"You're badly hurt. Lie still. I'll do what I can."

Rising, Dustin searched the cottage until he found the kitchen. Once there, he promptly located a pitcher, filling it with cold water and carrying it back to Sullivan's chambers. Next, he unearthed a pile of clean handkerchiefs, several of which he soaked in the water, the remainder of which he set aside to serve as bandages.

Sullivan groaned at the first contact of the cold cloth against his skin, but he didn't—or couldn't—fight Dustin's efforts. With a black scowl, Dustin confirmed that whoever had done this had been thorough as hell, inflicting injuries that were severe, but not fatal. It didn't surprise him. His guess was that the assailants wanted Sullivan alive enough—and frightened enough—to tell them Aldridge's whereabouts. Or, in the event he refused to cooperate, to alert Aldridge to the attack the instant he was able, thus leading them straight to Tyreham. Even if Sullivan were smart enough to do neither, the bastards would undoubtedly make sure Aldridge got word of the beating, knowing that loyalty would compel him to rush to his friend's side. At which point, they would descend upon him like a pack of wolves.

Dustin finished bandaging Sullivan's major wounds, then slipped a pillow beneath his head and covered him with a blanket. In truth, the jockey was light enough for one man to lift. But Dustin didn't dare hoist him onto the bed, for fear of worsening the injuries. Especially if there were broken bones or internal bleeding.

"Tyreham," Sullivan muttered again.

"I'm here."

One arm reached up weakly, plucked at Dustin's sleeve. "Don't . . . tell anyone."

Dustin nodded, understanding far more than Sullivan realized. "I know Aldridge is living at Tyreham," he said quietly. "Along with my new jockey. I've told no one. I intend to tell no one. I'm guessing that whoever did this to you suspects you know Aldridge's whereabouts and tried to convince you to share the location with them. Am I right?"

Despite his badly swollen features, there was no mistaking the surprise on Sullivan's face. "How . . . did . . ."

"It's a long story. We'll discuss it later. For now, let me summon a physician. I'll pay him enough to ensure his silence. But those wounds need to be professionally treated."

A long hesitation.

"Sullivan, Aldridge will have my hide if I don't take proper care of you."

Dustin's comment elicited a pained glimmer of amusement. "You're . . . right. Go ahead."

Squelching his myriad questions, Dustin rode into the village, returning in an hour with a man he'd discreetly learned was a skilled and trustworthy physician. He waited patiently while the man did his job, then had the Tyreham driver escort him home—after slipping a hundred-pound note in his palm and eliciting his promise never to discuss this incident with anyone.

Retracing his steps, Dustin found Sullivan propped up in bed, looking much improved, his breathing and color restored to normal.

"How are you feeling?"

Sullivan angled his head in Dustin's direction. "Better. What did you tell the physician?"

"Only that you owed a bit of money to some unsavory characters who extracted their pound of flesh." Dustin shrugged. "He understood how embarrassing it would be for you if the turf learned of the incident. That and the money I gave him was enough to ensure his silence. Don't worry, Sullivan. No one will hear of this episode."

"Thank you, my lord," Sullivan said, shoulders sagging with relief.

"No thanks are necessary." Dustin pulled up a chair. "However, a conversation is. Are you up for talking?"

A wary look crossed Sully's face—one that had nothing to do with discomfort and everything to do with loyalty.

"I'll begin by telling you what I know," Dustin offered. "That way, you won't feel you're endangering the Aldridges by having this chat." Noting the stunned lift of Sully's brows, Dustin grinned. "Yes, I know I'm housing both Aldridges. And, to be frank, your friend is less difficult to manage than his daughter."

A pained chuckle. "I expected as much."

"They wanted me to assure you they're both well, safely ensconced in a cottage at Tyreham, where Nick stays at all times."

"I'm sure he's thrilled with that arrangement," Sully inserted dryly.

"You're right, he's not. But he realizes he hasn't a choice. As for Nicole . . ." Dustin's grin widened. "She's playing her role to perfection. In everyone's mind but mine she's Alden Stoddard, a jockey who's so damned good, he'll be riding my stallion in the Derby. And believe me, that's no easy feat. Like Nicole, Dagger is a handful."

A faint, proud smile touched Sully's lips. "The Derby— Nickie's wished for that since she was barely more than knee-high, from the first time she watched Nick race."

"So I've heard. Well, she's going to get her wish. And more," Dustin added with an equal measure of pride. "Not only is she going to run that bloody race, she's going to win it." Intently, he returned to the issue at hand. "Sullivan, I'm privy to the reasons for Aldridge's concealment and Nicole's masquerade. And I have a strange feeling 'those reasons' were the ones who beat you within an inch of your life. Am I right?"

Slowly, Sully nodded.

"Did you tell them what they wanted to know?"

"Of course not. I didn't tell them a blasted thing."

"Then they're probably expecting you to dash off to alert Aldridge."

"Right. With them at my heels. I already thought of that.

That's why I'm not moving a muscle." Sully shifted, wincing as pain lanced through him. "Literally," he muttered.

"Do you want a drink?" Dustin suggested. "It will help ease the pain."

"Yeah, but not yet. I need a clear head for this talk."

Dustin nodded, admiring Sullivan's loyalty. "You're a good friend. The Aldridges are lucky to have you."

"It works both ways. Nick would do the same for me. So would the elf."

"I don't doubt it." Dustin leaned forward, gripping his knees. "Can you describe the men who did this to you?"

Sully's brows drew together. "One was heavyset and short."

"Blue eyes?" Dustin questioned. "Very pale blue?"

"Yeah. The other was taller, kind of leaner. He had those black, piercing sort of eyes."

"Dark hair? Dirty? Did the first one have a ruddy complexion, like he'd been drinking?"

A resigned nod. "I take it you've seen them."

"Oh, I've seen them, all right. They came to my home. They threatened me and my family if I hired Nick Aldridge."

"Dear God." Sully leaned weakly back against his pillow. "Does Nick know this?"

"Yes. His description of the scum who tried to blackmail him at Newmarket matches ours. Same men. Same method." Dustin rose and began to pace. "How long ago were they here?"

"I was only half awake when they broke in. The sun was just up. I'd say it was six A.M., maybe a little past. What time is it now?"

A glance at the clock on the mantel. "A quarter past ten. What else do you remember?"

"Not much. Other than demanding to know where Nick is, they didn't talk. Except with their fists." A pause. "Wait. When they were leaving, one of them called the other 'Archer.' I couldn't see which was which. My eyes were too badly swollen."

"Archer," Dustin repeated. "Good." Reaching into his pocket, he extracted the list Nick had penned. "Sullivan, I know you feel like hell, but I need your help. Aldridge gave me this list of jockeys who have been throwing races for money. He thought you might be able to add to it. If I read you the names, would you be able to concentrate well enough to do that?"

Sully blinked through slitted eyes. "Nick really trusts you, doesn't he?"

"I hope so."

"What do you aim to do with this list?"

"Visit every damned person on it until I find someone who's able to shed light on this scheme *and* the bastard who's orchestrating it. You and I both know that these jockeys, like the two ruffians who assaulted you, are just hired hands. I want their employer. Because whoever he is, he's not only tarnishing the reputation of the turf, he's endangering people's lives. People like Aldridge." Dustin met Sully's gaze. "And Redley."

That reference made Sully start. "Nick mentioned Redley?" A dubious pause. "What did he tell you?"

"Only that Redley was killed because he was stupid enough to try blackmailing his blackmailers."

"That's all any of us knows."

"Well, I plan to call on the Viscount Preighbrook, Redley's last employer, on my way back to Tyreham. Maybe he'll remember something of consequence."

"Um-hum. The St. Leger was Redley's last race, the one he threw riding Preighbrook's filly Nightingale." Sully cocked a brow, studying Dustin with shrewd comprehension. "I'm not a suspicious man, but I'm not a stupid one either. You gave Nick a place to stay knowing damned well his presence could put you in danger. You're letting Nicole run the Derby knowing damned well it could threaten your hard-earned, well-respected reputation as an owner and breeder. The truth is, you don't have to do either. You've got more than enough money to hire people who'll protect your family and keep your staff honest, which would shield you from this whole ugly mess. Why are you taking such a strong personal interest in the Aldridges?"

Staring at the list of names, Dustin smoothed the rumpled sheet. "My reasons, like my interest, are personal."

"I gathered as much." Sully's eyes narrowed. "I couldn't

help but notice the fervent way you talked about the elf. She wouldn't happen to be that 'personal reason,' would she?"

Dustin's head came up. "And if she is?"

"Then you've got me to answer to."

"Wonderful. That's two fathers I have to contend with."

A reluctant grin tugged at Sully's lips. "I'm as tough as Nick. Especially when it comes to the elf." His grin faded. "You care for her?"

"I do."

"I mean *really* care for her; you know—decently? Properly?"

"Honorably?" Dustin added wryly. *"I'm* not stupid either, Sullivan. I understood what you meant. The answer remains yes."

Sully pushed himself up a bit, ignoring the pain incited by his motion. "Then what are we waiting for? Read me that list. Then hand me that drink. We've got a lot to talk about."

It was nearly four o'clock when Dustin's carriage rounded the bend and pulled through Tyreham's iron gates.

With a final glance at the updated page of names, Dustin pondered the results of his day.

Stopping at Preighbrook had been a waste of time. The elderly viscount, who six months ago had been merely absentminded, was now totally senile, barely able to recall Dustin's name, much less the events of last fall's races. Questioning him had been futile.

So much for Preighbrook.

Sullivan, on the other hand, had been a great help. Not only had he added three names to Nick's list, he'd provided an update on every jockey's racing schedule, so that Dustin might be able to find them more easily. Armed with that, Dustin had taken his leave—but not before making the necessary arrangements to ensure Sullivan's safety.

To that end, he'd assigned one of the Tyreham footmen, Tuttle, to remain at the cottage, tending to Sully's needs and standing guard in the event the intruders should reappear. An unlikely prospect, to Dustin's way of thinking. Especially given the fact that they were probably lying in wait, watching for signs of Aldridge's appearance, or Sully's *disappearance*—should he happen to recoup enough strength to dash off and warn his friend.

Unlikely or not, Dustin wasn't taking any chances. Tuttle would remain with Sully for several days. At which time, Dustin would return, check on Sully, and apprise him of any developments in the investigation.

Despite a fine show of bravado, Sullivan had looked relieved as hell for the precautions, thanking Dustin profusely *after* he'd issued an hour's worth of advice on the proper way to treat Nicole.

That memory elicited a grin. Leaning back against the carriage seat, Dustin pondered Sully's sage, though pointedly virtuous, recommendations. How many years had it been since anyone presumed to advise him on the handling of a woman? Further, if someone had, would he ever have tolerated such interference, much less sat still long enough to hear it?

Never—until Nicole.

As it was, he found Sullivan's commitment to Nicole rather touching. Touching *and* revealing. Thanks to the injured jockey's sermon, complete with an array of details describing Nicole's upbringing, Dustin now fully understood the basis for her surprising ease with the male gender, despite her total lack of sexual experience. The reality was that, by growing up at the stables amid a host of men, she'd learned to regard them as family, if not in blood, then in fact.

Dustin had a sudden image of himself traveling to all of England's stables in an effort to solicit the blessing of dozens of skeptical surrogate fathers.

Ironic laughter rumbled from his chest.

He was still chuckling when the horses came to a halt in Tyreham's drive. Swinging down from the carriage, he glanced toward the far grounds and made an impulsive decision.

"Quinn," he called out to his driver. "Ask Poole to have my bag taken in. Tell him I'm stopping by the stables and will be back shortly."

"Yes, my lord."

Dustin was halfway to his destination when he spotted the subject of his preoccupation.

Nicole.

Astride Dagger, she was cantering the length of the course, her breeches and shirt damp and clinging to her slim, deliberately shapeless form.

Pausing, Dustin watched, impressed yet again by the fluidity of Nicole's movements, the keenness of her instincts. Head bent low, she was murmuring something in Dagger's ear, probably alerting him to the fence they were now approaching. The horse responded instantly, gaze focused on the barrier, limbs moving in conjunction with his rider's commands.

Nicole's eyes narrowed, her concentration intensifying as she gauged the distance to their goal, adjusted their pace. At precisely the right instant, she acted, leaning into position and urging Dagger up and over.

He responded effortlessly, gathering his legs beneath him and sailing over the fence, landing on the opposite side without ever breaking stride.

"Splendid," Nicole commended, giving Dagger a loving pat. Sighing, she gazed reluctantly at the position of the sun. "That's it for today, my friend. Let's cool down. We've got to rest up for tomorrow. Remember, we'll be galloping the course with Brackley timing us. And, if we're anywhere near as fast as I think we are, we're ready for Epsom."

"I agree," Dustin concurred, continuing toward them. "You're superb."

"Dustin!" Nicole's whole face lit up. "I didn't expect you home until tomorrow." Realizing how inappropriate her enthusiastic and spontaneous greeting sounded, she broke off, her gaze darting about to see if she'd been overheard.

"You're safe, Derby. No one is about but us." Dustin squelched the elation spawned by Nicole's joyous welcome. Coming up alongside her, he matched his pace to Dagger's ambling walk.

"Did you see Sully?" Nicole asked in a hushed voice.

"Yes." This time it was Dustin who glanced about. "We need to talk alone—your father, you, and I. Let's return Dagger to his stall and go to your cottage."

Nicole's brows drew together in concern. "All right."

They exchanged nothing more than casual conversation about Stoddard's preparations for the Derby until the stables were behind them and the cottage was in sight.

"Are you going to tell me what you learned?" Nicole demanded as they neared the entranceway.

"Once we're inside," Dustin muttered back. Noting her worried expression, he added, "Everything is fine, Derby. I promise."

Relief flooded her face.

"I wasn't exaggerating, you know," Dustin commented. "Your riding is magnificent. Watching you earlier was like watching a beautiful ballet unfold."

"Thank you." She glowed at the compliment. "Coming from you, that means a great deal."

"Starting tomorrow, you'll have the benefit of another professional opinion."

"Who?"

"Raggert, my new trainer. I don't know if you recall my mentioning him, but he arrives at Tyreham first thing in the morning."

"I recall." Nicole scooted up to the door and slipped the key in the lock. Turning, a mischievous spark lit her eyes. "Raggert—wasn't he referred to you by that incomparable source of information, the earl of Lanston?"

Dustin came to stand beside her, his lips curving into an indulgent grin. "Indeed. As for Lanston, he might be a virtual wealth of information, but he is also sadly lacking in subject matter. Why, I know for a fact that his previous study is out of the running, presently occupied with the blissful process of reforming."

"I see." Nicole raised her chin, lifting those incredible amethyst eyes to meet his gaze. "I'm glad to hear that."

Of their own accord, Dustin's arms began to reach for her. Forcibly, he checked the motion, clenching his fists at his sides, wanting nothing more than to drag her against him and kiss her senseless.

"Is Raggert's arrival the reason you returned to Tyreham so quickly?" Nicole asked, easing the door open.

"Ostensibly, yes. Truthfully? No." Dustin guided her into

the cottage, closing the door in their wake. "See how proficient I've become with my honesty?"

Another breathtaking smile. "I'm impressed."

"And I need to be alone with you."

Concern obliterated the smile. "Very well. I'll get Papa."

Dustin shook his head, staying her departure with his hand. "That's not what I meant. At least not this time." He drew an unsteady breath. "Nicole, come walking with me later tonight. After we've resolved today's happenings. After the rest of the estate is abed. Just us."

Warring emotions darted across her face. "I want to," she admitted softly. "Truly I do. But Papa . . ."

"I'll speak with your father. Assuming he agrees, will you come with me? *You*—not Stoddard. There'll be no risk. I'll make sure of it. We'll stroll the far grounds. No one will see us." His knuckles caressed her cheek. "I'll take care of you. I promise." Lowering his head, he brushed a swift, heated kiss across her lips. "Say yes."

"Yes."

His forefinger traced the fine bridge of her nose. *"Now* you may summon your father."

Shivering a bit, she nodded, taking a purposeful step backward as if that act alone could sever the currents running between them.

Pausing, she stared up at him.

"Later, Derby," Dustin vowed, answering the smoky request in her eyes.

Nicole swallowed and turned away. "Papa?" she called in as normal a tone as she could muster. "I'm home. Lord Tyreham is with me."

"Tyreham?" Nick took the steps two at a time. "You're back sooner than I expected. What did Sully say? And what happened with Preighbrook?"

"Preighbrook was of no use to us. As for Sullivan . . ." Dustin imparted the news as gently as he could. "It seems those hoodlums paid him a visit. When I arrived at his cottage, he was hurt."

"Hurt?" Nick blurted, ignoring Nicole's shocked gasp. "How badly hurt?"

"He's fine now." Dustin frowned, seeing the color drain

from Nicole's face. "Fine and in good hands," he added, wishing he could comfort her with more than just words.

"What did they do to him, dammit?" Nick exploded.

"Roughed him up. Enough to be painful but not fatal. It's a ruse, Aldridge. They're trying to ferret you out."

"Are they? Good. They can have me." Nick snatched his coat, simultaneously reaching for the door.

"Papa, where are you going?" Nicole reacted in a flash, grabbing her father's arm.

"To Suffolk. To see for myself that Sully's all right."

"Don't be a fool," Dustin warned, planting himself between Nick and the door. "They're waiting for you to do just that."

"Then I won't disappoint them. It's me they want, not Sully. I won't risk his life to spare mine."

"Papa, stop it." Stubbornly, Nicole tightened her grip. "Dustin said Sully's fine." She glanced at Dustin. "You did say that, didn't you?"

Dustin nodded. "He was beaten pretty badly. I persuaded a local physician to come to the cottage. He cleaned and treated Sullivan's wounds, then took his leave, promptly forgetting he'd ever been there. By the time I headed back to Surrey, your friend was sitting up and talking—even issuing advice. I left one of my carriage footmen behind to oversee Sullivan's needs and safeguard the cottage."

"Thank you," Nicole whispered.

"I'm glad I arrived when I did. Sullivan's a good man. He didn't divulge your whereabouts, not even when it meant sacrificing his own well-being." Dustin shot Nick a censuring look. "Are you going to reduce his heroism to nothing more than a wasted gesture by providing those bastards with precisely what Sullivan withstood a thrashing to conceal?"

"Dammit." Nick raked a hand through his hair.

"Let me put this another way." Dustin leaned back against the door, arms folded across his chest. "Sullivan insisted I keep you away. I gave him my word that I would. I don't break my word. Therefore, I'll wrestle you to the ground if I must. You're not dashing off to Suffolk." Studying Nick's anguished expression, Dustin felt a wave of compassion. "Aldridge, he's safe. He'll continue to be safe.

Tuttle is a large, powerful fellow. No one will get into that cottage. Besides, in a way this incident plays right into our hands."

That captured Nick's attention. "How?"

"If those men are watching Sullivan's cottage, they'll have seen my carriage arrive. It's hard to miss; my family crest is painted on the door, bold as hell. Thus, they'll know I visited Sullivan—and the condition I found him in. They'll wonder what we discussed, and if he told me what he refused to tell them—your whereabouts. Maybe they worried enough to follow me on to Preighbrook, in which case they're probably agonizing over whether I made a connection between your disappearance and Redley's death. And if they're still scrutinizing Sullivan's cottage, they'll see I left my manservant behind to guard against intruders. All in all, they'll be anxious enough to pay me another visit, which, if you recall, is exactly what I hoped they'd do. Because once they approach me, I intend to follow them to whomever they work for."

Nick mulled over Dustin's reasoning, then nodded, tossing down his coat. "That makes sense." He inclined his head. "You said Sully was well enough to talk. Did he fill you in on anything I couldn't?"

"He added three names to our list—Hills, Borley, and Garner—and provided me with every jockey's immediate schedule. I'll begin calling on them as soon as my new trainer is settled in."

"Dustin," Nicole inserted, chewing her lip apprehensively. "You're talking as if you're invulnerable. Has it occurred to you that these men are dangerous and might harm you?"

"It's occurred to me." Warmed by Nicole's concern, Dustin fought the urge to enfold her in his arms. "Don't worry, Derby. I'll think of a way to protect myself."

"Nickie's right, you know," Aldridge concurred. "I appreciate all you're doing for us, but I don't want you to get yourself killed."

"I don't intend to get myself killed. I'm a very resourceful man. Trust me." With that, Dustin confronted a far more personal challenge. "Speaking of trust, I'd like your permission to take Nicole out walking tonight. I realize my request is more than a bit improper, but circumstances preclude my following the rules of a traditional courtship. I promise to take excellent care of her and bring her home at whatever time you specify."

Nick started. "Walking . . . alone?"

"Yes. Alone."

A prolonged silence.

"You've entrusted me with your lives, Aldridge. I'm asking you to entrust me with your daughter. And I'm vowing that you won't regret it."

Uncertainly, Nick looked from Dustin to Nicole then back to Dustin again.

"She'll be safe," Dustin added quietly.

"Safe," Nick muttered. "From danger? Or from you?"

Dustin's lips twitched. "From both."

Again Nick searched his daughter's face, obviously affected by whatever he saw there. With a resigned sigh, he nodded. "All right. But only for an hour. No more."

"Agreed. And I thank you." Dustin glanced at Nicole. "Nine o'clock?"

Nicole blinked up at him, looking as if she didn't believe what had just occurred. "Nine o'clock," she repeated dazedly.

"Excellent. I'll collect you then." He turned to go, pausing to tug the brim of Nicole's cap. "And, Derby?" he murmured, for her ears alone. "Leave this home—along with Stoddard." A lazy grin. "You won't need either of them."

Nine

A surge of renewed energy accompanied Dustin back to the manor, every fiber of his being pulsing with the knowledge that tonight was going to fulfill another of Nicole's dreams.

A dream that, like her longing to run in the Derby, couldn't be bought in a store nor offered in a velvet-lined box.

But, oh, how cherished it would be.

Smiling, Dustin began planning the evening.

He was interrupted by the sound of Poole's anxious summons. "My lord." Standing in the drive, the butler sagged with relief when he spied Dustin. He whipped out a handkerchief and mopped his face, his gaze darting from Dustin to the entranceway door and back. "Quinn said you were at the stables. I've just returned from searching them, inch by inch. You were nowhere to be found."

"I was meeting with Stoddard. What on earth is wrong?"

"It's the duke, sir. He's been at Tyreham all day, awaiting your return. He arrived a scant quarter hour after your carriage departed. He's in quite a state about that missive we sent him."

"Yes, he certainly is." Trenton Kingsley stormed out of the manor, glaring angrily at his brother. "I thought I heard your voice. Where the hell have you been? And what's this about Alexander being in danger?"

"Hello, Trent," Dustin greeted him. "What took you so long? I expected you at Tyreham days ago." With a sympathetic glance at his butler, Dustin murmured, "Thank you, Poole. I'll take over from here." He climbed the stairs, laying a comforting hand on Trenton's shoulder, seeing beyond his brother's rage to the hollow fear beneath. "Stop bellowing. You're terrifying Poole—which you've probably been doing for hours. Let's go to my study. We'll have a drink and I'll fill you in."

With a terse nod, Trenton stalked through the house and into the study, waiting only until Dustin had joined him before shutting the door and leaning back against it. "Talk to me. Who's threatened Alexander? And why?"

Dustin filled two goblets with brandy, offering one to his brother. "Two men visited Tyreham a few days after I left Spraystone. They insisted—with their fists—that I not engage the services of Nick Aldridge who, if you recall, I was dead set on hiring."

"They barged in and threatened you?" A muscle worked furiously in Trenton's jaw. "That makes no sense. Whatever their reason for wanting Aldridge off the turf, it's immaterial now. He's in no condition to ride—for you or anyone. According to the newspapers, he's injured and recuperating in Scotland." Trenton broke off, suspicion narrowing his eyes. "Unless, of course, the newspaper reports are inaccurate."

"Evidently, my two visitors came to that same conclusion. To ensure my cooperation, they suggested that should I want Alexander to remain healthy, I avoid Aldridge at all costs. Their warning was unmistakable. As was my response—unmistakable and unfriendly." Dustin's mouth set in harsh lines. "I don't think they'll come near Alexander. The missive I sent you was simply a precaution." A swallow of brandy. "That's all I can tell you."

One black brow rose. "All you *can* tell me," Trenton repeated. "An interesting choice of words. Why do I think you're omitting a great deal?"

"If I am, that omission has nothing to do with my

nephew. Further, you can rest assured I'm in the process of terminating those lowlifes' careers. Permanently."

An assessing pause. "You know more about Nick Aldridge's disappearance than you told them, don't you?"

"According to the papers, he's recovering nicely."

"That wasn't my question."

"But that was my answer."

Trenton sucked in his breath. "You're up to your neck in something serious. Let me help you."

"I can't. Not this time." Dustin rolled the goblet between his palms. "I'd be violating a confidence."

"A confidence? Who the hell worth a damn would ask you to endanger yourself and your family? And to what end? You're not a bloody investigator."

That spawned a thought. "No, I'm not. Which gives me an idea." Dustin tossed back the rest of his drink. "Thanks, Trent. You've just helped more than you realize."

"You're not going to tell me another damned thing, are you?"

"I've told you everything you need to know. You have simply to keep a watchful eye on your family. By the way, where are my beautiful sister-in-law and my rambunctious nephew?"

"At Broddington. We returned from Spraystone this morning. Why do you think it took me so long to get here? I wanted to come the instant I got your note. But Ariana is too insightful. She knows how I savor our visits to Wight. If I'd left the isle abruptly, she would have guessed something was wrong. I don't want to worry her."

"Nor should you. She has enough to deal with controlling that eight-month-old tempest of yours. Speaking of which," Dustin tapped his upper lip. "Did you notice I shaved off my mustache? Your heir will now have to find a new distraction with which to torment me. That should take him, say, ten to fifteen minutes."

Trenton didn't smile. "You're evading the issue. Why? You're not in the habit of keeping things from me."

Silence.

"Is it Nick Aldridge you're protecting?"

"Trent, leave it alone. I can't say any more than I have.

You'll simply have to trust me." *Trust me.* Dustin's own words triggered a reminder of the evening ahead, an evening that was fast approaching. "I hate to be rude, but I have to cut this conversation short."

"Why? Do you have plans?"

"As a matter of fact, yes."

"Anyone I know?"

"No. At least not yet." This query Dustin met head-on. "But you will. Soon. The instant it's remotely possible."

Slowly, Trenton lowered his glass to the side table. "That sounds serious."

"It is. Or rather, it will be."

Surprise registered on Trenton's face. "When did this happen? You were at Spraystone a week ago, ornery and unattached."

"That was then. This is now."

"You became deeply involved with someone in a matter of days?"

"In a manner of minutes," Dustin corrected. He shot Trenton a pointed look. "As you did with Ariana."

"That was entirely different."

"Really? How?"

"Ariana needed help. I needed—her."

An ironic smile. "The situations are more analogous than even I discerned."

Trenton inhaled sharply. "Dustin, is this woman the cause of whatever crusade you're on? Because, if so . . ."

"Trent, you're beginning to sound like an overprotective parent. When I'm ready to disclose my secrets, you're the first one I'll seek out. Now, go home to Ariana. Stop worrying about your son—and your brother. We're both Kingsleys. We'll survive." His grin widened. "Better than survive, if I have my way."

"Are you implying . . ."

"Good night, Trent."

Throwing up his hands, Trenton complied. "All right, good night." Reaching for the doorknob, he paused. "You'll summon me if you need help?"

"When have I ever sought your help with women?"

"Very funny. I meant with the threats and with whatever those threats are dragging you into."

"I'll let you know the minute I'm free to discuss it."

A nod. "Dustin, be careful."

"I will."

Glancing back over his shoulder, Trenton regarded his brother with thoughtful understanding. "I can't wait to meet her. She must be extraordinary."

A smile curved Dustin's lips. "She is."

"A gown?" Nick Aldridge's mouth fell open. "You're wearing a bloody gown?"

"Stop making such a fuss, Papa." Nicole descended the steps, glancing self-consciously down at herself. "Do I look all right?"

The vulnerability in her voice penetrated her father's surprise. "You look beautiful. More than beautiful. Breathtaking. And not only because of the gown." He raised her chin. "There's a glow in your eyes that wasn't there before. A glow, I assume, caused by Dustin Kingsley."

Nicole lowered her lashes. "Is it that obvious?"

"Yes. But I wouldn't worry. He'll never notice. The man is so smitten with you, he can barely see straight."

"Do you really think so?"

"I know so. What I don't know is what he intends to *do* about his pent-up ardor." Worry furrowed her father's brow. "Nickie—"

"Papa, don't." She lay her forefinger across his lips, determined to squelch this particular subject before it began—again. The last thing she needed was a reminder of Dustin's womanizing ways or a lecture on how to ward off his advances.

Especially when her conviction to ward them off dwindled more by the minute.

A knock at the front door spared her further explanation. "Please, Papa," she soothed, reassuring him as best she could. "Have faith in my judgment."

"I do. It's the marquis's intentions I question." With that, Nick headed over and—hearing the requisite "It's Tyreham"—opened the door. "My lord," he acknowledged.

"Good evening, Aldridge." Dustin stepped inside, seductive as sin in his dark coat and trousers. "Is Nicole—?" He broke off, staring at Nicole as if she were an apparition.

"My reaction precisely," Nick commented dryly. He cleared his throat, stepping aside to let Nicole join her escort. "Have a nice stroll."

"Thank you, Papa," Nicole murmured. She walked toward Dustin, wondering how any man could be so heartstoppingly handsome. "Good evening, my lord. Shall we go?" When Dustin said nothing, merely continued to stare, she asked, "Are you well?"

"What I am is speechless."

Nicole felt her lips curve. "Somehow, I doubt that." She turned to her father. "I'll be home shortly, Papa."

"Yes. In an hour," Nick confirmed. "That's ten o'clock," he called after them, posted dutifully at the threshold.

Dustin began to chuckle. "Subtle, isn't he?" he inquired, taking Nicole's elbow and leading her away from the cottage.

"No, he's not." Nicole lapsed into silence, keenly aware of Dustin's touch, the proximity of his presence. Her own thoughts were a jumble of activity, her emotions raw and exposed. She'd anticipated tonight with all the giddy apprehension of a woman who knew her life was about to be forever changed by a man, a concept that both elated and terrified her.

She'd grappled with her feelings since yesterday, but it wasn't until tonight, while performing the uncharacteristic ritual of donning feminine attire, that the true significance of Dustin's words had found their mark.

Can you honestly tell me you don't come alive when we're together? Not only when we touch, but when we talk? When we laugh? Even when we argue? Ah, Derby, we can right life's wrongs and balance its inequities . . . together.

No, she couldn't deny it. Dustin had pervaded her life from the instant they'd met and not only during those brief, wondrous moments when she was in his arms. But along the Thames when they'd talked . . . on Tyreham's course when she trained . . . in this very cottage when he'd supplanted flattery with truth—for her. The affinity between them was rare, irrefutable, and no amount of trepidation could erase it.

It was then that the inevitable realization had struck— spawning those few, life-altering words.

She was in love with Dustin Kingsley.

The very acknowledgment, though unsurprising, heightened her misgivings to immense proportions, because whatever hope she'd had of shielding herself from Dustin's spell was now gone. The die was cast, the risk taken.

And her heart was no longer hers.

Now it was in the hands of fate.

Reflexively, her fingers went to her throat, brushing the soothing shape of her wishing locket where it hung gracefully—and, for tonight, openly—about her neck.

"You're very pensive," Dustin observed as they strolled through the woods.

"Am I?" Nicole blinked, raising her overheated face to the cool night air. "I'm sorry. I'm nervous."

"Don't be." Dustin's midnight gaze roved possessively over her. "You look exquisite. Precisely as you did the night we met."

"That's probably because I'm wearing precisely the same gown I wore the night we met," she replied, her heart drumming against her ribs. "I own only two. This one is a bit more stylish than the other."

"What made you decide to wear it tonight?"

Nicole averted her gaze. "I suppose I wanted to look like a woman, for once." The slightest of pauses. "For you."

"Thank you." Dustin's voice was husky. "I'm honored."

"Where are we going?" she blurted, noting the remoteness of this section of woods, now blocking the tenants' cottages from view.

"You'll see."

Staring at her slippered feet, Nicole contemplated what she should say next, and how in God's name she could speak past the lump in her throat.

"There." Dustin paused, pointing. "That's where we're going."

Her head came up, her brows drawing together as curiosity temporarily supplanted anxiety. "A cabin." She gazed questioningly up at Dustin. "Who lives there?"

"No one. At least not permanently." Looping an arm about her waist, Dustin urged her forward. "Come. Your father allocated one hour to this walk. I don't want to waste a moment of it."

Reaching the door, he eased it open, leading Nicole inside. Rather than lighting a lamp, he crossed over and threw open the wooden shutters, waiting as moonlight drenched the sparsely furnished room. "For you," he announced, beckoning her over. "A gift I've never shared with another. And, in our case, one I believe will mean far more than diamonds or sapphires."

Nicole walked over to stand beside him, staring, first out at the rapid descent of the trees, then upward to the starlit skies, her view of the heavens unmarred by so much as an oak or a church spire. "How beautiful," she breathed. "The moon and the stars. Brilliant diamonds cast across a sapphire sea. No jewels could compare."

"I agree." Silently, Dustin followed her gaze. "I built this cabin several years ago."

"*You* built it?"

"Um-hum. My father was an architect—a brilliant one— as is my brother Trenton. I dabbled alongside them. And while I cannot boast their genius, I absorbed enough knowledge to design a structure or two. This one is my favorite, simple though it might be. It's my own personal sanctuary."

"From what?" Nicole whispered.

"From the elaborate life you think I value so highly. You know—the lavish balls, the countless women, the frivolous parties." Moonlight drifted over his magnificently handsome features. "Here there are no balls, no vapid conversations, or meaningless liaisons. There's just me, my thoughts, and the night." He turned to her, his expression tender. "And now you."

Emotion constricted Nicole's throat as she savored the full extent of his offering. "I've judged you unfairly, haven't I?" she asked in a small, shaky voice. "There's so much more to Dustin Kingsley than the marquis of Tyreham." A breath of a pause. "Tell me about him."

"What would you like to know?"

"Whatever you'll share with me."

His knuckles caressed her cheek. "I'll share anything with you, Derby."

Nicole felt her insides melt. "Trenton—is he your only brother?"

"My only sibling. He's two years my senior." A twinkle. "The eminent duke of Broddington."

"An architect *and* a duke?"

"Um-hum. Also a dedicated, *faithful* husband who's hopelessly in love with his wife, and one hell of a good father. See? The Kingsleys follow paths of their own making, not those paved by the nobility."

Nicole flushed. "I suppose I deserved that."

"I meant to enlighten, not hurt, you. I'm demonstrating how little titles mean. Trent's the same fine man he was eight years ago, when Father died and bequeathed him a dukedom."

"And you? From whom did you inherit your title?"

"I didn't. It was bestowed upon me by Queen Victoria."

"Really?" Nicole leaned forward, fascinated. "When? Why?"

"About a decade ago. My father was a close friend of Her Majesty and the prince consort. Trenton and I often accompanied Father on his summer visits to Balmoral and Osborne House. During one of our trips to Balmoral, there was an attempt made on the queen's life. I was in the right place at the right time, and interceded. Her Majesty insisted on rewarding my efforts. She knew how I felt about Tyreham. Father designed this estate with me in mind. Accordingly, she named me the first marquis of Tyreham. End of story." Dustin studied Nicole's wide-eyed astonishment, and grinned. "Have I finally impressed you?"

"You saved the queen's life?"

"I gave her a very ungentlemanly shove as she alit from her carriage, then knocked down the culprit who was waving a pistol at her head. The man was clearly insane. He was seized by Her Majesty's guards and permanently confined to a madhouse."

"No wonder she was grateful."

"Ironically, she had occasion to be grateful again, only this time not to me but to Trenton. Two years ago he rescued Princess Beatrice from drowning in Osborne Bay."

"How did the queen reward him? He was already a duke."

A perceptive smile. "She gave him something far more valuable than a title. She gave him Ariana."

"His wife?"

Dustin nodded. "It's a long story, steeped in a lifetime of vengeance. Suffice it to say that my brother was ostracized for a crime he didn't commit—one that was orchestrated by a very twisted mind. Trent spent six years plotting his revenge. The man it was aimed at was Ariana's brother. So, when the queen offered Trent anything for sparing her youngest daughter's life, he asked for a royal decree commanding Ariana to marry him."

"He wed her just to punish her brother?"

"He thought so." A grin. "The truth is he fell in love with her the moment they met."

Nicole reacted to the obvious affection in Dustin's tone. "You love them both very much."

"I do. And their tyrant of a son, as well."

"They have a child?" Nicole's face lit up. "How old is he?"

"Eight months, and aging us all fast. His antics are enough to bring the British army to its knees. He crawls faster than I walk, and thinks of more things to destroy than I can count." Dustin's voice grew soft. "And I hope I have a houseful just like him some day."

Tears welled up in Nicole's eyes, and it was all she could do not to blurt out that she wanted those children to be hers.

"Now let's talk about you." Dustin changed the subject abruptly.

"What about me?" she managed.

"Well, I already know you began riding at the age of two, spoke French fluently by ten, and loathed needlepoint almost as much as you did sketching."

Realization made Nicole wince. "Sully," she muttered. "Lord, what else did he tell you?"

"Oh, a multitude of things, but he spent most of his time instructing me."

"Instructing you? Is that what you meant when you said he was offering advice?"

"Indeed. He wanted to be certain I realized how special you are, how well you should be treated. He grilled me thoroughly on my feelings for you and my intentions with regard to your future. The whole conversation was very enlightening."

Nicole wanted to drop through the floor—almost as much as she wanted to know what Dustin's answers to Sully had been.

"Then again, that's how I knew to bring you here," Dustin added, lifting her chin with his forefinger. "Sullivan told me how much you love stargazing. Stargazing and twilight." He caressed her cheek. "Next time we'll share twilight, but tonight I wanted you to see where I do my stargazing. I hoped you'd savor it as much as I do." His gaze fell to her mouth. "Tell me, Derby, is that what you were doing the night we met? Sitting along the Thames and stargazing?"

"Star wishing," Nicole breathed. She brought up her hand, fingers enveloping the locket that dangled about her throat. Solemnly, she held it out for Dustin to see.

"It's lovely," he murmured, leaning forward to inspect the delicate piece of silver.

"My mother gave it to me when I was five. According to her, it's a wishing locket."

"Is it?" Rather than amused, Dustin looked intrigued. "In what way?"

"Mama had a wondrous, fanciful mind. She believed that all the wishes I ever made would be stored inside this locket. After which, fate would decide when to make each wish a reality."

"What a remarkable thought." Dustin touched the clasp but made no move to open it. "Your mother sounds like an extraordinary woman."

"She was." Nicole's voice quavered. "That's who I was thinking of when you came upon me that night along the Thames. She gave me so much, and I miss her every day."

Dustin's fingers sifted through Nicole's hair, caressed her nape in warm, comforting strokes. "How long has she been gone?"

"Seven years." A sigh. "When you were describing Ariana's effect on Trenton, I couldn't help but think of Mama's effect on Papa. The way he tells it, he never did much wishing before she came into his life. Racing was his only passion and his only dream. He says Mama was his own priceless miracle." Teardrops glistened on Nicole's lashes. "I suppose once you've been given a miracle, it's far easier to believe they exist."

"That's true," Dustin concurred softly. "I'm discovering as much myself. Right here, right now."

Their gazes locked.

"My beautiful miracle." Dustin drew her against him, his muscles taut with emotion. "Let me hold you. Let me feel you in my arms." He covered her mouth with his. "God, how could anything be more right?"

Nothing could, Nicole thought silently, entwining her arms about his neck. She leaned into him, meeting his kiss with her own, parting her lips in silent invitation. Apprehension vanished, reservations scattered like leaves in the wind. At that instant, Dustin ceased to be a nobleman and she a commoner. He was a man, and for the first time in her life, Nicole felt very much a woman.

Whispering Dustin's name, she pressed closer, immersing herself deeper in his sensual spell. She shivered as his tongue possessed her mouth, swept her into a world of heady sensation and drugged desire. He lifted her off the floor, molded her body to his, and devoured her with a passion that was as tangible as it was consuming.

"Nicole . . ." He raised his head, his breath coming as hard and fast as hers, his magnificent eyes smoky with desire—a desire rooted in something far more profound than lust. His lips traced her neck, the curve of her shoulder, the pulse at her throat. When he seized her mouth again, there was a new urgency in his kiss, one he tried valiantly to control, but which Nicole felt nonetheless.

"Dustin, I want this," she breathed fervently. "I . . ." She struggled to form a coherent sentence. "I'm not afraid."

A harsh groan ripped from his chest, and he dragged his mouth away, shaking his head. "Nicole, this is not what I had planned. I didn't bring you here to seduce you."

"We're only kissing. You're not seducing me."

"Aren't I?" He set her feet on the floor, his expression stark with self-censure. "I want you so much I can't think. And, despite my best intentions, I seem to be using every technique I know to make you want me just as much."

"Is this wanting?" Nicole murmured, light-headed with sensation. "It feels wonderful." She drew his mouth back down to hers.

"Nicole, listen to me." Dustin buried his hands in her hair, tugged her head back to meet his gaze. "I meant what I said yesterday. I want more than tonight, more than this. I want you. All of you. Today. Tomorrow . . . and after."

"So do I," she said dreamily. "But right now I want to savor the dizziness that besieges me when you hold me, the ache I feel when we kiss." She gave him a quizzical look. "Is that wrong?"

"No, darling, it's not wrong. It's very, very right."

"When we touch, it's like there's a tiny flame inside me that flares higher with each passing moment. Is that a result of the technique you just described?"

An agonized sound. "God, I hope not." Instinctively, he bent to resume the kiss, then checked himself.

Nicole caressed his nape, realizing in some distant part of her mind that he was trying to protect her, flagrantly aware that at this precise minute, she wanted no part of that protection. Her fingers crept around to his jaw, caressed the warmth of his skin, feathered down his neck.

Dustin's muscles went rigid.

"Stop." He captured her hand, his own shaking violently. "Why?"

"Because I'm at the bloody edge of my control." His expression was a combination of wonder and amazement. "And you've barely even touched me." He kissed her palm, hesitated, then moved to her wrist, the inside of her forearm—waging an internal battle Nicole could actually feel. "You're so perfect," he muttered, capturing her other arm and repeating his caresses. "Soft. Warm. Intoxicating." He pulled her against him. "I can almost feel you under me." He buried his lips in hers.

Desire slammed through Nicole along with a loud, unheeded warning. "Dustin." She breathed his name, wrapping her arms about his neck. "Don't stop—not yet."

He tore his mouth away, but only to burn a blazing trail of kisses down her throat, the upper swell of her breasts. He descended further, his open mouth tracing the edge of her bodice. "The timing's all wrong," he rasped. "I have to bring you home."

"Just a few minutes then." Her hands slid beneath his coat, uncertain what to do, unwilling to forego doing it. "Show me," she breathed. "Please."

Something inside Dustin seemed to snap.

With relentless purpose, his fingers swept down the front of her gown, dispensing with the buttons in a few lightning-quick seconds, tugging the sides apart. He anchored one arm about her waist, leaning her backwards to give him greater access to her heated skin.

"Oh . . . God." Nicole's knees buckled when his lips surrounded her nipple, tugging it through the confines of her chemise. Flames shot through her, liquid fire pooling at her loins, and she scarcely heard Dustin's hoarse groan over her own whimper of pleasure.

But she felt him, oh, she felt him. Touching her, caressing her—his solid strength taking her weight, keeping her from collapsing to the floor. Trembling as violently as she, he shoved her bodice down to her waist and pushed aside her chemise, eliminating a portion of the intolerable barrier that separated them.

His greedy eyes devoured her.

"You're beautiful." He caressed her breast as if it were a priceless treasure, sending shards of pleasure shooting through her. "How could you bind down such beauty?"

Nicole's answer was a moan, as Dustin bent and claimed her with his mouth.

Had she thought his caress devastating before? If so, then now, without even a thin scrap of material between them, it was unendurable.

She cried out as his lips enveloped her nipple in velvet heat, tugged it into the damp haven of his mouth. Shrugging out of his coat, he paused only to cast it to the floor before lowering her onto it, following her down. Half covering her with himself, he bent to her other breast, laved it with his tongue.

And seared his mark on her soul.

As if from faraway, Nicole saw herself reach between them, unbuttoning his shirt and waistcoat, shoving the sides apart. Her palms glided over the hair-roughened surface of his chest to the broad width of his shoulders. "Let me feel your skin against mine," she managed.

Dustin complied, lowering his torso to hers.

The first contact was electrifying.

Dustin threw back his head, emitting a harsh growl of excruciating pleasure. "Derby . . . I . . ." He moved against her, dragging his chest across her nipples, shifting her legs so he lay between them, nestled in the cradle of her thighs. He seized her mouth, cupping the back of her head to fuse their lips more totally, his thumb tracing erotic circles on her breast.

Nicole whimpered, stroking the taut planes of his back, her lower body lifting instinctively to bring him closer. Dustin's body answered, thrusting forward, pressing deep, deep into the warm cavern he sought. His hips began a reflexive rhythm, nudging her thighs farther apart, driving him against her core with an agonizing motion thwarted only by their remaining layers of clothing.

Hot jolts of sensation coursed through Nicole, coiling low in her abdomen, pooling in liquid heat at the very spot where Dustin's hard ridge of flesh teased. Desperately, she sought more of the friction, matching his rhythm, arching each time he thrust, oblivious to everything but the need to ease the throbbing ache that only intensified with each frustrating roll of her hips.

"Nicole, don't. Ah, God . . . sweetheart . . ." Wildly, Dustin shook his head; his hands, in the process of shifting to his trouser buttons, halting, balling into fists on either side of her, fists that shoved him away even as his hips urged him forward.

"No." Nicole caught his forearms, totally beyond rational thought as she tried to stay his retreat. "Oh, Dustin, if you stop . . . I can't bear it."

"Nor can I." Sweat dampened his brow, his entire body quaking with unsquelched urgency. "But I have to stop. Derby, I'm going to shatter. I'm going to tear off your gown and take you right here, right now, and damn the consequences."

"I don't care."

"Yes you do. And so do I."

Dustin's words were a sobering douse of reality, and Nicole fell silent, blinking bewilderedly up at him.

"My God, Nicole." He gazed deeply into her eyes. "Have you any idea what you do to me? What you reduce me to?"

"What?" she whispered, torn between unfulfilled need and the rush of shame beginning to claim her.

"This." He indicated their position, half naked and entwined on a wooden floor, and shook his head in awed amazement. "This is what you do to me. I'm frantic. So crazed to have you I'm ready to erupt. I planned nothing more than to taste your mouth, and I've all but taken you on the bloody cabin floor. No wine, no flowers, no soft words." A self-deprecating pause. "The accomplished lover you fear is no more. He vanished the instant I took you in my arms."

Those words went straight to Nicole's heart, holding her humiliation at bay. "That is the loveliest compliment you could ever pay me."

"It's no compliment," he replied solemnly, kissing the hollow between her breasts. "It's truth."

She shivered. "I still ache," she confessed in a tiny voice.

"My beautiful, honest Nicole." With the greatest of efforts, Dustin left her, rising to his knees and tugging her clothes into place. "I ache, too."

Watching his fingers refasten her gown, Nicole blushed crimson, reality descending in a great, rushing wave. "I look like a wanton."

Dustin seized her chin, forcing her to meet his gaze. "Don't ever say that," he commanded fiercely. "Don't even think it. A wanton? You're a total innocent. What happened here was my doing, not yours."

Her smile was soft, starting deep within. "Thank you for your gallant attempt to spare my sensibilities. But I seem to recall participating quite fully in our . . . our . . ." Again she blushed.

"Lovemaking," he finished for her. "Call it lovemaking, Nicole, because with us, that's all it ever could be." His grip eased, his fingers shifting to caress her cheek. "Shame has no place between us. Neither does regret." He started to say more, then decided against it.

"Every time I think I've adjusted to these feelings you inspire, you incite new ones," Nicole admitted. "I'm constantly flailing about in uncharted waters . . . and drowning."

Dustin gathered her against him, his lips buried in her hair. "You might not believe this, Derby, but I feel exactly the same way. What's happening between us is astounding." His voice grew husky. "A miracle."

Nicole squeezed her eyes shut, moved beyond words by his implicit meaning, equally terrified by the enormity of what lay ahead—an enormity that was suddenly too great to bear.

Once the threats to her father were resolved, she'd no longer be able to hide behind the myth of Alden Stoddard, no longer be able to hold the future at bay. Presumably, she'd resume her life as Nicole Aldridge—leave Tyreham, the turf, and Dustin.

Unless she chose otherwise.

She knew, without question, that Dustin would expect some sort of decision from her with regard to their relationship. He'd stated over and over that he wanted her in his life, although in what capacity, she wasn't sure. But whatever her role, he certainly wouldn't settle for broken, isolated moments of privacy such as these. Neither, for that matter, would she.

So where did that leave them? Did he intend to offer her his name or only his bed and his protection? And, even if it were marriage he had in mind, did she have the strength—or the will—to sacrifice her way of life for his? To become, of all things, the marchioness of Tyreham? A role which, regardless of what Dustin claimed or how smitten he was, would involve relinquishing the stables for the manor, overseeing a staff, entertaining noblemen, taking tea with their wives.

Dear Lord, how could she abide such an existence, much less conform to one?

"Nicole?" Dustin caught her face between his hands, tilting it back to read her expression. "What are you thinking?"

Her lashes lifted. "That there are so many obstacles."

"I'll overcome every damned one of them." With that, he stood, tugging her to her feet, steadying her when she swayed. "I will, you know," he vowed quietly, rebuttoning his shirt and waistcoat. Tenderly, he reached forward, touching her wishing locket and giving her that bone-melting smile. "I'm not so foolish as to let a miracle get away."

Ten

The man frowned. The grounds outside Epsom were exceedingly muddy, leaving ugly stains on his fine leather shoes. That meant he'd have to return home and change—an annoyance that did not fit into his plans at all.

Whatever the cause for today's meeting, it had best be important. Damned important.

"I'm over here," came a raspy voice from a nearby cluster of trees.

The man veered toward it. "What is it, Cooper?" he hissed, glaring at the stable owner. "Have you found Aldridge?"

"Not yet, no."

"Then what the hell was so important that you sent for me? Haven't you learned from our previous complication that we're not to be seen together?"

"Yeah, I learned." Coop leaned against the tree, folding his arms across his chest. "But we have a problem you should know about."

"Well?"

"Archer and Parrish took care of Sullivan. He told them nothing, and so far, he's made no move to go to Aldridge. Neither, for that matter, has Aldridge come to him. But someone else did."

"Who?"

"Tyreham."

The man sucked in his breath. "Kingsley went to Sullivan? Why?"

"He must be snooping around, either to find Aldridge or to find out why someone else wants him so bad. I don't know the details—Tyreham didn't exactly invite Archer and Parrish in for tea and conversation, but Archer said Tyreham got to the cottage right after he and Parrish left. Obviously, he saw the kind of condition Sullivan was in. I'm sure the old jockey told him what happened. The question is, what does Tyreham plan to do about it?" He paused, massaging his scarred forearm. "And what do we plan to do about Tyreham?"

"Indeed."

"That's not all. After he left Suffolk, Tyreham made another stop on his way home. At Preighbrook's."

"Dammit." The oath emerged in an angry hiss. "He must have connected Aldridge's disappearance to Redley's death."

"Well, he sure as hell wasn't paying a social call. Preighbrook's so old he can barely stand up."

"True. But, being as feeble-minded as he is, he also couldn't have told Kingsley anything of importance."

The toe of Coop's boot dug into the ground, slashing blades of grass. "What do you want me to do, have Archer and Parrish thrash Tyreham?"

"I think not. Not yet." The man pursed his lips, idly fingering his silk neckcloth. "First let's see what the marquis has in mind. That should be easy enough to learn."

"How? You can't just walk in and ask him."

"I needn't do anything so rash as that. I have a new resource at Tyreham, remember?"

An ugly smile curved Coop's lips. "I'd almost forgotten. Yeah, that's right. You do."

"I'll contact that resource. In the meantime, tell Archer and Parrish to keep watching Sullivan's house. It's early yet. Perhaps news of the beating has yet to reach Aldridge—wherever he is. If I need further help with Tyreham, I'll summon you." A meaningful look. "Do not summon me."

His glance fell on Coop's forearm and, with a shudder of revulsion, he turned, retracing his steps over the damp grounds.

"You asked to see me, my lord?"

Poole stood at attention in the doorway to Dustin's study.

"Yes, Poole." Dustin rose from behind his desk. "Come in. And close the door behind you."

"As you wish, sir."

Dustin waited until the task was done, broaching the subject without further preliminaries. "You've been with me a long time, Poole. I needn't tell you how highly I value your abilities nor how greatly I rely upon your discretion."

"No, you needn't. But I thank you nonetheless."

"I require a favor."

"Anything, sir."

"One that must remain strictly between us."

"Of course."

Slowly, Dustin walked around front of his desk, perching on its corner. "This pertains to the missive we sent my brother, the one that brought him charging to Tyreham like a rampaging steed, and to the hoodlums that necessitated my sending it."

Poole's expression remained unchanged. "I gathered as much, sir."

"Your nephew, Thorne Saxon—he's still residing in Surrey, is he not?"

"He is." A flicker of comprehension. "He lives a mere ten miles away. And, if I might be so bold as to anticipate your next question, he's now a fine, seasoned investigator. In fact, he just recently left the employ of Mr. Hackberth to strike out on his own."

"Why? Hackberth is one of the most respected investigators in England."

"Indeed, sir. But, at the risk of sounding overly boastful, Thorne has acquired quite a following—clients who had begun making specific requests for his services. Mr. Hackberth was exceedingly proud. After all, he was the one who taught Thorne all his skills. He was also the one who broached the subject of Thorne's opening his own firm.

According to Mr. Hackberth, there were a dozen and a half clients who would be delighted to take their business to him."

"Impressive." Dustin's brows arched. "Also a generous display on Hackberth's part. Not that it surprises me. From what I know of Hackberth, he's a most gracious man. Heaven knows he has enough clients to spare a few. Still, giving Saxon his blessing was very kind of him." A pause. "And very fortunate for me."

"Shall I summon Thorne, sir?"

"If you would, yes. I'd like to hire him to be both a trained pair of eyes and a bit of brawn, should it be needed. As I remember, Saxon was powerfully built, even as an adolescent."

"Even more so, now that he's grown." Poole cleared his throat. "Are you in danger, sir?"

"I hope not. But I'm going to be delving into the matter of Aldridge's disappearance more fully. I'd like Saxon to accompany me." A slight smile. "I hope he's adept at handling a carriage."

"Sir?"

"I don't want whoever is behind this reprehensible scheme to know I've hired someone, or even that I'm taking precautions. Therefore, when Saxon travels with me, he must be disguised as someone easily overlooked."

Poole's eyes glittered. "Like a driver, for example."

"Exactly."

With a nod, Poole reached for the door. "I'll summon him at once, my lord. He'll be honored to serve you."

"Thank you, Poole."

Alone, and satisfied that he'd taken the necessary steps to ensure his own safety, just as he'd promised the Aldridges, Dustin resumed the line of thought that had preoccupied him throughout the night and into today.

Nicole—and their hour together in the cabin, sharing their thoughts, their dreams.

Their bodies.

With a harsh sound, Dustin reached for his coffee cup.

He'd be lying to himself if he denied that his contemplations had repeatedly converged on those exquisite moments on the cabin floor.

Moments as unrivaled as they were unplanned.

A surge of tenderness claimed him along with the wonder of discovery. He'd told Nicole she was a miracle, and she was, but so was what had transpired between them, sensations so utterly distinct, so different from lust that they redefined the parameters of passion as Dustin had known them. The smoky longing in her eyes, the absolute trust in her motions, the honesty in her words. During that precious time before he'd regained his sanity, there had been no doubts, no boundaries. There had been only the two of them and the extraordinary feelings unfolding between them. True, Nicole had no basis for distinguishing lovemaking from sex. But he did—thanks to her. The contrast was humbling.

As was the realization that had he not recovered his senses, she would have offered him her innocence.

And hated herself afterward.

Frowning, Dustin gulped down his coffee, confronting the gnawing anxiety that was as real, and as intense, as his elation—an anxiety that had hammered at his brain throughout the long hours till dawn.

What emotional damage had been done during those few poignant minutes? And how could he rectify it, overcome Nicole's guilt and regret, and convince her that what had happened between them was as right as dawn melding with day?

He'd never forget how bereft she'd looked, her awe transforming to shame even as they dressed—shame and self-reproach. Further, she openly placed blame for what had occurred not with him but with herself—a fact as untenable as her ensuing reaction. The result was that along with her gown, she'd restored that damned emotional barrier she'd erected between them, and no matter how valiantly Dustin had tried, he'd been unable to tear it down again. Not during those last seconds at the cabin, nor during their silent walk to her cottage. Several times his frustration had been so great he'd actually considered breaking his vow to Aldridge and spiriting Nicole away, just to rekindle her wonder, her dizzying joy, and, yes—if he were to employ that esteemed honesty she'd taught him—to keep her beside him, where she belonged. Lord, how he'd wanted to obliterate her self-condemnation, her qualms, her bewilderment; to see her face suffused with the exhilaration she'd displayed earlier.

And blame? Well, if blame were to be assigned, he should be its sole recipient. Because he was seasoned enough to have anticipated how devastating it would be to a virtuous young woman like Nicole to realize she'd come so close to surrendering her innocence. That unlike he—who understood that, despite the beauty of their physical encounter, their most profound sharing had occurred before they'd even touched—Nicole was too young, too naive to make that distinction. And, as much as he'd yearned to make her see the strength of what existed between them, he knew she wasn't ready. It was too soon to expect her to relinquish her doubts and fears, too soon for her to make the ultimate commitment he sought.

And yet he'd let things get out of hand anyway, knowing full well there'd be a price to pay. On their first evening alone, during their first moments of privacy—no, in light of all that, there wasn't a doubt with whom the blame rested.

With him.

It didn't ease his conscience one iota that she'd been as eager as he, nor that she'd unfurled more completely with each of his intensifying caresses. In fact, it made him feel all the more a cad. Because he was well aware she'd been drowning in her first taste of passion, lost to newly discovered sensations more acute than she'd ever encountered, much less overcome. Lord, she'd never even been kissed. In short, she hadn't a clue of the power desire wielded. *He* was the experienced one; *she* the novice. It had been his responsibility to set the limits, and he'd failed.

Dammit, he should have stopped sooner. Instead, he'd lost all control, nearly taking her virginity—and on the cabin floor, no less. With a half hour to return her to Aldridge's quarters.

Aldridge. His reception certainly hadn't helped matters. They'd arrived at the cottage to find him waiting like a cursed bloodhound, whipping open the cottage door so rapidly it left no doubt that he'd been pacing just inside it. And while Dustin had ensured that every article of Nicole's clothing, every hair on her head had been wholly restored, he could do nothing to repress her guilty expression, nor could he force her averted gaze back to her father's.

Aldridge's curt goodnight had been as cool as his countenance, filled with more than a touch of suspicion. Hell, Dustin hadn't a doubt that, were Nick not confined to his quarters, he would have stalked outside, dueling pistol cocked and ready.

And the bloody clock was first chiming ten.

Dustin slammed his cup to the saucer.

Why hadn't he followed his instincts and told Nicole what was in his heart—given her the words. Lord knew, he'd started to, not once, but countless times. *I love you.* Three words he'd never spoken to another, words that had been lying in wait for just the right woman.

For Nicole.

The question was a rhetorical one. He knew perfectly well why he'd refrained from uttering his profession of love aloud: because he hadn't a clue how Nicole would receive it. Especially offered in the aftermath of passion. Would she believe it? Embrace it?

Were she any other woman, Dustin's answer would have been an unequivocal yes. The women he knew would have swooned with pleasure to be offered his heart—especially because it would be one step closer to his title and his money. But Nicole wasn't other women. She wouldn't welcome such a declaration unless she deemed it true. And he wasn't at all confident she did—at least not yet. What he *was* confident of was the fact that she loved him in return, a certainty born of emotion, not arrogance. Yet, certain though he was of Nicole's love, he was equally convinced that the enormity of what was happening between them was escalating too fast for her to handle. Especially in light of the fact that she was still grappling with her preconceived notions of who he was, how he lived, not to mention the aversion she had to his bloody title.

Didn't she understand that he'd gladly relinquish it all for her?

The answer was, no, she didn't. Not fully. Not yet.

Therefore, expressing his love might have bound her to him or it might just as easily have driven her away.

The latter prospect had effected his silence.

But not for long. Because, precisely as he'd sworn to Nicole last night, he intended to overcome every obstacle in their path and, come hell or high water, make her his.

Soon.

"Pardon me, sir." Poole's reappearance interrupted Dustin's silent resolution.

"Yes, Poole?"

Poole stepped around the partially open door. "You asked me to advise you when Mr. Raggert arrived at Tyreham. Well, he's been shown to his quarters and is unpacking."

"Excellent." Dustin rose. "Are you off to your nephew's house?"

A nod. "But before I go, I have two unexpected visitors to announce."

Dustin went taut. "Is it those hoodlums again?"

"Oh, nothing like that, sir. These are welcome guests, not destructive—"

Before he could finish his sentence, the door jerked forward another notch, clipping Poole on the shoulder and, having caught him off guard, sending him off balance.

Unceremoniously, and seemingly without regret, Alexander Kingsley crawled swiftly into the study, casting a curious glance at the astounded butler who was in the process of regaining his footing.

A crack of laughter erupted from Dustin's chest. "Not destructive, you were saying?" Crossing the room, he scooped up his nephew at the same instant Ariana burst in. "Alexander? Where did you . . . ?" She halted, sagging with relief when she saw her son in his uncle's arms. "Thank goodness. I put him down only long enough to hand Poole my coat and admire that lovely new fern in your entranceway. When I turned, he was gone."

"Thirty seconds. That's all the time he needs." Dustin gave his sister-in-law a warm hug. "What a splendid surprise! To what do I owe the honor of this visit?"

"To the fact that your nephew's been demanding 'Un'l' since you left Spraystone. Evidently, he misses you." She turned to Poole. "Forgive me, Poole. Are you all right?"

"Perfectly all right, Your Grace." Poole had already

straightened his uniform. "Would you or the young marquis care for some refreshment before I take my leave?"

"Nothing, thank you."

"Then I'll be going. I shan't be long, my lord," Poole added with a meaningful look at Dustin. "If you need anything, just ring for Quinn."

"Quinn?" Ariana repeated in surprise. "Isn't he Lord Tyreham's driver?"

"He is, Your Grace. But prior to that, he was a footman. And, given the onslaught of guests we expect to arrive in conjunction with the races at Epsom, we'll need additional assistance in the manor. Thus, Quinn has been reassigned and a temporary replacement driver engaged. I'm off to fetch him now." Poole bowed. "Your Grace, Lord Tyreham, if you'll excuse me?"

"Of course. Thank you, Poole." Dustin bit back a smile. If Poole ever tired of his role as a butler, there was definitely a place for him in the theatre.

"Dustin?" Ariana glanced from the now empty doorway to her brother-in-law, looking totally perplexed. "Have we come at a bad time? I know that May is the heart of the spring meetings, but when Trenton returned yesterday, he announced that you wouldn't be participating in any other races until that jockey you were seeking, Nick Aldridge, had recovered and was back in England."

"Trent didn't stay long enough for me to update him on the situation," Dustin responded smoothly. "I've found another jockey, Nick Aldridge's protégé, as luck would have it. He's superb. Better than that. He'll be riding my stallion Dagger in the Derby. Not only riding," Dustin amended, "but winning."

"That's wonderful." Ariana transferred a wriggling Alexander from Dustin's arms to hers. "But, in that case, Alexander and I will be on our way."

"Nonsense. I'm not entered in the second set at Newmarket, nor any other race prior to Epsom. Further, I'm always delighted to see you—and my favorite little tyrant." A speculative pause. "Although I am a bit curious as to the timing of your visit. After all, Trent was here only yesterday."

"Alexander and I were en route to town," Ariana explained, averting her gaze to kiss her son's brow. "We stopped at Tyreham first."

"Ah." Dustin tapped his chin. "Interesting, the last I recall, Surrey wasn't a convenient stop when traveling from Sussex to London. Have they rerouted a few roads since last I visited Broddington?"

Ariana relaxed into a sheepish grin. "Very well. I used Alexander's adoration for you as a ruse. Trenton said you seemed a bit preoccupied. He mentioned something about a woman. He thought I might be able to help."

Dustin's lips curved. "I see. So you're here as my advisor."

"If you recall, you've acted as mine," she reminded him softly. "At a time when I most desperately needed one."

"I remember." Dustin nodded, sobering. "Although I sometimes lose sight of the fact that your marriage to Trent wasn't always as harmonious as it is now."

"Harmonious?" Ariana shot him an incredulous look. "Quite the opposite. At the onset, it was grim and mercurial, at best. But whenever I reached my lowest point, when I hadn't a shred of strength or objectivity left, you were there." She squeezed his forearm. "Let me offer you the same. Please."

Affection and relief converged inside Dustin's chest. "Truthfully, I could use some advice," he conceded. "Lord knows, I'm not doing too well on my own."

"Say no more." Ariana gestured toward the window overlooking the drive. "Mrs. Hopkins is waiting in the carriage. Suppose I have her take Alexander to that wonderful playroom you built for him. That will give us time to talk."

Another grin. "While giving Alexander time to demolish the new toys I've added." Dustin caught Alexander's fist in his own. "What do you say to that? You and Mrs. Hopkins can play for a bit, and then we'll all go to the stables. To see the horses," he added pointedly.

That had the desired effect.

Squealing, Alexander began to pump his arms and legs so vigorously that Ariana had to dodge to avoid his blows.

"I thought so," Dustin teased. "We now get to the real

reason you want to see 'Un'l'—my thoroughbreds. Very well, you may do both. First toys, then horses."

Ten minutes later, Alexander and Mrs. Hopkins were settled in the playroom, and Ariana and Dustin were comfortably seated in Tyreham's green salon.

"Tell me about her," Ariana began without preliminaries.

Dustin rubbed his palms together, considering the question carefully. "Ariana, this is a very complex situation. There's a great deal I can't say, simply because I've given my word not to. So I'll answer what I can and defer what I cannot."

"All right." A spark of curiosity lit her turquoise eyes, but she didn't question his odd conditions.

"I've never met anyone like her," Dustin began quietly. "She's the utter antithesis of every women I've ever been involved with—warmhearted, unaffected, and selfless. Quite frankly, I'd all but abandoned hope that such fineness of character, such inner beauty truly existed—at least for me." Images of Nicole—astride Dagger's back, gazing at the stars—flashed through his mind. "We have the same passions, the same dreams. We'd scarcely met, spoken, when I knew she was the one." Awed, he shook his head. "I never imagined feeling such intense emotion. I think of her constantly, spend most of my waking hours—which, over the past fortnight, have become numerous—devising schemes to make her mine." His fists knotted in his lap, his voice dropping to a hoarse whisper. "And, while I'm determined to succeed, I'm also terrified that I'll fail."

Tears glistened on Ariana's lashes. "If what you've described isn't love, I don't know what is." She rose, came to sit beside him. "Can you tell me her name?"

"No."

"Where you met? Or when?"

A nostalgic smile. "Several days after I left Spraystone. I was in London. That particular night, I'd accepted invitations to numerous parties. The prospect of attending even a single one of them left me cold. So I delayed the inevitable as long as possible, strolling aimlessly about town, wishing I could do so forever. I spotted her immediately. One doesn't miss the kind of beauty she emanates. She was stargazing on a bench alongside the embankment road. I joined her there.

We spent only a quarter hour together that evening, but I felt as if I'd known her all my life."

"That evening? Then you've seen her since?"

A nod. "But not often enough."

"Dustin, is it that she doesn't return your feelings?"

"To the contrary, I think she feels precisely as I do. And she's fighting it every step of the way."

"Why?"

Dustin inhaled, weighing his explanation so as not to reveal too much. "We're from very different worlds. My world intimidates her. So does my reputation."

Ariana's brows rose. "She knows of your reputation and she hasn't bolted? She must care for you a great deal."

"Very amusing."

"I wasn't trying to be amusing." A thoughtful pause. "Dustin, if I combine what little you've said with the fact that none of us, including yourself, has ever had occasion to meet this girl before now, I have to assume she's not of noble birth."

"Your assumption is correct. She lives a much simpler or, to use her words, more provincial life than we do."

"In which case, how can you blame her for being intimidated? Were I she, I'd be quaking in my shoes. Lord alone knows what she's heard about you. Most of which, I might add, is true—or have you forgotten?"

"I haven't forgotten. But how can I convince her that all that's behind me now? That she's different, special? That I'm so bloody in love with her I can't think straight?"

"That depends. Have you seduced her?"

Dustin started. "What kind of question is that?"

"A pertinent one. I infer from your description that the young lady in question is not experienced when it comes to men."

"As naive as you were."

Ariana grinned. "I'm not certain if that's a compliment or a condemnation, but it is an answer. Is she young?"

"Your age."

"But she's been protected by her family, I'm guessing."

"You can certainly say that, yes."

"Then I repeat, have you seduced her?"

"You, of course, assume that I have."

"Quite the opposite," Ariana demurred in her customarily serene fashion. "I suspect you're so eager to dispel her apprehensions that you've been unthinkably self-controlled—at least for you."

Dustin shot her a look. "I sense a barb beneath that supposed commendation, but I'll answer nonetheless. You're right. I'm doing my best to convey my feelings without compromising her or her values."

"I see." A tiny pucker formed between Ariana's brows. "Have you told her how you feel?"

"I've done all but utter the words. I'd gladly give her those, too, if I weren't so afraid she'd bolt." He raked a hand through his hair. "I don't know what more to do."

"Have you considered giving her time?"

Silence.

Ariana sighed. "Honestly, you Kingsley men are so . . ."

"I know—intense, impatient, and perpetually in search of a challenge," Dustin finished for her.

"Exactly. Well, Dustin, you've found the ultimate challenge, one that will change your whole life. But you can't approach it with mule-headed intensity, nor with single-minded haste. Some treasures, like flowers, need time to unfurl. You plant them, water them, and wait. Otherwise you destroy a miracle too beautiful to recreate, too delicate to recapture."

"A miracle." Dustin's features softened. "That's what she believes in. And that's what she is." He gave a deep, resigned sigh. "Do you really think time will help?"

"I do. And not very much time either. It sounds to me as if you've already made amazing headway. Just give her love a chance to overcome her misgivings. After which—" A twinkle. "I have a suspicion Tyreham will be hosting a wedding reception far more joyous than all your victory celebrations combined, including your anticipated taking of the Derby."

Your anticipated taking of the Derby. Ariana's particular choice of words struck home, although she could have no way of knowing why, and a warm glow pervaded Dustin's heart. Some Derbys could be taken, others had to be won not by siege but by trust. And since bone-deep trust took time to build, and time required patience . . . then patience he would find.

"Very well." With a decisive nod, he conceded to Ariana's suggestion. "I shall try to employ some of that nonexistent Kingsley patience you've described."

"You won't regret it," Ariana assured him.

Gratefully, Dustin brought Ariana's fingers to his lips. "Thank you. You're one hell of an advisor. Not to mention you didn't once grill me about how such overwhelming feelings could develop so quickly."

"I?" Ariana smoothed her skirts and rose. "I who fell instantly and totally in love with a man who did everything in his power to make me despise him?" A distant smile touched her lips. "Given my history with Trenton, I think it would be a bit unfair of me to denounce your feelings. After all, love is love, and strikes when and whom it chooses." She squeezed Dustin's forearm. "I'm so happy it's chosen to strike you at last. No one deserves it more." With keen insight, she studied his expression. "Your happiness shows, you know. You look—content. Tired and frustrated, to be sure," she added teasingly, "but content." A solemn note crept into her voice. "That restlessness that plagued you at Spraystone has vanished. Forever, I suspect. Yes." She nodded. "I believe, Lord Tyreham, your wandering days are over." With that, she glanced out the window. "Now, given what a lovely day it is, shall we collect Alexander and Mrs. Hopkins? The stables await and—" Breaking off, she frowned.

"What's wrong?" Dustin came to his feet.

"I'm not sure. Trenton has been acting so odd these past few days. This morning he very nearly forbid me to take Alexander to Tyreham with me. When I insisted, he commanded four additional footmen to accompany us. Look at them." She gestured toward the drive. "They're lined up outside the manor as if ready to do battle."

Dustin followed her gaze, warning bells ringing loud and clear inside his head. "They're probably waiting to accompany us to the stables."

"Why?"

"Because, although Trent loves Alexander with all his heart, you're his life. And, being that you're not exactly a strapping, muscular woman, he worries about your endurance. Why, in less than a year, your son has all but worn you out. And Alexander is getting older, more physically demanding. Trent is probably just ensuring you have enough help to get along."

Ariana planted her hands on her hips. "I'm slight, but I'm not exactly a weakling. Besides, *four* additional men? Plus the customary three, Mrs. Hopkins and myself, not to mention the staff at Tyreham? No child, energetic or not, requires an army to oversee him."

An offhanded shrug. "Trent has been more overprotective than usual lately. He all but swooned when I implied that I'd fallen in love so quickly and deeply. If he's fretting over me, he's bound to be a nervous ninny when it comes to you. Remember, Ariana, my brother's thoughts, like his love, run very deep. But that shouldn't surprise you. After all, you know how"—a grin—"intense we Kingsley men are."

"I suppose," Ariana murmured, chewing her lip.

"Don't give it another thought. Come. Let's head for the stables. I have a new trainer starting today. You can meet him, and Alexander can proffer a few cubes of sugar to the horses."

"That sounds wonderful." Ariana's somber mood lifted, precisely as Dustin had intended. "I'm also eager to meet this new jockey of yours, the one you're training for the Derby. Incidentally, it goes without saying that Trenton and I will be in the stands on Derby Day. In fact, we'll make a visit of it. We'll stay at Tyreham for the duration of the Epsom races. How would that be?"

"Splendid," Dustin heard himself say, feeling a frisson of apprehension as he realized that, simultaneous with Derby Day, Nicole would be exposed to the world's scrutiny for the first time. Hundreds of onlookers would see her race. What if she were recognized not by Ariana and Trent, who were completely trustworthy, but by someone else—the *wrong* someone? Countless jockeys knew Nicole Aldridge. What if a particularly competitive or unscrupulous one saw through her disguise and reported it? The ensuing disqualification, even the scandal, meant not a whit to Dustin, but Nicole's safety did. Was he endangering her life by permitting her to ride as a man?

Forcibly, he squelched his qualms, chastising himself for thinking with his heart, not his head. The truth was, there was nothing to fear. He'd known from the start that he needn't shield Nicole from the world. Her disguise was flawless, allowing no one a glimpse of Alden Stoddard's true identity. He was just overreacting—as Kingsley men apparently did when they were in love.

Nevertheless, just to be on the safe side, he'd implement the extra precautions he'd planned, not only on Derby Day but for the entire week the Epsom races were being run. The additional staff Poole was providing would ward off the reporters and the touts. *Especially* the touts, who'd be sniffing around Stoddard in an attempt to determine what odds to lay on Dagger's Derby performance. *If* they got near enough to make that discernment. Which they wouldn't, Dustin vowed silently, a muscle working in his jaw. In fact, as he'd promised Aldridge, Dagger and Stoddard wouldn't be approachable until they paraded up to the starting gate and swept the Derby.

"Dustin?" Ariana's expression was perplexed. "What is it? Will our visiting Tyreham during the Epsom races be too much for you? If that's the case, say so. Trenton and I will understand. We'll simply come another time and—"

"Nonsense." Dustin's composure reinstated itself. "I'd be insulted if you didn't stay for the duration. I'm just preoccupied. Let's gather Alexander and head for the stables." He turned, striding toward the door. "I'm eager to see how Stoddard is faring."

Stoddard was not faring at all well.

In fact, she was distinctly unhappy at the moment, and her unhappiness didn't stem from the upcoming race or from Dagger. It stemmed from Raggert.

From the minute the lanky, arrogant trainer had sauntered into the stables, Nicole had taken an instant dislike to him. It was nothing tangible, nothing she could put her finger on. His knowledge was thorough, his loudly boasted credentials impressive. There was just something about him—a cockiness, an icy condescension, that disturbed her greatly. Plus, his attitude toward her was nothing short of appalling.

"So, you're the fellow Lord Tyreham intends to sweep the Derby stakes," he muttered, his dark eyes assessing her. "How old are you, boy? Fifteen?"

"Twenty."

"That old, are you?" he taunted lightly, rubbing a blade of straw between his fingers. "Well, let's see what you can do, especially on that impossible stallion Tyreham insists on entering."

"You're familiar with Dagger?"

"Yup. I was with Lord Lanston when he bought him. Never saw much hope of reforming him. He was too far gone. I was relieved as hell when Lanston sold him. Personally, I think Tyreham's crazy for investing so much time and energy in a wild, reckless lunatic like that stallion. But—" A shrug. "That's the marquis's decision, not mine. In any case, let's get a stableboy to tack him up."

"He's already tacked up," Nicole replied, controlling her temper with the greatest of efforts. "I was about to take a trial run over the course when you arrived."

"Good. I'll oversee your practice."

"There's no need," Nicole heard herself say, despite the fact that Dustin had specifically mentioned to her that Raggert would be doing just that. "Brackley has arranged to time me."

A glint of annoyance. *"I'll* time you. Brackley can tend to the other horses."

"Very well." Nicole turned. "I'll lead Dagger out and meet you at the course's starting point. Are you familiar with the grounds?"

She could actually feel Raggert tense. "Don't be insolent, boy. I'm familiar with everything to do with my job. I make it a point to be. Brackley showed me around the grounds, including the entire course, before I came to find you."

"Fine. I won't be more than a few minutes."

Nicole stalked off, fury welling up inside her as she made her way into Dagger's stall. Deliberately instigating Raggert had been a stupid thing to do, but at that particular moment, she didn't give a damn. Who did the man think he was? Worse, what false veneer had he assumed to convince not only Dustin but Lord Lanston to hire him? Because, competent or not, no trainer could successfully relate to horses with an attitude like Raggert's. He lacked humility and compassion, supplanted instead by an overabundant— and undeserved—feeling of self-worth.

Stroking Dagger's velvet muzzle, she tried to bring herself under control and almost succeeded, until she glanced at the beautiful thoroughbred who was now nuzzling her palm. Raggert's ugly, inaccurate condemnation of Dagger sprang to mind, enraging Nicole anew. Trainer? The fool was no judge of horses. She had half a mind to march into Tyreham and . . .

And what?

She drew herself up short. In the name of heaven, she was merely a jockey, and an inexperienced one at that. Without using the leverage of their personal relationship, how could she run to Dustin and inform him he'd made a huge mistake in hiring Raggert? What grounds did she have—that he'd spoken harshly to her? She was, after all, a mere novice, and he, a seasoned trainer.

No. Alden Stoddard was here on merit and on merit would remain. Until and unless Raggert did something truly wrong, Stoddard's feelings would stay private.

Besides, bickering with the new trainer was the last hindrance Nicole needed right now. Her riding, most particularly her sessions with Dagger, were the only aspect of her existence that were stable, controlled. Her identity, her home, her world—and now her heart—had all been upended. In fact, her personal life was a tangle of complications, all centered around a man who dominated her thoughts like a fine, intoxicating wine.

Especially after last night.

She paused, her hand on Dagger's bridle, a tiny shiver of memory rippling through her. Last night. She'd been so consumed with her own vulnerability that she'd scarcely taken time to consider Dustin's.

He'd shared his dreams with her, opened his heart, and welcomed her in. Never had she imagined such tenderness, such sensitivity from a man of Dustin's ilk—or perhaps she had. Her heart had always viewed him as a man rather than as a marquis. Maybe it was time she heeded her heart's dictates.

Her thoughts shifted to those magical moments of sensual discovery.

Enfolded in Dustin's arms, she'd savored her first taste of passion, cast misgivings to the wind, and let emotion guide her. And, brief though their encounter had been, it had changed everything. After last night, nothing could ever be the same—*she* could never be the same.

Nor could Dustin.

She wasn't certain how, she just knew that to be true. Perhaps it was the wonder in his eyes, the helpless trembling of his body against hers. Or perhaps it was insight—the same insight that had drawn them together from the start and the same insight that was propelling her into the future—an unknown future with undetermined boundaries.

Dustin had sworn to conquer each and every obstacle that thwarted their way, make all her wishes reality. And, God help her, she was starting to believe he just might.

"Good morning, Stoddard."

That deep, unbearably seductive voice that had dominated her dreams resounded behind her.

Slowly, she pivoted—only to find that Dustin was not alone. Beside him was a beautiful, auburn-haired woman with turquoise eyes as clear as a cloudless sky. She was delicate and feminine, and Nicole felt a surge of jealousy so profound it shocked her.

"Good morning, Lord Tyreham," she replied, automatically lapsing into Stoddard's voice, keeping her face carefully devoid of emotion.

Dustin looked like he was biting back laughter. "I have a few people I'd like you to meet."

At that instant, a stout woman scurried up to Dagger's stall. In her arms was clasped the most precious tot Nicole had ever seen, a tot that was battling for his freedom.

"This is Ariana Kingsley, the duchess of Broddington," Dustin was saying. "My brother's wife," he added. "And the wild man in Mrs. Hopkins's arms is my nephew

Alexander." He turned to Ariana. "Meet Alden Stoddard, the incomparable jockey who's going to ride Dagger to fame."

"A pleasure, Your Grace," Nicole replied, her relief so acute it nearly brought her to her knees.

"Mr. Stoddard. I've heard a great deal about you." Ariana's smile emanated genuine warmth, and Nicole could understand why Dustin was so fond of her. "I hope you don't mind our dropping by. I promise we won't get underfoot. We'll only—"

As if to refute his mother's words, Alexander chose that moment to jerk free of his governess's arms, shimmy down her skirts, and crawl furiously off.

Dustin snatched him up before he'd gone ten feet. *"You are incorrigible,"* he proclaimed over his nephew's howling protest. "Would you like to meet Dagger?" Dustin pointed toward the horse. "He's new here. You have to be very gentle with him. You remember—I showed you with the others." In an exaggerated motion, Dustin demonstrated by smoothing his palm down the column of Dagger's neck. "Like this."

Alexander's squirming halted at once, his cobalt gaze fixed on Dagger.

"Would you like to try?" Dustin inquired, urging the child's arm forward.

Eagerly, Alexander reached out.

Nicole smiled, watching as what two minutes ago was a thrashing lion cub and was now a docile lamb petted Dagger's neck and back, his tiny fingers light as feathers, his expression awed.

"He's got an affinity for horses already," she murmured aloud. "I was like that at his age."

"The stables are the only place he's content," Ariana responded with a sigh. "Other than when he's sitting triumphantly amid his scenes of destruction."

"I was also like *that*," Nicole admitted with a grin. She turned to Alexander. "Would you like to watch me ride him?"

The child stared at her, as if attempting to discern the identity of this unknown stranger.

"I was about to take Dagger over the course," Nicole

explained to Dustin. "Raggert"—she nearly choked on the name—"is waiting to time me. If things go well, we'll be making trial runs at Epsom in several days, letting Dagger grow accustomed to the course. In any case, your family is welcome to watch this morning's practice. I'm sure your nephew would enjoy it."

Her eyes met Dustin's for the first time since last night, and everything inside Nicole went liquid with longing. Not only was he magnificent, but he looked so poignantly natural with a child in his arms, and for a fleeting instant, she found herself wishing Alexander were theirs. Recoiling from the realization of how dangerous such thoughts could be—not only to her heart, but to her identity—she averted her gaze, wondering how much longer she could endure this masquerade when she was so in love with Dustin it made her weak.

"That would be wonderful." Ariana beamed.

"Yes, it would," Dustin concurred quietly. He ruffled Alexander's dark hair, then placed him in his mother's arms. "Ariana, you know where the course begins. Why don't you and Mrs. Hopkins take Alexander there, and we'll lead Dagger out in a minute or two."

"Splendid." Ariana gave Stoddard a grateful smile. "Thank you for your patience."

Nicole nodded, watching them make their way out of the stables. "The duchess is lovely," she said quietly. "All you described and more."

"I didn't close an eye last night." Dustin's voice brushed her ear. "Are you all right?"

Swallowing past the lump in her throat, Nicole nodded. "Fine."

"You didn't speak a word the entire way home."

"I had a lot to think about."

"Dammit." Dustin's breath expelled in a hiss, his gaze darting about their section of the stables, now momentarily deserted. "We need to talk. Alone. Tell me when."

"I don't know. My father is not in a particularly generous mood today."

"He wanted to shoot me dead."

"That was my fault. I'm not sophisticated enough to conceal . . . certain things."

Dustin's swallow was audible. "I should have insisted on speaking with him."

"What would you have said?" Nicole asked softly, staring at the ground. She didn't wait for an answer. "Besides, the point is a moot one. Papa doesn't talk when he's angry, he shouts, except when he's truly outraged. In those cases, he stews for a while, then bellows. Evidently, this is one of those cases." She sighed. "Immediately after shutting the door in your face last night, he stalked off to bed. He hasn't spoken to me since. By this evening, he will."

"Derby—" Dustin made a move to hold her, then checked himself. "I'm sorry. I never intended to—"

"Please, Dustin, stop apologizing." On the heels of uttering his given name, and in her normal voice, she glanced about them, needing to verify that they were not being overheard. Reassured, she met his gaze, whispering, "I wanted those moments as much as you did."

Emotion—heated, drenching—surged between them.

"I meant every word I said," Dustin managed huskily.

"I know you did." Nicole had to fight the relentless urge to fling herself into his arms. "But now is not the time to discuss this." She wet her lips, her admission emerging in a breathless rush. "I'm having a hard enough time continuing this pretense in light of what's happened."

A vein throbbed at his temple. "I need to be with you."

"Give Papa a few days. Give *me* a few days to bring him around. Please, Dustin, give me some time."

Time. Her choice of words seemed to incite a private battle within him. Abruptly, he nodded, his intensity clearly unabated, yet somehow simmering beneath the surface. "Take whatever time you need. Whenever you're ready, I'll be here."

"Will you?" she heard herself murmur, searching his face for some palpable assurance.

Emotion darkened his midnight eyes to near black. "The fires of hell couldn't keep me away." His gaze delved deep into hers. "And Derby, in answer to that silent wish you made moments ago, one day the child I'm holding *will* be ours."

Eleven

"That was breathtaking."

Ariana shook her head in amazement, leaning back from where she'd been perched, whip-taut, on a fence near the course's end, straining to see Stoddard and Dagger complete their final lap. "I can't remember the last time I saw such an impressive display of horsemanship. Dustin, you're right." She climbed down to stand beside her brother-in-law. "The Derby is all but yours."

"Two minutes, forty seconds," Raggert called out from a dozen feet away, looking as astounded as Ariana.

"Two and forty," Dustin muttered, his expression pensive. "That beats last year's Derby winner by six seconds. Taking into account that Tyreham's course is similar in terrain to Epsom's, and only several lengths shorter, I'd say that's damned good. Damned, unbelievably good."

He loped over to his jockey. "Stoddard, you've outdone yourself. Do that on Derby Day and first place is ensured."

Nicole touched the brim of her cap. "I'll certainly try, my lord."

A broad grin split Dustin's face. "Do that." He glanced at Raggert, who had just reached them. "Do you still think Dagger is hopeless?"

Nicole blinked, astonished that Raggert had openly supplied Dustin with a negative assessment of Dagger.

The trainer's response astonished her even more.

"I owe Dagger *and* Stoddard an apology," he admitted. "I was too hard on them both. Sorry about that," he said directly to her, a note of respect in his voice. "I had no idea you could ride like that."

"Dagger's the one who makes it possible. But I appreciate your praise." With that, she glanced at Dustin. "I'm going to cool him down, if that's all right, sir. He's tired."

"He's not alone in that regard," Dustin noted aloud. "You look rather peaked yourself. You've been pushing pretty hard these past few days. After Dagger's cooled down, why don't you take a few hours off?"

"Thank you, my lord. I appreciate that." Nicole understood at once that Dustin was giving her the afternoon not only to recoup her strength but to work things out with her father.

"Are you staying at Tyreham?" Raggert was asking.

"Temporarily, yes," Nicole replied cautiously. "Lord Tyreham has been kind enough to let me use one of the vacant cottages while I'm training for the Derby. It allows me more practice time."

"Do you live far from here?"

The queries were innocent enough, but Nicole felt sweat begin to trickle down her back—sweat that had nothing to do with the exertion of galloping the course. "I live in London." She kept her tone as casual as she could. "The East End."

"Ah, that would take some travel time." Raggert bobbed his head sympathetically.

"Yes, too much travel time." She was being needlessly curt, and she knew it. But, apology or not, she couldn't shake her mistrust for this man. And his questions, well-meaning or not, were unnerving her terribly.

As if sensing his rider's unease, Dagger snorted, kicking the dirt.

"Sorry, boy." Nicole patted his back. "I'd best walk him, my lord. If you'll both excuse me . . ." She didn't wait to be formally dismissed. After all, her responsibility was to Dagger, who'd just reminded her he needed cooling down.

So did her father, she reminded herself a half hour later as she approached the cottage.

Taking a deep breath, she turned the key in the lock. "I'm home."

Silence.

Squaring her shoulders, Nicole braced herself for the tempest she was about to stir up. What she'd told Dustin had been the precise truth—her father hadn't uttered a word since she crossed the threshold last night. But the look he'd given her had spoken volumes and, although he'd retired to his chambers posthaste, she'd heard him pacing the floors until dawn.

Silently, she chastised herself for being unable to conceal her guilt and embarrassment until reaching the privacy of her own chambers. Being honest was one thing, being stupid quite another.

She peeked into each room on the first floor, only to find them empty. With a frustrated sigh, she mounted the stairs, bypassing her room and heading directly to her father's.

He was sitting in an armchair, staring off into space with an expression more brooding than angry.

"Papa, are you all right?"

A tired shrug. "I have no answer for you, Nickie."

The anguish in his voice tore at Nicole as his anger never could. Slowly, she crossed the room, kneeling beside the chair. "Dustin let me leave early so you and I could talk."

"That would be fine if I knew what to say."

"I have a wonderful way to begin." With renewed excitement, she seized his hands. "Dagger and I completed Tyreham's course in two minutes and forty seconds."

Her father reacted exactly as she'd prayed he would.

"Two and forty?" His head came up, triumph glittering in his eyes. "That's six seconds faster than last year's winner."

"Yes. And Dustin said the course here is only a few lengths shy of the one at Epsom."

"Bloody hell, you're going to win the Derby!" Nick erupted, nearly crushing her fingers in his. "I knew it. I could feel it. But now it's on the verge of happening." He shook his head in proud amazement. "Damn, I'm proud of you, Elf."

"Thank you, Papa." She held his gaze. "Your pride means the world to me. If I ever lost it, I don't know what I'd do."

One dark brow arched. "You think you're pretty clever, don't you? Bringing me around like that headstrong stallion of yours."

"You know me better than that. Horses excepted, I've never 'brought anyone around' in my life. I haven't the tact or the patience for it. And, even if I did, I certainly couldn't bring *you* around. You're twice as stubborn as Dagger. No, Papa, the reason I spouted out my news was because I wanted to share it with you and because it was the perfect way to break the silence that's separating us. We've always been able to talk, and now is no time to let that change. Shout at me if you must. Bellow out whatever anger or shame you're experiencing, but please don't erect a wall between us. I can't bear that."

"Shout? Bellow? I wish it were that easy." Nick drew a slow, unsteady breath, then exhaled, his words taut with emotion. "When you were three years old and you played too close to the back end of a horse, I shouted. When you were five, and you took it upon yourself to ride bareback without permission, I bellowed. When you were ten, and you sneaked out, spending the night in the carriage so you could accompany me to the Manchester races, I punished you. But you're twenty now, Nickie. You're a grown woman. I can no longer set things right with a word or a deed. Have you any idea how terrifying that is for a father? To realize his child is in danger, and there's not a bloody thing he can do to save her?"

"I'm not in danger, Papa."

"Aren't you? You're getting more and more deeply involved with a man who, quite possibly, wants nothing more than what to him would be a few days, weeks, or months of pleasure, but what to you is the most precious gift you have to offer—a gift that can never be regained or offered again. And I don't only mean the gift of your innocence, either. I mean all that goes with it—your heart, your soul, your spirit. You're just like your mother, Nickie. You can offer no less than all of yourself. Once. To one man. And God help you if it's the wrong man."

"It isn't."

"How can you be so sure?"

Nicole scrutinized her father, insight sparking to life. "You don't believe Dustin is the wrong man, Papa."

"Belief and certainty are very different. In this case, they're worlds apart." Nick scowled. "Besides, we're not discussing me, we're discussing you. I asked how you can be so bloody sure Tyreham is the right man for you?"

Wetting her lips, Nicole addressed her father's question in a way she prayed he'd understand. "You said I'm like Mama, at least in matters of the heart. Well, you're absolutely right. Mama fervently believed that instincts were miracles; gifts bestowed upon us as guides to our future. And how could I doubt her? After all, her instincts guided her straight to the most wonderful man on earth—you. I remember her telling me it took but one glance for her to determine you were her future, a certainty she didn't question once in fifteen years. Papa, I got that same feeling when I met Dustin, although I've spent every waking moment since then challenging my judgment." A shaky sigh. "I suppose that's because much of me is not like Mama but like you, practical, contemplative, considering every possible ramification. But, the fact is, no amount of logic or resistance can alter the simple, inevitable truth—I'm in love with Dustin Kingsley. He's the right man. He has to be because he's the only man I could ever feel this way about. I don't know how to convince you. All I have is a feeling, and feelings come with no tangible evidence to plead their case. They also come with no guarantees, although I understand how badly you want me to have one. Papa." Nicole's voice quavered, and she could taste her own tears. "I love him. I've tried not to. I've done everything I know how to protect my heart. But it's already lost—no, not lost, given. As for my virtue, which you forfeited a whole night's sleep fretting over, it's intact. The ironic thing is that the very man you mistrust is the one who made certain it stayed that way."

A brief flash of relief—gone as swiftly as it appeared. "This isn't only about . . . physical intimacy."

"I know," she answered simply. "Nor is my relationship with Dustin. There's something special between us, something I can't explain. An affinity, a magnetism, an innate understanding that's been there from the start. I don't know where our feelings will lead or even if I'll be able to endure the outcome when it occurs. But I know I must try. If I don't, I'll be empty for the rest of my life. Please, Papa, put aside your protective instincts long enough to remember what it was like between you and Mama. Once you do, help me. I need you now every bit as much as I did when you lifted me onto my first horse and held me so tightly I knew I'd never fall." A rueful smile shone through her tears. "Yes, I've grown. Unfortunately, my problems have followed suit. While I recognize that I must seek my own answers and find my own solutions, it's knowing your strength and love are there that gives me the courage to do so." Her voice dropped to a hush. "I love him so much, Papa."

A wealth of memories darted across Nick's face as he gazed soberly down at his daughter. "I know you do, Elf." Awkwardly, he groped for a handkerchief and dried her cheeks. "I don't mean to make it harder for you. I just"—he cleared his throat—"want so much for you to be happy."

"I realize that." Nicole caught the handkerchief, pressed it between her palms. "I'm a lucky woman. I have two extraordinary men in my life who want my happiness and who always seem able to dry my tears."

"I pray that lasts forever. But, Nickie, if anything should happen . . . if Tyreham should disappoint you, hurt you . . ." Another pause. "I'll be here. Of course, I'll tear him limb from limb first, but, after that—I'm not too old to hold you up and keep you from falling."

"Nor am I too old to ask you to," Nicole whispered. Reaching up, she gave him a hard, swift hug. "Thank you, Papa."

"You'll be wanting to see him again, I suppose?"

The gruff question made her grin. "You suppose right."

"Well, tell him he can come by tonight—for a little celebration." A spark of pride. "Two minutes forty seconds, you said?"

"That's what I said."

"That definitely calls for a drink. Tell Tyreham to be here at eight."

"I could invite him for dinner," Nicole suggested hopefully.

"Yeah? And who's going to cook it?"

Her lips twitched. "I could invite him to *bring* dinner," she amended. "Assuming his cook wouldn't mind supplying it."

Nick considered the request. "I do like that brown sauce she sent over when we first moved in." An exaggerated sigh. "Very well. Tell your marquis that *if* he brings more of that sauce with him, he can come for dinner. Say . . . seven o'clock."

"Yes, Papa." Securing her cap, Nicole bolted.

"That brown sauce tastes good on lamb," Nick called after her. "He can bring some of that, too. And those little iced cakes."

A peal of laughter was her reply, followed an instant later by the closing of the front door.

Moving aside the curtain, Nick glanced out the window, watching his daughter race toward her future.

"Alicia," he murmured softly, raising his eyes to the skies. "It's in your hands now. You gave me my miracle. Please . . . give Nickie hers."

Silence ensued.

But from behind a cloud a ray of sunlight shimmered.

"You and Alexander needn't rush off." Dustin grinned as he walked Ariana to her carriage. "Why, my nephew has much havoc left to wreak. Half the manor remains intact."

"But Mrs. Hopkins remains anything but," Ariana retorted, shifting Alexander from her arms to the carriage seat and indicating his governess, now collapsed against the cushions, snoring. "I only hope the poor woman doesn't tender her resignation the instant we arrive at Broddington."

"Doubtful. Your son is too precious to abandon—unruly or not." Dustin shook his head in amazement as Alexander began digging under the cushions for an undetected toy. "He doesn't even look tired." Leaning in, he ruffled the tiny dark head, chuckling as, for the sixth time that day, Alexander groped for his uncle's upper lip, looking utterly

185

perplexed by the absence of a mustache. "It's gone, little ruffian," Dustin informed him. "Thanks to you. You'll have to find another way to torture me."

"Fear not," Ariana said cheerfully. "He shall." Rising on tiptoe, she kissed Dustin's cheek. "Take care of yourself."

"I intend to. Tell my brother to stop worrying about me."

"Tell him yourself. We'll be back in a fortnight. For the Derby." Ariana's gaze flickered past Dustin, captured by a flash of motion. "I believe your brilliant young jockey wishes to speak with you," she observed, catching sight of Alden Stoddard as he rounded the corner of the manor at a dead run, then—having spied them—halted in his tracks.

Dustin's head jerked around, his brows arching in surprise. "Stoddard?" He cleared his throat. "Is everything all right?"

An awkward nod. "Forgive me, sir. Yes, everything is fine. I had a question, but it can wait. I didn't realize your family was still here. My apologies, Your Grace."

"Nonsense." Ariana waved her hand. "Whatever you need to discuss with Lord Tyreham is obviously important. Moreover, Alexander and I must be on our way." She smiled gratefully. "Mr. Stoddard, I appreciate your letting us witness that remarkable display of horsemanship earlier today. You can be sure we'll be cheering for you in the stands at Epsom."

"Thank you, Your Grace."

"I can't wait to tell my husband how splendidly you ride. We'll both be eager to share in your victory." Ariana's attention shifted to Dustin, her voice dropping to a murmur. "And eager to share in *both* of yours—the one you shall achieve on the turf, and, most especially, the one you shall achieve off it *if* you follow my advice." A poignant spark lit her eyes. "You will follow it, won't you?"

Solemnly, Dustin nodded. "Lord knows how, but yes."

"Good. Then we really will have much to celebrate." With that, Ariana gathered up her skirts. "I'd best get Alexander and myself back to Broddington before Trenton sends out a search party." She scooted into the carriage, rolling her eyes and laughing as Alexander immediately climbed into her lap and began tugging pins from her hair.

Even the coachman was grinning as he shut the door and took up his post at the back.

Dustin waited until the coach had rounded the bend and disappeared before he swung about to face Nicole. "Are you all right?"

"Yes." She kept her voice low . . . and distinctly Stoddard's. "Better than all right, actually. The reason I'm here is to extend an invitation to dinner. That is, if you're free tonight."

He looked utterly stunned. "Did you say an invitation to 'dinner' or to 'duel'?"

Her lips twitched. "Dinner, my lord."

"At your cottage?"

"Um-hum."

"Your father agreed to that?"

"Only if you bring some of your cook's splendid brown sauce." An impish grin. "And something to pour it over, preferably lamb, I believe Papa said. And iced cakes for dessert."

Dustin stared, then burst out laughing. "I see. Am I being blackmailed then?"

"It appears so, my lord."

"Very well. Since the rewards are so great, I'd be delighted to accept your invitation *and* your conditions. Cook's specified items and I will be on your doorstep at . . . ?"

"Seven o'clock," Nicole supplied.

"Seven o'clock it is."

"It's a celebration, by the way. My father was highly impressed by my running time today."

"He should be. You were incredible."

The entranceway door opened. "Pardon me, my lord," Poole announced from the threshold. "But you asked me to summon you as soon as the duchess had taken her leave."

"Ah. Yes." Dustin nodded. "Is Mr. Saxon available to see me now?"

"He's waiting in your study, sir. So, whenever you and Mr. Stoddard have completed your business . . ."

"We're finished now, aren't we, Stoddard?" Dustin asked, his tone as businesslike as if he were addressing his solicitor.

"Yes, my lord. Thank you for answering my question."

Nicole matched his impersonal demeanor with her own. "Good evening." She touched the brim of her cap and walked off.

For an instant, Dustin watched her retreat, marveling at the fact that the delicate, utterly feminine woman he'd held in his arms last night was the same person who'd just ambled off with the unmistakable stride of a boy, not a speck of femininity to be found.

Except by his body, he noted ruefully, shifting to alleviate the sudden constriction in his trousers. Disguise or not, his body hadn't a doubt that Nicole was a woman. He wanted her so much, he throbbed with it.

Poole cleared his throat politely. "My lord?"

"Forgive me, Poole." Forcing his attention back to the matter at hand, Dustin ascended the manor steps. "Have you filled Saxon in on any details?"

"Only that the matter is a delicate one, requiring both physical prowess and utter discretion. The rest I left for you."

"Thank you." Dustin paused. "See that we're not disturbed."

"Of course, sir."

Dustin entered his study, shutting the door and greeting Poole's nephew. "Good to see you, Saxon. I appreciate your coming on such short notice."

The tall, powerfully built fellow rose. "It's good to see you, too, sir. I'm delighted to be able to be of service to you."

"I hear you've established quite a glowing reputation for yourself."

"I enjoy my work, and I'm grateful for the opportunity to pursue it on my own."

"So your uncle mentioned." Dustin poured two drinks, extending one to Saxon. "I won't insult you with words like secrecy or confidentiality. I assume they're ever present in your line of work."

"Indeed they are, sir."

"Very well, then, here's my dilemma." Dustin proceeded to fill Saxon in on the entire situation, from the personal he'd placed in the *Gazette,* to Aldridge sending Stoddard in his stead, to the menacing intruders who'd invaded

Tyreham, to Sullivan's beating and Redley's questionable death—the whole ugly scheme he suspected was undermining the turf, everything except for the fact that the Aldridges were staying at Tyreham.

Saxon listened intently. "Obviously, what you want is to bring the men who threatened you out of hiding so they can lead you to whoever issued their orders."

"Exactly. I have a list of jockeys I suspect are taking bribes, throwing races for money. I intend to call on them."

A nod. "That will serve two purposes—gain information and upset whoever is in charge."

"Hopefully upset him enough to send those hoodlums back to beat me into compliance."

"You do realize, sir, that you're setting yourself up as a walking target."

"Um-hum. A walking target with a very capable carriage driver for an escort. A driver who insists on transporting me everywhere. Why, would you believe the faithful fellow refuses to indulge in even one day off lest I have to abide an inferior substitute? That's how loyal he is."

"A rarity indeed, sir."

"I thought you'd say that."

A corner of Saxon's mouth lifted. "Have you ever considered investigative work, my lord? You're quite good, you know."

Dustin grinned back. "I'm flattered. Now, the remaining question is, how well do you handle a carriage?"

"Nearly as well as I handle unsavory people."

"Excellent. We'll leave for Newmarket tomorrow. The second set is commencing. It'll run until May fourteenth. Most of the jockeys on my list should be there." Dustin tossed off his drink. "Get a good night's rest, Saxon. It's off to Suffolk in the morning."

"Reins in hand, sir."

"Thank you, Atkins. You can go now."

The astonished footman started at the unexpected dismissal, blinking first at Lord Tyreham, then at the closed cottage door, and last at the cart of food he'd just rolled from the manor to the tenants' quarters. "Don't you want me to carry in the trays, my lord?"

"I'll manage."

"But the cart is laden. Surely . . ."

"I'll manage," Dustin repeated firmly. "I appreciate your offer and your help. But Mr. Stoddard's father is ill and doesn't wish to be disturbed. The less fuss—or callers—that intrude on his solitude, the better. Don't worry. Stoddard will assist me. Between the two of us, we'll transfer these trays into the cottage."

"All right, if you say so, sir." With a dubious expression, the footman took his leave.

Dustin waited a full three minutes.

Then he knocked.

"I'm alone," he murmured.

Nicole eased the door open a crack, her eyes bright with laughter. "You're still far too smooth a liar, my lord."

"Let me in and I'll show you how honest I can be."

The door opened the rest of the way, keeping Nicole carefully concealed until Dustin—and the cart—were inside. Then it closed, and she emerged, wearing a simple beige gown, unadorned by anything save her wishing locket.

"Your other dress, I presume?" Dustin managed, drinking in her beauty.

"I'm afraid so. Not terribly impressive, is it?"

His reply was to glance restlessly about. "Where's your father?"

"He'll be down in a minute. He's . . ."

The rest of Nicole's words were stopped by Dustin's mouth. "Kiss me hello," he demanded huskily.

"Yes, my lord." She wound her arms about his neck, kissing him without hesitation or embarrassment.

Enfolding her against him, Dustin inhaled the scent of her hair, reveling in her softness. "I'm glad your father's on his way down," he muttered, burying his lips in hers for a deep, drugging kiss. "If he weren't, my resolutions to give you time wouldn't be worth a damn." He raised his head, his body taut with hunger. "Is that honest enough for you, Derby?"

She blinked, giving him a sensual look that frayed his control still further. "That was magnificent, my lord, as are you. So magnificent, in fact, that were my father not on his way down, I would suggest you burn your resolutions to ashes and kiss me until I forget all the obstacles that so plagued me last night."

Dustin searched her eyes, sensing a change that transcended the light, seductive banter in which they'd been engaging. "Nicole." He framed her face between his palms, frowning as he heard Aldridge's footsteps overhead. "I'm leaving for Newmarket tomorrow. I'll be gone several days."

She was instantly alert. "You're going to speak with the jockeys on Papa's list."

"Yes." He shook his head impatiently. "We can discuss all that in a minute—with your father present. But before he joins us . . ." Dustin glanced at the still-vacant stairway, then back at Nicole. "When I return, we need to talk. And I don't mean about the threats to your father, although I intend to get some answers while I'm in Suffolk. I mean about us and our future. I get the feeling that a few days will give you enough time. Please tell me I'm right, that that's all the time you need. Because, God help me, I don't know how much longer I can wait."

Slowly, she nodded, her amethyst eyes wide, vulnerable. "That's all I need. We'll discuss the future when you return."

God, he wished he had thirty seconds more. To erase the vulnerability from her face. To reassure her.

To tell her he loved her.

No. She deserved better than to hear those precious words blurted in haste. And, as a man who'd waited forever to say them, so did he.

Bending his head, he brushed a light kiss across her mouth. "Fear not, beautiful stargazer. Your father will resume racing in ample time to sweep the summer meetings. You have my word. As for those other obstacles, they're as good as gone."

Gently, he touched her wishing locket, then released her just as Aldridge descended the stairs.

"Hello, Tyreham." The greeting was not quite as stiff as Dustin had anticipated, and the man actually chuckled when he saw the abundant trays of food. "How many armies will be joining us for dinner?"

"None." Dustin grinned. "However, as I was telling Nicole, I'll be away for a few days. Hopefully, this will sustain you during my absence."

"Papa, Dustin is going to Newmarket."

Nick's grin vanished. "When?"

"First thing tomorrow. The second set will be ongoing for several days. I plan to make the most of that time, learn whatever I can. After which, I'll stop and check on Sullivan, then return home." He looked at Nicole. "Incidentally, I don't want you practicing at Epsom until I get back."

Her chin came up. "I'm perfectly capable—"

"I know you are, Derby. But the entire racing community, touts, bookmakers, handicappers, are waiting to descend on the unknown jockey I've entered in the Derby. We can't risk exposing you to crowds. With all their voices simultaneously hammering at you, it would be near impossible for you to remain silent. One wrong word might arouse suspicion, and I needn't elaborate on what that would mean to your Derby entry, not to mention the danger it would expose both you and your father to."

"How will that risk be lessened by your accompanying me?"

Dustin arched a brow. "I'm very resourceful. Trust me. No one will get near you or become suspicious of why they can't if I'm there to oversee the situation. Remember, I've been preparing for these possible complications from the moment I hired you."

"He's right, Nickie," her father inserted. Meeting Dustin's gaze, he added, "Don't worry, Tyreham. She won't go to Epsom. I'll make sure of it myself."

"What do you suggest I tell your new trainer?" Nicole questioned with a hint of distaste. "He's expecting us to move on to the course at Epsom immediately."

"I'll handle Raggert," Dustin assured her. "I'll simply tell him the truth without embellishing on it."

"Meaning?"

"Meaning I'll remind him that I don't want scores of money-hoarders converging on you at once. He needn't be aware that you're a woman to understand some of what you're up against. After all, Stoddard is an unknown jockey riding a questionable mount. I'm sure Raggert will see the prudence of delaying your public trials until my return. Besides, the Derby isn't until the twenty-sixth, and you're already timing well enough to win the bloody thing. Believe me, Derby, Raggert won't have a problem with my orders for you and Dagger to remain at Tyreham. I'll just instruct him to vary the path of the course so Dagger's trials don't become monotonous. We'll have more than enough time to practice at Epsom. The other horses won't arrive until the twenty-fifth, possibly a day sooner. By then, we'll have long since vacated the race course."

"And when do you intend us to return?"

A grin. "On the twenty-sixth. After the other contenders have left the paddock and are lining up. Just in time for the Derby to commence. Relax, sweetheart. I know what I'm doing."

The endearment slipped out of its own accord, and Dustin mentally kicked himself as he saw Nick's jaw tighten a fraction.

He steeled himself for an outburst, one that never came.

"The marquis is right." Aldridge shot Dustin a look that clearly stated he was squelching his personal feelings in lieu of resolving a more crucial matter: ensuring Nicole's safety. "We can't take any chances of being discovered. As it is, I'm uneasy as hell since Raggert got here."

Nicole's head came up. "You feel that way about him, too?"

"Of course. He's the first person staying at Tyreham who actually knows me. I'm skittish every time I go to the window, thinking that maybe he'll pass by and spot me."

"Oh." Nicole's face fell. "I thought you meant—never mind." Her voice trailed off.

Thoughtfully, Dustin studied her reaction. "You don't like Raggert. I sensed that on the course and again now. Why?"

An uncomfortable silence.

"I'd appreciate an answer."

"I'd rather not give one. As usual, I've inserted myself where I don't belong."

"Let me be the judge of that." A long pause. "Nicole?" he prodded.

She sighed. "I swore to myself that I wouldn't address this

issue. It is, after all, none of my business, but, if you insist, no. I don't like Raggert, nor do I trust him."

"Why?"

"Gut instinct. That and the fact that I don't agree with his training methods."

"His training methods?" Dustin's brows arched. "When did you see him train?"

"I didn't, but I've certainly heard him spout his opinions."

"Nicole, the man's qualifications are flawless, as are his references. He worked for Lanston for two years, and the only reason Edmund let him go was because his regular trainer returned from an agreed-upon leave of absence. I myself interviewed Raggert twice. He impressed the hell out of me. He's intelligent and knowledgeable. As for his opinions, we discussed those, too, including the techniques he employs with every manner of thoroughbred imaginable. No, we didn't agree on everything, but he was blunt about his weaknesses as well as his strengths, and I saw absolutely no indication that he was untrustworthy. Further, I've seen him handle horses, and he's more than capable."

Nicole rolled her eyes.

"It's apparent that our instincts conflict here," Dustin concluded. "And, at the risk of sounding pompous, mine are quite good."

"Obviously not as good as mine."

Dustin was torn between laughing and throttling her. "Aldridge?" He turned to her father for corroboration. "What's your opinion of Raggert?"

"I've already told you," Nick replied, with a puzzled glance at Nicole. "He's good. Oh, I've heard he's a little particular about the mounts he works with, but he makes no secret of that fact. If he likes what he's got to train, he's said to be one of the best. Not to mention the fact that he's been on the turf for years. If I remember right, I once heard something about him wishing he could have been a jockey. Unfortunately, nature had other ideas. He grew way too tall and lanky. So he took another path." A shrug. "He's obviously committed to his training."

"But not to what he trains," Nicole countered.

Her father eyed her with tolerant affection—and a dash

of pride. "Not everyone reveres horses as you do, Elf. To a lot of men this is a job. They do it well and with great integrity, but they don't necessarily have a personal attachment to each of their mounts."

"More fools they."

Dustin frowned, troubled by the intensity of Nicole's reaction. "Put intuition aside for the moment. Give me specifics."

"I have none. Other than the fact that he spoke of Dagger as if he were a wild and unwanted beast."

"Well, he was—with everyone but you."

"Raggert had no faith in Dagger's skill or potential."

"He told me that from the start. It was one of the things we disagreed about. I was fully prepared to leave Dagger's transformation to you and my other thoroughbreds to Raggert, but be fair. Raggert's reasons for doubting Dagger were sound. The poor man had endured months of unrewarded efforts at Lanston. He was quick to apologize today when he saw the amazing progress you'd made with our soon-to-be champion."

"Quick to apologize? I'm not a child, Dustin. I don't need pacifying. What I need is a trainer who believes as I do—that every horse can be reached if the right approach is used. He condemned Dagger as hopeless. That's inexcusable."

"To most everyone Dagger *did* appear hopeless."

"Raggert isn't everyone. He's a trainer, and a good trainer would have sensed Dagger's promise. You did. I did. Why didn't Raggert?"

"His instincts failed once."

"He *has* no instincts. Not for horses. He has competence but no instincts."

"Nicole, you're letting emotion interfere with logic."

"I'm seeing things as they are."

"You're unreasonable."

"I'm right."

"I'm hungry," Nick announced. "So if the two of you are going to stand here and bellow at each other, I'll roll that tray into the dining room and eat all the lamb myself."

Dustin's gaze met Nicole's, and, simultaneously, their glares transformed to grins.

"Truce?" Dustin suggested.

"Granted—but only because I don't want Papa to eat my portion."

The three of them pushed the cart through the hall and into the kitchen. Nick proceeded to make up plates of food, which Nicole and Dustin carried into the dining room.

"This must seem odd to you," Nicole commented, laying out the silver. "Setting a table. Serving yourself—in any capacity, much less at mealtimes."

A corner of Dustin's mouth lifted. "This is one argument you're going to lose, Derby. I'm actually more adept in the kitchen than you are."

"Really? When do you have the opportunity to frequent a kitchen?"

"Every time I visit Spraystone. That's Trent's Isle of Wight retreat," he explained, chuckling at Nicole's dubious expression. "I'll have to take you there sometime. It's on the isle's east coast, near the town of Bembridge and not too far south of Osborne Bay. The estate consists of a cottage, an enormous barn, every possible animal you can imagine, acres of land to explore, and a breathtaking charm that defies words. You'd love it. Trent and Ariana certainly do."

"They employ no servants there?"

"Only two, neither of whom live at the cottage. Much of the time Trent and Ariana are on their own. As am I, especially on those occasions when I travel to Spraystone alone, simply to bask in the peace and beauty it offers. On those visits, not only do I survive a total lack of servants but a total lack of even the most basic assistance. Why, not even Ariana and Trent are present to aid in my survival. Yet I do remarkably well—for a marquis, that is."

Nicole flushed. "Touché, my lord. I've done it again—branded you unfairly."

"I might forgive you—for a price."

A golden spark lit her eyes, turning them that magnificent shade of violet. "And what is your price?"

Leaning forward, Dustin hooked a forefinger beneath her chin. "Several minutes alone after dinner," he murmured too quietly for her father to hear in the kitchen. "The entirety of which will be spent kissing me good-bye."

"Such ambitious terms, my lord." She smiled. "I accept."

"Good." He stepped away just before Nick reentered the dining room. Waiting until the older man was seated, Dustin slipped into the kitchen, returning a minute later with a bottle of champagne and three stemmed glasses. "Before we eat, we must properly celebrate by toasting your extraordinary achievement today, Derby." He brandished the first piece of gleaming crystal, placing it on the table before Nicole. "Two minutes forty seconds—you are indeed astounding."

"I . . ." Nicole looked from the champagne to Dustin, her face alight with pleasure. "Thank you, my lord."

"You're welcome," he murmured, savoring her reaction. God, to see that joy on her face—he wanted to give her the world.

Forcibly, he averted his gaze, turning his attention to uncorking and pouring the champagne.

"To Alden Stoddard," he stated simply, raising his glass. "For the brief time he exists, may he take the Derby—and the *ton*—by storm, leaving them with a memory they'll never forget and a record that will go down in history."

"I echo that," Nick declared. "To Stoddard. May he be both the first woman and the fastest man to ever pass the winning post."

"Thank you," Nicole murmured, her voice choked. "I shall do my very best to make that wish a reality."

"Secure it in your locket," Dustin suggested tenderly, "but only for a fortnight. After that, it will be fulfilled and, thus, released."

Nick's glass lowered with a thud, his astonished gaze moving from Dustin to Nicole to her locket.

Abruptly, Nicole jumped to her feet. "This lamb is delicious," she proclaimed, taking up her plate. "I think I'll help myself to another portion. Excuse me." She bolted into the kitchen.

For a long moment, Nick simply gaped, his stare finding its way back to Dustin.

"You know about Nickie's locket?" he managed. "She's never told a soul . . ."

"I realize that." Dustin leaned forward. "Nicole's sharing the story of her locket with me was as precious a gift as the one her mother gave her. And I'm not referring to the locket itself, because what your wife truly gave Nicole, albeit intangible, was far more valuable than any piece of jewelry could ever be. She gave her the gift of dreams and hope and prayers. Well, Nicole has given the same to me. I intend to treasure those gifts not only now but always. More importantly, I intend to cherish—and sustain—the miraculous gifts that inspired their offering, Nicole's trust and, I pray, her love."

"I see."

"Do you?"

"Yes, Tyreham, I do." A glint of something—realization?—flickered in Aldridge's eyes. When it vanished, so did his tension. "I see and I remember. It hasn't been so very long since I fell in lo—ah, Nickie, you're back," he broke off, greeting his daughter as she reentered the room. "The marquis was about to pour another round of champagne."

Nicole blinked. "We've scarcely finished the first round."

"So what?" Nick grinned, handing Dustin the bottle with a definitive nod. "The way I see it, we have a lot to celebrate."

"What exactly happened between you and Papa while I was in the kitchen?" Nicole asked several hours later as she walked Dustin to the door. "For the duration of the evening you behaved like old friends. Also, why was he so willing to give us this time together?"

Dustin captured her hand in his. "This isn't the first time he's allowed us time alone."

"Allowed us, no. Urged us, yes. Dustin, did you hear him when he went upstairs? He was actually whistling. *Whistling*. What on earth happened that I missed?"

"Your father and I toppled one of those supposedly insurmountable obstacles you spoke of," Dustin replied, drawing her into his arms. "A most important one." He tunneled his fingers through her hair. "Kiss me."

"Dustin . . ."

"My price, if you recall." He covered her mouth with his. "Several minutes. That did not include conversation."

Laughing softly, Nicole twined her arms about his neck. "As you wish."

"Ah, my love, this is only the beginning of what I wish for us."

He took her mouth with a possessiveness he made no attempt to hide, fitted her body against his until she shivered at the blatant evidence of his arousal.

"Nicole." He breathed her name, his tongue stroking hers, his arms tightening, drawing her closer, harder, against him. "Do you have any idea how much I want you?"

She was shaking—and not with fear. "I think so," she whispered. "Yes."

"Tell me you want me."

"Oh, Dustin, you already know I want you."

"I dream about being inside you."

"Oh . . . God." Nicole shuddered, clinging to him as his hand shifted, easing upward to cup her breast. Her nipple hardened the instant his thumb brushed across it—once, twice—and without even realizing it, she leaned into the contact, invited more.

"I go up in flames just touching you. When I finally have you, I think I'll die." With the greatest effort, he lifted his head, watching her face as he continued to stroke her nipple. Slowly, he bent, surrounding the hardened peak through her gown, tugging lightly.

She whimpered, and Dustin acted at once, straightening to cover her mouth with his, capturing the muted sound. "You're beautiful," he managed in a voice too rough to be his. "And I'd best stop now before every shred of my sanity dissipates and I forget where we are."

"I've already forgotten," she admitted breathlessly. "But that comes as no surprise to you, does it?"

In answer, Dustin drew away, framing her hot face between his palms. "You have the mistaken notion that I've traveled this road before. I haven't. Ever. With anyone. What I'm feeling now is as new to me as it is to you and equally as precious. If you believe nothing else, believe that, because I'm not leaving this cottage until you tell me you do."

A dreamy smile touched Nicole's lips. "Then perhaps I'll alter my original decision to say I believe you. In that way, I can delay your good-byes indefinitely."

With a groan, Dustin lowered his head again, kissing her

until the very earth seemed to move. "Once I have you, there will be no good-byes," he breathed into her lips. "I'm going to stay inside you, fill you until we're one, pour my soul into yours until neither of us is ever empty again."

"For how long?" Even as the question tumbled out, her amethyst eyes widened with dismay, clearly conveying her desperate wish to recall it.

"Forever." The need was too great, the words emerging with a will all their own. "Nicole, don't you understand? I love you."

The declaration hovered, then sank in, feeling more right than even Dustin had imagined.

Nicole's lips trembled, and two tears trickled down her cheeks.

Irrational fear tightened Dustin's chest, and his arms locked about her, staying any chance of flight. "Sweetheart, don't be frightened. And for God's sake, don't pull away. You don't have to answer. You don't have to say a bloody thing. I promised you time, and I intend to give it to you. Please darling, don't cry."

"I won't pull away. I can't help crying. And frightened? I'm more than frightened. I'm terrified."

"Why? Because I love you?"

"No," she replied, her slender body quivering with emotion. "That alone wouldn't terrify me. The reason I'm terrified is because I love you, too."

Twelve

Newmarket was bustling with activity, much as Dustin had expected. With the second spring meeting commencing the next day, thoroughbreds were beginning to arrive, both from the nearby stables and from afar by rail, and anxious owners were muttering to trainers who, in turn, were issuing last-minute instructions to their head lads.

"Shall I accompany you, my lord?" Saxon inquired quietly as Dustin alit from the carriage.

"That won't be necessary, no. I have yet to delve deep enough to frighten whoever's at the helm of all this into ordering his hoodlums to stifle me. However, my *open* and intensive grilling of his conspiring jockeys should change that." Dustin's gaze swept the small crowd of people. "Even then, I doubt those bastards would be stupid enough to accost me in the center of Newmarket."

"Hardly, sir. Still, I won't venture far. Just in the event you need me."

"I appreciate that, Saxon." Dustin withdrew his timepiece and glanced at it. "I'll meander through the paddock and see who's about. Then, I'll pay a visit to the Jockey Club and finalize the details for my entries at Epsom. I don't expect to learn too much today. Many of the jockeys are still arriving. Still, it's a start. Tomorrow will be even more productive."

"Yes, sir."

With the impersonal nod one would give one's driver, Dustin strode off, making his way to the front of the stands along the Rowley Mile Course. Casually, he surveyed the thoroughbreds, sizing up their potential out of sheer force of habit.

"Tyreham."

A familiar voice brought him around, and Dustin turned to see a tall, impeccably dressed gentleman approach.

"Lanston," Dustin greeted his friend, "good to see you."

"And you." The earl reached his side. "I thought you were ensconced at Tyreham with the trainer I wish I'd never given away—least of all to you."

Dustin chuckled. "I was and I am. But I had business in Suffolk and couldn't resist assessing things at Newmarket."

"Are you entered in this meeting?"

"No. As you just pointed out, I'm preoccupied with getting things in order at Tyreham. So I withdrew all those entries I'd scheduled for the upcoming fortnight from this meeting at Newmarket straight through the Knowlet Stakes at Manchester."

"Why? Because you wouldn't win?" Lanston raised an amused brow.

"No, because I never do things by half measures, as you well know."

"Well, take heart. You wouldn't have won anyway, at least not at Newmarket. I've entered three of my prize mounts in the Two-Year-Old Plate, the Maiden Plate, and the Rous Stakes, respectively. I intend to sweep all three races."

"Excellent. I wish you the best of luck. May you do precisely as you proclaim."

Surprise flickered across Lanston's patrician features. "It's not like you to be so magnanimous, Dustin. Especially when I know bloody well that your plans for the remainder of the racing year hinged on retaining Nick Aldridge, who's injured and out of the country indefinitely."

"True. Well then, I suppose I'm far more charitable then even I realized."

"Hah." The earl's pale eyes glinted. "More likely, your

good nature spawns from the rumors I've been hearing about your anonymous Derby contender."

Dustin's expression was the epitome of innocence. "Anonymous? Really, Edmund. You, of all people, know who I'm entering. You sold Dagger to me."

"I wasn't talking about the stallion, although Lord alone knows how you expect that maniacal demon to take the Derby. I was referring to your new jockey—Stoddard, I hear his name is."

"You hear correctly. And, if I might be so bold as to offer some advice, I'd suggest that should you be entered in the Derby—withdraw. You'll only lose."

"That sure, are you?" Lanston inquired idly, brushing an imaginary speck off his sleeve. "I'm impressed. Tell me about this fellow."

"No."

Lanston started. "What?"

A broad grin. "You heard me. I'm not going to reveal one bloody detail about Stoddard, other than what's listed in the sheet calendar. You'll simply have to wait and see for yourself."

"Surely your strategic silence doesn't apply to your friends?"

"It applies to everyone. Stoddard is new at this, as you're aware, and I don't want anyone upsetting him or breaking his concentration. Not a tout, a backer, even a close friend who, despite our long-standing association, also happens to be a competitor. No, Lanston, this is one victory I mean to protect . . . and to savor." Dustin patted the earl's shoulder. "Once the race is over, Raggert is welcome to fill you in on every aspect of Stoddard's training. He timed the lad yesterday, as a matter of fact. Stoddard is already besting last year's winner by more than a nose, and that's without the advantages handicapping will afford us, given the meager number of races Dagger has taken part in."

Lanston kept his face carefully devoid of reaction, the ever-so-slight dilating of his pupils the only indication of his concern. "I see. Well, I'll keep that in mind." He cleared his throat. "And Raggert? He's working out satisfactorily, I presume?"

"He only started yesterday, but with qualifications such

as his, I expect he'll be an asset to Tyreham's stables." A knowing twinkle lit Dustin's eyes. "By the way, should your inquiry about Raggert—uttered on the heels of my refusal to discuss Stoddard—be a reminder of the colossal favor you did me, issued in the hopes of inciting my guilt, you may save your breath. I've saved your neck on more occasions in the past than I'd care to recount. So consider us even. If, however, you are truly concerned with my view of Raggert's skills, ask me again at Epsom. By then, I'll have watched his training methods long enough to render an opinion."

"You're certainly in high spirits," Lanston asked with a wry grin. "Even cockier than usual."

"I suppose I am." Abruptly, Dustin broke off, his gaze shifting to the paddock.

"What is it?" Lanston asked, following Dustin's stare to the two jockeys who'd appeared.

"Someone I'm most eager to speak with."

"Parker? Or Cralley?"

"Parker."

"Why? Are you thinking of retaining his services?"

"Hardly," Dustin muttered. "But I do have a host of questions for him." He swung back to face Lanston. "Have you seen Alberts, by the way?"

"At Newmarket, you mean?" Slowly, Lanston shook his head. "Actually, I haven't seen Alberts race since you discharged him. No one was particularly eager to take him on, knowing how displeased you were with his abilities."

"Well, I hope to discuss those very abilities with him. So, if you happen to spy the fellow, let him know I'm looking for him."

"Of course." Lanston studied Dustin thoughtfully. "You aren't reconsidering your decision to dismiss him, are you?"

"Not for a moment." Dustin cleared his throat. "Edmund, would you excuse me? I want to speak with Parker before he's immersed in preparations for tomorrow."

"Of course. Will I see you at the Jockey Club later?"

"Absolutely. I have to collect Stoddard's license and resolve a few details with the Stewards."

"And then?" A corner of Lanston's mouth lifted. "You do intend to stay for a portion of the meeting, don't you—to witness my triumphs?"

"I'll be here for a day or two. After which, I must get back to Tyreham and prepare for the Derby."

"Splendid. That's more than enough time for me to gloat over my soon-to-be victories."

"Hmm?" Dustin's mind was far away. "Oh, your champions, yes." He patted his friend's shoulder. "I'll buy the victory drinks. In fact, I'll begin with a prelude-to-victory drink. I'll meet you at the Jockey Club in an hour."

Leaving the earl, Dustin wound his way around to the paddock, strolling up to Parker. The jockey stood beside his mount, assessing the competition, his back to Dustin.

"What are you contemplating?" Dustin asked quietly. "How to win this race or how best to lose it?"

Parker's head snapped around, and he stared at Dustin as if seeing a ghost. "W-what?" He swallowed, obviously attempting to bring himself under control. "Aren't you the marquis of Tyreham?"

"I am."

"You must have mistaken me for someone else. Who are you looking for, m'lord?"

"You." Dustin glanced about the paddock. "How much did they offer you to throw this one? Five hundred pounds? More?"

Parker clutched the saddle of the thoroughbred beside him, his eyes darting about frantically. "No one's approached me on this meeting. I swear it."

"But they've approached you in the past?"

Sweat trickled down Parker's jaw.

"The way I see it, you can answer me now or I can address my concerns to the Stewards. With very little effort, I'll have your license revoked and ensure you don't ride anywhere for a long, long time."

"And if I answer?"

"Then I'll turn around, retracing my steps from this paddock and retaining my silence. Given, of course, that you assure me you've thrown your last race." Dustin's stare was icy. "Well?"

"Twice," the lad managed, his voice so low Dustin had to

strain to hear it. "I only did it twice. Once at Doncaster, once at York. They gave me two hundred fifty pounds the first time, four hundred the second."

"Who did? Who paid you?"

Again Parker's gaze swept the area. "I don't know their names."

"Describe them."

"Two men, one tall, the other heavyset with pale eyes and muscles thick enough to crush me. I know—he used them on me when I balked about throwing the second race." The boy's mouth trembled. "Please, Lord Tyreham, if they find out I told you this . . ."

"No one's going to find out. You're going to answer one final question, and then I'm going to walk away, and you can tell all your nosy pals, who at this very moment are straining to eavesdrop on our conversation, that I'm considering offering you a retainer for next season."

A frightened nod. "What's the question?"

"During these visits, did the men mention any names—most particularly the names of whoever sent them? Think, Parker. Think hard."

Brow furrowed, Parker struggled to remember. At last, he shook his head. "No, m'lord. Never. They didn't do much talking. They told me what they wanted, threatened me if I opened my mouth, and disappeared. I only saw them three times—when they made their first offer, when they paid me and ordered me to throw the second race, and when they paid me for that race. I haven't seen them since. And I don't want to." He dragged his forearm across his sweat-drenched face. "Please, m'lord. That's all I know."

"I believe you."

The jockey turned frightened eyes to Dustin. "Are you going to report me?"

"No. But, Parker, don't throw another race. Ever," Dustin warned, his lethal words a direct contrast to his tone and expression, both kept purposely affable for the benefit of passersby. "If those men should reappear, refuse them—threats or not. Otherwise, you can bid the turf good-bye. Is that clear enough?" He waited only for Parker's emphatic nod. "Excellent. Your colleagues will never suspect a thing.

Good day. And good luck in tomorrow's race. May you run fortuitously and honestly."

Turning, Dustin ambled off, satisfied that he'd acquired all the information Parker had to give.

Which wasn't a bloody thing more than he'd already known.

The next two days proved equally futile.

Other than chatting with Lanston and concluding the final details pertaining to Stoddard's Derby entry, Dustin was stymied at every turn. Of the additional seven jockeys he sought, three refused to say a word, their fear of physical harm obviously more powerful than their worry over losing their licenses; one took ill and didn't ride; and three provided descriptions of the blackmailers that were nearly identical to Parker's.

By the third day, Dustin was thoroughly disgusted, and more than a little uneasy. He hated leaving Nicole for so long, partially because he felt more secure when he was there to guard her tenuous role as Alden Stoddard, and partially because he missed her so much he ached with it.

For the umpteenth time in three days, his thoughts gravitated back to that crucial moment in the cottage doorway, the moment when Nicole had offered him her heart.

The reason I'm terrified is because I love you, too.

Her words, the look in her eyes, were ingrained in Dustin's mind with all the clarity of the most vivid rainbow.

He'd won her love.

Now it was time to obliterate her terror.

With a wave of gratitude, Dustin acknowledged the crucial support he'd gained during their celebratory feast. Nick Aldridge had, at last, crossed that invisible threshold between certainty and uncertainty, thus becoming an ally. In addition, Nicole had finally agreed to discuss their future together; hell, to even admit they *had* a future together.

Still, he was a long way from realizing that future. He had to resolve this blasted mystery, give Aldridge back his life, and, most importantly, convince Nicole that their love could—*would*—triumph over their differences, sustain whatever trials life had to offer.

None of which he was accomplishing here. In fact, he was wasting precious time that could be spent looking for his one-time jockey, Alberts, who had doubtless been alerted to Dustin's interrogation by now, and sprinted as far away as possible; time that could be spent preparing for the upcoming Derby.

Time that could be spent with Nicole.

He had to leave Newmarket. He'd stop only long enough to ensure Sullivan's well-being, then return to Tyreham.

Resolutely, Dustin headed toward the spot just outside the racing grounds where he and Saxon had prearranged to meet.

Halfway there, he stopped.

Directly before him, angled and empty, was his carriage, several hundred feet from where he'd left it. Alongside the carriage stood Saxon who, upon glimpsing his employer, signaled him by indicating the wiry man who was struggling to free himself from Saxon's iron grasp.

Evidently, Alberts hadn't bolted fast enough.

"My lord?" Saxon began as Dustin reached his side. "Forgive me, sir, but I was bringing the carriage around as you instructed, when this poor fellow—Mr. Alberts, I believe he said his name was—stepped in my path. I tried to veer off, but one of the horses didn't respond fast enough and clipped the gentleman's shoulder. Mr. Alberts is being most noble about this, assuring me he's unharmed." Saxon glanced at the sputtering man, whose head was lowered in a frantic attempt to avoid being recognized. "But I'd feel infinitely better if you would check for yourself. I wouldn't want to be responsible for injuring someone."

Dustin's stunned gaze flickered from Alberts to Saxon.

Saxon arched one brow ever so slightly.

Stifling laughter, Dustin joined in the game. "Of course I'll check. Alberts, did you say?" With apparent surprise, he caught the jockey's forearms, shifting him from Saxon's hold to his own. "Why, it *is* you. Alberts and I are well acquainted," he explained to Saxon. "In fact, he once rode for me. What a coincidence that it's my carriage he happened to stumble into."

"I didn't stumble," Alberts muttered, raising his chin as he realized his anonymity was gone. "This blasted driver of yours nearly ran me down. I was leaving Newmarket when he sped out of nowhere."

"Leaving Newmarket?" Dustin frowned, outwardly puzzled. "But I assumed you'd just arrived. I've been here since the onset and haven't seen any sign of you."

"I-I'm not racing." A dark look. "You, better than anyone, know why. You're the one who ruined my reputation when you discharged me."

"No, Alberts. That you accomplished on your own." A thoughtful pause. "If you're not racing, why are you here?"

"Is it against the law for a man to cheer his friends on?"

"Only if the reason he's cheering them on is because they're throwing races and sharing illegal profits with him."

A flicker of fear. "I don't know what you're talking about."

"Don't you? It makes good sense to me. If you can't get a job, you can't throw a race. But you can find substitute riders who, if they're willing to supply you with a portion of their earnings, you agree to introduce to the appropriate backers. Could you have come to Newmarket for that purpose?"

Again, Alberts began to struggle. "Like I said, I came to see my friends, but I changed my mind. I was leaving when this bloody madman almost killed me."

"Well, it appears you survived the ordeal," Dustin observed, glancing at the supposedly injured arm which, like its counterpart, was moving to and fro in Alberts's attempts to free himself. "Therefore, I needn't summon a physician. However, I have a fine idea. As it happens, I'm also on my way out. Permit me to escort you wherever it is you wish to go."

"I don't want you to escort me anywhere. I'll find my own way."

"Nonsense. Taking you to your destination is the least I can do. After all, it was my driver who nearly struck you down." Dustin shoved Alberts into the carriage and climbed in after him, firmly shutting the door in his wake. "Now, where was it you were heading? Or shall I say, fleeing to? And which of the jockeys at this meeting have you convinced to forfeit their races?"

Alberts groped at the carriage's other door handle, only to

find his escape blocked by Saxon's formidable presence. "What do you want from me?" he demanded.

"Answers." Abandoning the restraint he'd exhibited while in public, Dustin leaned forward, coiled and ready to strike. "You collected a thousand pounds for throwing my races at the fall meeting. Who paid you?"

"No one."

"Shall I beat the information out of you? I'd be delighted to. In fact, I'd feel vindicated."

The jockey paled, balking at the leashed violence in Dustin's tone. "What do you aim to do with me?" he asked, his fists clenching and unclenching in his lap.

"That depends on whether or not you answer me." Dustin's jaw tightened menacingly. "Consider this, Alberts. You're in my carriage, alone and unarmed. You're also without a job, thanks to your unscrupulousness. No one would notice or give a damn if you were to disappear—and I don't mean only from Newmarket. Now, I repeat, who paid you?"

Albert's pallor intensified. "Two men," he blurted. "Not counting their friend with the scars. They told me what they wanted, offered me enough money to make it worth my while, and disappeared."

Dustin had stopped listening an instant earlier. "Their friend with the scars?"

Recognizing his *faux pas*, Alberts again searched frantically for a way out, this time gauging the distance between Dustin and the door.

"Don't even consider it," Dustin warned, maneuvering himself until he was angled on the carriage seat. "Now, tell me about this scarred man."

"There's nothing to tell. He showed up at the paddock for a minute, gave the other men some instructions, then he left. The brawny one and the black-eyed one did the talking, at least to me."

"Their friend—describe him. Where were his scars, on his face?"

"No. On his forearm. Lots of them." Alberts shuddered. "It wasn't pretty. Neither was he. He was hard as hell looking, like he'd just as soon kill you as not. The kind you don't want to meet on London Bridge after midnight."

Renewed fear slashed across his face. "The kind you don't want to cross. Understand?"

Dustin lunged forward and grasped Alberts's shirt, dragging him up off the seat. "I understand. Now, it's time you did the same. I want you to tell me every bloody detail you remember about this scarred man. Then I want you to get on a ship and take an extended holiday. Not only because you're terrified of this scoundrel who, if he learns you've been talking to me, will take you apart piece by piece, but because your already floundering career will be over if you remain. Why? Because I'll report you to the Jockey Club and ensure that your license is revoked and that you don't work another day for the rest of your life. So, I'd suggest you take that vacation." Dustin slid one hand into his pocket and extracted some bills. "I'll give you two thousand pounds. Disappear until the fall meeting. Maybe by then those ruffians will have forgotten you, and, if I'm in a generous mood, I might help you get another retainer, albeit small. Maybe. And that's only if I feel confident that you never intend to act unlawfully again." Dustin dangled the money before Alberts's ashen features. "Well? Have we a deal?"

"Yeah." The jockey snatched the money. "He's tall, maybe a little bit shorter than you. He's got a thin nose and light brown hair. His build is only average, not real powerful or anything. But he's scary looking—it's something in his eyes. They're like chips of ice. Blue ice. Also, it's the way he moves. Like a cat about to spring for its supper."

"How was he dressed?"

A shrug. "Same as me. Only not in racing colors. He looked like a regular stable hand. He's not a blue blood, if that's what you mean."

"That's what I mean." Dustin searched Alberts's face, then flung him away. "I'm going to make sure no one is about who might ask questions. When I announce that it's safe, I want you to get out and walk away. Don't repeat this conversation to anyone and don't show your face in England until September. Now, do *you* understand?"

Nervously, Alberts nodded.

"Good." Dustin eased from the carriage and stretched, glancing idly about. Other than Lanston, who was chatting a short distance away with several other owners, the area was clear. Dustin leaned into the carriage, muttering, "On your way, Alberts."

The wiry man was out and gone in a flash.

"Did things go to your liking, my lord?" Saxon inquired, strolling around from the other side of the carriage.

"Yes. Finally, I learned something I didn't already know." Dustin's eyes narrowed. "But before I divulge the details, how the hell did you know who Alberts was, much less that I wanted to detain him?"

Saxon's lips curved. "Unearthing information is what you pay me to do, sir. While you've been probing for clues, I've been listening outside the stands. One of the benefits of being a driver is that in the eyes of the aristocracy you're invisible. Two of the Jockey Club Stewards wandered by me, engaged in conversation. When I heard your name mentioned, my ears perked up. They were discussing Alberts and his failing career. One of them brought up the fact that you'd dismissed him. I found myself wondering if he could be one of the jockeys you intended to interrogate. An hour later, Parker—who I believe was the first rider I saw you question and who, incidentally, was the pathetic lad who'd intended to throw a race and share the profits with Alberts—waylaid a man as he arrived at Newmarket. He called the fellow Alberts, informed him that their 'arrangement' was off, and suggested that he leave, given that you were grilling those you suspected of throwing races. As luck would have it, you were, at that moment, making your way from the course. I saw you. So did Parker and Alberts. Parker darted off. Alberts prepared to flee. I couldn't allow that to happen. So, at the right instant, I modified his plans. It was simply a matter of timing."

Dustin shook his head in amazement. "Your uncle was right. You are extraordinary."

"Just doing my job, sir. But, thank you." Saxon inclined his head. "I assume you were on your way to advise me that we'll be leaving Newmarket?"

"Definitely. I have one stop to make in Suffolk. Then, it's home to Surrey."

"Dustin?" Lanston strolled over, a perplexed look on his face. "Is everything all right?"

"Yes, why?"

"I saw Alberts leap from your carriage and bolt. I thought perhaps you'd had words."

"We did."

"About last fall?"

"About the differences that prompted my discharging him, which I hope I've now resolved." Dismissing the subject, Dustin clapped Lanston on the arm. "In any case, I was about to come looking for you to congratulate you again on your victories and to say good-bye. I must be heading back to Tyreham. My Derby preparations await. Will I see you at Epsom?"

The earl gave an adamant nod. "I wouldn't miss it. I look forward to witnessing this phenomenon of yours, this Stoddard fellow, racing Dagger." A challenging lift of his brows. "Who knows? Perhaps I'll offer you some healthy competition during the remainder of the meeting."

"Perhaps." With a broad grin, Dustin climbed into the carriage. "But I wouldn't count on it."

"You can't count on anything. That's the most important lesson I can teach you."

Nick Aldridge paced about the cottage sitting room, his brow furrowed in concentration as he instructed Nicole.

"I know that, Papa." She perched on the edge of the sofa. "After all these years of watching you, I've learned that one can rely only upon one's wits."

"Good girl. Because you can't control the weather, the conditions of the grounds at Epsom that day, or any unplanned complications that might occur during the race. All you can do is know that bloody course like the back of your hand and size up the other jockeys to the best of your ability." Halting, Nick leveled his gaze at Nicole. "We'll deal with how to handle the other jockeys—averting their various maneuvers to crowd you out, identifying the best ways to thread through their midst, and a host of other techniques—next week. But for now, let's deal with you. To begin, where would you ideally be situated if you had your pick of the lots drawn?"

"At the rail, of course."

"What if you weren't?"

"Then I'd look for the first opportunity to squeeze by and get there." She grinned, holding up her palm to ward off her father's oncoming admonishment. "'Look' is the wrong choice of words. Sense. I wouldn't spend an extra minute watching the other jockeys. I'd only give them an occasional glimpse to assess their respective positions. To avert my head would be distracting to Dagger and detrimental to our speed."

"Pacing," Nick corrected. "Pacing is what will ultimately win you this race, Nickie. And pacing does not always mean speed."

"No, it doesn't. Especially not on the Epsom course. I have to contend with that difficult turn at Tattenham Corner, not to mention the steep downhill section. Those are the times when I'll have to slow down, be precise."

"Exactly. Precise and smooth. The slightest hesitation could cost you the race. Now, combine your memories and your instincts and tell me, how would you take the Derby course?"

Nicole frowned. "I'd feel better about answering that question if I'd already ridden it."

"Don't start that argument again. You're not venturing from Tyreham until your marquis returns. Now, answer my question."

"Very well." She sighed. "The Derby course is in the shape of a horseshoe. The first section is on the ascent, and I'll reach the top of the hill upon rounding Tattenham Corner. Here's where my pacing must be perfect. If I ease Dagger around the bend without breaking stride or pushing too hard, we'll sail easily into the descent. If not, we'll fly into it awkwardly and either lose footing or momentum— either of which could cost us the race. The winning post is only a short distance from there."

"So you'll be prepared for it, there's a slight rise leading into the winning post. But if you've mastered the descent, that should pose no problem." Nick rubbed his hands together. "Having accomplished all that, at what point do you make your effort, breaking into a gallop that will leave the others far behind and award you first place?"

Nicole smiled at her father's obvious bias. "Fifty yards from the winning post."

"Excellent. Better than excellent." Nick positively beamed. "You've never even ridden the course, and your feel for it is exceptional. Between what I'm teaching you and your natural instincts, no other jockey has a prayer."

"Remember, Papa, count on nothing," Nicole teased, rising to hug him. "In all seriousness," she added, sobering, "my instincts alone wouldn't be enough—not without these sessions of ours. You know more about racing than anyone on the English turf. I'm blessed to have your guidance and your teaching, both of which are invaluable." A shadow flickered across her face. "At least some trainers are committed to what they do."

"We're back to Raggert again."

"He hasn't wandered from my side once during the past three days. And, believe me, his intentions aren't to praise Dagger or encourage me. All he does is grill me incessantly and inspect Dagger as if the poor stallion is bound to slip up and show his true colors at any given moment. Evidently, Mr. Raggert thinks I need constant supervision, and that with Dustin away, it's his job to provide it." She shook her head in frustration. "Honestly, Papa, if Raggert spent half as much time scrutinizing the horses as he does scrutinizing me, I might actually believe he's as splendid a trainer as you and Dustin claim."

"Is it that bad?" Nick scowled. "I hadn't realized he was asking you questions. About what?"

"Don't start worrying." Nicole patted her father's arm reassuringly. "He hasn't a clue who I really am. His questions are all for Stoddard—where Stoddard is from, where did he apprentice, how did he come to work at Tyreham, that sort of thing."

"What did you tell him?"

"That I'd apprenticed in Scotland, near the small village where I was born. That Lord Tyreham happened upon me during one of his summer visits to Balmoral and was impressed with my horsemanship. Therefore, when Nick Aldridge was unable to answer the personal, Lord Tyreham summoned me to England and to Tyreham. End of story."

"Did you mention this fanciful yarn of yours to Lord Tyreham before using it on Raggert?"

"It's not fanciful, Papa. It's as close to the truth as I could get, other than the part about my living in Scotland. As for discussing the details with Dustin, no I hadn't the chance, but I will. The instant he returns from Newmarket."

"You don't consider invented visits to Balmoral fanciful?"

"In Dustin's case, they're neither fanciful nor invented. His father was a close friend of Her Majesty's, so the Kingsleys spent many summer days at Balmoral. During one visit, in fact, Dustin saved the queen's life. That's how he acquired his title—it was bestowed upon him by Queen Victoria."

"I'm impressed." Nick regarded her intently. "More importantly, so are you, not by the title but by the way in which it was earned. Lord Tyreham saved someone's life, our queen's, no less. That's quite a feat." A satisfied nod. "As your father, I'm also very pleased that you and Tyreham have shared so many personal anecdotes. The acquiring of his title, your locket . . ." Her father shot her a meaningful look.

"All right, Papa, you've made your point. Yes, I told Dustin about the locket. And about Mama." A soft smile. "The memories just seemed to spill forth on their own."

"That's as it should be." Nick cleared his throat. "Let's get back to Raggert. Even if his questions are innocent, why the hell is he so curious about Stoddard? Jockeys aren't his business, horses are."

"My view exactly."

"Well, I intend to report this to Tyreham when he returns. He should be aware that Raggert is poking around where he doesn't belong." Another purposeful glance. "He should also be aware of the story you conjured up about Stoddard's background."

"I'll tell him." Nicole's eyes twinkled. "On the way to Epsom. Where I intend to dash off to the very instant Dustin sets foot on this estate."

As if on cue, a knock sounded at the door.

Nick tensed, his gaze darting toward the hallway.

"I'll see who it is," Nicole declared at once, reaching up to confirm that her cap was still in place. "But there's only one person who ever visits us here." She crossed the room in a flash. "Dustin must be home."

She reached the front door . . . then held her breath.

"It's Tyreham."

Those were exactly the words she'd waited to hear, and the voice she'd awaited speaking them.

Turning the key, she opened the door, her heart pounding as she gazed up at the man she loved, simultaneously trying to still her trembling.

"Welcome home, Lord Tyreham," she greeted him in Stoddard's voice.

Those midnight eyes delved into her with an intimacy that made her weak. "Stoddard."

Dustin stepped inside, shut the door.

And Nicole was in his arms.

"God, I've missed you," he murmured, seizing her mouth in a kiss of undisputed possession.

"I missed you, too." Reluctantly, she eased back, searched his face. "Are you all right?"

"Now I am." He cradled her against him for a moment, as if deriving strength from the very feel of her.

"Papa's right inside," she informed him softly.

"I assumed as much. Otherwise, I'd be doing much more than holding you." He tilted her chin up. "I'm taking you to the cabin tonight. We're going to talk."

Her insides melted. "Only talk?"

That devastating smile. "Knowing what happens when you're near me, I doubt it." His expression intensified, his knuckles tenderly caressing her cheek. "For now, I want to hear only two things. First, that you and your father are well and safe."

"We are."

"Next, that you love me."

Nicole's lips trembled. "I do," she whispered.

"Say the words."

"I love you."

"And I love you." Again, he kissed her, this time with a wealth of poignant emotion. "I'm never going to let you go, Nicole. Never."

"Nickie?"

Her father's voice intruded, and Nicole stepped away, as loath as Dustin to break the intimacy of the moment. "Yes,

Papa," she called back, her voice unsteady. "It's all right. It's Lord Tyreham." She gave Dustin a shaky smile. "That's as tactful as Papa gets. He knows it's you. He's announcing himself before he descends upon our privacy."

"I realize that." Dustin captured her hand, intertwined their fingers. "Will you come with me tonight? To the cabin?"

"You know I will," Nicole heard herself reply. Was it only wishful thinking or had she just offered him far more than a stroll?

"You're back." Nick emerged, relief flooding his features. "Is Sully well? Did you learn anything?"

"Lord, I didn't even ask you how Sully was," Nicole burst out, blushing profusely as she recognized the implication of her statement.

"You had other things on your mind," her father surprised her by saying—with a grin, no less. "I didn't."

"Sullivan is up and about, restless and irritable," Dustin reported, Nicole's hand still clasped firmly in his. "He and Tuttle have become fast friends. Evidently, in between Sullivan's grumbling, they play cards and argue over which one of them has cheated." A corner of Dustin's mouth lifted. "On the whole, your friend is very much himself. The bruises should fade enough over the next week or so for him to leave his quarters and resume his life without having to answer a lot of disagreeable questions. In fact, we're going to have him as a houseguest the week of the Derby."

"Sully's coming?" Nicole demanded, seeing her father beam from ear to ear.

"He is indeed," Dustin confirmed. "I've arranged for him to travel to Tyreham the day before the Epsom meeting commences. Should anyone inquire about his presence, we'll simply say he and I are discussing a retainer."

"You'd do well to make that ploy a reality," Nick declared loyally. "Sully's one of the finest jockeys in the business, successful, with years of experience. Honest as they come, too."

Dustin arched a brow. "What makes you think the explanation is entirely a ploy?"

"It isn't?" Nicole's eyes widened with pleasure.

"Absolutely not. Oh, it's a useful excuse, given the circumstances. But, that aside, I'd be honored to have Sullivan ride for me." His gaze returned to Nick, a sparkle of humor illuminating his eyes. "That is, if you're amenable to the idea. After all, since I mean to swiftly expose whoever's threatening you, you will soon be signing an exclusive retainer with me. And I'd never consider hiring anyone you'd prefer not to work with."

"I'll manage," Nick responded, visibly moved by the extent of Dustin's generosity. "Thank you, my lord."

"For what? For having two fine jockeys like you and Sullivan on retainer? It's I who should be thanking you."

Nicole tapped Dustin's sleeve. *"Two* fine jockeys? Where does Alden Stoddard fit into that list?"

Dustin's smile enveloped her in tenderness. "Stoddard is in a class by himself."

"Speaking of Stoddard, Raggert's been bothering Nicole," Nick announced.

Instantly, Dustin tensed. "Bothering her? How?"

Sighing, Nicole relayed the situation to Dustin as she had to her father, including the fictitious background she'd created to ward off Raggert's suspicions. "Perhaps I'm overreacting," she concluded, "but he makes me so uncomfortable. And I still can't rid myself of this feeling that he's not to be trusted."

"His behavior does sound odd." Dustin frowned. "I certainly never asked him to interrogate my jockey, nor to spend an inordinate amount of time watching Dagger, for that matter. I'm glad you mentioned this to me. I'll watch Raggert closely. Let's see if he continues to harass you now that I'm home from Newmarket. Oh, speaking of Newmarket . . ." Dustin released Nicole's hand, reaching into his pocket. "Your license, Mr. Stoddard," he proclaimed, flourishing the document.

Nicole stared. "You truly got it."

"Never doubt me, Derby. As I told you, when I want something badly enough, I overcome any and all obstacles." The look he gave her spoke volumes. "To that end," he continued, "I've also made arrangements for your discreet arrival at Epsom. You'll weigh out alone while the other riders are parading past the royal stand and cantering toward the paddock. You and Dagger will join them as they reach the starter." He gave the brim of her cap a teasing tug. "The rest, Stoddard—the race and the victory—are up to you."

"They're as good as yours, Tyreham," Nick assured him. "Nickie's understanding of the course at Epsom is amazingly thorough. Wait until she's able to combine her horsemanship and her knowledge—there will be no catching up to her."

"Which is going to be when?" Disregarding the praise, Nicole seized the opportunity to elicit a commitment from Dustin. "When may I run a trial heat on the Derby course? I've stayed at Tyreham the entire time you've been away, as I promised. Over the past few days, I've ridden three separate trials at your estate, and each evening Papa's instructed me thoroughly. But learning cannot take the place of firsthand practice. So, when are we going to Epsom?"

"Your logic is extraordinary." Dustin was clearly biting back laughter. "Have you been rehearsing this speech since I took my leave?"

"Dustin . . ."

"How about first thing tomorrow?" he suggested, precluding her from launching into her next set of arguments. "I'll escort you there myself. I'd do so today, but it's too late in the afternoon. By the time we traveled to Epsom and saddled Dagger, it would be dark."

"Today is impossible anyway," Nicole reflected aloud. "Dagger is exhausted. I exercised him twice today, each time for over an hour. He needs to rest."

"Tomorrow it is, then."

"At dawn," she amended.

A deep chuckle. "The moment the first ray of sunlight inches its way over the horizon."

"Tyreham, about Newmarket, did you talk to anyone, learn anything?" Nick interjected.

"Actually, yes." All Dustin's humor vanished. Quietly, he relayed the events of the past three days, beginning with Parker, touching on the unsuccessful encounters with the other jockeys, and ending with his confrontation with Alberts. "Nick," Dustin finished intently, "Alberts described this third man as a stable-hand type who was tall, with an average build, penetrating eyes, and an intimidating presence. Most distinguishing of all, one of his forearms is severely scarred to the point of looking disfigured. Have you ever seen someone who matches that description?"

Nick's brows drew together, concentration etched into his every feature. "I was about to say no, but I have a nagging feeling I shouldn't. Somehow, the mangled arm, the terrifying manner . . . it all rings familiar." He massaged his temples. "But why? Dammit, I simply can't seem to recall."

"Maybe you had the same experience Alberts did," Dustin proposed. "Maybe this scarred man accompanied Archer and his cohort when they threatened you."

"No." An adamant shake of the head. "Of that, I'm certain. I was only approached by those two men, the same ones who beat Sully and accosted you. No one else. So, under whatever circumstances I might have glimpsed that scarred bastard, it wasn't on those occasions." He raked a hand through his hair. "But I keep getting a flash of memory, thinking I've seen him. The question is when. And where."

"Nicole?" Dustin turned to her. "Does the description mean anything to you?"

"Not a thing." She frowned. "Horrible as he sounds, I wish I could say otherwise, but I can't."

"No, Nickie wasn't with me," Nick murmured with another frustrated shake of his head. "I'm pretty sure I was alone when I saw him—if I saw him. Give me some time to think, Tyreham." He turned, heading back toward the sitting room. "I'll remember, come hell or high water."

"I'm sure you will."

The clock in the hallway chimed five.

Dustin glanced from the clock to Nicole. "I suppose I should take my leave."

Neither of them budged.

"We have a bit of lamb left over," Nicole invited impulsively. "Would you like to stay for dinner? Then afterward we can take that stroll."

"I'd be delighted to stay—for dinner *and* our stroll." Dustin's reply was husky, his expression taut, filled with heated promise.

A shiver rippled through Nicole.

Along with the realization that her moment of reckoning had arrived.

Thirteen

"It's twilight," Nicole observed, looking out the cabin window and watching the sun make its descent.

"Delivered as promised." Dustin came up behind her, sliding his arms about her waist.

She leaned back against his solid strength. "That's right, you did promise we'd share twilight the next time we were together." A soft sigh. "It's beautiful. How did you convince it to await our arrival, given the lateness of the hour?"

"I wish I could take credit for that." His lips feathered through her hair. "But I can't. The credit belongs to nature." He kissed the fragrant hollow beneath her ear. "Speaking of credit, am I the reason you've donned a gown once again? Or have you taken a sudden liking to feminine attire?"

"Not likely." She smiled. "I just didn't think it would do much for the marquis of Tyreham's reputation as a womanizer if he were seen strolling the grounds with a boy." Fingering the folds of her dress, she added, "Although, without the layers of petticoats, these gowns aren't really *that* dreadful. I suppose I could wear one on occasion."

"I don't give a damn for my reputation, Derby. What I care about is that no one recognizes Stoddard's true identity or his gender." Dustin's arms tightened about her, his tone growing wicked. "As for the future, I'd just as soon you didn't develop a liking for gowns. Breeches give me a much better view."

Nicole's heart skipped a beat. "You, my lord, are incorrigible. What am I to do with you?"

"Tell me what's in your heart."

Delivered in the midst of their lighthearted banter, Dustin's solemn request caught her off guard.

"I-I don't know what you want to hear," she managed.

"Talk to me, Nicole. Let me drive the fears away."

Fears? She wanted no mention of fears—not now. Not when Dustin's arms were around her and twilight was theirs.

"Later," she replied in a small, shaky voice. "For now, let's enjoy twilight. It belongs to us for so brief a time each day."

For a minute, Dustin was silent, resting his chin atop her head as together they watched the fiery rays of sunlight dip lower on the horizon. "What goes through your mind during these precious moments when twilight unfolds?"

Nicole inhaled the fragrant air. "When I was small, I used to wonder what the sun did throughout the night. Since no one could see it, it was free to do as it pleased. So what did it do? Romp about? Rest? Or, like me, did it simply gaze upward and marvel at the miracle it had left in its wake?"

"Perhaps it wished it could stay in the sky and make daylight last forever," Dustin suggested softly.

"But why?"

"Maybe it knew how lonely nighttime was for those who were alone, how empty twilight felt when there was no one to share it with."

Nicole turned in his arms. "Is that really how you felt?"

"Not when I was a child, no. But lately, until I met you, without a doubt." His thumbs caressed her cheekbones. "I've been searching, Nicole. Searching for something—someone—I'd almost given up believing existed. That's when I found you, sitting on that bench, staring at the sky and wishing. And I knew, as you did, that I'd never be the same again."

Nicole swallowed past the lump in her throat. "Our lives, like our backgrounds, are very different, Dustin."

"But our wishes are not."

Her lips trembled as she searched his face. "I'm not sure all our wishes are meant to be."

"I am." He lowered his head, brushed her lips with his. "I love you." He drew her closer, tangled his fingers in her hair. "I never said those words until I met you. It humbles me to say them. It humbles me more to feel them." He tilted her head back, sealing their mouths in one heated motion. "Nicole, I want to give you your wishes, your dreams—the world."

She opened to him instantly, needing this exquisite moment as much as he did. Eagerly, she wound her arms about his neck, urging him closer, trembling as his tongue stroked hers. Her lashes drifted to her cheeks, every nerve in her body tingling and alive, attuned to the melding of lips, tongues, breath.

Hearts.

Something was different this time; or was that only for her? Something intangible: a change, a shifting, a transformation, an innate realization that after tonight there would be no turning back. Whether it was real or simply the consequence of her own heedless longing, Nicole didn't care. She welcomed it, wanted it, needed it desperately. Her body blossomed and awakened, rendering her breasts heavy and aching, liquid heat coursing through her, straining to be filled. Nothing mattered at that moment, not the past, not her values, not the future. Only Dustin. Dustin—and now.

No, it wasn't she alone who felt it. He sensed it, too, for he drew back, stared into her eyes with a bottomless hunger and a blazing intensity as heated as his kiss. "Nicole . . ."

"Shhh." She reached up, lay her hand against his jaw, stroking the harsh angles of his unbearably handsome face.

Reverently, Dustin turned his lips into her palm, fighting a battle Nicole could actually feel.

"Don't," she breathed, shaking her head. "Not tonight. Please, Dustin, don't."

His fingers slid beneath her hair, caressing her nape in slow, sensual strokes. "I haven't the strength," he bit out, shuddering. "Nicole . . . tell me to stop."

Stop? She hadn't a thought to comply. This twilight there was only this, only them, and right or wrong, she wanted to drown in all the pleasure she knew Dustin could bring her.

"No." She stood on tiptoe, untying his neck cloth and unbuttoning his shirt and waistcoat. Tenderly, she pressed her lips to his warm, exposed skin, tugging the sides of his shirt farther apart.

A groan rumbled from Dustin's throat. "Stop," he commanded as her fingers trailed over his hair-roughened chest. "God, Nicole, you can't—" Contradicting his own words, he captured her wrist, dragged her palm over his chest, across his nipples, down to his waist . . . and his trousers. There he halted, his grip becoming punishing as he battled once again for a control that was dissipating with every drumming heartbeat.

Nicole annihilated it entirely.

Easing her wrist free, she unfastened his trousers, her fingers sliding inside until she could touch him.

A whisper of a caress was all it took.

With a guttural sound, Dustin pulled away, flinging his coat, waistcoat, and shirt to the floor, seizing her mouth in a fierce, bottomless kiss that delved down to her soul. Urgently, he unbuttoned her gown, nearly tearing her chemise as he tugged it from her shoulders, shoving both the gown and chemise down to her waist. Gathering her in his arms, he walked three steps to the thick pile rug that defined the far corner of the cabin, then lowered them both to its softness.

He came to his knees, his gaze burning into hers as he cupped her breasts, defining their softness with worshipful strokes of his fingertips. Nicole's nipples hardened beneath his touch, his openly carnal stare, and she whimpered, stirring restlessly on the carpet, seeking more . . . more.

Dustin understood her plea, for his hands shifted to her waist, tugging her clothing past her hips, down her legs and off. Then he stopped, tearing his gaze from hers, taking in her nudity with an awed expression Nicole would remember for the rest of her life.

"Your beauty defies words," he said hoarsely, devouring her, inch by inch, first with his eyes, then with trembling fingers. "As I said, a miracle." With that, he lowered his head.

Nicole moaned aloud as his lips closed around her nipple, tugged it into the warm cavern of his mouth, lashed it with purposeful sweeps of his tongue. He repeated the motion again and again, until pinpoints of unbearable pleasure began to shoot through her, converging in a liquid pool between her thighs. Desperately, she tossed about, wanting to savor the magic, yearning to further it.

Again Dustin understood.

He left her breast, moving to sample its mate. This time he lingered only briefly before raising his head, raking her with eyes of midnight fire, the look on his face so profound, it hurt. "I'm drowning," he muttered hoarsely, barely able to speak. "Nicole, I'm drowning." His lips found the hollow between her breasts, blazing a trail down her waist, her stomach, her thighs.

Nicole wasn't certain she'd survive. Everywhere he stroked turned to fire, every unexplored inch of her clamored for his touch. When she heard him whisper, "Open for me, Derby," she did so without question, knowing she was behaving like a wanton, not giving a damn.

His fingers found her where she most ached for him, gliding through the satiny wetness he'd created. He groaned deep in his chest, a shudder wracking his powerful body as he circled and stroked and awakened the very essence of her.

"Dustin . . ." She sobbed his name when his finger slid inside her, penetrating ever so gently, withdrawing just as slowly, the sensual caress more than she could bear. He did it again and again, and Nicole twisted wildly, frightened by the clawing tension building inside her.

"God, you're like hot silk," Dustin rasped, watching her face. "Soft, sleek, beautiful." He bent, feathering kisses up the inside of her thighs to where his fingers probed, and Nicole cried out, clutching his shoulders, needing . . . needing.

His mouth found her, opening her to his lips and tongue in a way that made her scream, and arch, and plead with him to continue. Streaks of jagged heat raced through her, faster and faster, and everything on earth vanished beneath the unendurable ecstasy Dustin was unleashing inside her.

From far away, she heard his choked sounds of pleasure, his broken words of praise. But all she felt was his mouth, his unbearable, wonderful mouth, burning into the very depths of her, flames leaping higher and higher until they dragged her into a bottomless inferno.

The world unraveled.

Crashing pleasure, wrenching, saturating heat burst inside her, and she sobbed Dustin's name with each racking shudder. On and on the spasms went, until she collapsed, limp and drained, her soul no longer hers but his.

Opening her eyes was a colossal effort, but she managed to at last, only to see Dustin staring down at her, his chest heaving as he dragged in air, his forehead and shoulders slick with sweat.

Their gazes locked, and Nicole knew in that moment he was battling for control, determined to stop.

"No," she managed, reaching up to tug at his trousers. "Please . . . no."

"Sweetheart . . ." He could barely speak. "I didn't plan to . . ."

"I know." Her fingers found him, stroked the hot, rigid length of him, her eyes begging him to continue. "I love you," she breathed.

Her declaration was more powerful than his will.

With a strangled sound, Dustin capitulated, kicking free of his remaining clothes, lowering his body over hers until he lay in the cradle of her thighs. "Nicole." He cupped her face, kissed her cheeks, eyes, and nose with a reverence that defied his carnal urgency. Even as his hips were urging him into her, he covered her mouth with his, his words a fervid whisper that permeated her soul. "I love you . . . God, I love you." His hands slid down to her hips. "You can't imagine."

"But I can." Instinctively, she raised her knees to hug his flanks, wrapped her arms about his back. "Like this?" she murmured.

"Yes." The word was ripped from his chest. Head thrown back, he pressed into her, opening her body and possessing her until the beauty of it nearly made her weep. "How can anything feel so good?" he rasped. "God, how can any woman be so perfect?"

Nicole was lost in the same wonder as he. Nothing had prepared her for this exquisite feeling, this utter possession, and she reveled in the miracle of Dustin's body entering hers, melding them into one. Her eyes slid closed, her body softening, opening, sheathing him in its depths. She felt pressure, pressure that intensified into pain, but she didn't pull away, somehow sensing that beyond that pain was the most breathtaking miracle of all.

"Derby." Dustin must have felt it, too, for he froze, his whole body trembling with the cost of delay. "You're so small. So tight. I can't bear to hurt you."

Her eyes opened, and she drew his mouth down to hers. "Hurt me?" she repeated incredulously. "If you stop, I'll die." Her palms glided over his back, down to his buttocks, and she arched, urging him into her.

"Nicole." He shouted her name, thrusting deep, tearing her maidenhead and filling her to bursting.

How could pain feel so beautiful?

"Dustin," she whispered, an awed breath of sound, and she held herself utterly still for one breathless instant, memorizing every sensation defining this once-in-a-lifetime moment. Then, kissing his shoulder, she shifted to take him deeper into herself.

Dustin shuddered heavily, eased away, then pressed forward, burying himself inside her again. "The pain . . . is it . . ."

"Heaven," she managed.

Groaning, he repeated the motion, his hands gliding beneath her legs to lift them higher around him. She complied, enveloping him inside and out, wanting, aching, needing, more than she ever dreamed possible.

Her inner muscles caressed him, splintering the final vestiges of his control.

With a harsh growl, Dustin took over, surrendering at last to his primitive need to possess her, totally, thoroughly, unendingly. His thrusts became urgent, savage, taking all she had, giving all he was.

Their bodies moved in wild unison, arching and falling in cadence to the relentless pounding of their hearts. The escalating tension reignited in Nicole's loins, building and building until she thought she'd fly into a million scattered fragments. She clung to Dustin, begging him for things that would mortify her later, but for now were as necessary to her as breathing. In answer, he gripped her bottom, hauling her into his thrusts, opening her wider, more fully, with each motion, circling his hips until the friction on her—in her—was too excruciating to bear.

She reached her limit, dangled . . . and fell.

The contractions erupted, each wrenching spasm more potent than the last, gripping Dustin and drawing him into her core. Nicole cried out, shattering, dying, at the very instant that Dustin went rigid, shouting her name with a fervor that pierced her heart. His grip became bruising, crushing her to him with the frenzy of a drowning man. And then he exploded, pouring into her with great, pulsing bursts of release, seeking her womb in an inherent need to pour his seed as deep inside her as possible, to give her the very essence of himself.

It seemed to go on forever, this pinnacle of sensation, crashing and crashing like great untamed waves. Then, the waves subsided slowly, gradually, the aftermath drifting about them in dizzying clouds of fulfillment.

Awareness came gradually, in minimal degrees, contentment supplanting urgency as they lay together, still joined, gasping for breath, shaking with reaction.

Nicole began to cry, tears stealing from beneath her lids, trickling down her cheeks onto Dustin's shoulders.

He rolled to one side, staying inside her, reaching for his discarded coat and wrapping it about them. "Don't cry, darling," he murmured, stroking her back. "Please don't cry."

That only made her weep harder.

"Nicole." He took her face between his palms, thumbs capturing her tears as he gazed deeply into her eyes. "I didn't mean for this to happen—not here, not now. But my feelings for you . . ." He drew a shuddering breath. "Did I hurt you? Is that why you're crying?"

She shook her head.

"Then what is it? Regret? Shame? Because *those* reasons I could not, would not abide. What just happened between us was nothing short of a miracle, and miracles occur at their will, not ours."

"It's neither regret nor shame," she choked out. "I wanted this every bit as much as you did. I just never expected to feel so . . . so shattered." She looked up at him, bewildered and raw and achingly vulnerable. "Oh, Dustin, if I were terrified before, I'm panic-stricken now."

His expression softened, enveloped her in warmth. "And if I were sure before, I'm surer now."

"When you're *with* other women . . ." She swallowed. "Is it always like this?"

"Never. It's never like this." Tenderly, he kissed her. "Perhaps that's because I've never made love before tonight."

God, how she wanted to believe that his love alone could make everything right. "Tell me again that you'll overcome all the obstacles," she whispered.

"Every last one. Derby, tell me your fears, and I'll obliterate them."

"No." Nicole reached up, pressed her fingers to his lips. "Please, I'm not ready for this conversation—not tonight. Just give me the words."

He gathered her close. "The future is ours, Nicole. I promise you."

She grasped on to his pledge, closing her eyes and willing it to be so.

But in her heart she knew that just as twilight must descend to dusk, wishes must give way to reality.

"Two minutes forty-six seconds." Brackley snapped his timepiece shut with a flourish. "That was last year's winning time exactly."

"It was indeed," Dustin concurred, folding his arms across his chest as he watched Nicole bring Dagger around.

"You're not pleased?" Brackley shot his employer a puzzled look. "I know Stoddard's last run was six seconds faster, but Tyreham's course is shorter, not to mention more familiar. Considering this was his initial run at Epsom, two minutes forty-six seconds is good, my lord."

"It's better than good. It's excellent." Dustin's gaze was still fixed on Nicole. "However, bear in mind that it was achieved under unnaturally optimum conditions—good weather, no other horses to contend with, none of the pressure that will accompany the actual race. We need to provide a little authenticity to refine Stoddard's skills." He turned to Brackley. "Next session, bring Winning Streak. I'll ride her, simulate a two-contender race with Stoddard, and maybe throw a challenge or two his way."

Brackley heaved a sigh of relief. "For a minute I thought you meant to suggest Raggert for the job. I'm relieved you mean to do it yourself. Raggert and Stoddard don't exactly get along."

"No, they don't." Dustin shot Brackley a quizzical look. "What do you think of Raggert?"

A shrug. "He's all right, I guess. Does his job. Although, while you were at Newmarket, he spent hours and hours overseeing Stoddard. He seems to think the boy will take advantage if left to his own devices. I disagree. I've never seen a more devoted jockey."

"Did you mention that fact to Raggert?"

"Of course. But he insisted that with you away, it was his responsibility to make sure Stoddard was exercising Dagger right, riding him as often, but not more often, than he should. I stopped interfering. After all, it's not my place to tell a trainer what to do." Glancing in Stoddard's direction, Brackley frowned. "Did you mean to return with Winning Streak this afternoon, sir? Because if you don't mind my saying so, I think we should wait a day. Stoddard's not himself this morning. He's awfully pale, and he's got circles under his eyes. My guess is that with the Derby looming closer, he's starting to feel the strain. He's not the type to talk about his worries, he keeps them to himself. But I do think he's getting scared."

A stab of guilt accosted Dustin as the ironic truth of Brackley's statement struck home. "I couldn't agree more." Purposefully, he straightened, surveying the area just beyond the winning post where Nicole was cooling Dagger down. "Alert Saxon to ready the carriage. I'll advise Stoddard that we're heading back to Tyreham."

"Of course, sir." Brackley hastened off.

Dustin walked toward Nicole, thinking about the true reasons for her unsettled state, wishing he knew what to say, how to reach her. She'd been quiet and distant all morning, avoiding his gaze, not speaking to him unless it was necessary. Further, Brackley's observation of her depleted state was accurate. She *was* pale, with deep circles etched under her violet eyes. Obviously, she hadn't slept a wink. But, unlike Brackley, Dustin knew precisely why.

For the umpteenth time he berated himself for letting last night ensue without the preparation, the prelude, the formalized commitment he'd intended to elicit before joining his body to hers. He'd never believed himself capable of such a total and utter loss of control. But when she'd looked up at him with those smoky amethyst eyes, caressed him with those innocent, coaxing fingertips . . . Even now, he shuddered, just remembering.

Nonetheless, he should have resisted, knowing bloody well what the consequences would be. Last night had been devastating, overwhelming, and—to use Nicole's own description—shattering. Afterward had been the time for hushed words, all-night caresses, discussions of the future—*their* future. Oh, he'd made an attempt, but she hadn't been ready. It was too soon, her mind still dazed from the intensity of their union, her body still trembling as it struggled to recover. If only he could have held her longer, reassured her until her tremors had subsided and her mind had cleared. Then he would have enumerated the details he'd worked out to resolve their future, erased her fears, one by one, until she'd been as sure as he that they belonged together. But time was the one thing he hadn't had—not when they'd already been away from the cottage for hours. So what had he done? Helped her dress, brought her home, and left her to her thoughts . . . and her uncertainty.

And to a woman like Nicole, who couldn't give half measure, the only way to combat emotional uncertainty was with a wall of self-protection, a tangible barrier between them.

Given that reality, how the hell could Tyreham and Stoddard resume their casual rapport as employer and jockey?

"Hello, Derby." Dustin reached the object of his quest, falling into step alongside her and Dagger. "Nice run. Excellent pacing."

"But only adequate timing," she supplied, staring straight ahead.

"Two minutes, forty-six seconds. I'd say that's significantly better than adequate."

"Better but not good enough." Her brows knit, and she shifted a bit in the saddle. "I'll run the trial again later today. Perhaps by then my . . . concentration will improve."

"Your concentration was perfect," Dustin corrected. "You're just exhausted. And you won't run the trial again today. You'll run it tomorrow. With me as your competition, incidentally. That way we can work on your maneuvers as well as your concentration and pacing. As for today, we're going back to Tyreham. You're to do nothing but rest."

In response to his proclamation, Nicole's shoulders sagged with relief.

Dustin caught Dagger's reins in an inconspicuous manner, gently bringing Nicole around to face him. "Are you all right?"

She lowered her gaze, staring at the saddle and not pretending to misunderstand. "Yes. Just tired and—" She broke off, a flush staining her cheeks. Again she shifted, this time with a flinch.

Dustin tensed, a new worry intruding. "Are you hurt? Did you injure yourself?"

Her flush deepened. "No." A spasm of pain crossed her face. "May I dismount now?"

Realization struck Dustin with all the force of a tidal wave.

"Damn." He raked a hand through his hair. "I never thought . . . it didn't occur to me that . . . Derby, I'm such a bloody fool." He helped her dismount, silently castigating himself for his utter stupidity. He'd been so busy worrying about her emotional state, he'd completely overlooked her physical one. The way he'd taken her last night, with a bottomless craving he couldn't plunge deep enough to assuage, it was a wonder she could walk, much less ride. It had been her first time. And not only had she been a virgin, she'd been so small, so tight. What she needed today was to soak in a warm bath, not to gallop across Epsom Downs.

Had he lost his bloody mind?

"Derby . . ." He gazed down at her, seeing the discomfort on her face and loathing himself for causing it. "I'm sorry."

She reacted instantly to his self-censuring tone, a brief, reminiscent smile touching her lips. "Don't be. I'm not. As for the soreness, I'm sure it will be gone by tomorrow." Self-consciously, she glanced about. "Where's Brackley?"

"With my driver. Advising him that we're preparing to leave."

"What explanation did you give him?"

"None. It was his suggestion that you forego riding until tomorrow. He saw how exhausted you are. By now I'm sure he's also noticed the three touts that are combing the stands, scribbling down the incredible speed at which you just took the course, waiting to besiege you with questions. Derby, we can't leave things this way," he inserted abruptly. "We have to talk. Not now, obviously. And not later today, because I want you to have a warm bath and go to bed, but soon. Tomorrow. Before you've had too much time alone— time in which you'll doubtless convince that stubborn mind of yours to believe in truths that are, in fact, utter false-hoods."

Nicole absorbed his speech, understanding flashing in her eyes. "Very well, my lord. I'll have that bath *and* a good night's sleep, then early tomorrow morning, you may speak to me as kindly and convincingly as you know how. But be advised that no amount of persuasion will soften me into taking it easy with you. Should you presume to race alongside me at Epsom tomorrow, I shall beat you by at least five lengths."

Dustin blinked at the unexpected change in tenor. Then a surge of love rushed through him at the humbling realiza-tion that by resorting to spontaneous banter, Nicole was trying to console *him*. "Is that so?" he asked huskily.

"It is, indeed, not only so but a promise." She paused, holding his gaze. "And like you, Lord Tyreham, I never make promises I don't intend to keep."

"The duke and duchess of Broddington are here to see you, sir," Poole announced from the study doorway.

Dustin's head came up. "Here? It's nearly midnight." He

was on his feet, striding toward the doorway. "Is Alexander . . . ?"

"The young marquis is well and with his parents," Poole was quick to answer. "But His Grace is quite upset, as is the duchess. They wish to see you at once. Shall I send them in?"

"Of course. And have their rooms made up. It's much too late for them to travel back to Broddington tonight."

"That's already taken care of, sir. Mrs. Ladley is making up the rooms herself."

Footsteps pounded through the hallway, and Poole stood aside as Trenton stormed into the study. "We need to talk. Now."

"Where's Ariana?"

"Right here," she replied, walking into the room, her face drawn with worry. "Trenton, I let Mrs. Hopkins take Alexander upstairs to bed. I didn't want to, but he's half asleep. The instant we're finished speaking with Dustin, I'm going up there."

"What the hell is going on?" Dustin demanded as Poole left the room, closing the door in his wake.

"You tell us." Trenton glared at his brother, a muscle working furiously in his jaw. "And don't even think of putting me off this time. God damn it, this is my son we're talking about."

Dustin sucked in his breath. "Has someone tried to harm Alexander?"

"Not yet. But someone sure as hell intends to." Reaching into his pocket, Trenton extracted a folded sheet. "This arrived at Broddington not two hours ago. Read it."

With a sinking heart, Dustin took the paper.

Broddington:
Tell your brother to stop poking where he doesn't belong.
If he doesn't, you can bid your son good-bye.

"Dammit." Dustin scanned the page twice, then lowered it to his desk. "I never believed they'd actually involve Alexander in this. I thought they were bluffing."

"For the last time I'm asking, what are you involved in that's endangering my son?" Trenton slammed his fist on the edge of Dustin's desk. "Last time we spoke you told me two men had invaded Tyreham, assaulted you *and* threatened Alexander's well-being if you were to hire Nick Aldridge—who, the newspapers claim, is injured and recuperating in Scotland. When I pressed you for details, you said only that you were in the process of resolving the whole sordid matter. You refused to say more. You also assured me that Alexander would remain unharmed. Well, that no longer appears to be the case. Therefore, your silence is no longer acceptable."

"No, it's not." Dustin stared at the note, weighing his words *and* his loyalties.

"Dustin," Ariana said softly. "I realize we're putting you in a difficult position. But we have no choice. Alexander is our son. He means the world to us. If anything were to happen to him—" Her voice broke.

"Don't, misty angel," Trenton murmured, enfolding her against him. "No one's going to harm Alexander. I won't allow it."

"Nor will I." Dustin's heart lurched at their pain. "I'm going to be as honest with you as I can—tonight. I hope whatever particulars I omit now can be filled in tomorrow." *After I've gotten permission from Nicole and her father,* he added silently. "But that's neither here nor there, because what I'm about to relay will cover everything pertaining to Alexander." He glanced at Trenton. "I assume you've filled Ariana in?"

"On what? I've just specified every bloody detail I'm privy to. But if you mean, did I describe your original telegram and our first conversation, the answer is yes. This situation has far surpassed the point where I can protect Ariana from the truth."

"I agree." Dustin looked from Ariana to Trenton. "You can't repeat a word of what I'm about to reveal. People's lives depend on it." He waited for their nods. "Trent, when you came to Tyreham last week, you asked if I knew more about Nick Aldridge's disappearance than I was willing to say. The answer is, yes. Stoddard, my new jockey, is Aldridge's protégé. He saw my ad in the personals and responded to it. When I hired him, he told me the real reason behind Aldridge's disappearance."

"So I was right, Aldridge wasn't injured."

"No, he *wasn't*—yet, but he was about to be." Without pause, Dustin relayed the specifics behind Nick's disappearance, elaborating on Sullivan's beating, the list of dishonest jockeys Stoddard had provided, and Dustin's own decision to hire Saxon and travel to Newmarket to grill the disreputable jockeys—everything but his direct contact with Nick and Stoddard's true identity.

"Has Stoddard heard from Aldridge?" Trenton cut in. "Does he know his whereabouts?"

Dustin's jaw set. "That's one of the questions I can't answer until tomorrow."

"Hell, you know where Aldridge is." Trenton dragged a hand through his hair. "Dustin, these men aren't playing. You're going to get yourself killed."

"No, Trent, I'm not. Nor will those bastards harm one hair on my nephew's head. I might not have anticipated this note you received, but I am prepared to deal with it. Now, calm down and hear me out."

"Go ahead."

Dustin pointed at the note. "This tells me that whoever is overseeing this contemptible scheme obviously learned of my Newmarket inquiries and panicked. I expected just such a reaction. In fact, I counted on it. My only miscalculation was in assuming their retaliation would be aimed solely at me." A scowl. "I should have guessed they'd involve Alexander. Whoever is running this operation evidently knows enough about me to recognize that my family is my Achilles' heel." Dustin raised his head, an unwavering look in his eyes. "However, I still believe, as I originally did, that they'll strike directly. Mark my words, those two hoodlums will be back at Tyreham any day now to beat me into silence. After which, Saxon will follow them to whoever it is they report to and expose him."

"What do you mean 'after which'?" Ariana interrupted. "Are you saying you intend to *let* those men beat you?"

Dustin smiled faintly, touched by Ariana's unwavering softheartedness, despite her alarm over Alexander's safety. "Don't worry about me," he assured her. "I'm very resilient. I doubt they'll inflict too much damage. If things get out of hand, I'll yell for help. As for protecting Alexander . . ."

"Dustin, why are you doing this?" Trenton's cobalt gaze

delved into his brother. "And don't tell me it's to protect the turf. I know you better than that. You're principled as hell, but you wouldn't jeopardize your family for anything on earth. As I suggested last time, you're shielding someone. Who?"

Silence.

"It's Stoddard, isn't it?" Ariana murmured, watching Dustin's face. "You're safeguarding your new jockey."

A cautious nod. "Stoddard is twenty years old, Ariana, the same age as you. Nick Aldridge is all he has in the world. I feel . . ." Dustin searched for the right words, words that would be accurate but not revealing. ". . . responsible for him. I can't explain why, but if I'm able to help him, I must."

"You don't need to explain," Ariana surprised him by saying, precluding whatever furious response Trenton had been about to render. "We understand."

"We do?" Trenton demanded incredulously.

"Yes." Ariana's nod was strangely insightful. "We do."

"Thank you." Dustin gave Ariana a grateful—albeit puzzled—look. "Let's get back to Alexander. As I mentioned, I've hired an investigator. Actually, I did so right after meeting with Trent, who bluntly informed me I wasn't skilled enough to investigate on my own. He was right. I realized that the instant I interviewed and hired Saxon. Watching him do his job is an education unto itself. The man is exceptional. So, here's what I propose. You were planning to come to Surrey for the Derby anyway, you've merely arrived early. Stay on. Have your bags sent, as well. Let Saxon oversee Alexander. Believe me, no one will get past Poole's nephew."

"Poole's nephew." Ariana's brows arched in comprehension. "So that's why Quinn was relegated to his recent position as footman. You hired Poole's nephew as your new driver . . . and investigator."

"Precisely. In this way Saxon could accompany me to whatever racecourses I needed to visit, safeguard my well-being, and assist me at the same time."

"Trenton?" Ariana twisted around to glance up at her husband. "Dustin's suggestion does make sense. I'd feel much safer with Mr. Saxon keeping an eye on Alexander.

He is, after all, a trained professional. Not to mention that this way we can all be together, draw strength from each other. Perhaps you and I might even help. I'm sure Dustin is eager to resolve things as quickly as possible." Her gaze flickered briefly over Dustin before returning to Trenton. "May we stay?"

"You couldn't drag me out of here," Trenton retorted.

Ariana sighed with relief. "I'll ask Poole to send for our things. Then, I want to check on Alexander."

"And *then* you're going to bed," Trenton concluded. "Otherwise you're going to collapse." Tenderly, he kissed his wife. "Dustin and I will work out the remaining details."

"I'll even speak to Saxon before retiring," Dustin added. "He'll begin watching Alexander tonight. How would that be?"

Ariana crossed the room and kissed Dustin's cheek. "You're a fine man, Dustin." A flicker of a smile. "The woman in your life had best know how lucky she is." Squeezing his arm, she retraced her steps, pausing only to receive Trenton's brief, reassuring embrace and his murmured, "I'll make everything right, misty angel," before hastening from the study.

The instant the door closed behind her, Trenton turned back to his brother, his former intensity restored. "This conversation is far from over."

"I never thought otherwise," Dustin returned dryly. "I assumed your intention was to ease Ariana's mind enough so she'd agree to get some rest, then to continue this discussion in private."

A terse nod. "Ariana is taking this whole situation very hard. I won't keep things from her, but I needn't immerse her in unnerving specifics either. The fact is that, unless she believes we've eliminated all cause for worry, she'll post herself at Alexander's bedside until dawn, and become ill in the process."

"I feel guilty as hell."

"Don't feel guilty. Just tell me everything. What did you learn at Newmarket? What more do you know about those hired hands who came to Tyreham? What can I do to help? And what the hell can't you tell us?"

"You can pour me a drink while I ask Poole to summon

Saxon—after which I'll address your first two questions. Also, you can understand, or at least accept, that what I can't tell you must wait until tomorrow."

"That's an untenable request."

"I wouldn't make it unless I had to."

Sucking in his breath, Trenton relented. "Very well. I'll wait until morning." He stalked across the room, pouring two goblets of brandy. *"Early* morning," he called after his brother, who'd stepped into the hallway to speak with Poole.

"How can I be of assistance, my lord?" Poole inquired quietly.

"You can tell me if Saxon has retired for the night. I need to speak with him."

"He headed off for bed mere minutes ago, sir. Would you like me to summon him?"

"If you would. It's critical, or I wouldn't disturb him at this late hour."

"He'd expect nothing less. I'll fetch him at once." Poole hurried off.

Confident that Saxon would soon be joining them, Dustin returned to his study.

Tyreham's entranceway door eased open silently, a lone figure assessing that the hallway was, at last, empty. Hearing Lord Tyreham's study door click shut, he crept in the direction of the sound. Upon reaching his destination, he pressed himself to the wall outside the room, straining to hear the conversation unfolding between the marquis and his brother.

Oblivious to the intruder's presence, Dustin and Trenton resumed where they'd left off.

"Here's your brandy." Trenton handed Dustin a goblet. "I've already downed half of mine. God knows I need it."

"Everything will work out, Trent. I'm certain of it." Dustin accepted the proffered goblet. "You asked if I discovered anything of consequence at Newmarket. The answer is yes. Do you remember Alberts?"

"Your jockey?" Trenton halted, the reason for Dustin's question snapping into place. "Was he one of the names on that list? Did he throw your races?"

"He most certainly did. And, as luck would have it, I stumbled upon him at Newmarket."

"Who foolishly engaged his services?"

"No one. He wasn't entered. In fact, he's been unable to secure a position since I discharged him. He was there to blackmail one of the other jockeys into sharing his illegal winnings with him."

"The bloody scoundrel."

"A scoundrel, yes, but an informative one. I convinced him to describe the two men he dealt with."

"And?"

"They were the same men who visited me. Everything Alberts revealed about them I already knew. However, in the process of relaying his experiences, he disclosed a new and interesting fact. It seems that during one of their visits, they brought a companion with them. An unsavory sort with a horribly scarred arm. Alberts described him quite thoroughly." Dustin slammed his goblet to the desk. "I intend to find this bastard—whoever he is."

Still listening intently, the intruder scowled, wondering how much more time he had. His answer came in the form of approaching footsteps that alerted him to the butler's imminent return. Instantly, he retraced his steps and slipped out the front door to avoid discovery.

Fortunately, the grounds were deserted.

Raggert darted off into the night.

Fourteen

"Raggert, what the hell do you want? It's two in the morning." Coop rubbed his unshaven face, glowering at the trainer.

"When you hear why I've come, you won't care what time it is. Now are you planning to let me in?"

Eyes narrowed, Coop swung open the door. "This better be good."

"Oh, it is, all right." Raggert wiped the sweat off his forehead, striding into the shabby hall and pacing restlessly about. "Broddington and his family are at Tyreham. They showed up a couple of hours ago in a snit about something. I couldn't get close enough to hear what they were saying, not for a while anyway. I finally got my chance—so I sneaked in and listened."

"So?"

Raggert blinked. "Aren't you surprised?"

A shrug. "About the duke bursting into Tyreham? Not particularly. Our employer said something about going after Tyreham through his family, especially after the prying he just did at Newmarket. I don't see why—all Tyreham learned was what he already knew, but I couldn't calm our nobleman friend down. He muttered something about planning to send Broddington a telegram about his son. That's probably what got him and his family so riled up." Coop shot Raggert a dark look. "Is that the only reason you're here?"

"No, although it explains a lot. I wish you two would tell me your plans. It would be nice to know what's going on since I'm the one who's supposed to be keeping an eye on Tyreham's estate and his jockey. Speaking of Stoddard, he's a cocky, insolent—"

"I don't give a damn about Stoddard," Coop growled, rubbing his scarred arm. "He's your problem, not mine. Just tell me what the hell you're doing here, then get out and let me go to bed."

"You're wrong about Tyreham not learning anything at Newmarket. In this case, our source did a lousy job."

Coop's massaging motions slowed. "Our *source* is not about to miss anything—not when he's got more to lose than we do."

"Well, he missed one conversation, that's for sure. Did he mention that Alberts was at Newmarket?"

"Yeah, he said something about Tyreham scaring him off. Why?"

"Before he ran off, Alberts did a bit of talking. He told Tyreham about the time Archer and Parrish brought a friend with them. 'A terrifying man with a horribly scarred arm,' I think were Tyreham's words."

With a vile oath, Coop slammed his fist into the wall.

"Still sorry I came?" Raggert taunted.

"Shut up," Coop snapped. "We're going to have to speed up our plan. I'll contact Archer tonight, tell him and Parrish to get over to Tyreham and beat the hell out of our friend the marquis. Maybe then the bastard will mind his own business. The last thing I need is for him to come looking for me."

"Bloody right," Raggert agreed, frowning. "Archer and Parrish had better be damned convincing. Because if they aren't—if they don't manage to scare Tyreham into staying out of things—this whole scheme could explode in our faces."

"You made your point." Coop jerked open the door, nearly shoving Raggert out. "Now get back to Tyreham before someone notices you're missing. I'll get dressed and find Archer and Parrish. By tomorrow, Tyreham will either cease to be a problem or cease to be."

Dawn had yet to begin making its entrance when Dustin left his chambers the next morning. Time was short, and he intended to make full use of it. If he didn't get to Nicole and her father by half after five, Nicole would leave for the stables and Trenton would begin pacing the floors, demanding answers that were his right to have.

Arising early had been more of a relief than an effort, given that Dustin hadn't closed an eye all night. Between his worry for Alexander and his preoccupation with Nicole's physical and emotional state, slumber had evaded him entirely.

Both issues would be confronted today; the latter tonight, the former in a matter of minutes.

Making his way downstairs, Dustin paused only to gulp down two cups of fortifying coffee before leaving the manor. Saxon had agreed, albeit reluctantly, to allow his employer this unexplained and unsupervised morning excursion. Dustin fully understood the investigator's concern: sufficient time had passed since Dustin had stirred up a hornet's nest with his inquiries at Newmarket. He was now a walking target. Nevertheless, he meant to walk to the tenants' section alone. His reasons were twofold: one, he refused to permit Saxon to leave Alexander's side; and two, he was determined to keep the Aldridges' whereabouts a secret, to fulfill the vow he'd made when he'd hired Nicole.

Until—and *unless*—they modified that vow.

He didn't dare consider what he'd do if they refused. He could never betray Nicole.

He could never look Trent in the eye if he didn't.

Troubled, he crossed the grounds, making his way to the Aldridges' cottage before the first rays of sun appeared.

A customary silence greeted his knock.

"It's Tyreham," he announced, once a short interval had elapsed.

The door opened, and Nicole gazed up at him, her expression apprehensive beneath her concealing cap. "My lord? Is something wrong?"

"Forgive me for coming by so early, but, yes, I must speak with you and your father at once."

"Of course." She paled but admitted him without further question.

Dustin shut the door in his wake, clasping Nicole's narrow shoulders and fighting the nearly unbearable urge to envelop her against him to ease his aching conflict.

"Dustin?"

She looked so frightened and so vulnerable. Memories washed over him, and he searched her breeches-clad form for signs of lingering discomfort. "Are you feeling better?"

With a flicker of embarrassment, she nodded. "Yes. Much better. The bath and rest worked wonders."

"I almost came by last night," he told her huskily. "Three times, in fact. I wanted to see for myself that you were all right, but I resisted the urge to do so. You needed rest, not company. However, that doesn't mean I wasn't thinking of you. I was. All night."

A soft smile. "Worrying about me, you mean." She reached up, lay her palm against his jaw. "Thank you. But I'm fine. Truly. And we will talk. I promise."

He turned his lips into her palm. "I've turned your life upside down, haven't I? And God help me, I'm about to do so again. Have you any idea how frustrating that is, given the fact that all I want to do is make you happy?"

Trepidation flashed in her eyes. "What's happened?"

"They sent a note. To Trenton. A direct threat to Alexander's life if I don't stop delving."

She needed no explanation for who *they* were. "Oh, my God." Her arms dropped to her sides. "I'll get Papa."

"You don't need to. I'm here." Nick Aldridge descended the stairs, belting his robe. "I heard you mention a note. To whom? Saying what?"

"To my brother. Threatening my nephew's life if I don't stop asking questions."

"Dammit." Nick's mouth thinned into a grim line. "When did this happen?"

"Late last night. Ariana and Trenton arrived at Tyreham close to midnight. They brought Alexander with them. Needless to say, they're terrified."

"Of course they are." Compassion swept Nicole's features. "He's their child. What can we do to help?"

A surge of love erupted inside Dustin at Nicole's use of the word "we." For the first time, she was integrating her life with his . . . *and* when he needed her most. "Thank you," he said humbly. Clearing his throat, he added, "Fortunately, Alexander is in good hands. I haven't mentioned this to either of you, but several days ago I hired an investigator. He accompanied me on my trip to Newmarket. As of now, he's standing guard over Alexander."

Nicole's eyes narrowed. "Why didn't you mention this?" She answered her own question. "You didn't want us to know how much danger you've put yourself in. *We've* put you in," she amended.

"Nickie's right, Tyreham," Aldridge concurred. "And I let you talk me into it. But you're a grown man. An innocent babe is another thing entirely. I won't be the cause of your nephew's life being jeopardized."

"You aren't," Dustin interrupted. "The bastards orchestrating this scheme are. The only way to ensure Alexander's well-being—*and* yours—is to expose them. Nick, I appreciate your compassion. In fact, I'm counting on it. But I didn't come here to upset you, I came to elicit your trust."

"My trust?" Nick cocked an ironic brow. "I think I've more than demonstrated my trust in you, Tyreham, not only professionally but personally." A subtle glance in Nicole's direction.

"Yes, you have." Dustin felt a pang of guilt as he contemplated what Nick's reaction would be to the knowledge that he'd taken Nicole's innocence.

Staunchly, he deferred that issue for later.

"The duke must have had a million questions," Nicole murmured.

"He did." Dustin met her gaze. "And I explained a great deal, including the fact that Stoddard was Aldridge's protégé and had come in his stead when Aldridge went into hiding. But I couldn't tell Trent all he needed to know—where Nick Aldridge was hiding, why I was so personally involved . . ." A pause. "Who I was protecting. And why. Those questions, I couldn't answer without betraying your confidence, which I will not do."

"That's why you're here," Nicole stated softly.

"Yes, Derby. That's why I'm here." He drew a harsh breath. "Nicole, as you yourself just said, Alexander is Trent and Ariana's son. Do I truly have the right to deprive them of all the facts surrounding the telegram they received? The answer is no. Yet that's what I'm doing—unless you allow me to do otherwise. It comes down to the trust I just alluded to. If you trust me, you'll believe in my instincts—that both my brother and Ariana will guard your secret with the same integrity as I. You have my word. I'll say about them what you've said about Sullivan. I'd place my life in their hands." With that, Dustin offered the decision to Nicole and her father. "What shall I do?"

Nicole's reply came in a heartbeat, which was all it took to elicit her father's nod. "Tell them."

Waves of relief radiating through him, Dustin caught Nicole's fingers, brought them to his lips. "You have my thanks." He glanced over at Nick. "Both of you. Mine and my family's. Now I can ensure everyone's safety *and* get to the heart of the matter at the same time."

Nicole's whole body tensed. "I don't want you hurt," she said fiercely.

"Stop worrying, Derby." Now he was able to grin. "Besides, you've got more important things to worry about. Like fulfilling that claim you made yesterday."

"What claim?" Nick demanded.

"I'm racing alongside Nicole today at Epsom," Dustin informed him. "To add some healthy competition and a few obstacles to her run. She's boasted that she'll beat me by at least five lengths."

"Arrogant chit," Nick chuckled.

"Arrogant, perhaps." Nicole's eyes sparkled. "But right." She rolled up her sleeves. "Give me a quarter hour to drink my coffee and eat a bite of breakfast. I'll be at the stables by six. Ready to best you on the Derby course." Sobering, she added, "Tell your family that I'm sorry. If there's anything I can do . . ."

"You already have." Dustin squeezed her hands then, reluctantly, released them. "A quarter hour, Derby. I'll be waiting."

* * *

But he wasn't.

Nicole paced about the stables for ten minutes. Then she started worrying.

"Calm down, Stoddard." Brackley shot her an exasperated look as he tacked up Blanket, their newly purchased mare, in preparation for her morning exercise. "The marquis is a busy man. He knows where we are. He'll be here."

"He said he'd be at the stables at six."

"Maybe he's giving us time to ready Dagger and Winning Streak. Or maybe he overslept. When the hell did you become so skittish? It's only ten minutes past the hour."

Pressing her lips together, Nicole fell silent. She couldn't very well say she knew Dustin was awake because he'd been at her cottage less than thirty minutes ago, now could she?

Something was wrong.

She knew it. She felt it. It wasn't the amount of time that had elapsed, for Brackley was right; ten minutes was negligible. It was intuition.

The same intuition that told her Dustin needed her.

"You're right, Brackley," she forced herself to say calmly. She stroked Blanket's velvet muzzle, soothing her as she stomped about the stall. "Clearly, both Blanket and I are full of nervous energy. Why don't I take her out and exercise her? It would ease your head lad's morning schedule and divert my attention to something useful. I've already tacked up Dagger and Winning Streak. That leaves me nothing pressing to do before we depart for Epsom. So this would benefit us all. I won't venture far. You can send for me when Lord Tyreham shows up."

"Sure. Good idea." Brackley grinned. "Only don't use up *too* much of that energy. You want to beat Lord Tyreham and Winning Streak."

Feigning a smile, Nicole gathered up Blanket's reins. "I won't."

She led the mare from the stables, abandoning all pretense the moment the door closed behind them. Gazing across the grounds, Nicole considered riding directly to the manor, then dismissed the idea. If something had happened at the house, something that would have altered the training schedule, she and Brackley would have been advised.

Mounting Blanket, she followed the impulse that commanded she head back toward her cottage, this time not across the open grounds but by way of the woods.

She was halfway there when she heard the struggle.

"Happy, Tyreham? You're not tough enough to take us both," a deep voice growled.

"Come on, Parrish," another voice—this one taut with pain—inserted. "My side is killin' me. And your head is bleedin' bad. Let's go."

"In a minute." A sickening thud, followed by a groan. "That one was for my head." Another punch. "That one's for Archer's guts." A final blow, more vicious than the others. "And that last one's to remind you to stay the hell out of things that don't concern you. Cut out the late-night talks with your brother, because the next time it won't be your blood, it'll be your life. Yours and your nephew's."

Nicole felt bile rise to her throat. Swiftly, she dismounted, tying Blanket to a tree, intentionally rustling the branches and making as much noise as possible.

Her ruse worked.

"Someone's comin'," she heard the lowlife named Archer mutter. "Let's get outta here."

Swift movements, followed by a grunt of pain. "I can't run. I think he broke my ribs."

"Then limp."

An answering oath, followed by slow, unsteady footsteps that grew fainter, more distant.

The instant she sensed it was safe, Nicole dashed forward. She saw Dustin's huddled form twenty feet away.

"Dustin." Dropping to her knees beside him, she eased him onto his back. With quaking hands, she smoothed hair off his bruised forehead, her insides twisting with fear.

He blinked, trying to focus. "Derby?" Reflexively, his head turned in her direction, and he groaned.

"Don't move." Nicole stabbed in her pocket until she found a handkerchief.

"I heard . . . hoofbeats. Did you ride here?"

She could scarcely think, much less answer. "Yes." Her voice trembled as she dabbed the handkerchief to Dustin's bloodied jaw. "Blanket is tied to a nearby tree."

"Derby . . . listen to me." Dustin gripped her wrist, halting her ministrations and shuddering at the resulting pain he caused himself. "This might be . . . our only chance to stop them. They're hurt, and they're on foot . . . until the main road. Ride to the manor. Tell Poole . . . to get Saxon. To follow them. Race, Derby. As if this were the course at Epsom."

"I can't leave you like this."

"Go, dammit!"

The urgency of his tone convinced her. Jumping to her feet, Nicole rushed back to Blanket. An instant later, rider and horse tore off through the woods, not slowing until they'd reached the manor.

Dismounting, Nicole dashed up the steps and pounded on the door.

"Stoddard." Poole greeted her with a disapproving frown. "You needn't hammer. What can I do for you?"

"Get Saxon," she said, remembering the name Dustin had said. "Now, Poole. Lord Tyreham's been hurt. Hurry, please."

Poole went sheet white. Without another word, he stalked to the foot of the stairway and did the unthinkable: "Thorne!" he shouted.

Seconds later, a tall, formidably built man shot down the steps.

"You're Saxon?" Nicole demanded.

"I am."

"Two men just attacked Lord Tyreham. He sent me to get you. He wants you to follow—"

"Where was this?" Saxon interrupted. "Show me the direction. I'll find them."

"In the woods just east of the tenants' section." She pointed. "They're hurt and moving slowly. They were fleeing by foot to the main road. Take my horse."

Saxon was down the steps and mounting before she'd finished, blasting across the grounds like a storm wind.

"Where the hell did Saxon go?" A thunderous voice from the second floor landing brought Nicole's head around. "He was ordered not to leave my son."

Poole reacted at once, retreating to the foot of the stairs and angling his gaze upward. "It's Lord Tyreham, sir," he informed the powerful, dark-haired man whose uncanny physical resemblance to Dustin left no doubt as to who he was. "Stoddard says he's been hurt."

The duke took the steps three at a time, descending on Nicole like an avenging angel. "Where is he?"

"In the woods, Your Grace. He's been beaten, badly I think. I wasn't with him long enough to judge. He sent me to fetch Saxon—to pursue the assailants, which he just rode off to do."

Alarm slashed across Trenton Kingsley's face, and he turned to Poole. "Stay with my wife and son. I'll go with Stoddard."

"Of course, Your Grace."

Nicole led Trenton across the grounds at a dead run.

"He's through those trees." She pointed.

Trenton lunged forward until he'd reached his brother's side. "Dustin?"

One eye cracked open. "Did Saxon . . . ?"

"Stoddard delivered your message," Trenton supplied. "Saxon went after those filthy bastards. He'll find them. In the meantime, let's put you back together."

"Good." Dustin seemed to relax, then tensed again. "Stoddard—where is he?"

"Right here, my lord." Nicole walked forward, stifling a cry as she saw the small pool of blood that had gathered alongside Dustin's head. Her hands balled into fists of impotent rage, and she struggled to repress her anger and her fear. If ever she needed to display the control one expected of a man, it was now, and not because she felt compelled to shield her identity from Trenton, for he'd know soon enough who she was, but because she wanted to offer Dustin the strength he needed.

Puffy eyes didn't seem to dull Dustin's insight, at least not when it came to her. "It's not as bad . . . as it looks," he managed. "They got mostly my head and my mouth . . . those areas bleed a lot." A semblance of that devastating smile. "Besides, if you think I look bad . . . you should see them."

Relief surged through her, mirrored simultaneously on Trenton's face.

"Stoddard, can you help me carry him?" Trenton asked, turning to Nicole.

"Of course."

"No, Trent." Dustin inched his head from side to side. "Derby's too . . . slight."

"Derby?" Trenton frowned in noncomprehension, looking as if he were trying to determine whether or not his brother were delirious.

"Lord Tyreham calls me Derby because he hired me to win the Derby," Nicole explained as briefly as possible. Now was *not* the time to pour out her whole story, reveal who she was. "And I'm perfectly strong and capable. If we make a seat with our arms, we can carry him without worsening any of his injuries."

Trenton nodded. "Good idea."

"You take most of my weight, Trent," Dustin muttered.

"Stop worrying about me," Nicole retorted, helping Trenton boost Dustin from the ground. "I'll be fine."

"Who's worrying about you?" Dustin eased into the makeshift seat with a grimace, gritted his teeth as they moved carefully toward the clearing. "It's me I'm worrying about. You might drop me."

God, he was actually trying to make her laugh.

The generosity of his action spawned a rush of love in Nicole's heart so intense, so profound, it brought tears to her eyes. And suddenly, with the clarity of a flawless diamond, she realized that all her objections, her half-hearted attempts at self-protection, were for naught. Even if the adaptations she faced were next to impossible, even if her heart ended up shattered, she loved Dustin Kingsley far too much to walk away. He was her fate, her future. And for however long Dustin's "forever" lasted, in whatever capacity he wanted her—she was his.

Odd that so monumental a decision would strike now, under these unlikely circumstances. All her other firsts with Dustin had been in wildly romantic settings as magnificent as the man with whom she'd shared them. They'd met on a starlit night along the Thames, made love in a secluded cabin, shared twilight and stargazing in sensual, stolen moments. Yet here she was, silently committing herself to him for—what in her case could mean nothing less than the rest of her life—and it was under the most *un*romantic, harshly realistic circumstances imaginable.

Maybe it wasn't so odd after all, she decided, sagging with relief as the manor drew near. Maybe it had taken the shock of seeing Dustin vulnerable, needing *her,* that had made her realize how badly she needed him.

And need him she did. Enough to bid her former life good-bye, to become a mistress, even—God help her—a marchioness, if by some miracle he asked.

A soft smile touched Nicole's lips. The moment Dustin was able to have that talk, she was ready.

"Just a bit farther," Trenton muttered. He glanced at his brother. "How are you holding up?"

"I've been better." Dustin's jaw was dotted with sweat, mixing with a fine trickle of blood. "Derby?" He tried to turn his head, then gave it up.

"I'm quite well, my lord," she assured him as they neared the entranceway steps. "And you had best be, too. Oh, I'm not totally unreasonable. I'll agree to postpone our Epsom competition for a day or two, but that is my absolute limit. After which, I intend to beat you by those five lengths I boasted. Perhaps six lengths, given the fact that you're not quite yourself."

Trenton's head snapped around at the flippancy of her tone; and Nicole realized how cheeky she must sound—a jockey speaking with such familiarity to his employer.

In contrast, Dustin emitted a pained chuckle. "Don't make me laugh, Derby. It hurts."

"Take the stairs slowly," Trenton instructed, turning his attention back to the matter at hand.

Poole flung open the entranceway door, rushing out to assist them. "The duchess and marquis are fine, sir," he informed Trenton, assessing Dustin's condition as he helped guide him inside. "They're with Mrs. Hopkins in the nursery." He frowned. "Lord Tyreham?"

"Hello, Poole." A corner of Dustin's mouth lifted ever so slightly. "I'm in bad need of a brandy."

"I'll bring one at once, sir." With obvious relief, Poole glanced at Trenton. "Quinn went to fetch Dr. Welish. They should be back within the half hour."

"Excellent." Trenton gestured for Nicole to veer with him toward the staircase. "In the interim, I'll take Lord Tyreham to his chambers and clean his wounds. Bring me some towels and a basin of water."

"Very good, sir."

Nicole walked gingerly up the stairs, helping Trenton balance Dustin's weight. Finally, they reached the landing and rounded it, facing an endless hall.

"Which way, Your Grace?" she asked.

Trenton jerked his head in the direction of Dustin's room. "It's the last one on the right."

Minutes later, they lowered Dustin to his bedcovers, where he gratefully lay back.

"The blood's soaked down to his shirt," Trenton bit out. "I'll peel it away so it doesn't stick to whatever bruises are beneath it. You get his boots and breeches."

Nicole froze. "What?"

Trenton tossed her an exasperated look. "I said, get his boots and breeches off. It will expedite things for Dr. Welish. I'll handle the shirt, which is a more delicate task."

That depends on who you're asking, she almost blurted out.

Feeling Dustin's eyes upon her, she glanced over, realizing by the slight twitch of his lips that he'd read her thoughts as clearly as if she'd spoken them aloud.

"All right." Ducking her head to hide her flaming cheeks, Nicole tugged off first one boot, then the other, wondering how the duke would react once he learned who she was.

"Let Stoddard go, Trent." Evidently, Dustin had decided to take pity on her and salvage her modesty. "He looks worse than I do." The statement ended on a groan, and Nicole's head shot up, all nonsensical thoughts vanishing in the wake of his pain.

"Just a little more," Trenton appeased, inching the shirt down Dustin's arms, lifting him enough to yank it free, leaving a dozen angry bruises in its wake. "There. Done." He looked up as Poole hurried in, carrying a basin and some towels, a bottle of brandy tucked beneath his arm.

"Dr. Welish is here, sir," the butler announced.

"Good." Trenton glanced at Nicole. "You do look shaken, Stoddard. Go to your quarters and rest."

"No."

The word was out before she could restrain it.

Trenton's dark brows rose. "Pardon me?"

"It's all right, Trent," Dustin murmured weakly. "Let him wait in the sitting room."

With an astonished shake of his head, Trenton conceded. "Fine. Wait in the sitting room."

An hour later, Poole came to summon Nicole. "Lord Tyreham wishes to see you."

She leaped to her feet. "Is he all right?"

"Yes, thank heavens. His lordship's excellent physical condition prevented him from sustaining a more serious thrashing." A smug lift of Poole's brows. "It also helped him deliver an unexpected, and most certainly unwelcome, retaliation."

Nicole found herself grinning. "How unfortunate for his attackers."

"Yes, wasn't it?" Poole sniffed. "In any case, the marquis is experiencing a bit of pain, but the brandy is already alleviating that. Overall, he's doing remarkably well." A brief flicker of emotion crossed Poole's face. "Thank you, Stoddard. From all of us at Tyreham. Your swift and courageous actions spared his lordship further injury. We're grateful." He drew himself up, protocol restored. "You're welcome to see him now."

Swallowing, Nicole nodded. Then she hurried into the hall and up the stairs to Dustin's room.

Trenton answered her knock. "Stoddard." There was a definite gentling to his tone.

Had Dustin told him?

No, Nicole decided, studying the duke's face. There was no indication that he knew.

"Trent, let me speak with Stoddard alone." Dustin's voice was tired but definite.

His brother's jaw tightened. "If this is about Aldridge . . ."

"Later, Trent," Dustin interrupted. "Give me a few minutes. You'll have your answers."

With a curt nod, Trenton left, closing the door in his wake.

Nicole crossed the room in a heartbeat, kneeling beside

the bed. "Are you all right?" She reached out, touched the bandage that traversed Dustin's ribs, her lashes damp with the tears she could no longer suppress.

His hand lifted, fingertips catching the moisture on her cheeks. "You're beautiful. And, yes, I'm fine."

She kissed the hollow at the base of his throat, one of the few exposed spots that wasn't reddened, swollen, or bandaged. "At the moment, I'm anything but beautiful. I'm murderous. I want to kill those animals myself."

She felt his chuckle ripple against her mouth. "Had I known how fiercely protective you are—and how adept at transporting me around—I wouldn't have hired Saxon." He framed her face, lifting it so their gazes locked. "Do you think you got to Saxon in time?"

Nicole nodded. "Yes, I do. Your attackers were badly hurt, creeping away rather than fleeing. The one named Archer was groaning that his ribs were shattered, and the other one—Parrish—apparently had a bleeding head. You were most effective in maiming them, my lord." She attempted a smile. "I, too, was most effective. As you requested, I raced to the manor in record time. I only hope I manage to be as swift on Derby Day. The same applies to Saxon, who wasted not an instant, mounting Blanket and dashing off mere seconds after hearing my story. Further, it stands to reason that he found Archer and Parrish. If he hadn't, he'd have returned to Tyreham by now, which he hasn't. So I'm sure he's following them, just as you wished."

"Nicole." He looked deeply into her eyes. "I needed this moment alone for two reasons. First, to convince you I was fine, to see you, to touch you, to have you beside me. And second, to make certain, before I reveal everything to Trent, that this is still truly what you want."

"It is," Nicole answered softly. "For all our sakes, I want them to hear the truth." Her palm gently caressed Dustin's jaw. "Incidentally, your brother is a wonderful man. A bit severe, but wonderful. He loves you very much."

"The severity is a facade. You'll soon see that for yourself." Dustin kissed her fingers. "Thank you, Derby, not only for sharing your secret but for coming to my rescue."

"I knew," she whispered. "Somehow I knew you needed me."

"Does that surprise you?" he asked, his voice husky. "That's fate, my darling. Fate and love. Just as your mother described."

Trembling with emotion, Nicole touched her lips—ever so lightly—to his swollen mouth. "Heal quickly. We have much to discuss."

An intense expression crossed Dustin's face, awareness penetrating the effects of the brandy, alerting him to the fact that something had changed. "Today, Nicole. We'll talk today. I don't care what time or how, but I can't go through another night without resolving things between us."

"Nor can I."

He caught her hand. "Stay at Tyreham today. I don't want you at Epsom without me."

"What will you tell your staff?"

"The truth—or part of it. My bruises will be visible for some time, so we can't avoid revealing the fact that I was beaten. We'll say it was an attempted robbery and that you and Blanket made enough of a commotion to frighten my assailants off. I'll tell Brackley you're too shaken up to ride. How's that?"

"I shouldn't miss a day of practice."

"You won't be. You rode Blanket like a demon from hell. It's enough for one day. Nicole, if I can't be there to shield you, you can't go."

She saw beyond his command to the love that inspired it. "All right."

"No argument?"

"No argument. I'll simply conserve my energy for tomorrow, when I defeat you at Epsom."

"I have a better use for that energy, Derby, one I intend to explore soon. Very soon," Dustin repeated huskily, his eyes darkening as he took in her revealing flush. "You'd best go get Trent now, because in exactly one minute I'm going to forget my injuries and our whereabouts and drag you into this bed."

Nicole scrambled to her feet, propelled not by embarrassment but by the realization that, should Dustin do precisely what he'd just professed, she wouldn't have the strength, nor the inclination, to stop him.

Taking a deep breath, she crossed the room and opened the door.

It was no surprise to see the duke pacing back and forth in the hallway.

"Your Grace?" she said quietly. "Your brother would like to speak with you. You—and your wife and son." She glanced up and down the hall, ensuring they were alone. "To address your unanswered questions."

"I'll get Ariana." With that, Trenton strode off.

"The Kingsley men are unnervingly single-minded," Nicole muttered as she returned to Dustin's chambers.

A grin. "When we want something badly enough, yes, we are."

"Your brother's gone to fetch his family. Would you like me to leave?"

"No." Dustin's answer was instantaneous. "I want you beside me. We'll explain the situation to them together."

Together. The very word warmed her heart. "All right."

Footsteps sounded, grew closer.

"Don't look so frightened, Derby," Dustin murmured, studying Nicole's face. "You're in for a surprise."

"Thankfully, Ariana is not as intimidating as your brother, or I'd be quaking under the bed," she returned, perching in a nearby armchair.

"Now that Dr. Welish has proclaimed me well, you'll see another Trenton," he vowed. "Watch."

On cue, the door swung open and Ariana broke out of Trenton's embrace to dash in, Alexander in her arms. "Dustin." She reached the bed, her turquoise eyes clouded with worry. "Trenton just told me what happened. Are you all right?"

"I'm a lot better than I look," he teased.

"That's not much consolation," Trenton declared cheerfully. "You look like hell." He grinned, amazing Nicole with his lighthearted banter. "Then again, knowing you, this is a ploy to entice women to your bed, allegedly to minister to your wounds."

That Nicole didn't find at all amusing.

Ariana appeared equally unamused—but for different reasons. "Why did you go out alone?" she grilled Dustin.

"You knew those horrible men would be coming to Tyreham."

"I had to take that chance," he replied frankly. "For many reasons." With that, he gestured toward Nicole. "I had to visit my soon-to-be Derby winner."

Following Dustin's motion, Ariana spotted Nicole and broke into a brilliant smile. "Forgive my rudeness—" A pause. "Mr. Stoddard. I didn't see you. Thank you for coming to Dustin's rescue. We're very grateful."

"No gratitude is necessary," Nicole murmured, rising as Ariana approached her.

Five steps later, Alexander, realizing he was near enough, reached out, snatching the rim of Nicole's cap and tugging.

The cap didn't budge.

"Mama," he exclaimed.

"No, Alexander," Ariana scolded gently, prying his fingers loose. "You cannot do that."

"I was wondering what took him so long," Dustin commented from the bed. "Appendages of any kind offend him, be it mustaches or hats."

"Mama," Alexander repeated. Ignoring the adult conversation, he yanked his hand free of his mother's, leaning forward to pull, once again, on the unyielding brim. He gave a frustrated squeal when it refused to give.

"I'll relieve you for a while, misty angel," Trenton said with a hearty chuckle that made Nicole wonder why she'd ever found him intimidating. "Sorry, Stoddard," he added, lifting his son into his arms. "My son is as stubborn as a mule."

"I wonder who he could take after," Ariana mused wryly.

"Mama." Alexander continued to stare at Nicole's cap.

"Mama is exhausted," Trenton informed him. "She'll hold you again later."

Vehemently, the child shook his head. "Mama," he insisted, pointing at Nicole.

"He's not referring to me, Trenton," Ariana noted, her lips curving. "He's referring to Mr. Stoddard."

"Wonderful." Trenton rolled his eyes. "Not only does he call every female on earth 'Mama,' he's now extended the title to men as well."

"I don't think so." Ariana gazed calmly at Nicole, and,

with a start, Nicole realized Dustin's sister-in-law knew the truth. She knew, and she was asking permission to share that knowledge.

With an admiring nod, Nicole granted it.

Eyes sparkling, Ariana crossed over to shut the door and lean back against it. "Dustin." She folded her arms across her breasts, inclining her head in Nicole's direction. "You have quite a bit to share with us . . . wouldn't you say?"

Dustin blinked, easing up on his elbows and glancing from Ariana to Nicole. "You know."

"I know. From the onset, in fact. But evidently no one else does. Except, of course, my brilliant son."

"What is it you all know that I don't?" Trenton demanded, looking from one of them to the other.

Ariana arched an amused brow at her brother-in-law. "You summoned us here to fill in the missing pieces. Perhaps you should begin by introducing us to this lovely woman you've been protecting—whatever her name might be."

"It would be my greatest pleasure." A proud, relieved smile curved Dustin's swollen lips. "Trent, Ariana." He held out his hand, waiting until Nicole had crossed over to clasp it. "I'd like you to meet Nicole Aldridge." His voice was a whisper of a caress. "My very own miracle."

261

Fifteen

Silence greeted Dustin's announcement.

Nicole watched Trenton stiffen with shock, and he shifted Alexander's weight, staring at her as if she were a ghost. "Stoddard is . . . ?" He blanched, as the next reality struck. "Nicole *Aldridge?*"

"Yes, Your Grace." Purposely, Nicole abandoned Stoddard's voice in lieu of her own. "I'm Nick Aldridge's daughter."

"Of course," Ariana breathed, nodding. "Now it all makes sense. No wonder Dustin is so fiercely committed to resolving these crimes." Warmly, she added, "It's a pleasure to meet you, Nicole. I hope you know your secret is safe with us."

"I've been a bloody fool." Trenton moved closer, studying Nicole's face at close range. "But it never occurred to me . . ."

"It wasn't supposed to," Nicole replied with an impish grin. "I worked long and hard perfecting Stoddard's boylike mannerisms. Remember, I had to convince everyone— even Poole."

"Which you did," Dustin commended. He brought her palm to his lips, making no attempt to hide his feelings. "Everyone but me, of course."

"Had you and Dustin met prior to the onset of this masquerade?" Ariana asked Nicole.

"Once." Nicole replied. With a deep breath, she recounted the entire story, from their meeting at the Thames, to the threats on her father's life, to her answering Dustin's personal as Nick Aldridge's protégé.

"Nicole is every bit as good as Aldridge's letter claimed," Dustin put in proudly. "You should see her ride."

"So Ariana's told me," Trenton responded.

"When I applied for the position, I had no idea that the gentleman I'd met and the notorious marquis of Tyreham were one and the same," Nicole confessed. "If I had, I would have dismissed this whole deception as an impossibility."

"Then I'm glad you didn't realize the truth," Ariana declared.

"Nicole, where is your father?" Trenton demanded.

A heartbeat of a pause. Then, "He's staying at Tyreham. With me."

Trenton's jaw tightened. "Does anyone know this?"

"Other than those in this room and our friend Sully, no."

"Sully?"

"Sullivan," Dustin supplied. "He's the jockey I told you about. The one Archer and Parrish thrashed in an attempt to find out where Aldridge was."

"He told them nothing," Nicole inserted loyally.

"Parrish?" Trenton swooped down on the name. "I thought all we had was the name Archer."

"Until this morning, that was true. But Nicole and I both heard Archer call his cohort Parrish. So we now have his name as well."

"How did Nicole happen upon you during your beating?" Trenton asked. "You'll forgive me, but I'm beginning to doubt it was mere coincidence."

"It wasn't," Nicole answered honestly. "It was a combination of tangible misgivings and emotional instinct. You see, I was the last one to see Dustin before he was attacked. He came to my cottage before dawn to tell Papa and me about the telegram you'd received and to ask our permission to reveal the entire truth to you. We agreed. As he was leaving, he said he'd meet me at the stables at six. I assume he intended to use the intervening time to speak with you. When he didn't arrive, I knew something was wrong. Gut instinct compelled me to ride Blanket through the woods toward the cottage. That's when I heard those men. I made as much noise as I could to scare them off. It worked."

Trenton cleared his throat. "Forgive my abruptness, Nicole. I don't mean to interrogate you. It's just that . . ." He glanced at the wriggling child in his arms.

"You needn't explain, Your Grace. I fully understand. That is why I agreed to divulge the truth to you about my identity and Papa's. We'll do anything we must to keep your son safe."

An unsteady nod. "Thank you." Trenton's glance shifted to his brother. "So all we're really sure of are the names Archer and Parrish, and the fact that they have a scarred associate. We won't know another thing until Saxon returns."

"Wait." Nicole's grip on Dustin's hand tightened. "A thought just occurred to me. Dustin, do you recall what Parrish said to you before he staggered off? During those last few punches?"

Dustin frowned in concentration. "Something about one punch being for his head and one for Archer's guts."

"Yes. And the final one, he said, was to remind you to stay out of things that don't concern you. He warned you that if you wanted to save yourself and Alexander, you'd better 'cut out the late-night talks with your brother.'" Nicole inclined her head in Dustin's direction. "Now how would he know you and the duke had a late-night talk?"

A heartbeat of silence.

"How indeed," Dustin repeated at last. "Unless someone told him."

"Someone who was inside the manor at the time of our talk." Trenton scowled. "Not only inside the manor but right outside the study. How else could he have eavesdropped on our discussion? Dustin, you and I were behind closed doors. Our voices were low. Hell, the window wasn't even ajar."

"And no one gets by Poole." Dustin's hands balled into fists. "So whoever this informant is could very possibly be a resident of Tyreham." He shot up—and groaned in pain.

"Where the hell do you think you're going?" Trenton demanded. "You're hardly in shape to stagger downstairs and interrogate the staff—unless you want to swoon at their feet."

"Dustin," Nicole said softly. "Determining who eavesdropped on your conversation is a delicate matter. You need to mull over the possible suspects, then narrow down that list. Next, you must devise the most effective course of action to take, so as not to alert the culprit or upset your staff. I know how badly you want to resolve things *and* how impatient you are to do so. I'm equally as impatient. But you've been confined to bed for the day. Since your tactics require planning anyway, and since you'll do a far better job of effecting those plans once you're healed, why not use today to think and tomorrow to act? Also, remember that by then you'll have another crucial piece of the puzzle, Saxon's report." Nicole gave the man she loved a tender smile. "Wait a day. Then you'll work your magic."

With a sigh, Dustin sank back against the pillows. "All right, Derby. One day."

"No wonder you called her your miracle," Trenton observed dryly. "I've been your bloody brother for two and thirty years and haven't once been able to placate you like that." He shot Nicole an admiring look. "What's your secret?"

"I'm in love with him," Nicole returned softly.

Trenton's expression softened. "So I see."

A tiny spark lit her eyes. "Then perhaps you'll turn away that stream of women when they arrive to minister Dustin's wounds."

Ariana laughed aloud. "If Trenton doesn't, *I* will."

"Also, Your Grace," Nicole continued, straight-faced, "I hope you won't hold it against me that I'm terribly inept at removing boots. Men's boots, that is."

While Nicole's first quip had only succeeded in making Trenton look sheepish, her second one caused his mouth to drop open. "Lord," he muttered, realizing the significance of his earlier actions. "Not only the boots, but the breeches." He actually flushed. "I apologize. I had no idea . . ." He leveled an accusing stare at his brother. "Why didn't you say something?"

"I did . . ." Dustin grinned. ". . . eventually. Until then, I was having too much fun watching Nicole squirm."

"What shocking incident did I evidently miss?" Ariana demanded.

"Nothing much, misty angel." Trenton continued to glower at his brother. "Only the fact that I ordered Stoddard to strip Dustin so I could cleanse his wounds, which poor Nicole began to do."

"Dustin"—Ariana's shoulders were shaking—"that's unconscionable, even for you."

"Yes." An unrepentant chuckle. "It is, isn't it?"

"Nicole," Trenton declared, catching Alexander's flailing fist. "You have my permission to trounce my brother at Epsom. I hope you beat him by twelve lengths, not six."

Her eyes twinkled. "I'll certainly try, Your Grace."

"Trenton," he corrected.

"Trenton."

"You've acquired a welcome ally, Nicole," Ariana said warmly. She met Nicole's gaze. "Actually, two."

"Thank you, Your Grace," Nicole murmured. "And please forgive me for the danger I've put your family in. I'll do everything I can to eliminate it."

"My name is Ariana. And you're as much a victim as we are. We'll resolve this situation together. After which"—her whole face lit up—"I anticipate a most festive future."

It was nearly noon when Saxon returned to Tyreham. He was immediately shown to the marquis's chambers.

"At last. Come in." Dustin rose stiffly from the armchair in which he'd been sitting.

"Are you in pain, my lord?" Saxon inquired with a furrowed brow. "My uncle apprised me that your wounds were, thankfully, not as bad as they could have been."

"I'm sore. I'm also losing my mind—with boredom *and* worry. Now tell me what you found."

A competent nod. "I found your assailants without too much trouble, thanks to Stoddard's directions. As we suspected, they made their way to the main road, where their horses awaited. To your credit, sir, it took them long minutes to mount, given the injuries you inflicted. I followed at a discreet pace for one and one-half hours, at which point they stopped."

"Where?"

"At a run-down stable just outside London. It was dingy and dark, and once they'd entered the stable, I could make out only their forms. I could, however, hear their words. They entered, met with a third man who was clearly their superior, judging by his denigrating manner. The conversation was brief. They announced the job was done. He threw some pound notes at them, courtesy of their employer who, he said, was feeling generous but who would not pay another cent until they found Nick Aldridge. He then tossed them out. They limped to their mounts and bid a hasty retreat." Saxon opened a thin portfolio. "At that point, I could have rushed right back to Tyreham, but it stood to reason that I should stay long enough to catch a glimpse of this third colleague."

"Did you?"

"Yes. When he emerged into the light, alone and unaware that I was present and crouched behind his newly arrived bales of hay, I got a thorough look at him." With a quick glance at his scribbled notes, Saxon elaborated. "He was approximately five feet ten, of average build, unkempt and unshaven, his hair a light, filthy brown. His eyes were pale blue, icy and penetrating. Most significant of all, he had a massive scar on his left forearm. Quite hideous looking, as your one-time jockey described." Saxon lifted his head. "The lad who delivered his hay referred to him as 'Coop.'"

"Coop." Dustin jumped on the information. "At last we have a name. You said his stable is on the outskirts of London?"

"The East End, to be exact, sir."

"Dammit." Dustin began to pace, then winced and stopped. "I want this Coop watched. I want to find out who visits him, how long they stay, and what they talk about. What I *want* is his bloody employer. *He's* the one with the influence necessary to back a scheme as costly as the one we're contending with."

"I quite agree. The sophistication of this operation, not to mention how long it's been in effect, leads me to believe that this Coop's employer is a man of some intelligence and power. In order to put an end to his conspiracy, we must put an end to him—in the figurative sense."

"Right now our only link to this anonymous bastard is Coop."

"True. So we must lie in wait for him to show up at Coop's stable."

"But who do I send to survey the stable?" Dustin wondered aloud. "Who do I *trust?* Moreover, who'll do the job right besides you? Damn." Dustin made another attempt to pace, this time disregarding the resulting pain. "I promised Trent you'd watch over Alexander. I also want you to keep an eye on Stoddard. I'm more worried than ever about him. With those lowlifes hunting so hard for Aldridge, they're bound to learn Stoddard is his protégé. After which, the lad's life will be endangered as well." A grim pause. "Especially now."

"Now, sir?"

"Yes. That's what I meant when I said 'Who do I trust?'" Dustin inhaled sharply, turning his head towards Saxon. "During those final seconds when Parrish was punching me, he warned me to stay out of things that don't concern me, more specifically, to discontinue my late-night talks with my brother."

"Did he?" Saxon's brows rose. "Given my uncle's vigilance at the manor's entranceway, and the fine sentry duty performed by the guards at your front gates, Parrish's comment makes me wonder if Coop might very well have a pair of ears stashed right here at Tyreham."

"Exactly. And I need you to discover the owner of that pair of ears, as well as look out for Stoddard and Alexander." Dustin scowled. "Which brings us back to the problem of scrutinizing Coop's stable."

"The problem's been resolved, sir. Effecting its solution was the other cause for my delayed return to Tyreham." Saxon cleared his throat. "After pondering the exact line of reasoning you just expounded upon—other than the final item, which I had yet to learn—I knew it was infeasible for me to be away from your estate. So I took the liberty of summoning a longtime associate, William Blaker, who began with me at Mr. Hackberth's investigative agency, and who now has a small agency of his own. Blaker is both thorough and trustworthy. We often assist each other when a situation requires more than a single investigator. Still, as I had yet to obtain your approval, I refrained from divulging the details of the case. He knows only what he's to do, that is, to observe Coop's stable, keep track of all comings and goings, as well as every caller and the details of his visit. All other specifics—why this needs to be done and for whom— remain undisclosed. Blaker is already posted outside the stable, and intends to remain there until I advise him otherwise. I hope that meets with your satisfaction, my lord."

"Saxon," Dustin replied, a glint in his eye, "remind me to increase your wages. I don't think I'm paying you enough."

The investigator's lips twitched. "I'll remember to do that, sir." His smile faded. "I'd like your permission to take the next logical step, one I'd intended to take when we returned from Newmarket, had this commotion not ensued."

"What step?"

"I'd like to question Stoddard."

Trenton's knock was firm.

He waited the full minute Dustin had advised him, then knocked again, this time murmuring, "It's Broddington. I need to speak with you."

Another prolonged silence, not a rustle of movement from within the cottage.

"Stoddard, open the door," Trenton added quietly. "Lord Tyreham sent me. I must talk to you."

The lock turned, and the door inched open, violet eyes assessing that it was, indeed, Dustin's brother.

"Come in." She opened the door enough for him to slip through, then shut it tightly in his wake.

"Nicole"—Trenton turned to face her—"I realize you weren't expecting me, but . . ." His voice trailed off, and he blinked in astonishment as he encountered Nicole Aldridge, her dark hair flowing loose about her shoulders, her fine features unobstructed by a jockey's cap. "Damn," he muttered.

A tiny smile played about her lips. "Does that mean my disguise is effective?"

"It means I must have been bloody blind."

"Don't be so hard on yourself. There's quite a bit of Stoddard in me." She indicated her shirt and breeches.

"Yes, but . . ." Trenton shook his head in amazement. "No wonder Ariana is still laughing over the expression on my face when Dustin announced who you were. I don't blame her. Until now, I'd always considered myself to be a perceptive man."

"Perception isn't the issue here," Nicole observed softly. "Even if I'd been dressed as myself, your awareness of me would have been casual, at best. In truth, the only woman you really *see* is your wife. Which is how it should be."

Trenton studied her intently—not her appearance but something more. "Ariana is right. I can see why Dustin feels about you as he does. When this nightmare is behind us, I hope you'll give us a chance to get to know you better."

"I'd be delighted, Your Gr—Trenton," she corrected herself. "At which time I promise to let Alexander tear my cap from my head."

He chuckled. "That will give my son a great deal of satisfaction. He never did manage to yank off Dustin's mustache, despite eight months of trying. My poor brother ultimately gave in and shaved it off, right before he met you."

"You're being here . . . Dustin's all right, isn't he?"

An emphatic nod. "He's fine. Stubborn as hell, but fine. He made three unsuccessful attempts to descend the stairs and traverse the hallway, with the intentions of crossing the grounds and coming here, before he finally agreed to let me stand in for him."

Nicole blinked. "Stand in for him?"

"Yes, to tell you that Saxon has requested the right to talk to you, or rather, Stoddard. Dustin wants it to be your choice as to whether or not you do so—now, if at all."

Thoughtfully, Nicole chewed her lip. "I suspected this might happen when Dustin told me he'd hired an investigator. Since I'm allegedly Nick Aldridge's protégé, it stands to reason I'd know a great deal about him, perhaps even something I don't realize I know. Saxon wouldn't be very thorough if he didn't interrogate me." She frowned. "The question isn't whether or not I'll speak with him, it's whether or not I should tell him everything. On the one hand, I want to protect Papa, on the other hand, perhaps I'd be doing both him and you a disservice if I limited Saxon's facts. Assuming, of course, I'm even able to convince Saxon that I'm a boy. We're talking about a seasoned investigator, not an average person. So how do I handle this?"

"You tell him the truth."

Nick Aldridge's voice came from across the hall. "Nickie," he added, walking over to them. "We've come too far to back down. We're on the brink of discovery, and to keep things from Tyreham's investigator would be to impede his progress and keep the duke's son in danger." Turning to Trenton, he extended his hand. "I can tell without asking that you're Tyreham's brother. You look just like him. I'm Nick Aldridge."

Trenton grasped Nick's fingers in a firm handshake. "I've seen you race. You're extraordinary." A smile tugged at his lips. "As for family resemblance, perhaps earlier today I could have said the same about you and Nicole. But not now."

"Ah, you're seeing Nickie for the first time," Nick realized aloud. "Well, no offense taken. Other than her love for horses and a few less admirable traits, she is, overall, not me but very much her mother."

"Trenton," Nicole interrupted. "Did Saxon learn anything new?"

The barest hint of a pause. "Nothing monumental."

"In other words, Dustin instructed you not to say anything."

"In other words, Dustin informed me he'd discuss it with you later. Right now, he wants you to redon your disguise and come with me to the manor."

"I thought you said he was letting me make the decision about whether or not I speak with Saxon."

"He is." A twinkle. "But he's *not* letting you make the decision about whether or not you speak with *him*. Apparently, you and he scheduled a discussion for this evening. He intends to hold it. He also intends to have someone escort you to the manor. And I've been appointed."

"That settles it," Nick put in. "Go with the man, Nickie. Talk to this Saxon. Answer his questions—*all* of them. Then do the same for the marquis." He held her gaze. "And, Elf, afterward, should Saxon wish to speak with me, the answer is yes."

"Papa, are you sure?"

"I'm sure. He's welcome to come here and ask whatever questions he chooses."

"Very well." She glanced down at her shirtfront, realizing she lacked her requisite binding, and headed off to effect her transformation. "Excuse me." She snatched her jockey's cap from a nearby side table. "Alden Stoddard will be down in a moment."

"Thank you, Broddington," Nick said when they were alone. "I don't think Nickie realizes how vulnerable she is right now. I worry every minute she's by herself."

"You can rest easy," Trenton replied. "I know my brother. And he won't let any harm befall Nicole. Ever. Moreover, it's *I* who should be thanking *you*. By trusting us, you're taking a risk. All I can say is, you won't be sorry."

"No, I don't expect I will be."

"One last thing. Does the name Coop mean anything to you?"

"Coop?" Nick frowned. "Not offhand, no. Should it?"

"That's the man with the scarred forearm. Dustin thought the name might trigger something."

"I wish it would." Nick rubbed his chin. "That damned man's been on my mind since Tyreham first brought him up. But for the life of me, I can't figure out where I saw him. That doesn't mean I've stopped trying. I haven't. And I'll remember yet."

"I'm sure you will." Trenton glanced up as Nicole descended the stairs, tucking pins beneath her cap. "Well, Tyreham's famous jockey has returned. Shall we go?"

"Yes. Immediately." Nicole drew an unsteady breath. "Before I lose my nerve."

"Don't be so skittish, Stoddard." Saxon flipped through his portfolio, frowning as Stoddard paced circles about the library. "I'm merely going to ask you a few routine questions."

"I'm sure you are." Nicole came to an abrupt halt. "But my answers are going to be anything but routine."

A pucker formed between the investigator's brows. "Why do you say that?"

Crossing the room, Nicole tugged open the library door, peering into the hallway. Relief flowed through her as she saw Trenton posted on the opposite wall, standing guard as he'd promised. He gave her a nod of encouragement, and, smiling shakily, she retreated back inside, closing the door in her wake.

"The duke is protecting our privacy," she told Saxon. "As I'm sure you've been informed, there's a possibility that someone at Tyreham is untrustworthy. And it's imperative that no one overhears this conversation. Only the marquis and his family are privy to what I'm about to tell you."

Saxon lowered his portfolio. "With all due respect, I've been provided with full details of . . ."

"No, you haven't." Nicole approached him, lowering herself to the leather settee. "Not because Lord Tyreham didn't trust you but because he was protecting me."

"You're Nick Aldridge's protégé."

"I'm Nick Aldridge's daughter."

The portfolio struck Saxon's lap with a thud. "Pardon me?"

Quietly and without hesitation, Nicole filled in the pieces Saxon had been denied. "Lord Tyreham gave us a place to stay, an income, and his word that no one would know my identity or Papa's whereabouts. But now that you're privy to both, I hope it will help."

"Well," Saxon said after a moment, "so much for my questions about whether or not you've heard from Aldridge. Obviously you have"—an ironic lift of his brows—"daily."

"Papa's offered to speak with you. At the cottage."

"Excellent. I'll do so first thing tomorrow."

"Please, sir." Nicole leaned forward. "Come before I leave for the stables at six. I won't let Papa answer the door, nor would it appear natural for you to be visiting Stoddard's father."

"I agree. However, given that you'll be traveling with Lord Tyreham to Epsom tomorrow, and given that I've been hired to act as Lord Tyreham's driver, it would be perfectly logical for me to visit Stoddard to make arrangements for the trip." Saxon rose, closing his portfolio with a flourish. "I'll be there at half after five."

"Thank you." Nicole rubbed her palms against her breeches. "There's one thing more."

"Yes?"

"I haven't discussed this with the marquis yet, but I intend to." She met Saxon's gaze. "I could be completely wrong, but I'd rather be wrong than negligent. As of this week, a new trainer has begun working at Tyreham's stables."

"Raggert."

"Yes, Raggert. He comes highly recommended and with a wealth of experience."

"But . . . ?" Saxon urged gently.

"But, frankly, I don't trust him. He hovers about me every moment he can, asking personal questions about my background, my association with Nick Aldridge, my training. He spends far less time with the horses than he does with me."

"You'd like me to keep an eye on him?"

"I'd *like* you to prove me wrong. But, given the fact that there might be an informant right here at Tyreham, I don't think we can afford to overlook anything—or anyone."

"Consider it done. And Miss Aldridge—pardon me, Mr. Stoddard," Saxon corrected himself purposefully. "It goes without saying that this entire conversation will remain confidential. Moreover, while I realize that your decision to tell me the truth wasn't an easy one to make, rest assured, you did the right thing. Your candor will enable me to keep all the residents of Tyreham safe and assist me in solving these crimes and restoring order to the turf."

"I'm counting on that, sir."

Dustin's bedchamber door opened on the heels of Nicole's first knock.

"Are you all right?" she demanded.

"At last." He drew her in, shutting and bolting the door behind her. "I've asked that we not be disturbed."

"What?" Nicole's baffled gaze moved from Dustin's face to his silk dressing robe. The deep vee at his chest revealed the bandage across his ribs was still in place, but much of the swelling on his face had receded, and his motions were far less stiff than earlier that day. "Poole said you were too weak to come down, that you'd requested I visit you in your chambers."

"I did."

Nicole's brows rose as he drew her against him, his palms smoothing over her shoulders and back. "You don't seem terribly weak to me. In fact, you seem much stronger than before."

"I am." His smile made her bones melt. "I fabricated the part about being weak. I wanted you up here." He bent, his lips brushing the side of her neck.

A quiver of pleasure ran through her. "Don't you want to hear about my conversation with Saxon?" she murmured. "Aren't you going to tell me what he found out from following Archer and Parrish?"

"Later." Dustin hooked an insistent forefinger beneath her chin. "Kiss me."

"Dustin . . ."

"Kiss me." He covered her lips with his, wincing a bit as his bruised mouth protested the pressure.

"You're going to aggravate your injuries." Tenderly, she stroked his jaw, eased away. "We should talk."

"You're right, we should, but not about Saxon." With that, Dustin scooped her up—ignoring the twinges of pain that resulted—and made his way across the room. Reaching the cushioned armchair, he seated himself, Nicole settled comfortably on his lap. "There."

She blinked. "There . . . what?"

"There—you're not budging and we're not digressing until we've had our discussion. And I don't mean about the crimes of the turf."

Nicole leaned back, regarding him from beneath the brim of her cap. "You really mean that."

"I really mean that. It's time we talked about us—about our future. We've waited too long already." Dustin angled her face to his, his midnight eyes dark with emotion. "Nicole, when you left me this afternoon and that brandy took effect, I slipped into a kind of half slumber. Do you know what I dreamed?"

Mutely, she shook her head.

"I dreamed you were carrying my child."

"Oh God." Nicole began to tremble. "I hadn't even considered . . ." She swallowed. "I was so preoccupied with my own feelings, I never even pondered the fact that I might be . . ."

"Does the possibility upset you?"

Two tears slid down her cheeks. "No," she whispered with aching candor. "It doesn't."

He kissed the tracks of her tears. "Shall I tell you how it makes me feel? Ecstatic. Elated. Awed and humbled all at once." His lips sought hers, brushing once, twice, feathering over her cheeks and nose, returning to her mouth in a whisper of a caress. "Tell me, darling," he breathed into her parted lips, "what events can I change, wrongs can I right, inequities can I balance? Tell me and I'll make them happen."

Forever, Nicole wanted to shout. *I want forever—and all that goes with it.*

Slowly, she drew back, determined to follow through as she'd intended. Nothing had changed, other than the wonderful new awareness that she might be carrying Dustin's child. And that awareness should only serve to strengthen her resolve. She belonged with Dustin—on whatever terms he would have her.

Her fingers clenched tightly in her lap. "Before I tell you my dreams, before you enumerate all the dragons you're willing to slay for me, there's something you should know, something that might make your sacrifices a little less drastic, your decisions a bit easier."

One dark brow rose. "Go on."

"Do you remember my saying I'd never be your mistress? That I'd never accept such a role, cherished or otherwise?"

"I remember."

"Well, I've changed my mind." She gazed up at him, her emotions bared for him to see. "Pride, ideals, even wishes vanish in the wake of feelings such as these. The simple truth is, I love you. I don't want to live without you. So I'll take my chances, be anything you want me to be, and pray that your love for me will endure."

Something profound flashed in Dustin's eyes. "Thank

you, Derby. That's the most beautiful gift I've ever been given. Unfortunately, it's not enough."

She blinked.

"I'm sorry to disappoint you," he continued, his voice hoarse with emotion. "But I won't settle for some. I want it all—marriage, children, grandchildren—and I want it with you. I want to put my ring on your finger and shout to the heavens that you're mine. I want to take you to bed and pour my soul into yours, hoping each time that our child is being conceived, a child born of the miraculous love his parents have for each other. I want to live with you, laugh with you, grow old with you. I want to awaken each morning with you beside me and go to sleep each night with you in my arms. No, Nicole—" Dustin shook his head definitively. "I won't settle for having you as my mistress. I want you for my wife. Marry me."

Nicole drew a shuddering breath. "Marriage is forever, Dustin."

"So are we."

"Forever is a long time."

"Not nearly as long as waiting for it."

A choked sound escaped Nicole's lips. "I won't share you," she whispered shakily.

"I don't want to be shared. I don't want other women. I want only you. It's been that way from the moment we met. It will be that way for the duration of time."

"What if I'm unable to make the transition from stables to manor? I know you insist titles mean nothing to you, and I believe that they don't. But, dear God, Dustin—a marchioness. I'm totally unprepared . . ."

"Fine. I'll renounce my title."

"You'll what?"

"Renounce my title. Relinquish it. Give it up. Although, in my opinion, you'd make the most spectacular of marchionesses. Still, if it causes you distress, consider it done."

"Just like that?"

"Just like that. Her Majesty, of all people, will understand. She loved the prince consort with all her heart." Dustin gave a dismissive wave of his hand. "So much for my title *and* my way of life. What other supposedly insurmountable obstacles are troubling you? Ah, the parties. I'll decline them all. The *ton?* I'll snub them. I'll even burn all my money if it will make you feel better. We can buy a farm, raise horses, live without servants or visitors. You can wear breeches every day, sleep naked in my arms each night . . ."

"Stop." Nicole pressed her fingers to his lips, too shaken to speak. She'd known he loved her, but never in her wildest imaginings had she fathomed the depth of that love, the enormity of what he'd be willing to sacrifice. God, she had to be the luckiest woman alive.

Abruptly, all her apprehension vanished.

"I don't want any of those things," she whispered, willing him to see beyond the words, to feel the wealth of emotion that spawned them. "I just want you—as you are."

Perception ignited Dustin's eyes, eased the rigidness from his shoulders. "Would you reconsider the part about sleeping naked in my arms each night?"

She gave him a watery smile. "Well, perhaps that."

"Nicole." He kissed her fingertips. "Say yes. Say it and by month's end you'll be Mrs. Dustin Kingsley."

"By month's end?" That made her start. "Dustin, that's five days after the Derby."

"All right," he conceded reluctantly. "I'm not unreasonable. I'll give you a fortnight to recover from the Derby or from the day we resolve the crimes plaguing the turf—whichever is sooner."

Joyous laughter bubbled up inside her, spilled out. *"That's* not unreasonable?"

"Very well, it is." A corner of his mouth lifted. "But as you noted earlier today, the Kingsley men are unnervingly single-minded when we want something badly enough, and I want you more than life itself. I intend to make you my wife—before you change your mind, before you conjure up new and equally nonexistent differences between us that would preclude our happiness."

"I have no other differences to name," she reassured him, wondering if it were possible to explode from exhilaration. "You've obliterated them all, just as you promised."

"I have, haven't I?" A self-satisfied grin. "To continue. I'll go to your father at dawn, secure his permission and his blessing. Then, I'll arrange for a special license to be delivered posthaste so it's ready and waiting. In the meantime, you make whatever wedding plans you choose. Large, small, formal, informal—I'm amenable to whatever sort of ceremony and reception you want. So long as when it's over, you're mine."

"I'd like a church wedding," Nicole answered softly, laying her cheek against his robe. "And a reception right here at Tyreham, but not in the manor."

"In the stables?" he queried huskily.

"Close. On the grounds. Where you and I walked, and rode, and created our first memories. At twilight. With all those we love present—our families, our friends, and the stars that brought us together."

"And your wishing locket?"

"And my wishing locket."

Smiling, Dustin wrapped his arms about her in a way that clearly stated he meant never to let go. "Am I going to have to prove myself to dozens of indignant jockeys and other assorted horsemen who love you as Sullivan does?"

"No. All they'll have to do is look at me to see how happy you've made me, and they'll welcome you with open arms."

"That's a relief." He rested his chin atop her cap. "Anyone else you'd like to invite?"

"Mama," Nicole managed in a choked voice. "But she'll already be there. As will your parents," she added, tilting her head back to gaze up at him.

"I love you." Dustin's breath grazed her lips. "I'll spend forever fulfilling your wishes."

"I love you, too." Nicole twined her arms about his neck. "And speaking of forever, my answer is yes." She smiled against his mouth. "After the Derby, Stoddard plans to retire, which is just as well. Because, all of a sudden, I find myself surprisingly eager to become the marchioness of Tyreham."

Sixteen

The earl of Lanston stepped gingerly into the stable, frowning at the muck that settled around his shoes, the stench that greeted his nostrils. It was a damned good thing he only had to come here once in a long while. More than that, he couldn't abide.

"Where are you, Cooper?" he called.

"I'm here. Hold on a minute." Coop stepped out of a stall, wiping his hands on the sides of his breeches, and leveling an ice blue stare at his visitor. "Well, I was wondering when you'd finally get here. The Derby's in three days. I haven't seen a sign of Raggert since he showed up on my doorstep over a week ago. What the hell's going on? How do you want this handled?"

"Raggert was a bit put out by the reception you gave him. He came directly to me with his report."

"The reception I gave him? Hell, Lanston, it was the middle of the night. What did he expect?"

"He was just doing his job, Cooper. In case you've forgotten, he works for me. As you do."

Coop wiped sweat from his face, a lethal glint flashing in his eyes. "Whatever you say. So what did Raggert tell you?"

"First of all, it appears Archer and Parrish were successful. Tyreham has restricted himself to licking his wounds

280

and preparing his contender for the Derby. He's made no further inquiries into the situation on the turf. So, for the time being, that's one less noose around our necks." The earl shifted his weight, scowling as he sank deeper into the ground. "Don't you ever clean this place?"

"It's a stable, Lanston, not a ballroom." Coop massaged his forearm. "So we're rid of Tyreham—for now. What about his jockey?"

A scowl. "Unfortunately, it appears Stoddard is every bit as good as Tyreham boasts. Arrogant, but good. Raggert detests him."

"Raggert hates anyone who's got a better way with horses than he does."

Lanston shrugged. "In any case, Raggert's been studying Stoddard for weeks, hoping to detect a weakness in his technique—something we might use to our advantage—but the blasted boy seems to be a model horseman."

"So we need him in our corner is what you're saying."

"Exactly. You and I both know my horse *must* win that Derby. Our pockets are counting on it."

"Are you sure your mount's good enough?"

"Oh, he's good enough, all right. Demon is as fast as they come. As is Baker, who's riding for me. Without Stoddard for competition, we'll win by a dozen lengths."

"Then we've got to bring Stoddard around."

"Indeed. I don't think it will be a difficult task. To begin with, Archer and Parrish will have no trouble finding him for their little talk. Stoddard practices at Epsom daily, accompanied by Tyreham and Brackley. Tomorrow Raggert will be joining them as well, supposedly to provide last-minute suggestions."

"Supposedly," Coop repeated. "I take it you want him there for another reason."

"I certainly do. Tomorrow is the final day of Stoddard's test trials. The Epsom meeting begins on the twenty-fifth, which will preclude further practices. Thus, tomorrow is also the day for Archer and Parrish to pose their business arrangement to Stoddard. And I want Raggert to overhear the outcome of that chat."

"What if the outcome isn't to our liking?"

"Should that happen—and I don't believe it will—I've made provisions to ensure the race anyway."

"Yeah? How?"

"That's my concern, not yours."

Coop's mouth thinned into a menacing line. "Getting paid is my concern."

"You'll get paid, Cooper," Lanston assured him. "We'll all get our long-awaited money." Pensively, he smoothed his neck cloth. "Now, to continue: I intend to be in the stands at Epsom tomorrow morning to keep Tyreham occupied. Instruct Archer and Parrish that they're to waylay Stoddard during that time. Tell them to make the offer attractive and the alternative terrifying. My guess is, the lad will be an easy target. He might love his work, but he's poor, he's naive, and he's alone. With the right incentive *and* the appropriate threat, he should give us no trouble."

"That's what you said about Aldridge."

Lanston bristled. "Aldridge was an entirely different matter. He's an established jockey, perhaps the finest one on the turf. He was seasoned, financially secure, and disgustingly ethical. Tact was what was needed to sway him, something you and your lowlifes lack. I should have handled that one myself."

"Really?" Coop bit out. "How? By marching into the paddock and announcing you're running this whole scheme? By telling everyone you'd have been bankrupt if you hadn't recouped your losses from this illegal operation? Now *that* would have given you high marks at the Jockey Club."

"Shut up, Cooper." Beads of perspiration dotted Lanston's brow. "I may be a thief, but at least *I'm* not a killer."

"No?" Coop inquired in a low, taunting voice. "Funny, I thought that was what you meant to do to Aldridge when you got your hands on him."

"Damn you." The earl took out a handkerchief and dabbed at his forehead. "If you hadn't murdered Redley, I'd never have to—"

"If I hadn't murdered Redley, he'd have blackmailed us out of every pound we earned or turned us over to the magistrate," Coop snarled. "So shut your bloody aristocratic mouth. I did what had to be done *and* took care of the whole thing without dirtying your noble hands. The entire procedure will repeat itself when we find Aldridge—this time *with* your blessing. So let's stop playing games, Lanston. Just do what you do best—issue the orders, let me carry them out, then pay me."

"If the process is that simple, why haven't your men found even a clue as to Aldridge's whereabouts?"

"Because you wanted the cheap way out. Because, as you well know, Archer and Parrish are brainless fools, useful only for browbeating terrified jockeys. Let me handle the job alone. I cost a lot more, but I'll get it done—fast."

Lanston wet his lips. "How much and how long?"

"Twice what you're paying them, plus the cut I usually get for being the middleman. Give me a week once we're done at Epsom. Not only will I find Aldridge, I'll eliminate him." A scathing laugh. "And you'll never have to hear the details or feel guilty when you go to church."

"All right. Do it." Lanston dragged a shaking arm across his brow. "But I can't stop wondering—what if Aldridge didn't hear us talking at Newmarket? What if he has no idea you killed Redley? What if we're murdering the man for nothing?"

Coop spat at the ground. "We've been over this a dozen times, Lanston. I don't know if Aldridge heard us or not, but he sure as hell *saw* us. And that's enough to make him one big walking risk."

"If he knew something, wouldn't he have gone to the authorities by now?"

"Maybe. Maybe not. It depends on how scared he is. It's a hell of a lot easier to disappear than to die."

"But he didn't disappear, at least not immediately."

"He was probably hoping we hadn't noticed him that day at Newmarket. Even when Archer and Parrish started pressuring him into throwing races, he most likely prayed he was only another jockey on our list, instead of a potential obstacle whose loyalties we were testing. But once Parrish painted that death threat on the stall, he knew we were after him. He panicked and bolted."

"If only he'd agreed to throw those damned races, then we'd be certain he wasn't a threat to our discovery."

"But that didn't happen. Aldridge refused to cooperate. And we don't know if it was just his damned ethics standing in the way, or something more, something he meant to hold over our heads—like murder." Coop spat again. "Take my advice, Lanston. Shed your conscience. Newgate's an ugly place. I've been there. I know."

"Hell," Lanston muttered, rubbing his throbbing temples. "One damned meeting. *One*. In all these months. I was so careful about where and when. Ten full days before the onset of the first spring meeting. At bloody dawn. No one was about. We were at the far end of the stables in a deserted stall. Why the hell did Aldridge have to pick that time to check out his mount?"

"He's the finest jockey on the turf, remember?" Coop mocked. "And soon he'll be the deadest."

"Enough!" Lanston exploded. "I've agreed to let you take care of him. I've offered you an exorbitant sum to do it quickly. But that doesn't mean I have to listen to the details."

An evil sneer. "Suit yourself."

"I intend to. In the interim, we've got the Derby to focus on and to win. Contact Archer and Parrish. Get them to Epsom tomorrow by seven A.M."

"They'll be there."

"Good. I'll be in touch." Lanston turned on his heel and strode away.

Blaker flattened himself against the stable wall, waiting only until the earl had climbed into his phaeton and urged his horses off, leaving a cloud of dust in his wake.

Then he slipped off to report to Saxon.

"Do you know, my lord, you're surprisingly good for an amateur—an amateur horseman, that is." Nicole's eyes danced as she handed Dustin a cup of tea, then lowered herself to the settee beside him. "This morning, I only beat you by five lengths, and that included the two times you managed to edge me away from the railing and the three times you cut me off. That was a fine improvement from yesterday, when I beat you by seven lengths, and you had to work considerably harder to impede my concentration and my speed. Of course, I'm sure you would have progressed far beyond that point had your wounds not precluded your beginning our challenging sessions until five days ago, rather than the originally scheduled eight."

A corner of Dustin's mouth lifted, and he set down his cup, tugging Nicole into the circle of his arms, her back curved into his side. "Your father's right. You're an arrogant chit. Beautiful, and one hell of a rider, but arrogant." He nuzzled her hair.

"Thank you, sir." She snuggled closer, cherishing these few isolated moments alone as much as he did. "Coming from a man whose very smile causes women to swoon, I consider your praise of my physical attributes to be the highest of compliments."

Laughter rumbled from Dustin's chest. "'Whose very smile causes women to swoon?' You've been talking to Ariana."

"Ariana has been pointing out the changes she sees in you. In the process, she filled me in on your varied and colorful past, yes."

"That's my *past*," Dustin emphasized softly. "You, Derby, are my present and my future. I *have* changed—permanently. Wait and see. I'm going to be the most devoted, faithful husband in all of England—possibly in all the world. In fact," he murmured, brushing aside her hair to kiss her nape, "based upon my sordid past, I feel it's only fair that, once wed, I demonstrate my devotion to you—repeatedly—until you're fully convinced." His lips sought the pulse point at her neck, punctuating each word with a breath of a kiss. "I'll use all the countless and diverse techniques I know to win you over." A heated pause. "Every last one."

A shiver rippled through her. "A most prudent idea, my lord. I look forward to this thorough and prolonged demonstration of your devotion."

Dustin made a harsh sound, and his embrace tightened, all humor having vanished. "God, Nicole, have you any idea how long it's been since we've been alone?"

His hoarse question found its mark, Nicole's clamoring body screaming that it had been a lifetime since he'd held her, filled her. "Not counting these precious minutes Papa allows us? Eleven days."

"An eternity," he confirmed, nibbling at her ear. "Derby, if I'm not inside you soon, I'm going to explode."

She moaned softly. "Dustin, please. Papa and Sully are right in the kitchen. If they hear you, they'll shred the marriage license you so painstakingly acquired and call you out."

"They won't hear me," Dustin murmured, unperturbed. "Sullivan arrived a mere two hours ago. He and your father haven't seen each other in a fortnight. They're catching up on news, paying not a whit of attention to us." His hand slid up to cup her breast through the barrier of her shirt. "Just let me touch you."

With a whimper of pleasure, Nicole shifted closer, biting her lip as Dustin's thumb teased her hardening nipple.

"I love how you respond to me," he muttered, continuing his exquisite torture until tiny bursts of pleasure began to tug at Nicole's loins, converging in a damp pool between her thighs. Dustin groaned, somehow sensing—and sharing— every inner ripple as her body prepared to receive him. "I can almost feel you wrapped around me."

"Dustin." Nicole's head fell back against his shoulder. "Don't."

"Don't what? Touch you until you melt? Or tell you how perfect it feels when I'm inside you, buried in your softness? So hot. So tight. So wet."

Nicole's breath exhaled in a rush. "Don't say things like that. I can't bear it."

"Wait until our wedding night, my love. I'll say things that will make you blush—everywhere." Turning her into his arms, Dustin raised her chin to meet his burning midnight gaze. "Don't make plans to see a soul for the first month of our marriage," he commanded fiercely, "because I intend to make love to you for at least that long, and that will only appease our initial urgency. After that, we'll begin exploring every exquisite nuance in existence and invent a few of our own."

"I think I'll die waiting," Nicole confessed heatedly, twining her arms about his neck.

"So will I." Dustin's mouth seized hers in a poignant, hungry caress.

Their kiss was interrupted by a loud knock on the front door.

Breaking apart, they stared at each other.

Another knock, equally as purposeful.

"It might be Trent. Or Saxon," Dustin said, coming to his feet.

Nicole scrambled up, snatching her jockey's cap and following Dustin through the hall. From the corner of her eye, she spied her father and Sully, poised in the kitchen doorway.

Dustin reached the entranceway . . . and waited.

"It's Saxon," the voice on the other side declared. "I must see you, my lord."

Easing open the door, Dustin ensured that it was indeed Saxon, then admitted him. "What's wrong? Is it Alexander?"

"No, my lord. Everyone is well." Saxon shut the door, moved farther into the cottage. "Miss Aldridge," he greeted Nicole. His gaze shifted to Nick, then narrowed as it found Sully.

"Saxon . . . Sullivan." Dustin provided the introductions.

"Ah." Saxon visibly relaxed, nodding at the familiar name.

"Saxon's the investigator Lord Tyreham hired," Nick explained to his friend.

"Does that mean you've found something?" Sully demanded.

Glancing at Dustin, Saxon waited for permission to continue.

"Speak freely, Saxon. What have you learned?"

"Thank you, sir." Saxon extracted some notes from his inside coat pocket, his brows drawing as he scanned them. "Blaker just provided me with a report that contains precise and incriminating information. It seems that Coop—whose full name is Farley Cooper and who, incidentally, has a lengthy prison record—received a visitor today. A most prominent visitor. And while Blaker could only hear snatches of their conversation from his position outside the stable, he heard enough to know they were discussing the blackmail scheme on the turf. He distinctly heard Aldridge's name mentioned several times, as well as those of Archer and Parrish. His impression was that plans of some kind were being made, although he wasn't sure precisely what they were." An uneasy pause. "One thing he was sure of. These plans—whatever they might be— involve Stoddard."

"Dammit." Dustin's jaw tightened. "Who?" he demanded. "Who was Coop's visitor?"

"I'm sorry, sir," Saxon replied simply. "It was the earl of Lanston."

All the color drained from Dustin's face. "Lanston?" he repeated. "You're sure?"

"I'm afraid so, my lord. Not only that but, upon leaving the stables, Blaker stopped to make a few inquiries before filing his report. It seems that Lord Lanston owes a great deal of money—a *great* deal of money—to colleagues, business establishments, even employees. In short, he's very nearly bankrupt. So the motive to blackmail these jockeys is indeed there."

"Lanston," Nick muttered, a light dawning in his eyes. "Tyreham, that's who I saw that Coop person with. It was at Newmarket, maybe a month ago—no, more—it was before the first spring meeting even began. I went to the stables before dawn to check on Oberon. He'd been a bit out of sorts the last day or two. I heard quiet talking in the empty stall next to his. Naturally, I was curious who was using an empty stall for a predawn chat. So I glanced in. It was Lord Lanston and that man with the scarred arm. Obviously, they were talking about something private, because they broke off the minute they saw me. I took the hint and reversed my tracks. At the time, I remember thinking it was kind of odd for the earl to be taking up with such a lowlife, but then, who am I to figure out the nobility? I dismissed it, never gave the matter a second thought. Until now."

"They were discussing their blackmailing scheme— doubtless in full detail," Dustin surmised. "Why else would they take so drastic a step as to threaten your life simply because you might have overheard their conversation? Lord ... I can't believe I'm talking about Lanston." Dustin averted his head, shaking it bewilderedly from side to side. "He and I have been friends for years." A hollow laugh. "At least I thought so. What a fine judge of character I turned out to be."

Nicole lay a gentle hand on his forearm. "Dustin, people keep sides of themselves concealed. If one of those sides happens to be ugly, that person's character will deteriorate when he's backed into a corner, often without anyone recognizing it. Don't blame yourself for not seeing through the earl. He's obviously proficient at hiding his weaknesses."

"I was with him two weeks ago at Newmarket. We talked about . . ." Abruptly, Dustin went taut, and he pivoted, gripping Nicole's shoulders. "We talked about Stoddard. Lanston asked a lot of questions. I boasted to him that you'd effortlessly take the Derby." A muscle worked in Dustin's jaw. "One thing about Lanston I *do* know—he never aspires to the mundane. Between that reality and the fact that Blaker's report says Stoddard's name was mentioned, I'd be willing to bet that whatever my bastard of a friend is planning, it pertains to the Derby."

"Your reasoning is sound, sir," Saxon noted, scrutinizing a separate page tucked amid his notes. "And this item in the latest copy of the *Racing Calendar* would seem to support your theory." He extended the sheet to Dustin. "It appears that your confident assertion to Lord Lanston that Stoddard's victory is a *fait accompli* didn't deter the earl. He did indeed register for the Derby Stakes."

"At the last minute," Dustin muttered, scanning the information. "He entered his stallion Demon, who's a remarkably swift mount—fast, seasoned, intelligent."

"Who's the jockey riding him?" Nick quizzed.

"Baker."

"Baker's damned good. Been around a long time. The combination of him and that stallion you just described would be enough for Lanston to take the Derby." Nick's worried gaze drifted to his daughter. "*If* Nickie weren't racing."

"But I am racing." Nicole's chin came up. "And I don't intend to back out."

"I don't think they expect you to, Miss Aldridge," Saxon mused aloud. "I think they expect you to race as planned—with one alteration."

"They expect me to throw the race."

"Precisely. My guess is they'll approach you tomorrow during your final practice and pressure you to do just that."

"Let them. I won't cooperate."

Despite the gravity of the moment, Saxon's lips twitched. "I rather suspected you wouldn't."

"Nicole—" Dustin began.

"Dustin, please." Nicole gazed up at him, her heart in her eyes. "Don't ask me to withdraw from that race. Certainly don't ask me to throw it. You and Papa know how much winning the Derby means to me. Please don't ask me to discard my dreams and my principles." She glanced from Dustin to her father. "Papa, I can't. I can't and I won't."

For a long moment, silence prevailed.

Oddly, it was Saxon who broke the silence. "Forgive me for intruding, my lord, but there's another aspect of this situation we have yet to discuss, that being the matter of proof. The way things stand, we have nothing but Blaker's word that Lanston is running this scheme. True, Aldridge saw the earl meet with Cooper, but that in itself is evidence of nothing. And yes, it's safe to assume these criminals believe Aldridge heard far more damning information than, in fact, he did, and that they intend to eliminate him because of it. But, with Aldridge alledgedly missing, no attempt on his life has yet been made. In fact, the only culprits who have inflicted actual violence—at least, violence we can attest to firsthand—are Archer and Parrish. There could be countless more offenders involved in this conspiracy, including, for example, someone right here at Tyreham. Remember, we have yet to resolve that possibility, despite my discreet inquiries. And observations," Saxon added, with a pointed glance at Nicole. "I did keep my promise to you, Miss Aldridge. Over the past week, I've observed Raggert as often as I conceivably could without neglecting my responsibility to the young marquis. But, aside from being more than a tad overbearing, Raggert has done nothing either illegal or unethical. He hasn't even left the estate, other than on his day off. So the question of how many others, and which particular others, are involved in this scheme, remains. And, to be frank, I'd like to see each and every one of them join Archer and Parrish in Newgate." He turned back to Dustin. "Wouldn't you, my lord?"

"You know I would." Dustin's eyes narrowed. "What is it you're suggesting, Saxon?"

"A plan of our own, sir. A chance for Lord Lanston to undo himself. Let his hoodlums approach Stoddard and fail to gain his cooperation. That should put the earl in a fine state of panic. He can't very well break into Tyreham and do the boy harm—not that any of us would allow it. So he'll have to withdraw his mount or lose his money. In either case, he's bound to be agitated—and vulnerable. Trapped like that, there's no telling what he might do."

"And we'll be there to see him do it."

"Precisely, my lord."

"But there's no guarantee Lanston will betray himself as we hope."

"No, sir, there isn't. On the other hand, we can't very well seize the man with no firsthand proof of his crimes."

Dustin nodded, weighing the options, considering the risks and the potential gains.

In the end, it was the imploring look in Nicole's eyes that spawned his decision.

Slowly, he turned to meet Nick's troubled stare. "If I were to instruct Saxon to move to your cottage, to travel with us to Epsom, and to remain with Nicole every minute—lest those thugs approach her—*and* if I were to vow that I would personally kill anyone who laid a hand on her, would you agree to let her race as planned?"

"Would you?" Nick shot back. "Given how much you love her?"

"Because of how much I love her—yes. If the conditions I outlined were implemented, I would let her race."

Nick swallowed convulsively.

"Papa," Nicole beseeched, her eyes damp with emotion. "The whole reason we brought Alden Stoddard to life was because you refused to do the very things you're now contemplating I do, compromise my ethics or surrender my ideals. Can you ask any less of me than you asked of yourself?"

"All right," Nick relented, slicing the air with his palm. "I'll probably age ten years between now and Derby Day, but, yes. Run the bloody race."

"Thank you, Papa." Nicole ran to him, hugged him tightly.

Then, she stepped away, walked over to her future husband. "Thank you," she whispered, raising up to kiss his cheek. "You're my very own miracle, too."

Seventeen

"Ah, there's Lord Tyreham. Thank you, lad."

Every muscle in Dustin's body went rigid at the sound of Lanston's approaching voice. Not that the bastard's arrival at Epsom came as any great shock. Thanks to Saxon's shrewd predictions, Dustin had been stationed in the stands since dawn, steeling himself for precisely this moment throughout the entirety of Nicole's final practice. It was Saxon's belief that Lanston would surface today, ostensibly to chat with Dustin, actually to divert his attention so Archer and Parrish could find Stoddard and do their dirty work.

Remember, my lord, Saxon had cautioned, *it's imperative that you behave as you ordinarily do. It's completely natural for the earl to seek you out, to advise you he's decided to enter the Derby Stakes. You've been friends and healthy competitors for years. In his mind, nothing has changed. Give him no reason to believe otherwise, or our entire plan will be jeopardized.*

"Tyreham, good morning."

Swallowing his hatred, Dustin pivoted, facing the man he had once called friend with a forced smile and a deceptively surprised expression. "Lanston, hello. What brings you to Epsom? The meeting doesn't start until tomorrow."

Lanston pointed at the course. "I'm here to size up the competition. Especially your Stoddard. He's very impressive, every bit as remarkable as you claimed he was."

"I agree," Dustin managed, fighting the urge to choke Lanston to death. Reflexively, his gaze shifted to Nicole and Dagger, now cooled down and heading for the paddock, accompanied, thankfully, by Brackley and Raggert. Most reassuring of all was the knowledge that, concealed behind the far end of the paddock was Saxon, pistol ready, should Nicole find herself in over her head. "Tell me, Lanston"— Dustin turned back to the earl—"Why are you so interested in Stoddard's performance?"

An enthused lift of Lanston's brows. "That's the other reason I'm here—to see you. I wanted to forewarn you that Stoddard is going to have some unexpected competition."

"Really? Who?"

"Baker."

"Baker? I thought he was on holiday, enjoying his winnings from Newmarket."

"He was. I convinced him to return a bit early, made it worth his while to do so. He'll be riding my stallion Demon. After all, how could I resist your blatant challenge?"

"I don't recall issuing a challenge."

"Ah, but you did. Not a direct one, of course, but then that's never your way. You boasted of Stoddard as if he were virtually unbeatable. So how could I help but try to beat him? Especially with the added incentive of Demon's performance this racing season. Why, that stallion of mine has taken every bloody race he's run. So, consider your challenge met, my friend. And advise your lad Stoddard the same. Baker will be riding Demon—to victory, I hope."

"I see." It took every fiber of Dustin's self-control not to pound that arrogant smile off Lanston's face.

"Tyreham?" The earl inclined his head quizzically, as if trying to discern the reason for Dustin's uncustomary brusqueness. "Does my decision upset you?"

"Of course not." Dustin took a firm hold of himself. He had to squelch his enmity, for Nicole's sake. "In fact," he added, with a magnanimous sweep of his arm, "I'm relieved as hell. Stoddard will be, too. Until now, it appeared the lad .would win with such ease that his victory would be lacking in fanfare. Baker's participation will lend just the excitement needed to make our triumph truly distinctive."

"Touché." Lanston's smile reappeared, his gaze flickering briefly to the paddock before returning to Dustin. "We'll see who reaches the winning post first."

"Shall we make a small wager?" Dustin asked in a silky tone. "Say, five hundred pounds?"

"Why not?" Lanston nodded, a glint in his eyes.

"Excellent."

Another glance at the paddock. "Tell me, Tyreham, is Stoddard running only in the Derby? I understood your reluctance to enter him in any races prior to that. After all, he is new and he was training. But, with the Derby behind him, your unease should vanish. And there will be a few more days remaining in the Epsom meeting. So why not enter him in the Two-Year-Old Stakes or the Oaks Stakes?"

You greedy bastard, Dustin blazed silently. *How many races did you intend to browbeat him into throwing?* "The Two-Year-Old Stakes is out of the question," he said aloud, shaking his head. "It's the day after the Derby, and Stoddard needs and deserves time to recuperate from his rigorous training schedule."

"Perhaps. But the Oaks isn't until the day following that. I'm sure the Stewards of the Jockey Club would permit you a last-minute addition, given your sterling reputation on the turf."

Dustin pretended not to notice the definite tinge of sarcasm. "I'll consider it."

"I would, were I you. Stoddard is superb, good enough to win any number of races. Plus I'm sure the poor lad could use whatever money would be spawned by those victories. After all, he's barely begun his career. He can't have accumulated much of an income." With that, Lanston's gaze shifted, once again, to the paddock. Dustin saw his eyes flicker just before he pivoted about to casually survey the row of carriages behind the stands. "I should be off. It's nearly noon, and I need to make certain Demon is primed for his victory. Until Derby Day, my friend."

"Until Derby Day." The words tasted like chalk, and Dustin uttered them automatically, his rage having been supplanted by a powerful rush of fear. If Lanston were hastening off after his subtle, but repeated, perusal of the paddock area, he must have just spied Archer and Parrish taking their leave. If so, they'd already confronted Nicole with their offer. And, Saxon or not, Dustin needed to see for himself that she was safe.

He waited until Lanston was out of sight.

Then he made his way to the paddock, mentally rehearsing the credible sequence of events Saxon had outlined for them to follow: Nicole was to feign a sore muscle. He was to respond to it and usher her out to the waiting carriage, instructing Brackley and Raggert to stay behind and tend to Dagger. With the noon hour almost upon them, Epsom was far from deserted. So, until the carriage left Epsom, nothing was to be discussed; Nicole was to remain as Stoddard, Dustin as a concerned employer, and Saxon as their driver.

God, let her be all right.

Heart pounding, Dustin strode directly toward the shadowed corner of the paddock where Nicole had positioned herself to await Archer and Parrish's arrival.

He spied her slight form, and his knees nearly buckled with relief. "Stoddard?"

She turned, taking a few hobbling steps in his direction. "Yes, my lord?" Her voice was calm, reassuringly even. But she was white-faced, her eyes huge, and Dustin knew instantly that those filthy lowlifes had approached her.

"I saw you massaging your thigh," Dustin continued on cue. "Did you injure it?"

"Yes—slightly, sir. I believe it's only a strain. But I would like to soak the leg as a precaution. Saxon happened by a moment ago, and I took the liberty of asking him to ready the carriage. If you don't mind, may I return to Tyreham?"

"Certainly." He was desperate to hold her, ensure himself of her well-being. "The Derby is two days away. We can't take any chances of your muscles tightening up. We'll leave for Tyreham right away." Purposefully, he scanned the area. "I'll instruct Brackley and Raggert to see to Dagger." Catching sight of Brackley, he waved him over.

"Yes, my lord?" Brackley inquired.

"Stoddard's left thigh is bothering him. I want to have it treated at once, before it becomes a problem. I'm taking him back to Tyreham. Can you and Raggert finish up?"

"Of course." Unaware that the injury was fictitious, Brackley gave Nicole a paternal scowl. "I thought I saw you favoring that side when you dismounted. Is it bad?"

"No." Nicole shook her head. "Just sore."

"Well, you're sheet white. Go ahead with Lord Tyreham." Brackley surveyed the paddock. "I saw Raggert a few minutes ago. He's around here somewhere. I'll find him, my lord. And we'll see to Dagger."

"Splendid. I'll send the carriage back for you." Dustin led the way from the paddock, Nicole limping alongside him. He was silent, not trusting himself to converse until they were alone and he could speak freely.

"Is the carriage ready?" he asked Saxon as they approached.

"Yes, sir." Helping to ease Stoddard in, Saxon waited until Dustin had followed suit. Then he closed the door behind them, climbed into his own seat, and slapped the reins.

The instant the carriage was moving, Dustin turned to Nicole. "What happened? Did they hurt you?"

"No." Adamantly, she shook her head. "It was the two men you and Papa described. They waited until I was alone and out of view. Then they cornered me and informed me that I would throw the Derby. They gave me two reasons to do so—one, they'd pay me fifteen hundred pounds, and, two, if I didn't, I'd never walk—much less ride—again."

Dustin sucked in his breath. "And what did you do?"

"I waited, as we planned, until I heard Saxon round the paddock and head toward me. Then I thanked them for their kind offer—and refused it. I limped over to Saxon and asked him to bring the carriage around. The entire encounter lasted less than a minute."

Reaching over, Dustin pulled the curtains at the windows. Then, he tugged Nicole into his arms. "You're shaking. Derby, I don't want you frightened."

"I'm not frightened. I'm furious. I wanted to kill those animals for threatening Papa and for hurting you."

Dustin started, and laughter, a welcome balm to his frazzled nerves, rumbled inside him. "My precious Derby," he murmured, touched beyond words by the fact that this tiny, delicate woman would take on two brawny lowlifes to defend him. "My beautiful, fierce lioness. Protecting her cubs."

Nicole leaned back far enough to give him an offended look. "Are you mocking me?"

"Never." Dustin enfolded her closer, stroked her back. "I never imagined being loved so deeply. Thank you, Derby."

Nicole sagged against him, gripping the lapels of his coat and accepting the comfort of his embrace. "Now what happens?" she whispered.

"Now you go home and rest, secure in the fact that there are a host of able-bodied men protecting you and each other. And the day after tomorrow you do what you've waited all your life to do—you win the Derby."

"Whatever made me think I could win the Derby?"

Pacing the sitting room, Nicole glanced from her father to Sully, never breaking stride as she readjusted her cap for the twentieth time.

"Stupidity, probably," Sully replied with a straight face.

"Or arrogance," Nick proposed, sipping his coffee.

"Yeah, that, too. The elf is known for both."

"Perhaps we could withdraw her entry," Nick suggested thoughtfully, glancing at the clock. "We have nearly two hours before the race begins. That would give us ample time to explain to the judges that Stoddard is really inept and that Lord Tyreham and his entire stable staff were wrong when they deemed him the most brilliant young jockey to come along in years. After all, what do they know?"

"For that matter, what do we know?" Sully added. "We have no eye for talent. Why would we? We ourselves have little experience in the saddle. Therefore, we're in no position to deem another jockey extraordinary, to state our belief that he'll win the Derby by such a wide margin that the spectators will be gaping long after the winning post has been passed."

"True." Nick shook his head sadly. "Pity, isn't it, that arrogance and stupidity should so foolishly influence someone's thinking?"

"Are you two enjoying yourselves?" Nicole demanded, her lips curving in spite of herself.

"We got you to smile, didn't we?" Sullivan grinned, setting down his cup.

"Yes, you got me to smile. Now if you could only race Dagger for me . . ."

"Nickie." Her father rose, soberly placing his hands on her shoulders. "You've waited for this day all your life. You're ready as hell for it. You know that Derby course better than you know your name . . . *both* names." Smiling tenderly, he lifted her chin. "If I didn't think you could do it, I would have put a stop to this long ago. Do you think I don't understand the panic you're feeling right now? That Sully and I haven't felt it dozens of times?"

Nicole blinked. "Neither of you ever panics. You don't even seem nervous."

"We're good actors." Sully came to his feet. "It wouldn't soothe the men paying us if we paced about the paddock, wringing our hands before each race, would it? But don't kid yourself. We're as skittish as you, wanting to do the best we can every time we get in that saddle. But, Elf, your best is all you can ask for. Yours and Dagger's. You've readied both you and him in every way possible. Be proud of that. Race proud because of that. And leave the rest to fate."

"Fate," Nicole repeated. Abruptly, her eyes lit up. "My wishing locket." She dashed upstairs, returning instantly with the necklace. "I need this with me today. Since I dare not wear it as Alden Stoddard, I'll carry it in my pocket. Then, I'll feel as if Mama's with me throughout the race."

"She's always with you, Elf," Nick said softly. "As am I."

Nicole clasped her father's hands. "I wish you could truly be there, accompany us to Epsom and watch me compete in my one and only race."

"I know, Elf." For a brief, uncharacteristic moment, Nick enfolded her against him, gave her a hard hug. "But Sully will be standing in for me. And just as Alicia can see you, so can I, and we're both very, very proud."

"Thank you," Nicole murmured into his shoulder. "Armed with that knowledge, I'm sure to succeed."

Nick kissed the top of her capped head. "I never doubted it."

Slowly, Nicole drew back. "I love you, Papa," she whispered. Turning, she squared her shoulders. "I'm ready now."

Saxon frowned.

Something was bothering him. And that something was Raggert.

Until two days ago, his opinion of the trainer had been much the same as Nicole Aldridge's—and with equally as little solid fact upon which to base it. He didn't like the trainer, didn't trust him as far as he could throw him; but, as he'd explained to Miss Aldridge, being distasteful did not necessarily designate someone a criminal. And, after scrutinizing Raggert for weeks, doing everything short of following the trainer to his quarters at night, Saxon had found nothing illegal about the man's actions.

But Raggert's behavior these past two days had altered. He'd become skittish, jumpy, keeping mostly to himself rather than hovering about Stoddard. More distressing was the fact that this change had first occurred directly after Stoddard's final practice at Epsom.

His scowl deepening, Saxon gazed out his bedchamber window. The duke and duchess of Broddington had settled themselves beside Stoddard in the Tyreham carriage, and the very object of Saxon's deliberation—Raggert—was climbing into the rear seat, ready to embark on his Derby Day excursion.

He always seemed to be at the right place at the right time, didn't he? Just as he'd been in the paddock at Epsom throughout Stoddard's encounter with Archer and Parrish. It was more than possible he'd heard every word they said. In fact, if Saxon were to heed his instincts, he'd swear Raggert had been *trying* to hear every word.

Immediately thereafter, the trainer had disappeared—at the precise moment as had Archer, Parrish, *and* Lanston.

A staggering and less than believable coincidence.

Where the hell had Raggert gone? And why?

To report to Lanston.

The possibility reared its ugly head for the dozenth time since Monday. Could Raggert be working for Lanston, sent here to gather information on Stoddard? Was he spying on the jockey's activities, asking pointed questions to report back what he learned? If so, Nicole Aldridge's suspicions had been well-founded, and Raggert was, indeed, the informant they sought.

The theory made a world of sense. If Lanston were losing money, it would help to know how to beat his most noted competitor, the marquis of Tyreham—especially in light of the fact that Tyreham had just hired an unknown and reputedly spectacular new jockey. What better way for Lanston to keep up on Tyreham's thoroughbred stock and be apprised of Stoddard's riding potential than to refer a splendid but unscrupulous trainer to work for the marquis?

But all that was minor compared to the more sinister and immediate likelihood at hand: the integration of Raggert's unique position at Tyreham with Lanston's desperate need to win the Derby.

That led Saxon back to pondering Raggert's close proximity to Stoddard at the time when Archer and Parrish proposed their little business deal. If Raggert were assigned to eavesdrop, he'd probably rushed off to inform Lanston that Stoddard had no intention of throwing the Derby Stakes. At that point, with monetary ruin at stake, Lanston would have panicked, having no choice but to ensure Stoddard lost the race anyway. And who better to secure that loss than Raggert, who not only lived at Tyreham but hated and resented Stoddard?

Saxon gripped the window ledge. Had Raggert done precisely that? And, if so, was it too late to thwart whatever plan he'd set into motion?

Restlessly, Saxon peered out, counting the occupants of the carriage. Trenton and Ariana Kingsley, Raggert, Stoddard, Sullivan, and Lord Tyreham. Brackley had already ridden off astride Dagger in order to give the thoroughbred a brisk mile-and-a-half walk in preparation for the race.

All those attending the Derby were accounted for.

And since Saxon's own job was to stay behind and, along with his uncle and Mrs. Hopkins, oversee young Alexander, all he had to do was wait.

By the time he'd collected his pistol and slipped a metal

file in his pocket, the carriage had disappeared around the drive, along with the very suspect he intended to investigate.

Determinedly, he headed for Raggert's quarters. Pausing at the doorway, he glanced about to ensure he was alone, then extracted his file and, with one swift slide, gained the entry he sought.

There was enough light shining from the window to guide his way, and Saxon moved about, checking the drawers, wardrobe, even the pockets of Raggert's clothing for signs of anything incriminating.

He found it beneath the bed.

There, wrapped in a concealing sheet and shoved beneath the bed's far corner, was a horse's girth—complete with billet straps and covers—distinguished by a tiny gold plate engraved with one word: "Dagger."

Saxon stared at his findings, his mind already at Epsom. Swiftly, he stuffed the girth back into the sheet and restored it to its hiding place. Relocking the door, he took the grounds at a dead run.

Minutes later, having alerted his uncle to the urgent nature of his business, Saxon leaped into the phaeton and took off for the Derby.

The starting flag rose . . . and hovered.

Rather than the dread she'd anticipated, all Nicole could feel was an acute surge of relief. She was undiscovered. Thanks to Dustin's planning, she'd successfully fooled the Clerk of the Scales, the starter, and the other jockeys. At long last, the race was about to commence. Now she had only one thing left to do.

Win.

"We can do it," she informed Dagger softly. "I know we can."

The flag dropped.

And the Derby had begun.

Urging Dagger forward, Nicole glanced neither to the left nor the right. She was oblivious to the crowds and the cheers, focused only on Dagger and where she intended him to go.

They were out in front, leading everyone but Baker who was directly to her left, closer to the inside rail. Dagger was taking the ascent beautifully, but it was her job to determine the best place to move forward and, ideally, over—to dominate the inside rail in order to shorten her distance to the winning post.

Pacing, Nickie, she could hear her father say. *Don't avert your head. It will confuse Dagger and slow you down. Trust your instincts. Then follow them.*

Leaning forward in the saddle, Nicole pushed Dagger for a spurt of speed. He complied, and an instant later, they shot ahead of Baker and Demon, then over to the inside rail.

Tattenham Corner was just beyond the curve of the horseshoe. That meant the sharp descent would soon be upon her. She had to take the curve slow and easy, pace Dagger as they shifted downward, then hold that pace as they headed into the straightaway that would take them to the winning post.

It was at that moment Nicole felt her saddle slip.

The slightest of motions, she felt it nonetheless. And so did Dagger. He missed a step, then regained it, as Nicole fitted herself more snugly against him. The saddle was loose, there was no doubt about it. But why?

Legs gripping Dagger's sides, Nicole forced herself to concentrate on the course. They were rounding the curve now, shifting into the decline as Tattenham Corner loomed just ahead.

The saddle jerked to a side.

"Something's wrong." In the grandstand, Dustin came to his feet like a bullet, his gaze fixed on the deep green color of Nicole's cap.

"What do you mean?" Ariana demanded.

"I mean, Stoddard is off balance. Something's wrong."

"Dustin," Trenton said quietly, "that corner is known to be brutal. Surely—"

"Something is bloody wrong," Dustin ground out. Shoving past his family, he barely heard Sullivan's grunt of agreement. Threading his way through the crowds, he could think of but one thing: getting to Nicole. Whatever the hell was happening, it was out of her control.

Nicole was thinking much the same thing.

As Tattenham Corner bore down on her, Nicole frantically examined her options. She was still ahead—but not by much. Her wide lead had been cut down to about several lengths, she'd guess, and that promised to diminish further with her saddle impeding her speed. It was sliding freely now, the girth slipping beneath Dagger's body, the straps holding the left side of the girth in place growing more and more slack.

They were going to give out entirely. And, if they did, her saddle would launch out, probably injuring another horse, definitely impeding the other jockeys and getting her disqualified from the race.

Those prospects were intolerable.

Hugging Dagger's flanks, she eased around Tattenham Corner, then, as the other mounts slowed into the curve, she took advantage of her slim lead by maneuvering as quickly as she could to the far right, as close to the outside rail as possible.

Baker shot past on her left, breaking into the straightaway at a dead run just as her billet straps gave a telltale snap.

Don't be distracted by the other riders, Nickie, her father would say. *Do what you have to do. You'll regain speed later.*

Glancing quickly around to ensure no one was beside or behind her, Nickie eased her weight, letting the saddle and girth fly free. They whirled off to her right, striking the outside railing and hitting the ground fifteen feet to the right of any rider.

Beneath her, Dagger tensed, swerving away from the rail, losing his momentum as he struggled to steady himself.

Vaguely, she heard the startled shouts erupting from the crowds in the grandstand: "It's the saddle!" "Baker's ahead by four lengths!" "Not a hope of Stoddard recovering!"

Disregarding the uproar, Nicole gripped Dagger's reins more securely, molding herself to his back as she fought to both reassure him and to regain control. "Easy, Dagger," she murmured. "It's over. We're fine. Now let's go for that post."

Instantly, Dagger responded, recovering his balance and, a split second later, his speed.

A roar went up from the grandstand as Nicole and Dagger burst forward, leaving the rapidly approaching third-place jockey far behind and breaking into the straightaway.

Shutting out the commotion, Nicole had but one thought: catching up to Baker, then beating him.

Eyes narrowed with purpose, she leaned forward and squeezed Dagger's sides, commanding the extra speed she needed.

The stallion blasted onward, galloping at a breakneck pace, reaching his competitor sixty yards shy of the winning post.

For the next few seconds she and Baker raced at a dead heat.

"I know, Papa," Nicole muttered, a spark lighting her eyes. "That telltale burst of speed fifty yards from the winning post. Right . . . now."

In a heartbeat, she and Dagger shot ahead, edging by Demon and flying by the winning post—victorious by a neck.

By the time she slowed down enough to bring Dagger around, the crowd was on its feet and a substantial argument—as she'd anticipated—was under way at the judges' box, a mere ten yards away.

As Dagger's owner, Dustin was right in the middle of it.

As Demon's owner, so was Lanston.

Fleetingly, Dustin's gaze darted to Nicole's, his expression fierce with anger and worry.

"I'm fine." She mouthed the words with a shaky grin, touching the brim of her cap to salute their victory—acknowledged or not.

His relief transmitted itself to her as clearly as if he were standing right beside her. With a solemn salute, he mouthed back, "You're a hell of a lot better than fine."

Then he returned to the battle at hand.

"How does it feel to be a Derby winner?" Dustin asked, entwining Nicole's fingers in his.

She settled against the cottage settee, totally spent from the past few hours of grueling questions, hearty congratulations, and, upon her arrival at Tyreham, frenzied worry and furious outbursts from her father—followed, finally, by a warm bath and change of clothes. "I still can't believe I won," she murmured, grateful beyond words for Dustin's intentional efforts to relax her. "How does it feel? Wonderful. Better than wonderful. Even better than the bath I soaked in."

He pressed her palm to his lips. "You were astonishing. I've never seen such extraordinary riding in my life."

"Neither have I," Sully agreed, following Nick out of the kitchen while casting repeated, worried glances at him.

"Here's your tea, Nickie." Nick handed her a cup, still white-faced with the realization that his precious daughter could have been killed today. "Tyreham, do you and Saxon want another brandy? I'm having a third. Lord knows, I need it." Even as he spoke, he was sloshing brandy into a glass. "I still can't believe Raggert cut those straps."

"Well, he did," Saxon said quietly from the armchair in which he sat. "Although no one besides us and the duke and duchess of Broddington knows it. I'm only sorry I couldn't get to the race in time to spare Miss Aldridge from her harrowing experience."

"I'm not," Nicole assured him, sipping her tea. "Much as I detest Raggert *and* what he did, I loved every minute of that race—even the most challenging seconds when I was scared silly. If you'd arrived in time to delay the starter's flag, you would have had to provide an explanation. Lanston might have eluded us, and I would have had to forfeit my entry and my victory."

"Not necessarily in that order of importance," Dustin commented, his lips twitching.

"Speaking of Lanston," Sully chimed in, "how did he behave during that bitter battle for first place?"

"Like a drowning man fighting for air," Dustin supplied. "Oh, he was gracious as hell when the judges' decision was announced, offered repeated congratulations to both Stoddard and me, but his pretense was far from convincing. In truth, he was white with fury. I think he wanted to kill me."

"How could he think the judges would rule in his favor?" Sully barked. "The elf not only won bareback, she took the time and care to move aside so no one would be hurt or even slowed by that saddle when it sailed off. She lost ten good seconds doing that, if you ask me. Her winning time should have been reduced to two minutes twenty-nine seconds."

"Two minutes thirty-nine seconds is fine with me," Nicole demurred, "as is winning by a neck. My dreams were to run in the Derby and to win it. In committing those wishes to my locket, I didn't specify an exact distance by which I needed to win nor a specific time frame in which I had to do so."

Throughout Sully and Nicole's exchange, Nick had been staring broodingly into his brandy. Now, he slammed his goblet onto the side table, facing Dustin with blazing eyes. "Tyreham, what the hell is the matter with you? You allowed everyone on the turf to believe that some unknown, jealous mischief maker tampered with Dagger's tack when you know damned well that bastard Lanston paid Raggert to hurt my daughter. Not only are you letting them both walk free and unaccused, you're sheltering that son of a bitch Raggert under your roof, letting him keep his job. Have you lost your bloody mind?"

"Papa." Nicole emitted a tolerant sigh. "Please stop bellowing and try to be rational. What good would it have done for Dustin to accuse Lord Lanston? What proof do we have? The tack Mr. Saxon found only condemns Raggert. Lanston could simply deny knowledge of the whole crime and walk away virtually unscathed. And since *he's* the one we want, we have to tread very carefully."

"Your daughter is right, sir," Saxon concurred.

"I don't give a damn." Nick continued to glare at Dustin even as he addressed Nicole. "Elf, you could have been killed. It seems to me that protecting you and punishing the men who threatened your life should be first on the list of your husband-to-be."

"Papa . . ."

"It's all right, sweetheart." Dustin squeezed Nicole's fingers and released them, leaning forward to meet Nick's gaze. "Your father is right. It's time I shared my plan with him—and with you."

"Plan?" Nick demanded. "What plan?"

"The one Saxon and I worked out."

"Actually, Lord Tyreham is being unduly modest," Saxon inserted. "The idea was, for the most part, his. I merely elaborated on it." A grin. "As I said, sir, you'd make an excellent investigator."

"Dustin?" Nicole set down her teacup, brows drawn in puzzlement. "You didn't mention any plan to me."

"I intended to—after you'd had a chance to recoup your strength and I mine." He stared into his empty goblet, his voice growing hoarse with emotion. "I don't think I'll ever recover from the dread I felt watching you slide wildly from side to side as you tore around that corner. I was so terrified you'd—" He broke off, swallowing.

"Well, by the grace of God, Nickie is fine," Nick said in a mollified tone. "So tell us what plan you're talking about."

Dustin looked up, the predatory fire in his eyes burning away all traces of vulnerability. "The plan that begins with my feigned ignorance of Raggert's guilt in severing those straps, despite the fact that I'd like to break every bone in his contemptible body, and culminates in sending him, Lanston, and all their filthy colleagues to prison. The plan that will further result in reinstating you as England's finest jockey and in giving me the miracle I've awaited forever—your daughter as my wife."

Eighteen

"Stoddard! Are you up to being at the stables this morning?" Brackley tossed aside Blanket's saddle and hurried up to Nicole.

From the corner of her eye Nicole saw Raggert step out of Blanket's stall.

"I'm fine, Brackley. Thanks." She gave him a faint smile. "Although I'm not eager to relive yesterday."

"I don't blame you. You could have been killed." He patted Nicole's shoulder. "Like I said yesterday, you're one hell of a jockey. That Derby will go down in history."

"I hope so. Because it's my first and my last."

In the distance, Raggert's head came up.

"What do you mean?" Brackley asked, rubbing his chin.

"That's really what I came here to tell you, and what I intend to tell Lord Tyreham." A resigned sigh. "Brackley, I'm not suited for racing. I have the skill, but I haven't the grit or the strength. I'm totally spent from weeks of nonstop training. My nerves were raw enough just thinking about competing in the Derby. Then yesterday— well, I could have died or killed someone else. That reality did me in. Affinity for horses or not, it's not worth it. So I'm packing away my Derby victory and bidding the turf good-bye."

"Stoddard, you're talking crazy. Do you know how good you are? What kind of future you're passing up?"

A nod. "Yeah, I do."

Brackley drew a sharp, inward breath. "Lad, the race only happened yesterday. You're still reeling from the shock. Why not take some time off—hell, maybe even skip the whole summer racing season. Then in the fall, you can reconsider." An attempted grin. "Not every race is as exciting as yesterday's Derby. I'll bet you find most of them uneventful and boring. But you're too damned good to walk away."

"Right now, I have to."

"Look—I have an idea," Brackley tried, gesturing about the stables. "I need more hands around here than I can count. How about if I arrange with Lord Tyreham for you to work with me, exercise the horses, maybe break in the new foals. Temporarily, of course. Until you feel up to racing again. The money won't be as good as a jockey makes, but you won't starve either. And you'll be able to stay where you're happiest, where you belong—around horses."

Nicole felt a surge of warmth at the generous offer Brackley was extending—maybe even at his own expense. If Brackley assumed that taking Stoddard on meant the lad would get a portion of the work, he probably also assumed he'd get a portion of the pay. *I wish I could tell you, my friend,* she mused silently. *But I can't. Not yet. Still, your kindness won't be forgotten. Soon I'll be able to repay you.*

Her own reflection spawned an inner smile. It appeared there would be definite advantages to becoming the marchioness of Tyreham, after all.

"Stoddard?" Dustin flung open the door to the stables. "Ah, there you are." He stalked over to where she and Brackley stood. "Are you feeling better today?"

"Yes, my lord. I am. However . . ."

"Excellent. Because I've just arranged for the most extraordinary opportunity."

"Sir?"

"During your final practice at Epsom, Lord Lanston put a splendid idea in my head. After seeing you race yesterday, I was more than eager to realize his suggestion. I've done precisely that. I spoke to the Stewards early this morning, and, given your superb performance at the Derby yesterday, they've agreed to allow us to enter the Oaks Stakes, which is taking place at Epsom tomorrow."

Nicole blinked. "But it's too late to enter . . ."

"I've been granted special permission. The Stewards unanimously agreed you're too bloody good a jockey to limit to one race." Dustin glanced at Brackley. "The Oaks, as you know, is for three-year-old fillies. I've entered Winning Streak. She and Stoddard will take the race without batting a lash."

"I'm sure they will, my lord." Brackley cast a questioning look at Nicole, who lowered her gaze to the ground.

"My family's waiting, so I must be getting back to the manor," Dustin concluded, apparently oblivious to Stoddard's less than enthusiastic reaction. "But as soon as Winning Streak is tacked up, I want you to take a few trials on her. Oh . . . Raggert." Dustin seemed to spy the trainer for the first time. "It's a good thing you're here. This situation concerns you, too, on a most crucial level."

The trainer inadvertently stiffened.

"I don't like to upend your schedule without notice," Dustin continued, seemingly unaware of Raggert's tension. "Therefore, I shan't expect you to assist Brackley and me in working with Stoddard today, but tomorrow I have a conflict. Long before I realized I'd be entering Winning Streak in the Oaks, my brother and I arranged a business meeting for tomorrow morning. And, as the duke and his family will be departing for Broddington directly after the close of the Epsom races, there is no other time for us to conduct this meeting. Therefore, I'll need you to oversee Stoddard during his final trial tomorrow morning. Brackley will time him. I'll be back before the race, after which, you're free to take the rest of the day off. Does that present any problems?"

"No, sir," Raggert replied, nearly sagging with relief. "I'll make sure they're ready to do their job at the Oaks."

"I'm sure you will, Raggert." With a cool nod, Dustin turned. "Congratulations again, Stoddard. You were amazing."

With that, he was gone.

* * *

"What the hell is the matter with you, Stoddard?" Raggert barked from alongside the course. "You're riding like you've never been in the saddle."

"Why don't you stop badgering the poor lad," Brackley asked, struggling to control his anger. "He's obviously not himself."

"Not himself?" Raggert blinked in astonishment. "The bloody Oaks Stakes is in six hours. All I asked him to do was trot Winning Streak over the last lap of the trial, just to give her a bit of exercise. If he can't do that, how the hell can he race?"

"Raggert's right, Brackley." Nicole brought Winning Streak around, patting her neck fondly before dismounting. "It's no use. I've tried, for Lord Tyreham's sake, but I'm taut as a bowstring in that saddle. I feel it, and so does Winning Streak. My entering the Oaks is a mistake. I'll only embarrass Lord Tyreham, and I won't do that, not after all he's done for me." She sighed, wiping perspiration from her brow. "Brackley, thank you for your kind offer yesterday morning. I might even have taken you up on it, but I can't face the marquis. Especially not after what I'm about to do."

Brackley paled. "Which is?"

"Bolt," Nicole stated simply.

"Bolt?" Raggert's mouth fell open. "You mean you're not competing?"

"That's what I mean. Listen to me, both of you. No one but the Stewards of the Jockey Club know Lord Tyreham is entering the Oaks. The *Racing Calendar* made no mention of it. So far as the world of the turf is concerned, Winning Streak is not a contender." Nicole turned to Raggert. "Lord Tyreham gave you the afternoon off. Knowing how loyal you are to him, I'm asking you to use that time to ride ahead and alert the Stewards to the change in plans. Tell them the truth, sparing neither me nor my cowardice. That way, Lord Tyreham's reputation will be unscathed, which is all I really care about anyway."

"Stoddard, think of what you're doing," Brackley inserted.

"I have." Her shoulders slumped. "I'm sorry, Brackley. I can't face another race. I'm . . . terrified."

"I'll leave this instant," Raggert announced, a gleam in his eyes.

"So will I," Nicole murmured. "By the time the Oaks commences, I'll be miles away." With an odd expression, she surveyed the grounds, then looked from Raggert to Brackley. "I don't expect either of you will be seeing me again. Thank you, Brackley." She extended her hand, clasping his firmly. "You've been a good friend. And, Raggert—" She inclined her head in the trainer's direction. "Working with you has been quite an experience. Conflicting, to say the least. But at this moment, when so much is at stake, I can't tell you how much your cooperation means to me."

"Think nothing of it." Raggert was already backing away. "Good luck, Stoddard."

Brackley watched him hurry off, took an inadvertent step after him.

"Don't," Nicole said quietly. "Trust me, Brackley. This is for the best. Let him go. And me, as well." She tucked Winning Streak's reins into Brackley's hands, then turned to leave. "I'll see you soon, my friend."

"Stoddard?"

Nicole glanced over her shoulder, smiling at Brackley's quizzical expression. "Yes?"

"I thought you said we won't be seeing you again."

"I did. But I said nothing about my seeing you."

A half hour later, Ariana Kingsley whirled a soft blue day dress from her wardrobe. "This is perfect." She squinted at Nicole, still clad in dirty breeches and shirt, and a self-satisfied smile curved her lips. "You, Miss Aldridge, are going to take the *ton* by storm." Lowering the dress to her bed, she began to laugh. "After all this time, Dustin is finally going to get his comeuppance. I can hardly wait to see the expression on his face when the besotted admirers strewn at his feet are men, and the one they're gazing at with lovesick eyes is you."

Nicole frowned dubiously. "I wouldn't count on that, Ariana. I'm not a natural beauty like you."

"You're not, are you?" Ariana pointed to the bathroom.

"Wash the dirt away, then give me a half hour. You'll bring every breathing male in England to his knees."

Crossing over, Nicole fingered the gown's soft bodice. "It's beautiful," she breathed. "Are you sure you don't mind my borrowing it?"

Ariana seized her hands. "Nicole, I've awaited this day for two years. You're the most wonderful thing that's ever happened to Dustin—the woman I've prayed for to make him whole. And, selfishly, I'm looking forward to calling you my friend—and my sister. So, please, anything I have is yours."

Swallowing, Nicole murmured, "Thank you."

A sharp rap sounded at the bedchamber door.

"Who could that be?" Again Ariana gestured toward the bathroom—this time worriedly. "Hide."

"All right." With a mysterious grin, Nicole complied, reaching up to tug the pins from beneath her cap. "But I don't think it's necessary."

An instant later, Trenton Kingsley strode into his wife's chambers, Alexander in his arms.

"Trenton?" Ariana frowned, puzzled. "It's not time to leave yet. Nicole and I aren't finished dressing."

"I know." He shook his head bemusedly. "But Nicole asked me to stop by your room an hour before we head for Epsom and to bring Alexander with me. So here we are."

"Yes, right on time." Nicole stepped back into the room, tugging her last few constricting hairpins free. Eyes twinkling, she walked over to Trenton. "I believe I made your son a promise, one I intend to keep." She leaned forward, taking Alexander's tiny fist and unclasping it to place his chubby fingers on the rim of her cap. "Go ahead, my little lord. It's all yours."

Grinning broadly, Alexander yanked, tugging the cap free and sending Nicole's dark curls cascading out in a dozen directions. "Mama," he declared, waving the cap around.

"I hope so," Nicole replied solemnly, kissing his brow. "As soon as the wedding's over and your Uncle Dustin and I can arrange it. You'll be the first to know." She shifted his hand over to his own head, placing the jockey's cap atop it, where it promptly swallowed him down to his chin.

From beneath the concealing fabric came a coo of delight.

"Oh, Lord," Ariana muttered. "Another natural-born horseman. Just what we need."

Nicole smiled tenderly from Alexander to Trenton to Ariana. "Thank you," she said simply.

"For what?" Trenton questioned.

"For keeping my secret. For offering me your friendship. For welcoming me into your family. And, as a result of all that, for making it incredibly easy to bid Alden Stoddard good-bye."

"Good-bye, Raggert." Slumped in a chair, Lanston lifted the bottle of madeira from his desk and dismissed Raggert the instant the trainer burst into the room. "I'm not seeing anyone. Not today, tomorrow, or ever." So saying, he tossed off another in a countless stream of drinks. "Hence, you can show yourself out."

"I don't think you'll feel that way once you've heard what I have to say." Raggert shut the study door and crossed over to grip the edge of the desk. "In fact, I think you'll put down that bottle and get yourself to Epsom."

"Care to bet on it?" Lanston inquired, his voice unsteady.

"Yeah." Raggert gave a triumphant nod. "Because I'd win."

Lanston laughed bitterly and refilled his goblet.

"Listen to me, Lanston. Our worries are over. We've got the perfect opportunity to recoup your money—hell, to make a fortune. And the ironic thing is, we didn't have to do a bloody thing. This investment opportunity just fell in our laps."

Blinking, Lanston rubbed a hand over his bloodshot eyes. "You must be drunker than I am. Investment opportunity? Raggert, I don't have a shilling to my name. I have nothing to wager other than the shirt on my back and the breath in my body." A gulp of madeira. "The latter of which our friend Cooper will soon remedy. He's probably on his way over here right now, ready to go for my throat like a bloodthirsty vulture. Well, he can slit it, for all I care. I've tried everything I know how to make the odds work for me—thrashing that damned stallion Dagger, who didn't become a champion until I sold him to Tyreham, paying you to help me undermine the incomparable marquis, blackmailing every available jockey who'd take the bait. Not to mention Cooper, who's done things that would make your skin crawl. But after that unexpected disaster at the Derby, my losses are too vast to recoup. I'm finished." Lanston made a harsh sound of defeat. "If you think about it, it's almost humorous. I've been outdone by a scrawny boy who turned out to be a hero."

"A short-term hero," Raggert retorted, smirking as he leaned closer. "Would you listen to me? It's about Stoddard. Yesterday, Tyreham got the Stewards of the Jockey Club to agree to let the boy race again—today, in the Oaks Stakes. Tyreham said it was your idea."

"It was. Have you come to congratulate me?" Lanston arched a sardonic brow.

"No. I've come to remind you that your filly Chloe is the prime contender in that race, especially with a bloody fine jockey like Baker riding her."

"I don't give a damn. And even if I did, you just told me Stoddard's been entered. He outran Baker once; no doubt, he can do it again."

"No, he can't. Because he's not running."

"You're talking in riddles, Raggert."

"Then I'll make it simple, let you know something Lord Tyreham doesn't. As of a half hour ago, Stoddard quit."

The glass paused midway to Lanston's mouth. "Quit?"

"Yeah, quit. As in backed out, ran away, fled. He's scared to death to ride since those billet straps gave out on him. I just left him. He's so stiff in the saddle, he can't even get Tyreham's horse into a trot. So, rather than embarrass the marquis, he bolted."

Lanston came slowly to his feet. "And you're telling me Tyreham knows nothing about this turn of events?"

"Now you're catching on. No, Tyreham left early this morning for some business meeting with his brother. He won't be back until right before the race. Stoddard appealed to me to alert the Stewards to the situation in order to save Tyreham's reputation. In fact, that's where I supposedly am right now—getting them to withdraw Tyreham's entry so the poor marquis won't be publicly embarrassed."

A slow smile spread across Lanston's face. "But you're not with them."

"No, instead I'm here advising you to bet a fortune on Baker and Chloe. She's one hell of a filly, and you're about to be one hell of a rich man."

"The possibilities are limitless," Lanston laughed, shoving aside the madeira. "Why, I think I'll make my way over to Epsom early, before Tyreham has a chance to arrive and learn about Stoddard's desertion. In addition to my official wager, I'll make Tyreham an enormous personal wager, which the stupid, arrogant fool will take, having not the slightest idea that he'll be forfeiting the race *and* all his funds." Enthusiastically, the earl clapped Raggert on the back. "You, on the other hand, will soon be collecting a substantial sum as a token of my gratitude."

"I thought you might say that."

"I'd better bathe and get dressed." Lanston glanced distastefully down at his own rumpled apparel. "You hasten back to Tyreham's estate, lest the marquis return early. We can't have him discovering our little secret yet, now can we?" A bitter smile. "But when the time is right, when Tyreham does show his pompous face at Epsom, I'll be waiting. My good friend Dustin has quite an afternoon in store for him."

Several hours later, Dustin was thinking much the same thing . . . but for reasons of his own.

His mood was buoyant as he settled himself in the box at Epsom, leaving two empty seats between Trenton and himself. "Today's events are going to yield wonders," he informed his brother. "I'm feeling extraordinarily lucky this afternoon."

"I'm glad to hear that." It was Lanston who answered, having sprinted over the instant he saw Dustin and Trenton arrive, before they had time to learn of Stoddard's unexpected departure from the turf. "I'm feeling much the same." A cocky grin. "I've come to congratulate you on taking my suggestion and entering Stoddard in the Oaks. I'm sure it will prove to be a lucrative move."

"Ah, so you heard about that," Dustin replied. "Well, I have you to thank for the idea. As you pointed out, Stoddard is far too splendid a jockey to restrict to one race." Glancing down at the list of scheduled entrants, he added,

"I see Baker is running for you again, astride Chloe—a wise choice."

"She's magnificent; a perfect racehorse. I've just wagered a small fortune on her victory."

"Really? Even knowing Stoddard's racing Winning Streak against her?"

A smug nod. "As I said, I'm feeling lucky today. Speaking of which, shall I pay you what I owe you for the Derby?" Lanston reached into his pocket, then paused. "Or shall we raise the stakes and wager it all on the Oaks?"

"Raise them to what?"

"Oh, say fifty thousand pounds."

"Fifty thousand pounds?" Dustin's brows shot up, as did the volume of his tone. "You *are* feeling lucky." He turned to the cluster of noblemen behind him. "What do you suggest, gentlemen?"

"Go for it, Tyreham," one of them declared with a chuckle. "Even if you lose, you'll never miss the money. Besides, it will make the race that much more interesting for us."

A murmur of agreement from the surrounding group.

With a good-natured grin, Dustin extended his hand to Lanston. "Why not," he determined with a flourish. "It'll be gratifying as hell to beat you twice during the course of one meeting."

"*If* you beat me," Lanston qualified, shaking Dustin's proffered hand with an equal measure of exuberance.

"The flag is about to go down," Trenton observed, glancing about. "I wonder where Ariana and Nicole are?"

"Nicole?" Lanston inclined his head quizzically in Trenton's direction. "Who is . . . ?"

"Here they are now." Dustin gestured, and he and Trenton came to their feet as the two women approached. "We were getting concerned about you."

"I'm sorry, darling," Nicole said sweetly, letting Ariana precede her, then taking the seat beside Dustin's. She smoothed her skirts, glancing up in time to see the flag descend and the race commence. "Ariana and I stopped by to wish Papa luck."

"He won't need it," Dustin assured her. Capturing her

hand in his, he brought her attention to their guest. "Nicole, I think it's time you met the earl of Lanston."

"Lord Lanston." Nicole acknowledged the introduction with a cool nod.

"My, my." Lanston stared, making no attempt to disguise his openly sensual appraisal.

Dustin's fingers tightened around Nicole's. "Lanston, I'd strongly suggest you erase that provocative expression from your face. Nicole is my betrothed."

"Your betrothed?" That surprising piece of news diverted Lanston's attention—both from his hungry assessment of Nicole and from the race. "When did this happen? I knew nothing about it."

A warning glint flashed in Dustin's eyes. "Ah, that's because I know far more about you than you do about me."

A shout from the crowd made Lanston whip about, alerted him to the unexplained excitement rippling around him, as well as the status of the ongoing race.

Awareness dilated his pupils. "Who's that in front?"

"Hmm?" Dustin was deeply absorbed in the race. "Why, Winning Streak, of course."

"Winning Streak?" Lanston turned sheet white.

"Lanston, I'd suggest you get your pound notes ready," Trenton recommended icily, staring straight ahead, seemingly mesmerized by the event. "Winning Streak is already leading by a full length."

Sweat drenched Lanston's brow. "But I thought . . ."

"You thought?" Dustin prompted.

Abruptly, Lanston's eyes narrowed on the more heavily muscled legs gripping Winning Streak's flanks. "That's not Stoddard."

"No, it isn't. But then, you already knew that, didn't you—from Raggert?"

Lanston jerked about as if he'd been struck, a vein throbbing at his temple as he faced Dustin. "What do you mean?"

"I told you, Lanston. I know a great deal about you. In fact, I know everything." Enmity tightened Dustin's features. "Everything."

"He's in front by three lengths, Dustin," Trenton announced. "And that's after being absent from the turf for weeks. I'm impressed."

"Absent from the . . ." The earl weaved, clutching the rail beside him. His wild-eyed gaze darted back to the course and froze on the jockey who was racing Dustin's filly to victory. "Tyreham," he rasped, "who's riding Winning Streak?"

"I think you know the answer to that."

"Who, dammit?"

"The most brilliant jockey on the English turf." It was Nicole who answered, her chin coming up, pride and hatred converging in her tone. "My father."

"Your father? Who the hell is—?"

"Oh, that's right," Dustin interjected. "I never did have the chance to complete your introductions. Lanston. My betrothed." A lethal pause. "Nicole *Aldridge.*"

Lanston seemed to crumple before their very eyes. "Oh, my God," he whispered.

"It's too late to pray," Dustin bit out. "Further, I doubt God aids murderers."

"I didn't murder anyone." Lanston took an inadvertent step backward, looking like a trapped animal who sensed his own doom. "I know what Aldridge heard. He thinks I killed Redley, but I didn't. Nor did I order Cooper to kill him—he took that upon himself. And he never would have if Redley hadn't threatened to expose us. That's the only reason Cooper silenced him. I never wanted anyone hurt. It was just the money." He dragged a handkerchief from his pocket and began mopping at his face.

As if on cue, the crowd gave off a cheer.

"Well, Lanston," Trenton pronounced over the commotion, "speaking of money, you'd best go home and amass yours. As of now, you have enormous debts to satisfy. Aldridge just took the Oaks—by more lengths than I can count."

"Money?" Lanston repeated woodenly. "I've nothing left."

"In that case, besides being an animal and a culprit, you're also a pauper." For the first time, Trenton met Lanston's gaze head-on, letting the earl see the undisguised fury blazing inside him. "If you hadn't already hung yourself, I'd kill you for threatening my son, you miserable bastard."

Lanston sank to the bench. "Dustin, help me," he managed.

"Help you?" Dustin could barely control himself long enough to bait Lanston into finishing what he'd begun: tightening his own noose. "You're scum, Lanston. You might not have killed Redley, but you sure as hell hired men to kill Aldridge. Cooper, Archer, Parrish—they're all out on the streets, looking for the very man who just took the Oaks Stakes. And let's not forget Raggert. You referred him to me, sent him to Tyreham as your eyes and ears and eventually your muscle. You ordered him to stop Stoddard from winning that Derby any way he had to. But for the grace of God, that poor boy could be dead, too. So could any of the other jockeys he rode against, had Stoddard not been skilled enough to release that saddle where no one would be struck. In short, Lanston, each action I've re-counted translates into attempted murder."

Without pause, Dustin began counting off on his fingers. "Now let's enumerate your other forms of violence. You hired men to beat Sullivan within an inch of his life, then rehired them to do the same to me. You also sent a warning note to my brother, threatening his son with physical harm. And we have yet to detail the theft, fraud, and blackmail that were involved in your unscrupulous scheme to coerce jockeys into throwing their races. And you're asking me for help?"

"It wasn't meant to be like that." Lanston was shaking now, dragging his hand through his hair. "No one was supposed to get hurt, only frightened enough to succumb to our demands. I explained to you what happened with Redley. Aldridge was . . . a necessity. I wish to God he'd never walked into Newmarket that day, never overheard Cooper and me discussing Redley's death, but he did. Still, if he'd only cooperated with us, demonstrated his allegiance by throwing those bloody races, I wouldn't have had to instruct Cooper to kill him. But, as things stood, I didn't know what his position was. Did he intend to blackmail us like Redley did? Or worse, did he intend to use the truth about Redley's death to undo us, turn us over to the authorities? I agonized over these questions for days, gave Aldridge every chance to change his mind, but he didn't. Instead, he disappeared. So what choice did I have? I had to have him found and eliminated. As for Stoddard, I told Raggert not to hurt him, only to stop him."

"And how did you intend for him to do that—with a polite request?" Dustin shot back incredulously. "You're twisted, Lanston, deluding yourself into believing that paying others to kill isn't the same thing as killing. But it is. You're as guilty as Cooper and Raggert."

"No, I'm not. I never killed anyone. I couldn't kill anyone. It's just that I'm drowning." Lanston's voice took on an hysterical tone. "I have more outstanding notes than I can count. Everywhere I turn, I owe hundreds of pounds. I tried everything, but time after time I encountered failure. Even with that bloody stallion. I bought him, beat him into compliance, and what was the result? For me he was a savage, for you he became a Derby winner. I sent Raggert to Tyreham not to harm anyone but to study your breeding methods, keep me apprised of your latest contenders, and hold you back long enough for me to win some races, recoup some of my losses. With Aldridge unavailable, I expected it to be easy. Then Stoddard showed up and ruined everything."

"You didn't anticipate Stoddard's level of skill, did you?" Dustin grilled. "Nor did you expect him to refuse Archer and Parrish's offer. Just as you didn't expect Nick Aldridge to be so principled that he'd rather desert the turf than cooperate with criminals. But then, why should that surprise me? You can't understand principles, Lanston. You have none."

Lanston emitted a strangled sound. "It was survival, Dustin. Please . . . you must understand."

"Oh, I understand, all right." Dustin pivoted in his seat, glancing behind him to receive Saxon's definitive nod. "We all understand," he added, pointing.

Following Dustin's gesture, Lanston leaped to his feet, becoming aware of his surroundings for the first time. He blanched as Saxon stepped away from his box, revealing the men his presence had concealed, the Stewards of the Jockey Club. Behind them, and all around the Kingsley box, clusters of noblemen muttered among themselves, shaking their heads in disgrace.

Dazedly, Lanston looked at Dustin. "You planned this?"

"Every bit of it," Dustin confirmed. "Right down to eliciting the assistance of the Stewards in setting up this performance. These fine men have no more desire than I to have a criminal in their ranks." Dustin turned to Saxon. "I presume we have enough evidence for the authorities."

"More than enough, my lord," Saxon assured him. "Right before you arrived at Epsom, I was handed a missive written in Blaker's hand. He's apprehended both Cooper and Raggert. It seems our 'Coop' is wanted in two English and three Scottish towns in connection with a series of violent crimes. As for Raggert, he's terrified by the thought of Newgate and is more than happy to cooperate in any way that will reduce his sentence, including filling in any details we have yet to acquire. Archer and Parrish will be ferreted out by day's end. And it will be my pleasure to escort the whole bloody lot of them to Scotland Yard."

Lanston blinked, as if trying to make sense of something. "If you've had Aldridge all this time, why did you wait until now and go to such extremes to confront me? Why didn't you end this weeks ago?"

"That's the ironic part of it," Dustin supplied caustically. "You see, Lanston, Nick Aldridge never heard your conversation with Cooper, never knew you murdered Redley. All he discerned on that day he strolled into the stables at Newmarket were two unlikely people having a private conversation. He was as bewildered as we by your sudden urge to kill him."

With a low groan, Lanston buried his face in his hands. "Oh, my God. All the risk, the anguish, was for nothing." Slowly, he raised his head, realization flickering in the hollow depths of his soul. "If Aldridge heard nothing, you had no actual proof of my guilt."

"Precisely. Until now, that is. You've done an exceptional job of incriminating yourself." Dustin glanced at Saxon. "He's all yours."

"As I said, a pleasure, sir." Saxon grasped Lanston's arm, led him off.

"Thank you, Tyreham." Lord Chisward, the eldest of the

Jockey Club Stewards rose solemnly. "I think I speak for everyone when I express my horror at the fact that corruption such as this was tainting the turf. But it's over now, other than amassing the disreputable jockeys involved. Which, between the list you've supplied us and the results of our own investigations, we shall do posthaste. At which point the guilty parties will be dealt with—swiftly and severely. You have my word on that. Again I thank you for helping to bring Lanston to justice."

"No thanks are necessary, Chisward," Dustin responded. "In truth, I'm equally relieved to put this behind us, not only for the sake of the turf but for the sake of my betrothed"—he tucked Nicole's arm through his—"and her father."

"Miss Aldridge," Chisward turned to Nicole, "please extend our deepest apologies to your father. And tell him we welcome him back with the greatest of enthusiasm."

"I will," Nicole answered faintly. "Thank you."

Hearing the tremor in her voice, Dustin glanced over, frowning when he saw tears glistening on her lashes. "Nicole?" His knuckles brushed her cheek. "What is it, sweetheart?"

"He beat that beautiful, spirited horse," she replied in an aching whisper.

Dustin needed no further explanation. "Never again," he vowed quietly. "He'll never abuse Dagger—or any other horse—again."

"Yes, I heard that admission as well," Chisward chimed in, with a hard shake of his head. "And from a renowned breeder, no less. Well, fear not, Miss Aldridge. With the list of crimes the earl has committed, he won't be free to hurt anyone or anything for many years to come."

"Thank you, sir," she said, attempting a smile.

Lord Chisward surprised them by abandoning his ever-present reserve and smiling back. "You, my dear, are a breath of fresh air after a sordid display like the one we just suffered. Tyreham is a lucky man. I wish you the best of luck, and I look forward to making a toast to that effect at your wedding. Now, run off—both of you—and congratulate your father. He's earned himself another splendid victory."

"I will, sir. And again, I thank you." This time, Nicole's smile came naturally.

"Oh, Tyreham?" Chisward prompted.

"Yes?"

"My only lingering regret is that you couldn't convince Stoddard to stay on and further his racing career. Is there any chance he might reconsider?"

"Doubtful," Dustin countered soberly, wrapping his arm about Nicole's waist. "He was adamant when he left Tyreham, wouldn't even leave a forwarding address. He said something about retiring from the turf to pursue a long-awaited dream. No, Chisward, I don't expect we'll be seeing Stoddard again."

With a resigned nod, the elderly man made to leave. "Such a pity," he murmured aloud. "A lad like that could have become another Nick Aldridge."

"I don't doubt that for a moment," Dustin concurred. He arched a quizzical brow at Nicole. "Don't you agree, love?"

"Oh, I don't know." Nicole gazed up at her future husband, undisguised love shining in her eyes. "Being a dreamer myself, I understand Stoddard's need to follow his." She glanced toward the paddock, beaming as she witnessed her father's joyous homecoming. "Besides," she stated without the slightest tinge of regret, "Stoddard *was* exceptional, but, ultimately, there's only one Nick Aldridge."

Nineteen

Leaning out the bedchamber window, the new marchioness of Tyreham reveled in the warm night air. Sounds of merriment still clamored loudly from the far grounds of the estate, equal amounts of champagne and ale being consumed as the party prevailed full force, despite the fact that the bride and groom had made their exit an hour ago.

Mrs. Dustin Kingsley.

Reverently, Nicole touched the golden band on her finger, wondering if it were possible to burst with happiness. At last, after a frenzied and interminable fortnight, she had, mere hours ago, walked down the aisle on her father's arm and been joined with the man she loved.

The celebration that followed had been perfect, boasting a fascinating mixture of guests ranging from the distinguished Stewards of the Jockey Club to the joyful, raucous jockeys themselves.

A true melding of her life and Dustin's.

Smiling, Nicole recalled one of the highlights of the festivities: the moment she and Dustin had taken Brackley and Poole aside to a secluded cluster of trees in order to tell them the truth.

Solemnly, Dustin had explained that, as Brackley and Poole were more family than servants, he'd wanted to personally introduce them to his bride. Both men had been deeply moved, and Brackley had begun by humbly thanking Lord Tyreham for inviting him to this momentous occasion.

"My lady," he'd then stammered, bowing awkwardly to her. "I'm honored to meet you."

"And I as well, Lady Tyreham," Poole had echoed, with a more practiced bow.

"Meet me?" With feigned surprise, Nicole had inclined her head quizzically. "Why, you both act as if we're strangers." Seeing their baffled expressions, she'd leaned forward, purposely lowering her voice to become Stoddard's. "At least Dagger had the good sense to recognize me."

Would she ever forget the looks on their faces?

"Damn." Brackley's mouth had dropped open. "I mean . . . forgive my language, my lady. I mean . . ."

"I know what you mean." Nicole had squeezed his arm, adding in a conspiratorial whisper, "Now this must remain our secret. I have no intention of relinquishing my Derby victory."

Poole had stared for a full minute before speaking. "All this time . . ."

"All this time," Dustin had assured him cheerfully.

Somehow, Nicole doubted poor Poole would ever recover from the fact that he hadn't guessed the truth.

The bride's musings were interrupted by a quiet click from behind her.

Pivoting about, Nicole's heartbeat accelerated at the sight of her husband leaning back against their connecting bedchamber door, studying her from beneath hooded lids. Clad only in his dressing robe, he surveyed her hotly, drinking her in from the crown of her dark, unbound hair to the soft curves of her body, visible through her thin lace-trimmed nightgown.

"At last," he said huskily. "The ultimate wish fulfilled."

Crossing over, he drew her away from the window and into his arms.

Nicole gripped the lapels of his robe, her palms opening over the smooth silk. "And what wish is that?" she asked softly.

"You." Tenderly, his thumbs caressed her cheekbones. "Do you know how many times I've stood in that doorway, scrutinizing this room and wondering if I'd ever find a reason to cross its threshold, a woman to fill its emptiness—and mine?" His gaze fell to Nicole's wishing locket, and he caught it in his palm. "Perhaps your locket's magic has extended to me, as well."

"I'm sure it has," Nicole breathed. "Everything about tonight is magic."

Dustin's midnight eyes darkened, his fingers tunneling through her hair. "Did I allow you enough time to get ready?" he asked in a tone that clearly said he had no intentions of granting her even one second more.

"Oh, indeed you did, my lord." Nicole gave him a radiant smile. "I'm beginning to see the benefits of a lady's maid. It's amazing how much faster one can dress and undress with the proper assistance."

"Really? Well, I hope you haven't become overly accustomed to your new maid. You won't be seeing her for many, many days. Then again—" Dustin's hand tightened on his wife's nape, urged her forward to receive his kiss. "You won't be dressing, either."

Nicole's eyes drifted shut as Dustin's lips brushed hers, a brief, heated caress that made her body tremble, her breath expel in a rush.

"My beautiful bride," he whispered, "I've nearly died dreaming of tonight."

"I've nearly died *waiting* for it," she confessed, twining her arms about his neck.

He kissed her again, this time more deeply, caressing the delicate line of her spine and exploring her mouth with tenderness, desire, and a carefully leashed restraint that Nicole wanted no part of.

"Dustin—" She drew back, searched his face. "It's been forever."

"Longer," he corrected. "But I want our wedding night to be everything you ever wished for."

"It already is. It became that the instant we were pronounced man and wife."

"Ah, Nicole." Dustin's embrace tightened, and he seized

her mouth with a kind of raw desperation, opening it to his tongue, his taste, his possession. "I love you. God, I love you so much."

She pressed closer, thinking that nothing could be more right than this exquisite, incomparable moment—only to find that the next one surpassed it. With uninhibited joy, she gave herself up to her husband's spell, kissing him back with all the fervor in her soul.

Dustin groaned, lifting her up and into him, devouring her mouth with an urgency that far transcended the physical. His tongue sought and found every tingling surface, stroked them with tender, heated caresses that branded them as his. Molding her to fit against him, he held her there, cupping her bottom and pressing his rigid erection into the warm haven between her thighs, kissing her again and again until neither of them could think, or talk, or breathe.

Nicole's head was spinning, her body liquid with longing as the hard ridge of Dustin's flesh throbbed against her yearning core, burning through the fine layer of her nightdress. She wanted to part her legs to him, feel him thrust deep inside her, fill the hollow void he'd created and only he could fill. Instinctively, she moved against him, and he made a rough sound deep in his throat, crushing her closer still, his hands moving reverently over the hidden curves of her body.

"Dustin." She tore her mouth from his. "Please—take me to bed."

Her plea was more than enough.

Wresting himself away, Dustin seized the hem of her nightdress, pulled it over her head, and cast it to the floor. "You're even more breathtaking than I remembered," he managed hoarsely, his ravenous stare raking her with a need that made the throbbing inside her quicken.

With a heated shiver, Nicole reached forward, unbelting his robe and pushing it open. He flung it alongside her nightdress, then swept her into his arms and carried her to the bed.

"I want you more now than I did before—more than I've ever wanted anything in my life," he rasped, lowering her to the sheets. Ever so lightly, he traced the curves of her breasts, brushed the hardened peaks of her nipples, then stopped, fanning her hair out over the pillow and standing back to make love to her with his eyes.

Nicole's breath was coming in shallow pants, her whole body flushed with arousal. Lying perfectly still, she surveyed her husband, wondering at the incredible sexual magnetism he exuded, as natural to him as breathing. He wasn't even touching her, yet her body was throbbing in conjunction with each shift of his intensifying scrutiny. She nearly sobbed aloud when his gaze found the core of her femininity, his expression growing taut with strain, hot with desire. "Dustin." She was hardly aware she'd said his name, her own greedy stare instinctively dropping to his rigid manhood, now huge and pulsing with its need for her. Awed, her gaze returned to—and locked with—his.

Dustin took an inadvertent step toward the bed, then checked himself, his jaw clenched against the tide of sensation they both knew was already out of control. "No," he attempted, giving voice to the words. "I want to make this last for hours, days . . ."

"Dustin . . . please," Nicole whispered, opening her arms to him.

Restraint vanished.

With a growl of capitulation, Dustin covered Nicole with himself, seizing her mouth in a kiss so openly carnal that Nicole moaned with the dizzying impact, arched instinctively against him. "Yes," she breathed as his lips left hers, blazed a trail down her body, igniting an inferno every place he touched.

"Perfect," he muttered against her breast, drawing the aching nipple into his mouth. "You're heaven."

"Oh, Dustin." Nicole's eyes drifted shut, and she shivered, holding his head to keep him there even as her body arched to lure him further along his path.

He captured her hands in his, intertwined their fingers as he shifted to her other breast, bathed it in liquid fire, then inched his way down the bed, worshipping her with reverent strokes of his mouth.

Abruptly, Nicole needed to share the magic, to discover

the warmth and textures she'd been unable to explore during their one all-too-brief joining.

Wriggling free, she urged her startled husband to his back, running her palms over the powerful breadth of his shoulders, down the contours of his hair-roughened chest. "It's my turn," she whispered, gazing up at him.

Excitement flashed in Dustin's eyes. "I'm all yours," he murmured huskily, stretching his arms overhead.

Nicole felt a surge of exhilaration. She shifted her hands, teased his nipples with her thumbs, and was rewarded by his low groan of pleasure, the tightening of his nipples beneath her touch. Venturing downward, her fingers traced the steely muscles of his abdomen, the corded muscles of his thighs, and her gaze returned to his, saw the shimmer of anticipation reflected there.

She answered it.

Dustin went taut when her fingers closed around his shaft, stroked its rigid length. A hard shudder wracked his body, and he groaned—a primal sound of male need—before he seized her wrist, taught her the pleasure she was capable of bringing him, then relinquished himself to her magic.

Eagerly, Nicole complied, glorying in her husband's blatant masculinity, her own wondrous sense of abandon as she teased him with featherlight strokes of her fingertips, more purposeful sweeps of her palm. A sudden thought struck her, and on impulse, she lowered her head, murmuring, "The way you made love to me in the cabin—with your mouth—would that please you as well?"

"I won't survive," he ground out, trembling as her hair swept his thighs.

She paused, giving him a siren's smile. "Try," she breathed, taking him into the warm cavern of her mouth, tasting him as he had her.

Dustin nearly launched off the bed. Whip-taut, he arched like a bowstring, gripping the headboard to steady the harsh tremors wracking his body. "Nicole, I can't." Even as he commanded her to stop, his hips lifted, begging her to take more of him.

Recalling her own helpless ecstasy when he'd done this to her, Nicole ignored her husband's protests, concentrated on the mysteries of his body and the miracle of his response. She savored his size, his velvety hardness, the warm droplets of fluid he was unable to repress.

"Nicole . . . God, sweetheart, you're killing me." Desperately, Dustin fought to withstand the exquisite torture, broken love words escaping him, his knuckles white with the strain of holding back.

With a hoarse growl, he reached his limit.

"No more." Dragging her from him, he rolled her onto her back, pressing her thighs wide apart. He knelt between her legs, staring down at her, his forehead slick with sweat, his midnight eyes nearly black with passion. "I'm about to explode." He leaned forward, his fingers finding and opening her, sliding inside.

Nicole's breath caught in her throat as Dustin stroked her delicate tissues, stretched her narrow passage to receive him. Sensuously, his fingers glided in and out of her heated wetness, his thumb circling and teasing the tight little bud that cried out for his possession.

"Now—oh, Dustin, now." She sobbed aloud, twisting on the pillow, reaching for him.

"Not yet," he muttered, his chest heaving with the exertion of holding back. "I'm too close to the edge. The minute I go into you, I'm going to erupt. I need you with me."

Drowning in passion, Nicole shook her head, realizing on some impalpable level that he was worried about giving her pleasure. *Dustin, please* . . . she wanted to shout. *I'm already over the edge. Please* . . . *please* . . .

All words and thoughts vanished as he bent down, utterly possessing her with his mouth, his fingers continuing their unbearable assault as his lips and tongue devoured her sweetness.

Nicole shrieked, sensation slamming through her, screaming along her nerve endings, hurtling to a crashing peak beneath her husband's sensual onslaught. "Dustin!" she sobbed, her entire being shattering in a wild, unbearable release.

Instantly, he raised up, thrust deep inside her, erupting even as he did. His climax intensified as Nicole's tremors convulsed around him, and he surged forward, pouring into her in wild, drenching bursts of completion. "Nicole . . . hold me," he ground out, lifting her legs higher, wider, needing to be as deep inside her as possible.

Nicole wrapped herself around him, gasping his name with each flood of his seed, each spasm of her body.

They collapsed in each other's arms, Dustin's head dropping into the crook of her neck, his weight pressing her into the mattress, his body buried inside her still.

Eyes closed, Nicole drifted, stroking her husband's damp back, conscious of every magnificent nuance—his lingering shudders, his harsh, rasping breaths, but, most of all, the warm wetness of his seed inside her, the tangible evidence of their union. "I love you," she whispered.

Shakily, Dustin raised up, gazed solemnly into his wife's eyes. "God, how I love you, Mrs. Kingsley. And I was right. You *are* a miracle. *My* miracle."

Tears glistened on her lashes. "You're quite miraculous yourself, my lord."

They fell silent, savoring the aftermath, awed by the total oneness spawned by their lovemaking.

Long moments later, Dustin stirred, sifting strands of Nicole's hair through his fingers, and smiling that lazy, bone-melting smile that made her breath catch.

"What?" she murmured.

"I was just thinking that you did away with my noble intentions once again. I meant for this, our first joining as husband and wife, to be all I denied you the first time— slow, tender, prolonged. It was anything but."

"That's true. Are you disappointed?"

Again, that heart-stopping smile. "I'm drunk with discovery. Ecstatic with happiness. And insane with love. But disappointed? No." He brushed her lips with his. "Besides, we have countless opportunities ahead of us tonight. This was but the first."

Nicole shivered, her pulse quickening. "Also true. Tell me, my lord, how long must we wait before taking advantage of our second opportunity?"

Dustin chuckled, moving sensuously against her, stirring as if the past frenzied moments had never occurred. *"You* tell *me,* my lady. Is now too soon?"

"Now would be ideal," she assured him, lifting her arms around his neck.

"Good. Then perhaps this second time will be slow and tender." His words ended on a groan as Nicole arched up, took him deeper into herself. "Then again," he amended huskily, "perhaps not."

Long, languorous hours later, Nicole curled contentedly in her husband's arms, whole and happy and utterly replete . . . despite the fact that they had yet to master slow, tender, and prolonged.

"Sleepy?" Dustin murmured, kissing her shoulder.

"Yes and no. Too tired to stay awake, too exhilarated to sleep. Besides," she added, sighing, "I don't want to sleep. I want to make this night last forever."

"It will, darling. I promise you, it will." He propped himself up on one elbow, gestured toward the window. "The stars are out," he observed.

"I know. I've been watching them shine down on us."

"Have you? And have you also been wishing?" he prompted softly.

She smiled, shaking her head. "I have no need to. All my wishes have been fulfilled." A slight pause. "All but one."

"And what wish is that?"

With aching tenderness, Nicole touched her locket, met her husband's gaze. "To have your child."

A look of profound emotion crossed Dustin's face. "I love you, my beautiful stargazer," he said huskily. "And there's only one wish that means more to me than your having my child, and that wish is right here in my arms."

"I'm no longer a wish," she breathed, laying her palm against his jaw. "I'm very much a reality."

"Not merely a reality." He turned his lips into her palm, renewed desire shimmering to life. "A dream come true."

This time, at last, was slow, tender . . . and very, very prolonged.

Afterward, they slept in each other's arms, neither of them aware that, as a result of their last precious union, the wishing locket was blissfully empty, the fulfillment of Nicole's ultimate wish nestled safely in her womb.

But the locket knew. That final wish soared forth, an unknown but nonetheless tangible dream come true, deemed by fate to join the miracles of twilight and stargazing.

There it twinkled in the darkness and sailed joyously on the wind.

Author's Note

The only thing more difficult than making Dustin's story all you asked for is realizing it's at an end. (These good-byes don't seem to be getting any easier.) Nevertheless, I leave Dustin in Nicole's loving hands, knowing he's found the happiness he so deserved. Oh! An interesting historical tidbit before I close: Sugar cubes didn't come into being until 1878, three years after the date in which *Wishes in the Wind* is set. Just the same, I took the liberty of offering a few cubes to Dagger. He deserved the license fiction affords, wouldn't you say?

And now, it's back to Regency England for me, to a secluded estate in Devonshire where my next Pocket historical, *Legacy of the Diamond,* is unfolding. Slayde Huntley, the earl of Pembourne, is being thrust headlong into the echoes of a dark legacy that has haunted the Huntley family for generations and, as fate would have it, hurled straight into the path of a beautiful and unexpected complication: Courtney Johnston—the woman destined to change his life and awaken his heart.

I hope you enjoy the preview of *Legacy of the Diamond* Pocket Books has provided and that you, like I, will be eager to share Courtney and Slayde's poignant story.

Remember, I cherish your letters! You can write to me at:

P.O. Box 5104
Parsippany, NJ 07054-6104

(Include a legal-size SASE if you'd like a copy of my latest newsletter.)

With love,
Andrea

**POCKET BOOKS
PROUDLY PRESENTS**

*LEGACY
OF THE DIAMOND*

ANDREA KANE

**Coming soon
from
Pocket Books**

**The following is a preview of
Legacy of the Diamond. . . .**

Devonshire, England
May 1817

It was the third ransom note this week, the fifth in a fortnight, but only the second that rang true.

> Pembourne:
> The exchange will be made tonight. Eleven P.M. Ten miles due south of Dartmouth—in the open waters of the English Channel. Take a small, unarmed boat. Come alone, accompanied only by the diamond. Heed these instructions or your sister will die.

Shoving the terse message back into his coat pocket, Slayde Huntley, the ninth earl of Pembourne, gripped the wheel of his fishing vessel with one hand, simultaneously tilting his timepiece toward the dim light of the lantern. By his calculations, he'd traveled more than nine of those ten miles. He steeled himself for the confrontation ahead, maneuvering deeper into the fog-shrouded waters of the Channel—waters far too choppy for a boat this size.

He should have brought the brig. Every instinct in his body cried out that not only was this craft unsuited for rough seas, its very construction left him utterly vulnerable to the enemy. But the kidnapper's message had been precise. And, instincts or not, Slayde dared not disobey for fear of jeopardizing his sister's life.

Aurora.

The thought of her being held by some filthy pirate made Slayde's skin crawl. For the umpteenth time he berated himself for falling short in his responsibilities, for allowing this unprecedented atrocity to occur. In the decade since he'd become Aurora's guardian, he'd successfully isolated her from the world and, despite his own frequent and prolonged absences, ensured her safety by hiring an army of servants whose fundamental roles were to keep Aurora occupied and Pembourne safeguarded against intruders. Events had proven the latter easier to accomplish than the former. Still, as the accountings he received each time he returned bore out, seldom did Aurora manage to venture beyond her revered lighthouse without being spotted and restored to Pembourne. So how in the hell had this happened?

Vehemently, Slayde shoved aside his frustration and his guilt. In a crisis such as this, there was room for neither. Interrogation, self-censure would come later. Now they would only serve to dilute his mental reserves, thus lessening his chances of accomplishing what he'd sailed out here to do: deliver the ransom and recover his sister.

Ransom—the detestable black diamond whose legend had dug its talons into his past and refused to let go, whose curse haunted the Huntleys like some lethal specter—a specter whose presence did nothing to dissuade hundreds of privateers from stalking the coveted gem.

Pondering the glittering black stone now wedged inside his Hessian boot, Slayde's knuckles whitened on the wheel. What made him think the claims of this ransom note were not mere fabrications invented strictly to procure the jewel? What if, like most of its predecessors, this message were a hoax? What if this pirate didn't have Aurora at all?

Again, Slayde abandoned his line of thinking, refusing to contemplate the idea of returning home without his sister. There had been three generations of blood spilled already. Aurora would not fall victim to the greed and hatred spawned by that loathsome jewel. He wouldn't allow it. Come hell or high water, he would find her.

The sound of an approaching vessel breaking the waves made Slayde go taut. Eyes narrowed, he searched the murky waters, seeking the outline of a ship.

At last it came.

Steadying his craft, Slayde waited while the ship drew closer.

As anticipated, it was a brigantine, moderate size but well manned and, doubtless, well armed. The whole situation was almost comical, he thought, his mouth twisting bitterly. Here he was, miles from shore, alone and unprotected in a meager fishing craft, being challenged by a hostile vessel ten times his size that was now closing in, primed and ready to blast him out of the water in a heartbeat.

And there wasn't a bloody thing he could do to save himself.

Except surrender the gem and pray Aurora was on that ship, unharmed.

"Pembourne, I see you followed instructions. All of them, I hope." The kidnapper's raspy voice cut the fog as his ship drew directly alongside Slayde's. "Did you bring the black diamond?"

Slayde tilted back his head, wishing the mist would lift so he could make out the bastard's features. "I have it."

"Good. If that's true, you'll remain alive. I'll send my first mate down to fetch it."

A whooshing noise followed by the slap of a

rope ladder as its bottom rungs struck the deck of Slayde's boat.

"Where's Aurora?" Slayde demanded, his fingers inching toward his waistcoat pocket—and the pistol he'd concealed there.

"Halt!" the kidnapper's order rang out. "Touch that weapon and you'll die where you stand."

An electrified silence.

Slowly, Slayde's hand retraced its path to his side.

"A wise decision, Pembourne," the raspy voice commended. "As for your sister, she's being brought topside. Ah, here she is now."

As he spoke, two men dragged a struggling woman onto the main deck. She was slight of build, her arms tied behind her, a strip of cloth covering her eyes and upper face.

It *could* be Aurora—but *was* it?

Slayde squinted, intent on discerning the woman's authenticity.

He had little time to do so, for she was shoved unceremoniously into a sack, bound within its confines, and tossed over the shoulder of the first mate.

"Wait," Slayde instructed as the man began his descent down the ladder's rungs.

The first mate paused.

Addressing the shadowy form on the deck above, Slayde inquired icily, "What proof do I have that the person in that sack is my sister?"

"None," the captain returned, a taunt in his tone. "It appears you'll have to take me at my word."

Slayde's jaw set. He was on the verge of denying his earlier claim that he'd brought the diamond with him, ready to swear that it was, in truth, ensconced at Pembourne Manor, when his gaze fell on the grappling sack on the first mate's arm. From the partially open end at the top several long tresses tumbled free—hair whose color not even the fog could disguise.

A shimmering golden red.

Aurora.

Reassured that his efforts were about to reap their reward, Slayde nodded his compliance, now eager to complete the transaction and be gone. Aware he was being scrutinized, he allowed none of his impatience to show, instead remaining impassive while the first mate completed his descent and paused three rungs above Slayde's deck.

"The diamond, m'lord," the sailor requested, extending his hand.

Wordlessly, Slayde studied him, noting—with some degree of surprise—the twinge of regret on the first mate's face, almost as if the rogue were being forced to act against his will.

"Please, Lord Pembourne," the sailor reiterated, balking beneath Slayde's probing stare, "the stone."

"Very well." Deliberately, Slayde leaned forward, slipping his hand inside his boot. "I'm fetching the diamond, not a weapon," he clarified, taking pity on the cowering fellow. "My Hessian is unarmed." So saying, he extracted the gemstone, holding it out so the first mate could see the truth to his words.

Relief flashed on the weathered features.

"Take it, Lexley," the captain bit out.

With a start, Lexley jerked forward, snatching the diamond from Slayde's palm.

Simultaneously, the woman in the sack began struggling furiously, catching Lexley off guard and toppling from his arms.

With a sickening crack, the sack smashed against the boom of the fishing boat, the impact hurling it outward, where it plummeted down to the railing below.

It impacted with a hollow thud.

Slayde lunged forward, grasping nothing but air as the small craft pitched, upsetting his balance and butting the sack yet again, this time overboard.

A glint of silver struck his deck.

Then—an ominous splash as the sack plunged headlong into the rolling waves and vanished.

"Dear God." Lexley made an instinctive move toward the water.

"Get back on board," the captain bellowed. "Now."

The first mate froze. "M'lord"—he turned terrified eyes to Slayde—"you must . . ."

Slayde never heard the rest of the sentence. Having regained his balance, he charged forward, pausing only to gauge his distance to the enveloping swells that divulged the sack's location.

Then he dove.

He sliced the surface in one clean stroke and was swallowed up by darkness.

"Please, God," Lexley prayed, staring at the foam in Slayde's wake, "let him save her. And, God, please forgive me."

With that, he scooted up the ladder and onto his ship, dragging the ladder in his wake.

Slayde propelled himself downward, groping blindly in the pitch-black seas. The eclipsing combination of fog and night made it impossible to distinguish anything. He could only pray his calibrations had been right.

Perhaps his prayers were heard.

With a surge of triumph, Slayde felt the coarse edge of the sack brush his fingertips. He latched onto it, hauling the cumbersome bag against him, locking it securely to his body. Kicking furiously, he battled both the weight of his own waterlogged clothing and the additional constraint of his unwieldy bundle.

After what seemed like an eternity, he broke the surface. Gasping in air, he heaved the sack over the edge of the deck, then hoisted himself up after it.

The sack thudded softly, then lay motionless.

Kneeling, Slayde was only minimally aware of the rapidly retreating brig, far too worried about Aurora to concern himself with the fate of his gem. His fingers shook as he gripped the loosely tied cord atop the sack, cursing as the wet fibers resisted, ripped at his flesh.

He whipped out his blade, slashing the material from top to bottom, shoving it aside to give him access to the woman within.

She lay facedown, her breeches and shirt clinging to her body, masses of wet red-gold hair draped about her.

He rested his palm on her back.

She wasn't breathing.

Shifting until he was crouched at her head, Slayde folded her arms and pillowed them beneath her cheek. Then he pressed down between her shoulder blades—hard—finishing the motion by lifting her elbows in a desperate attempt to force water from her lungs, replace it with air.

He repeated the action five times before he was rewarded with a harsh bout of coughing.

"Sh-h-h, it's all right." Relieved as hell, Slayde shifted again, trying to soothe the wracking shudders that accompanied her coughs, determinedly helping her body expel all the water she'd swallowed and replace it with air.

At last, she lay still, unconscious but breathing, battered but alive.

Gently, he eased her to her back, now taking the time to assess her injuries, simultaneously releasing her from the confines of imprisonment. Broken ribs were a certainty, he thought with a grim scowl, given the force with which she struck the boat. A concussion was a distinct probability as well. Not to mention cuts, bruises, and Lord knew what else. His mind racing, Slayde untied the cords that bound her wrists and, tucking aside her hair, pulled the obscuring cloth from her face.

Blinding realization was followed by a savage curse.

The young woman was not Aurora.

Look for
Legacy of the Diamond
Wherever Paperback Books
Are Sold
Coming Soon from
Pocket Books

Let
Andrea Kane
romance you tonight!

Dream Castle 73585-3/$5.50

My Heart's Desire 73584-5/$5.50

Masque of Betrayal 75532-3/$4.99

Echoes In the Mist 75533-1/$5.50

Samantha 86507-2/$5.50

The Last Duke 86508-0/$5.99

Emerald Garden 86509-9/$5.99

Wishes In the Wind 53483-1/$5.99

Available from Pocket Books

Simon & Schuster Mail Order
200 Old Tappan Rd., Old Tappan, N.J. 07675
Please send me the books I have checked above. I am enclosing $_____ (please add $0.75 to cover the postage and handling for each order. Please add appropriate sales tax). Send check or money order–no cash or C.O.D.'s please. Allow up to six weeks for delivery. For purchase over $10.00 you may use VISA: card number, expiration date and customer signature must be included.

POCKET BOOKS

Name _____

Address _____

City _____ State/Zip _____

VISA Card # _____ Exp.Date _____

Signature _____ 957-05

New York Times
Bestselling Author

Kathryn Lynn Davis

☐ **All We Hold Dear**
73604-3/$6.99

☐ **Sing To Me of Dreams**
68314-4/$5.99

☐ **Child of Awe**
72550-5/$6.50

☐ **Too Deep for Tears**
72532-7/$6.99

Simon & Schuster Mail Order
200 Old Tappan Rd., Old Tappan, N.J. 07675
Please send me the books I have checked above. I am enclosing $_____ (please add $0.75 to cover the postage and handling for each order. Please add appropriate sales tax). Send check or money order--no cash or C.O.D.'s please. Allow up to six weeks for delivery. For purchase over $10.00 you may use VISA: card number, expiration date and customer signature must be included.

POCKET
BOOKS

Name _____

Address _____

City _____ State/Zip _____

VISA Card # _____ Exp.Date _____

Signature _____ 1081-02

JULIE GARWOOD

Ten *New York Times* bestsellers—including her latest, *For the Roses*—verify what Julie Garwood's fans have always know: she is a masterful storyteller. "Julie Garwood attracts readers like beautiful heroines attract dashing heroes," says USA *Today*. Now, returning to the enchanting world she created in *The Bride*, she delights us again with another fascinating tale of love, adventure, and soaring ambitions, set in twelfth-century Scotland....

The Wedding

Available in Hardcover
from Pocket Books

POCKET
B O O K S

1196-01